THE KNAVE OF SECRETS

THE **KNAVE** OF **SECRETS**

ALEX LIVINGSTON

SOLARIS

First published 2022 by Solaris
an imprint of Rebellion Publishing Ltd,
Riverside House, Osney Mead,
Oxford, OX2 0ES, UK

www.solarisbooks.com

ISBN: 978 1 78618 607 2

10 9 8 7 6 5 4 3 2 1

A CIP catalogue record for this book is available
from the British Library.

Designed & typeset by Rebellion Publishing

Printed in the UK

NOTABLE LOCATIONS OF
THE
IMPERIAL
BORDER
AND THEIR FAVOURITE GAMES

A GENERAL MAP OF
THE INDEPENDENT NATION
VALTIFFE

WITH POLITICAL NOTATIONS

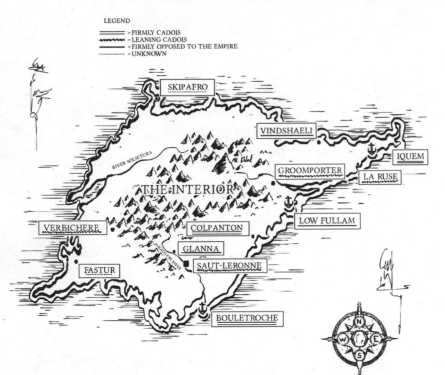

LEGEND
======= = FIRMLY CADOIS
~~~~~~~ = LEANING CADOIS
——————— = FIRMLY OPPOSED TO THE EMPIRE
·············· = UNKNOWN

SKIPAFRO

VINDSHAELI

IQUEM

RIVER SOLSETURA

Mt. Elfed

GROOMPORTER

LA RUSE

THE INTERIOR

LOW FULLAM

VERBICHERE

COLPANTON

GLANNA

FASTUR

SAUT-LERONNE

BOULETROCHE

For Sue and Ann,
who never let me win
(to my knowledge).

Of all of the varied games of chance played by the people of Valtiffe—be they descendants of the savage race that scratched a living from the black beaches of an unforgiving steel sea, or those citizens of our Cadois blood whose forefathers brought much-needed sophistication to those shores—the one diversion in which this author can find no qualities to recommend it to serious players is the game of bluffs and wagers known as *clips*.

A corruption of our native game littre, clips would be suitable only for children were it not for the large sums of money which often accompany it. Coin encourages a seemly excitement of the blood, surely; but skill is the saucer which cools the tea in games of chance, and in clips that virtue is all but completely absent.

A word of caution: it is easy to think oneself skilled at clips after a night or two of accidental winnings. It is at this point that one becomes susceptible to the devices of cardsharps and cheats.

"A Brief Chapter on Clips, or 'Fool's Littre,'"
The Gente's Manual of Card and Dice Entertainments,
M. Jerôme de Tabanne, 3rd edition.

I
VALEN

NEVER STAKE MORE than you can afford to lose. One of the cardinal rules of gambling, and one which Valen Quinol was utterly breaking in a casual game at a highwayside inn.

This was the sort of place that people stopped at to get out of an unforeseen rainstorm: a converted stone stable with a useless fireplace, oilpaper windows which threatened to light on fire every time a candle came near, and a rickety stack of cots which served mainly as a breeding ground for the type of biting insects usually associated with livestock. This was a little extra cash for some mangy shepherd, not a place to lose your fortune.

Yet the stakes had risen remarkably quickly. Now Valen had to play his way out of it.

One of Valen's opponents flicked his fan of cards with a fingernail, each tap accompanied by a jingle of silver from his coat buttons. This gentleman was the source of the unusually large piles of coins in the center of the table—not a very good player, but he had pockets deep enough to push the rest of the table around.

A few hours prior, this man had burst into the inn, spectacles fogged and color high in his cheeks, demanding a dry place by the fire for his rifle. Out for a day's hunting, apparently, and the success he hadn't found in chasing gray foxes across the landscape he planned on finding at the clips table. He seemed indifferent to the persistent barks and howls of the dogs he had left outside in the rain.

A cold vanity. That was the hunter's weakness. One which Valen had spent the night exploiting.

"While we're young…" the hunter chided, looking pointedly over the tops of his glasses at the player to his left, a quiet woman of thirty or so with skin a sickly white tinged with blue. It was plain she was trying to hide her foreign appearance with a high-collared riding coat and a tricorn. Drops of rainwater would occasionally fall from the point of her hat, much to Valen's annoyance. The deck was his, after all. He would prefer the cards not be soiled.

The woman played her turn without acknowledging the hunter's remark, placing her seven of coins face up beside Valen's six on the weathered shard of barn door that served as the table in this establishment.

"Oh, to every hell." Valen tossed his knave of keys on the discard, useless. He grimaced at the man to his right, a slim-shouldered fellow in his late twenties who looked as if he had just walked in from the fields. He wore no wig on his stubble-shorn head, and did not even wear a neckcloth. "And you, monsieur? I don't suppose you have the eight?"

The man frowned around the whalebone toothpick he had been chewing at through the entire game. "Not me. You three figure it out." He rose without another word, prompting the other players to stand and bow, then walked out into the pounding rain without so much as a jacket.

A jingle of silver as the hunter sat again and played a well-timed six. "Leaving mid-hand. No way for a gentilhomme to behave."

The woman in the tricorn laid down the five of coins silently. A perfect play, and the win of the hand.

Valen clapped his hands and smiled at her. "Wonderful play, mademoiselle! Just wonderful. And now I fear I must be heading off as well. Not a kron left to play with and I've no patience for just watching."

The hunter nodded politely, but his eyes were on the cards. "Thank you for the diversion, monsieur. Now we will see if I can win some of my inheritance back from this charming lady. You don't mind leaving the deck, do you? I neglected to bring one, and I can't imagine this place has anything so refined."

"Of course," he replied. "It is a small matter, after all. Perhaps you can leave it here when you're done. Donate it for the hospitality of future wayfarers. The gods know there is naught else to do in this hovel."

It was not, in fact, a small matter. The deck in play was one of Valen's marked decks, specially pressed at the sort of expense it takes to convince a printer that destroying his reputation might not be so bad of a risk. Letting it out of his sight and into the scrutiny of the public at large would require a solution. But he would have to deal with that later.

An abrupt stop in the sheeting of rain against the thatched roof interrupted the pleasantries. The woman looked to the hunter and smiled winningly. "I'm afraid I shall have to take advantage of this momentary break in the weather to continue my ride," she said. Her Mistigri accent was light but unmistakable, a trait which would set her apart anywhere in the world. "I do hope to meet you around the clips table another time. Such a fine player!"

She looked at the towers of currency on the table and gasped as if she had forgotten about them. "Oh, and the pot! What do you say, shall we split it?"

Valen looked to the hunter and waited. No gente would allow himself to do such a thing. But silver buttons don't give a man a title.

"Nonsense," the hunter sputtered. The color had risen in his checks again and something about his neckcloth was troubling him immensely. "The winnings are yours."

The woman raised her hands in protest. "But I am leaving the table before the game has ended! That is no fair play at all. As you say—no way to behave. At the very least let us cut for it. I shall take my half, of course, and we shall cut for yours. Lowest card wins?"

Again, a perfect play from this pale woman. Her proposal was the only solution which would allow both players to maintain dignity. Only winnings gained by chance or skill were to be allowed at any game involving decent people.

She took a packet from the top of the deck and held it up for all to see—the ten of hands.

"Ah." She frowned. "Well, that is likely that, then, is it not?"

The hunter hid a smirk as he made his cut. He held the packet face down and moved his arm across the table dramatically. This little flourish gave Valen plenty of time to make his move.

He lowered his eyelids and carved the outlines of the shapes on the empress of hands into his conscious mind. He mouthed a word in three languages without speaking it.

The hunter rotated his wrist and revealed the king of lamps. Valen's spell hadn't worked. His accidental magic—the magic of chance—never seemed to work when money was on the line.

In the end, it hadn't needed to. His associate Marguerite, the most talented card-marker and dice-loader he had ever met—and who, as luck would have it, happened to be his wife—had trimmed the edges of all of the cards in the deck but the honours, which all but guaranteed that the fingers of anyone making a cut would naturally pull a knave or higher. Valen had argued against the modification at the time, seeing it as redundant with a custom-printed dishonest deck, but was now rather glad she had persisted.

"That's just fine, isn't it?" the hunter grumbled. "Just fine."

The woman hesitated for a moment, then began to gather the jingling coins into a small felt purse. The hunter watched with his arms at his sides. Valen kept a close eye on him. He had seen more than his share of losers catch fire over a bad night.

Before long, the purse was too full to close and there was still nearly half the pot left on the table. The hunter barked a laugh. "I suppose you want my purse now, too. Well, that I shall keep. It cost more than twice this pittance. True leather from the continent, sewn with wire finer than you've ever seen."

"Come now, monsieur," Valen scolded. "There's no need to be sore. You must admit, she is a fine player."

"Aye, fine. Fine enough to win three men's money and walk with it. Remarkable fine luck, I'd say."

If the woman was offended by the veiled allegation of sharp play, she showed no sign of it. She simply thanked the men for the game and walked out. A moment later the clomping of horse hooves against muddy stone passed the inn.

Valen stared down the hunter until the sound had faded. He was no fighter, but he was sure he could keep things from getting troublesome by putting up a good front.

"Good night, then," Valen said. He picked up his deck of dishonest cards, slid them into a pocket, and turned to the door.

"That blueskin took everything you had on you," the hunter said. "Every kron. The entire payment for your meager crop, you said. Doesn't seem to bother you."

Valen stopped with the door half open and spoke over his shoulder. "My own fault, not hers. If I didn't want to lose it, I shouldn't have played it. You can never tell who you're going to meet out here on the road."

With this, he gave the man a knowing wink and stepped out into the rapidly cooling night.

VALEN HADN'T RIDDEN, and now faced an hours-long walk back into Saut-Leronne. Perhaps some kind person marching a cart through the flat pasture lands would let him jump in back. If he was lucky. The hunter's ignored dogs had growled at him as he passed, jealous of his dry clothes.

The road had held up well in the downpour. Water filled the deeper wagon ruts, but for the most part the bare earth took Valen's weight. The fields of low grass that flanked the road drank deeply of the rain, and in turn fed the livestock which made up much of the economy of Valtiffe. More rain meant fatter sheep, which meant better-fed shepherds, better-dressed merchants, and drunker financiers for him to gamble with. He, like most of the people of this island nation, loved the rain.

THE FIRST SHOT hummed past Valen before he had gone an eighth of a mile. He spun to see the silhouette of the hunter against the glow of the torch light, the man's spectacles making grim red disks of his eyes. He was reloading.

When Valen had heard that the Baron de Niver's dissolute son was going to be hunting on his own the night after the Sjogur Festival, Valen had figured the little peacock would stop at the farm inn for refreshment, especially in the case of rain. He had not figured, though, that the bastard would take it upon himself to start shooting at people when he lost. While it was certainly not unheard of—or truly even frowned upon, by the people of Valtiffe—Valen simply hadn't expected the man to have it in him. He was a gente, after all, of noble family and fine upbringing and all that. Surely his fine old tutors had taught him not to murder a man over a game of cards.

Not the first time he'd misread a player, but if he didn't come up with something quick it might very well be his last. Pivoting right, he jumped a low stile and ran into the darkness of the uneven field. Craggy hills dotted with sheep rose in front of him a short way off; if he could make those hills, he might find something to hide behind between shots.

The rain started again, and Valen laughed through painful breaths. Surely the de Niver heir wasn't good enough to hit him at this distance in the storming dark.

At least that seemed likely until pain exploded in his shoulder. The impact threw him off balance for a second, but he regained his stride with some help of a conveniently placed boulder. No organs in the shoulder. He would deal with the bleeding after he was sure he wouldn't be getting a matching wound in his skull.

Someone tackled him from the side as he ran, utterly knocking what little wind was left in his lungs out into the worsening weather. The two of them landed against the rocky ground in a painful pile, and his assailant shoved his face into the mud.

"Did you say something smart?" It was the poorly-dressed farm boy, one of Valen's co-conspirator Jacquemin's favorite roles. "Again? You just can't help it, can you?"

"It would appear I cannot," Valen mumbled, his nose jammed in grass-covered loam.

"Aye. Next time we run a simple con and you feel like boasting to an armed drunk, you best remember having your face... hells, did he hit you?"

Valen felt Jacquemin's fingers probing the bloody patch on his coat. "Unless one of these sheep is a sharpshooter, yes, I'd say the stuck-up noble with nothing better to do with his time than practice shooting at helpless things running away from him has put a bullet in me. He should be happy; I'm his first success of the day."

Jacquemin removed Valen's neckcloth and pressed it firmly against the wound. Valen was proud of himself for not yelping too loudly.

"We're not outrunning this maniac with you wounded," Jacquemin said. "So we stay here until he gets bored."

"Or finds us."

"Well, if he spots two fellows lying prone in a pasture under these clouds, he's got better eyes than anyone I've ever sailed with."

Something small shrieked over his head. Valen stole a look back at de Niver, whose spectacles still danced with firelight.

"Hardly sporting," he wheezed. "Can't you strike him with lightning or something?"

"You can count yourself lucky I got that storm going at all. Y'know how hard it is to get the rain to start and to then convince it to *stop* again later on?"

"Well, you know what they say about the weather around here; if you don't like it, wait…"

He left the remainder of the old saw unsaid as the whine of another bullet very rudely interrupted him.

Jacquemin poked his head up for a look. "He's reloading every twenty-seven seconds on the mark, and that while walking in the dark at night over slick rocks. He's good."

"I'd like to defer any awe at the man's prowess with firearms until after we're done being on its business end. For now, I recommend we move. Next time he fires, we bolt up, run, then drop at the twenty-sixth second. Indeed, let us say the twenty-fifth, for safety's sake."

"Beats the lightning idea. Hells, we can hide behind some sheep. Bastard can't have that many bullets left on him after blowing them all day."

They waited the twenty-seven seconds, but no bullet came. Valen raised an eyebrow, but Jacquemin just shrugged. Thirty seconds. More.

A new sound spattered across the sodden field. Hoof beats.

Tenerieve was on them in moments, her tricorn off and her purse bouncing with the weight of de Niver's money. She led another horse behind her by the reins.

"Jaq, with me," she ordered. "You're smaller."

Jacquemin pointed at Valen's shoulder. "He's wounded,"

"Badly?"

"No. A graze, but it's a deep one."

Tenerieve looked at Valen for a heartbeat, then over her shoulder at the other horse. "Can you handle this one on your own, Valen?"

"I fear that depends on whether or not I'm being shot at."

"We no longer have need to worry about de Niver's rifle. His dogs, though...."

Valen mounted the young gente's horse without further interrogation, and did his best not to faint from the pain in his back as he and his fellow cheats raced back to the road and toward the city with a horde of poorly-treated hunting dogs in tow.

Card-table talk of sizable sums lost to innocent-eyed Mistigri youths can be heard at any club of quality. These pallid transients shamble into honest towns accompanied by the sounds of their rough music and rougher dialect, and leave jingling with the hard-earned wages of their prey.

Lord d'Alhambere, with whom I have had the pleasure of partnering in many a night of fine play, tells a story of a time when he thought to find a night's entertainment by teaching a dull-witted Mistigri horseman to play two-hand beaufils. It could only improve the vagrant's mind, and perhaps allow him access to a finer set—were he to dress the part. My friend soon found himself beaten quite handily, despite the Mistigri's mumbling and head-scratching. An unlettered migrant had beaten a gente whose name appears on the tournament rolls of the best clubs of Soucisse!

Being a gente, d'Alhambere did not quarrel with the brute who had so clearly snowed him, but reached for his purse to pay what he owed. As any astute reader by now has guessed, his purse had been cut; only cord and a rag of cloth remained. The horseman howled for his due until another patron paid the debt.

The Mistigri are cheats and scoundrels; no person of decent name would engage them in play.

Dishonest Play and Players,
M. Jerôme de Tabanne (pamphlet)

II
TENERIÈVE

IN MANY WAYS, Tenerième's life began in Voet, the great port city on the western coast of the empire of Cadogna. This was several days' sail from Valtiffe, a day's trip up the Magdalene river to the old city of Saut-Leronne, and then a good two-hour ride to the shepherd's inn where she had just taken de Niver for every livre he had on him.

Most people in her line of work, that being dishonest gambling at the expense of others, could claim a youth of beggary on the streets, the gray life of an orphanage, or some great calamity which separated them from happiness. She could claim no such history. Her family was a merchant family, after a fashion, and she'd lived in relative ease—if not comfort—in the warmth of caravan campfires swapping barbs with her several-score cousins. They'd traveled the Rushed Road between the mountain cities of the north and their seafaring counterparts, their horses and wheels serving where wind and sails could not reach, and if their bellies were not as full as they might have liked, at least they were alive.

They were Mistigri, refugees from the northlands ravaged by

a volcanic eruption during the Fire War a century past. The conflict between the Empire of Cadogna and the L'Ombrian Queendom had been hard enough for them, but the flames of Mt. Senecin had left them with no home but ashes. They had made a life on the move, working as they could and never truly welcomed anywhere.

The adults knew her as a cold, quiet child. Never one for troublemaking or ill-planned adventures, nor for warm embraces and easy laughter. As often happens in such cases, one of the elders took a shine to the silent child who sat by the kitchen fires while her contemporaries splashed in muddy rivers just out of the hearing of the adults. Her great-aunt Lucie, seen herself as distant by her family, often happened to have a book on her for Tenerième to borrow or some delicate task for which most young hands would be too impatient or clumsy.

Lucie also introduced Tenerième to the oracular use of cards. She knew enough craft to be regarded as something of a seer among the caravan, though not enough to be considered a true diviner, not in any serious definition of the word. She used the L'Ombrais Fanzago deck, not the Satique deck used in Cadois society, which only added to the mystery.

Fortune-telling with cards, dice, or sticks was as close as an uneducated person could get to the divination magic of the Brothers of the Séminaire. There was no blood in most cases, though some said it could help. Any magic involving blood, no matter how beneficial, would label its practitioner as a witch anywhere in the world; the Mistigri had enough troubles without adding that to the list.

Séminaire magic was a matter of abstraction—of words and rhythms—while witchcraft used the innate powers of the natural world: blood, herbs, rare stones and metals. Cards were their own matter. Any prognostication involving them was more likely to be considered charlatanism than magic.

True Divination was the work of the Brothers. These wisemen worked magic into every aspect of life across the known world. They enchanted the glowstones that lit dark nights and the prows of ships to make them float upstream unaided. They saw futures clearly in still water, and never answered in riddles and half-truths.

Like the Mistigri, the Séminaire held no allegiance to crown or scepter. Their buildings of learning could be found throughout Cadogna, L'Ombre, and any of the small nations those two rivals had yet to encompass, but they operated independently of all of them.

This was one of the reasons Tenerième decided at a young age that she would join them.

Gaining entry into one of the Séminaire academies was difficult for anyone, but it would be especially so for her. The Brothers of Saut-Leronne had never accepted a woman into their order to her knowledge, and not a one of their number had the cobalt-porcelain skin of the Mistigri. And yet it was to the Séminaire in Saut-Leronne that Tenerième desired to go.

Aunt Lucie recognized that her niece's interest was tending more towards intellectual pursuits than a life of carting cabbages was likely to provide. Her parents resisted, of course. She was choosing a difficult life, and one which would take her away from the family. When Tenerième told her parents she planned on going regardless of their concerns, her mother asked her father where they had gone wrong.

They had wanted Tenerième to marry some fool from one of the Cadois towns they passed through and add to the clan. This was of no interest to her, but she bore them no ill will. She knew that those who choose to marry and have children wanted others to know their happiness.

Tenerième could have applied to the school in Voet, but everyone knew the best Séminaire in the Empire was in Saut-

Leronne. She sailed with little more than a scrap of paper bearing a name. A letter of introduction, calling in a long-unpaid debt. She was offered housing with the Hoques, a trader family of that riverside city. She shared a room with the daughter, Marguerite, and by some luck managed to become friends with her.

The application process at the Séminaire was no small endeavor. There were interviews for personal character, tests of linguistic ability. Every Brother Tenerième encountered expressed their doubt that she would succeed. She ignored their concerns and answered their questions. A life of changing personae to fit the expectations of different towns had given her some skill at guessing what a person wanted to hear.

These men had power, she came to learn. Not the power of empires, but they held some measure of influence over every matter of importance. Nearly every home held their handiwork, be it a warming hearthstone or an unbreakable lock, and battles had been decided by the quality of their martial enchantments. She never saw them using their pull outwardly, but it was ever-present in the way they carried themselves, the way the people of Saut-Leronne stepped aside when they walked by.

People had spit on her in her old life. No longer.

It was at school that she had met Valen, an intense young man with some unconventional ideas about magic. She struggled, as a Mistigri woman in a Séminaire academy, but Valen befriended her. Things were worse for her when he left, the circumstances of his sudden and irrevocable departure making any connection with him a black mark. The teachers made it quietly clear that she would never be made a full Brother now. The home she had chosen was now lost to her due to the one friendship she had made there.

She had tried to make a living telling fortunes in the dockside bars, but few credit a soothsayer and even fewer trust a Mistigri with a deck of cards. Even in far Valtiffe, the assumption that her kind would fleece honest folk and disappear in the night could be heard in every whisper when she sat at a table. Valen found her one day and offered her what he called an 'unorthodox job,' which she assumed he had done out of guilt for her situation. It had not truly been his fault, in fact, but such was his way.

The world had no place for her. She knew she must find something at the edges. At the gaming tables, at least, she could be independent. Her opponents might insult her, but they could not deny she had beaten them. The irony of learning how to be a cheat—the only Mistigri cheat she knew—was not lost on her.

Marguerite insisted on meeting Valen, for Tenerième's safety. With time, in late-night conversations and quiet moments, Margo spoke of Valen to Ten more and more. He was clever and diligent, which Marguerite said reminded her of her father in an odd way. She simply enjoyed his company. Ten watched as the love grew from there.

And now, after a rainy night of gambling in the farmland, Tenerième was racing back to the safety of Marguerite's home once again, dogs at her heels and her friend's husband bleeding.

Thieves. Pirates. Ne'er-do-wells. Where one finds the lowest sorts, one also finds dice. Noisy and fast, most games which involve throwing the cube attract those who take no pleasure in mental exertion but prefer instead the animal rush of high stakes and little direction. Some dice games excite a commendable passion in persons of status, to be sure, but no serious player devotes much time to them.

In addition, dice are notoriously easy to rig. Many a journeyman cheat gets his start shaving sides and loading pips. Some tables still use bones from the ankles of sheep after the Valtivan fashion, and no confidence is to be had as to their honesty.

The Gente's Manual, etc.

III
VALEN

EVEN AFTER THEY were fairly certain they had outlasted de Niver's menacing hounds, Valen and his crew kept silent, aside from the occasional word of concern for his injury. As they neared the riverside and the bridge city they called home, the turf-roofed stone huts of the pasture lands gradually gave way to more recent buildings of imported Cadois wood.

There seemed to Valen to be more of these new-styled structures than there had been the last time he had left the comforting bustle of the city. The old ways of wool and ivory and grim steadfastness, the life of the Hvallais people who had lived on Valtiffe for millennia, survived mainly in the rural lands now. Émigrés from the river-faring empire of Cadogna had brought their own fashions—and wealth—for the last few hundred years. The cities of Valtiffe were hardly Valtivan any more, but imperial money meant better-funded gamblers, which suited Valen just fine.

Unlike Cadogna and L'Ombre, Valtiffe was not ruled by a monarch, or even a family of nobles. Everyone who owned land on the island had a vote in the governing body, known in typically stark Hvallais fashion as 'Parliament.' They all stood on an equal footing, small homeowners along with the vastly wealthy and well-familied, although not equally securely: to lose one's land was to lose one's vote.

This was the question of the eventual Tipping Point, the last drop which would make the vase overflow. Many thought the Cadois would vote to turn Valtiffe into a proper Imperial arrondissement, another pearl for the Empress's necklace of countries. It didn't matter much to Valen. He paid his taxes to whomever could punish him for not doing so. As with many people in Valtiffe, he had both countries in his blood.

The windows of Valen's building were blessedly dark. The three compatriots walked up the stairs to the second floor as quietly as two people all but carrying another could be expected to. Tenerièhe chose that moment to start telling her version of the events of the evening, the crux of which was that the shepherd had intervened when de Niver had started shooting.

Valen's drawing room chair, indeed his favorite chair in all of the world, provided little comfort when Jacquemin and Tenerièhe deposited him in it, still bleeding and still uncomfortably drenched from the night's activities. The wound on his shoulder detracted from any feelings of homely relaxation. He idly wondered if he'd be able to smoke a pipe any time soon. Perhaps as a final act.

Jacquemin's eyes—one pale blue, the other brown—searched Valen's body for additional injuries. He had gone tense in preparation for the magic he was about to perform, but hid it with a smile. "The shepherd...?"

Ten clomped across the wooden floor in her boots, and Valen frowned at the noise. "Do try and be a touch quieter, would you?" he whined. "I'm positive the landlord is a hair's breadth from throwing us out of here. It would be hard to keep up my cover with alley fleas on my waistcoat."

"Let her finish her story, old man," Jacquemin said. "Near as I can tell it involved some shepherd saving our lives, and I'll bet she's got a flea or two."

"The shepherd." Tenerième's accent had returned in full, the amiable performance replaced with her customary severity. "Yes. She and her husband ran with clubs and beat the fool, all the while shouting that he was a poacher. He set his poor dogs on us and ran off."

Jacquemin chuckled as he worked Valen's coat off a little too roughly for its owner's tastes. "Young de Niver, the Night Poacher. There's a tale needs a skáld's song, I say."

"You may sing it at my funeral," Valen groaned. "Unless you think we should see to this bullet hole I seem to have developed."

"Give a man a moment," Jacquemin said, still struggling to pull the coat off Valen's tall frame. Jaq had the lean, tanned body of a young man who spent most of his days climbing ropes and reefing sails. He reminded Valen of a fighting dog: small, but dangerous. "Not being a very good host, old man. You've not offered us any refreshments."

"Nor are you being very good guests. We really must keep quiet. I don't want to spend the last moments of my poor life getting evicted."

The tall windows allowed the late moonlight to join them as it made its way over the mountains, making it easy for Valen to find his buttons and remove his shirt. The room was tailored for the comfort of guests, with a small table and oil lamp at every seat. Of course, Valen never *had* any guests save Tenerième and Jacquemin, and they were more suited to the card table cunningly folded and hidden behind a screen. Valen had started to notice scuffs in the finish of the floor where Jacquemin's seat could normally be found. That said, if he left bloodstains all over the furniture, a few scuffs would be least of his concerns.

"Perhaps my bedroom would be a better place for this," Valen offered. "I could lie down, and my bedclothes are of no great value."

Some piece of furniture scraped against the floor behind him. Tenerième was on all fours, proudly holding a tiny mouse. "And wake Margo?"

"Too late for that, I fear."

This new voice belonged to Marguerite Quinol, who appeared through the inner door fully clothed in one of her plain dresses and a dark pelisse trimmed in fur. "And the drawing room will be quite adequate, thank you. The light is better here."

Valen smiled, a genuine smile, and rose from his seat. "Good morning, my love. You'll forgive me for appearing in such dishabille in the drawing room, but I simply could not wait to get home and see you."

"I'm sure your friends are in a great rush to see you clothed again." She raised an eyebrow at Jacquemin. "You couldn't have done this sooner, Jaq?"

Tenerième cut Jacquemin off before he could retaliate. "We thought it best to get home before de Niver came back with a crew of fops, Margo." Jacquemin had a way of perceiving slights in every word Marguerite spoke, and Tenerième's close friendship with her often put her between the two. "You know how difficult they are to avoid once they've set their bored, useless minds on a thing."

"Oh, she knows quite well," Valen said, smiling weakly. "She has been suffering my attentions for years. Now." He motioned to the mouse wriggling in Tenerième's gloved hand. "Ten, give the man his weapon, would you?"

Jacquemin took the mouse and stood quite still. "Alright, old man. Sit back down. You could probably use a firewine."

"After." Valen lowered himself to his chair and tried not to think about what was going to happen next.

"As you like. You know, I think I'll join you. Could use a good belt after this."

Even after years in the learning halls of the Séminaire, where the hours were spent watching others work magic of all manner in the service of education, Valen was always impressed by witchcraft. He had seen little of the art outside of Jacquemin's occasional sailorly ministrations and weather-working, but still he respected it. An unpopular opinion, to be sure.

Jacquemin held the mouse to his lips and squeezed until the little thing got agitated and bit him. He ran a finger over the wound, collecting a dollop of blood, which he then ran along the mouse's back. The animal let out a neighbor-waking squeal as Jaq dug a finger into its belly until it burst, after which he applied the thing's guts to his own eyes without blinking. Then it was in the mouth, swallow, and the mouse was gone like a festival bon-bon.

A maddening itch replaced the pain as the skin of Valen's wound knitted itself back together. Only a fresh pink scar remained, a few moments later. Valen thanked Jacquemin, who was rubbing desperately at his eyes, and dressed.

This spellcraft differed from the cerebral works of the Séminaire. Jacquemin's magic was witch magic, a bartering of power, the kind the Séminaire detested but turned a blind eye toward. They could easily have used their influence to make witchcraft a crime and give themselves a monopoly on the magic arts; Valen was never sure why they didn't.

Unlike the witches telling fortunes on street corners or working their hexes over crops, Jaq used a type of magic specific to sailors, all salt and wind and blood. It never sat well with Valen, but when you add a former pirate to your list of associates, that sort of thing is bound to happen.

Marguerite's offer of firewine was interrupted by a quiet rapping from the door.

"All the hells," Valen whispered. He was only barely dressed, quite stained with blood, and entertaining two sopping wet visitors in the very late hours. The tableau was not one he would want his landlord to witness.

Jacquemin pushed him into the back rooms before he had the presence of mind to head there himself. Tenerième followed, bloody clothing in her arms.

The three of them stood facing each other in the dark as Marguerite told the downstairs neighbor she hadn't been able to sleep and had bumped into the furniture a few times. This downstairs neighbor happened to be the landlord's ill-tempered and ague-afflicted old uncle, who took every opportunity to rail against the dissolution of society he had seen in his long years, the inference naturally being that married people who raised no children and kept odd hours were a prime example of said trends. He did not hide his attempts to get the Quinols thrown out; indeed, he took great pride in them.

Valen needed this place. When he had won enough for the rooms here in the bourgeois Gouvernor Pole, he could at last build a believable cover story which gave him access to the decent clubs. Hard to do when you walk the wrong direction home every night.

It had nearly bankrupted them to do it, and they had accepted the risk. As long as they kept money coming in regularly, they would be fine. Valen may have come home wounded, but at least he and his crew had won some cash. He imagined the look in Margo's eyes if she had to pack their possessions for a move back down to the Docks, back to her parents' house to take that room they were always offering. Valen had ruined the homes of enough of his loved ones. He wasn't going to do it again.

And anyway, he liked this place.

The door closed, and the three gamblers walked back into the light of the drawing room without speaking. Marguerite poured two brandies and handed them to the men without a smile. "You beat him, then? De Niver?"

She gave Valen a hard look for a moment, and he tried to guess what she was feeling. She never liked having to shut the neighbors up, but this time was different. Was there something else troubling her?

"We did," Jacquemin said. "Us dumb peasants took him for every coin he had on him. I might have got some of those fancy silver buttons off him if we'd kept going."

"We did not get his buttons, but I did take these," Tenerième said. Between two slight fingers she held de Niver's gold-rimmed spectacles by a rim. "The shepherd's first clout knocked them off of his nose. If we're going to have a gente after us, we may as well take everything we can. Try them on, Valen."

Valen wanted his associates to leave so he could speak plainly with Marguerite. They had just risked themselves for him, though, so he supposed he had to play host a while longer. He took the spectacles from Tenerième's hand and balanced them on his nose. He saw nothing of note through the glass.

"They don't seem to magnify much. His vision must be fair."

"Think back to school, Valen." Tenerième had studied Divination at the Séminaire for two years by the time Valen had stumbled into the quiet old place. Despite being several years his junior, she treated him as a novice, then and now. "This man shot you under impossible circumstances, and he was wearing these when he did it."

Cursing himself for not realizing it immediately, Valen saw the tell-tale signs of enchantment on the lenses, the faint tinge of a color he couldn't describe. It was unmistakable once he looked for it.

Tenerième pulled a deck of cards from a pocket of her coat, slipped a single card out of it, and held it in front of her with its back toward Valen. "Now," she said. "What card do I hold?"

The trouble with an unfamiliar enchantment was trying to figure out what it was for. Valen stared at the card back, wondering if he would be granted a vision of the other side, or if some aura would give him suit and number. Seven gossamer hands floating in a circle around Tenerième's head or some such thing.

When nothing appeared, he looked closely at the patterns on the card back...

Absurdly close. It was as if he was inches away from the delicate whorls and figures of the card's design. If it was marked, no matter how faintly, he could have seen it plainly even in the dimmest candlelight.

The corner of Tenerième's mouth rose a degree. "That's not it."

He looked up from the card for a moment to meet Tenerième's smug eyes. Eyes in which he could plainly see the card reflected.

"Nine of cups," he declared, and snatched the card out of Tenerième's hand to confirm it. "That bastard was cheating us."

"Surely," Jacquemin grunted. "Rich ponce out for a laugh, bit of the rough life, stealing money from the common folk as if he didn't do that enough already. Cliché as they come."

Valen removed the offending glasses and handed them back to Tenerième, happy to rid himself of them. "I think I'd be bored to sobbing. Where's the fun if you know all the cards?"

"Fun enough for you, apparently," Marguerite countered. "You play with marked decks."

"Well, yes, but with these glasses there's not even any craft to it. No deft fingers and fast eyes. We play with rigged cards, certainly, but to interpret them takes cleverness."

"Cleverness? It's a simple code, Valen."

"Simple? My dear, nothing about your marks is simple. You try remembering the meanings of dozens of different miniscule marks subtly integrated in the design on the back of a card...."

Jacquemin interrupted in the sing-song cadence of a child memorizing something. "'If the branch in the corner has three twigs, it's a lamp. Two, a key.' But that's only on that blue design from Droulet's. On another deck...."

"I know," Marguerite said impatiently, "I made them." She was still frowning. This was very much unlike her indeed.

Valen smiled. "And a fine job you did of it. But it takes a careful mind not to mix all that up when you need to win a hand to keep from losing all you have." He took the deck from Ten's hands and started shuffling. "Cardsharping is a skill like any other, mastered through careful study and persistent practice. It took me years before I was confident enough in my hook cut to use it in public." He performed this trick cut with the cards face up, showing how it kept the last card on the bottom of the deck as he rearranged the rest of the cards. "De Niver just... spent some of his allowance for enchanted glasses."

Tenerième smirked. "And even then the fool could not win."

"How much do you think these things cost, Ten?" Valen asked. "They must have come direct from the Séminaire; no glazier would admit to selling these in the open. Custom made for our night poacher, most likely."

"It has been some time since I've seen any of the fees charged by the Brothers, but I assume an amount which would buy these rooms outright."

"He'll want them back, I wager." Jacquemin leaned his chair back, which Valen was certain would leave marks on his floors. He really did need to get a bigger rug. "Probably a shit hunter without them, too. Best not run into him again."

"Agreed," Valen said with a laugh. "Between that and the new scar on my shoulder I feel quite safe in saying I plan on declining any invitation to the de Niver estate for the season."

Marguerite did not join the mirth. "This was not a good enemy to make. The favorite son of a powerful family."

"Yes," Ten said, surprising Valen with her agreement.

"You knew he was a gente, Ten." Valen's jaw tightened. "You didn't see fit to mention any concerns before. And aren't you the one who made off with his spectacles?"

"After he shot at you. Yes. We were meant to take his money and leave. We could have just walked off and been done with it. But something happened. Why did he start the shooting?"

"That'd be 'cause Valen opened his mouth," Jacquemin grumbled. "Just can't help yourself, can you?"

"I teased the fool a little," Valen said hurriedly. "A little jab. That's all."

Tenerève stood as still as a post, angry eyes on his. "He will want satisfaction. We must avoid him. He will tell his friends also: a short young man who dresses terribly, a Mistigri woman, an older man who talks too much. They will look for us."

"Excellent," Valen forced a smile to his face. "Then we shall take their money, too. We shall play them for every kron over the course of years. We will let them win just often enough to make them think they have a chance, and we'll drink honeyed wine as we take what we wish from them."

Marguerite took a step to her friend's side. "You might. If they don't bring their hunting rifles."

Having assured themselves that Valen was not going to collapse from his injury and the hard ride, the group settled in for firewine and exchanged their thoughts on the night's adventure. Valen once again found himself a bit house-proud. The Gouvernor Pole building was a decent hôtel with a view of the bridge and proximity to the main thoroughfares, without being so close as to hear the clatter of hooves on stone all day and night.

These rooms were, aside from being a convenient addition to his cover story, Valen and Marguerite's first real home together.

The life of a gambler had kept them on the road for most of the ten years they had been married. In those heady, fun years they'd moved from town to town with the ready ease of the young. Few possessions, few needs. Valen gambled and Marguerite traded; there was always room in the shops for a new style of fabric at a good price. They had a standing joke that Marguerite's speculation in the value of the various trade goods they carted from home to home made her more of a gambler than Valen ever was.

As middle age settled in, and their contemporaries—short-lived friendships they maintained in the towns they frequented—started having children, they felt the draw of a steady hearth of their own. In the two years they had spent at the Pole, they had outfitted the place modestly but with some of the taste and style they prided themselves upon. Nothing that did not befit their alleged station; Valen had Saut-Leronne convinced he was a financier's clark.

Everyone knew him to be a man of finance, but no one was ever *his* client. To the people of Saut-Leronne, he was ever someone *else's* accountant. He referred business to actual moneyhouses when pressed, claiming conflicting interests or some suitably boring excuse. And money-changing was considered to provide a decent enough income and leisure time suitable to be seen— nay, expected—at the gambling tables.

Marguerite's efforts in managing the finances of their little cabal required no cover story. Her family, the Hoques, had been successful ivory-traders for generations.

As it was just the two of them, few rooms were required. Marguerite made use of a study for her affairs, as well as her remarkable skill at marking cards, and Valen required no workspace.

"Monsieur Arbelan came by today." Marguerite provided no context and revealed no opinion on the matter.

Any attention Valen was paying to his décor was now firmly on his wife.

"Here?"

"He said he would return in the morning. Dawn."

Valen tried to keep his tone light, but failed. "Not for a duel, I hope?"

"No," Marguerite said, and Valen stopped holding his breath. Hugues Arbelan ran a small but ardent gang in the Hillside neighborhood, The Naughty Knaves, and had secured his position as their leader by dueling anyone who crossed him. He was a quick hand with the smallsword, but lacked any of the education necessary to understand the finer strategies of the duel, relying on his native speed. An artless fool with a cruel streak.

"What could he want?"

"Perhaps he looks to finish some unresolved business," Tenerière said. "His choice to come at dawn seems portentous."

Marguerite shook her head. "No, if he had intended a duel he would have named his choice of weapons and place."

"It wouldn't be the first time, would it?" Valen said.

The last time he had seen Arbelan, Valen had utterly trounced him at a game of joccas to the tune of a few months' rent. Arbelan had called him a cheat and insisted on a duel, which he would almost certainly have won—Valen's dexterity did not extend to swordplay. Valen had refused, though it was not strictly necessary; by the rules of decency, he would have had to have made the challenge himself, as he was the insulted party. When Arbelan would not relent, Valen offered a roll of the bones. Odds they fight, evens they part ways.

As the knucklebones clattered over the table, Valen cast a spell. The dice rolled two and four: evens. Arbelan's cronies had pulled their boss away. Even among criminals, there is only so far one can push the boundaries of etiquette.

He counted that as one of his first great successes with his self-made magic, though he could never be sure it was truly his doing.

"I can handle Arbelan." Valen turned to Ten and Jaq. "Either way, there is no need for you two to be implicated in whatever nonsense he has come to spin. I'll see you at work."

Tenerième and Jacquemin lingered on their brief goodbyes, clearly hesitant to leave, but Valen wanted a moment with Marguerite before the miscreant arrived.

Once they were alone, they put aside the easy masks they wore for the others and sat on the couch facing each other.

"There aren't any big events coming up, are there?" Valen asked, avoiding the more difficult questions. Hugues Arbelan in his home; this was not a sign of happy days to come. "Anything he would need extra hands for?"

"Nothing," Marguerite said, exasperated. "The Sjogur Festival just ended. No holidays, no elections. Munnrais has the docks, Arbelan has the hill, and we all sleep soundly."

Munnrais. The leader of the gang calling themselves Les Royaux, and Arbelan's biggest rival. It disgusted Valen that he even knew the man's name. Street gangs and territories—this was no way for a man of quality to live.

"What does that bastard think he's up to, coming by here?"

Marguerite sighed with exasperation. "There is only one reason he would come to you."

"Money."

"Control. There are much faster ways for him to get money than harassing a gamester. He wants you in his côterie."

Valen shook his head. "I doubt that. He detests me. I'm not one of his up-from-the-gutter cases. Hells, who knows how much money I've won from people in his employ?"

"The man is a pompous lout, but he can lead. He recognizes what people can do for him and makes it worth their while. He'll be happy to tell you so."

"I can't imagine he has anything I want." Valen frowned deeply. "Nothing is worth working with him."

Marguerite pointed to a spot on the back of Valen's chair. "I'm glad to hear you say it. Staining the upholstery with blood from a gunshot wound smacks a bit much of the violent criminal element."

Valen held back a snappish response. The path of this argument had been well-trod already, and nothing new was to be gained. The line between harmless cardsharp and jaded criminal thinned in places, and Valen wasn't always successful at treading the right side of it. "De Niver is a gente, Margo. I chose him precisely for that reason. No more dockrats and would-be thieves. Step by step until we can open our casino."

Saving enough to open a casino in Saut-Leronne after the fashion of those in the Queendom of L'Ombre had proved to be a challenge. This was the goal the Quinols had set for themselves years prior, and the closest thing they had to a plan.

Once they opened the casino, Valen could practice his luck magic constantly. He wouldn't even need to play; no one would mind the owner walking around and watching the games. He would develop his new discipline in safety.

With land ownership tied to the vote, one did not see many opportunities to purchase, and certainly not for a price the Quinols could come close to affording. Most deals of this kind were done in private among friends and like-minded individuals, the majority of whom were on the better side of well-to-do. Keep the right people in, and all that.

The right people don't spend their time rolling the bones in filthy alleyways or playing for small stakes in bourgeois bars. Valen needed to make acquaintances of a higher standing.

"With you manning the books, we'll have enough soon," Valen said.

Enough. That most elusive amount.

Marguerite frowned, disbelieving. "Not all that soon."

"Sooner than you think, I promise," He lightened his tone. "I was looking at places downtown. That carambol club your father's a member of is in a nice enough neighborhood."

Marguerite laughed. "You want to open a casino next to The Herringbone? The oldest carambol club in Saut-Leronne?"

"A little healthy competition would suit us well." Valen smiled back at her. He was glad to be steering this conversation away from Arbelan and his sword. "And no carambol will be allowed in our place; I never could stand the cracking balls."

The laugh on Marguerite lips died quickly. "Let's focus on dealing with Arbelan first. See what he wants and learn what we can. More information is always better. Whatever it is he's after, I can't imagine we'll end up on the winning side of it."

Valen wanted to make some charming quip that would make it all seem just so trivial, but he had to agree with her.

The Fanzago deck has been the standard for playing cards in casinos, taverns, and clubs throughout the Ombrian coastlands and the adjacent countries for over two centuries. Originally manufactured in the port city of Anillar and sold to sailors for petty coins, the Fanzago worked its way from the crumbling docks of Mola to the noise and color of sunny Torreçon as naval trade grew in the relative security of the post-war decades (circa 1010-1030), and has made an indelible mark on our cultural history[1].

Each card in the Fanzago deck bears an illustration of a pastoral scene, all cleverly drawn so that the images on the cards align perfectly when placed next to each other. Distant mountains form an uninterrupted horizon behind foreground depictions of farms and castles, beasts and streams. Rearranging them to form pretty landscapes and little stories is a common diversion in both nurseries and salons, but their main use is, and has always been, in gameplay.

---

[1] You will not find the Fanzago deck in use in any decent clubs in Cadogna. This limits our skills at carré, perhaps, but that odd game is the only one played in L'Ombre to which a gente might bend his mind. The loss is not too keenly felt.

The Fanzago Deck: A Brief History,
Grandee Ariadna de Alodesal y Juegon,
Gamesmaster of Torreçon,
Translated, and with annotations by,
M. Jerôme de Tabanne

IV
RIA

THE BREEZE THAT stole into the great marble room of the casino was too weak to disturb a single card. The thick curtains hung heavily in their ties as powders and perfumes contended with the lifeless reek of noblemens' sweat at every table. Ria's light undertunic, cunningly ruched to keep its wearer cool, clung to her back regardless. Her brother had offered to work a cooling enchantment into the undertunic for her in his Séminaire atelier, but Ria avoided such displays of wealth; modesty befits a servant of the people.

The night's clammy atmosphere would make palming a card a few shades easier, so she made certain to be seen at every table to discourage such ideas. Everyone on the casino floor of her mother's arcada knew who she was, be they peer or paisan, and knew her reputation for spotting a cheat.

She hardened her features against the mugginess, an appropriate skill for Gamesmaster to the Corte of the sunny coastal city of Torreçon, one of the greatest ports of Ombria. Dona Ariadna de Alodesal y Juegon—'Ria,' to the few who knew her well—was known for the stillness of her face both in high-stakes games at the casino and higher-stakes negotiations at the Palacio. And if she heard a few choice items at the former which could be of use at the latter, well, who could blame her?

Ria's position made her a gambler by vocation, but she was not one of the gilded sots who came to the fine marquetry tables to show how little they cared for something as common as currency. Ria was a professional. She won and lost as she chose (and as the best interests of her family directed) through patience and skill, not blood-pumping wagers. Her tools were caution, memorization, practice; techniques which a student of any craft did well to adopt.

Juan Burqu, the best of Ria's pit bosses, stepped over to her with far less noise than a man of his size should have been able to. He was the sort of man who shook hands sideways, his arms too muscular to extend straight from the chest. There wasn't a trace of sweat on him.

Burqu's hard eyes glinted toward one of the tables. "He's up to it again, Dona."

Dona. A smile of friendly frustration rose to her lips. Try as she might, she could never convince Burqu to leave off his formality. He had served her family since before she was tall enough to see the felt tops of the tables in her mother's new casino. She used to pretend Burqu was a giant and she the brave caballero sent to slay the grim fiend who stomped between the table-mountains and tower-chairs.

Rumors—legends, really—of the man's past placed his broad, bearded face at most of the more exciting battles of the previous generation, when pirates backed by the Empress of Cadogna ravaged the Ombrian coasts. 'The Culling of the Corsairs,' the war was called, and Juan had apparently done more than a little culling himself. Ria's mother told her once over a glass too many that he had entered the family's service on a temporary basis after he lost a big wager against her father, but stayed on when he found he enjoyed the work. This seemed likely; most of Don Juegar's greatest coups had taken place over dice. The man had a gift for making people happy to risk whatever he wanted them to.

Juan Burqu addressing Ria as a noble felt to her like an eagle calling a canary 'Queen.' Still, he had never made a peergild. It was appropriate for him to address her by her title.

"Who's up to what again, Juan?" Ria asked, only partly teasing. "We should make certain we're conniving about the same person."

"At the mirror table, Dona. You know him?"

She followed his glare to see a lean, stooped don in his sixties smiling winningly at the other players around the carré table. The great gold-framed mirror on the wall behind him gave her a view of all of his opponents.

"Oh yes. Don Sesio de Vicenns," Ria recited. "Mining. First-generation noble. He donated the marble for the Granplaza as peergild. Unbeatable at carré."

Juan nodded. "Yes, Dona. And with him is a man named Lucas Sartian."

"A paisan?"

"For now. Could be a peer already if he'd stop losing to Vicenns," Juan shook his bald head. "That seat the don is in is the favorite of every cheat in the house. Sit with a mirror to your back, they think you're too foolish for false play."

Ria allowed her eyebrow to rise a degree. "Perhaps. Or perhaps it sets the other players up. A quick flash of your cards above the table is enough to tempt anyone into trying to spy them in the reflection. An honest player feels ashamed at that, and is too confused about his own morals to bother thinking about yours."

"If that's his game, then it's working," Juan grunted. "He's kept Sartian coming back night after night."

"To win his money back," Ria said with a nod. An old story.

"Not exactly, Dona. He has not lost much at all, but he has yet to win. Vicenns is keeping him right on the cusp. Each night the fool paisan returns, thinking that his skill is improving. Each night Vicenns toys with him. Several times now there have been pots large enough to change Sartian's life. But each time, Vicenns manages it so that he breaks even."

"You think he's cheating?"

"If I could say so for sure, I would have thrown him down the stairs."

"Hardly worth the risk for a don, I think," Ria said. "The man is a master carré player, Juan. Even in the stuttering games they play in the lowest of taverns, they know of him. Strategies have been named after him. Unless this Sartian is a prodigy, Vicenns is in complete control of that table at all times. And he is using his skill to keep Sartian playing. Why?"

"Sartian's a successful merchant, Dona."

"Ah. And successful enough to make peer. I see what's happening here."

Juan shrugged, then turned to scowl at a knot of youths making more noise than he approved of.

Ria kept herself from frowning. Vicenns was trying to keep Sartian from joining the peerage. If there was one thing she hated about her own class, it was how many of them wanted to keep their number as small as possible. Elitist bastards.

It was not meant to be this way. Social mobility based on public service was the cornerstone of Ombrian society. In order to be a member of the nobility, and thus part of the voting class, a person needed to perform some great public work, a 'peergild.' Parks, healing homes, schools—all were supported by the peergild system. Ria's mother had built the first floor of the arcada when she was twenty and expanded it regularly.

A cynical person would say that her mother kept improving

the place to make sure her nobility was never questioned; if a peer did not continue to donate public works throughout her life, she could be voted out of the nobility. Ria knew, though, that her mother truly believed that the populace needed open spaces to meet and pleasant diversions from the strains of life. No one in Corte would challenge an Alodesal, after all.

Even the children of nobles needed to perform a peergild to be allowed a vote, though this often took the form of an augmentation to the family's works. At her mother's suggestion, Ria held a city-wide festival and tournament of games in the distant, frigid city of Saut-Leronne on Valtiffe, open to all comers for free. She took pride in paying for the event herself. Her mother would have helped her with the finances, of course, but there was no need to risk the condescending looks of other peers later on. She had done it the old-fashioned way.

The event was such a success she was made Ambassador to the backwards country, which was in essence a Cadois colony at this point. She had yet to hold another tourney. Indeed, she had not visited since the first, making do with the occasional dinner with the Valtivan Ambassador in Torreçon.

She watched this paisan Sartian in the mirror, deciding her next move. A not-unhandsome fellow, paler of skin than she and with his hair swept up in the latest fashion. He wore simple black clothing. A single silver brooch was his only adornment. The clean, conservative look of a paisan among peers. Best not to look as if one was trying too hard.

The undertaking of a peergild was the only way for a paisan of Ombria to elevate himself. A recognized public act afforded the person a seat in Corte and a vote on matters of state. One could barely walk a half-mile in the city without passing a stadium or soup kitchen built by a person who woke up one morning as 'señor' and went to bed that night as 'piaron.' Ria loved to see it.

Don Vicenns turned, blocking her view of Sartian's reflection. The thin man held a glass of wine to his lips for a long moment, only barely sipping at it, then smiled broadly at Sartian as he slid a stack of coins across the table.

Not all of the nobility felt as Ria did. Her family were grandees; they had been peers for centuries, since before the neighboring countries fell to paisan revolutions and the peergild was instated to ensure the needs of the populace were tended to. If anyone had the right to look down their nose at an ambitious paisan, it was an Alodesal. Yet it seemed to her that those people of families which had only recently become nobility—within a generation or two—were the ones most likely to undermine those who tried to do the same.

Ria pressed Burqu's arm and whispered to him. "So Vicenns takes pleasure in keeping this fine paisan down, is that correct? Well, that simply will not do. Not in my casino."

"Agreed, Dona," Juan said with a short nod. "Shall I find cause to remove him?"

"Absolutely not. Any action on our part will reveal we have guessed his game and open us to retaliation at Corte. We will simply have to see that he loses."

Burqu's wide forehead wrinkled. "That Don Vicenns loses at carré? I have yet to see that happen. You just called him a master yourself, Dona."

"Then I suppose I must play well."

Despite Burqu's smothered blustering, Ria directed a passing servant to refresh the mirror table's wine at the expense of the house. She walked over to the game, Burqu's impossibly light footfalls following her.

By the time she reached the table, all six players were clapping politely and smiling at her. Ria smiled warmly at them, the perfect host.

In a casino, a deck of cards is the standard unit of measurement.

Ria's quick hands were nearly as narrow as a deck's width. Don Vicenns' ruff collar was as thick as a deck is tall. The stack of coins in front of Sartian was no taller than a deck lying on its face.

Decks came and went with as little notice as that given to a napkin. They were replaced at the first sign of wear, at the request of a player, or at the will of the croupier, whose reasoning for the change was inscrutable and unquestioned. The casino's reputation depended on the honesty of its cards.

Ria had several decks of cards on her person at any given moment, as did most of her staff. It caused no surprise whatsoever at the table when she pulled one out of a pocket, only a small increase in the volume of the applause.

"Ah, will the Dona grace us with a hand?" Don Vicenns asked, careful not to knock over his stack of coins as he spread his hands in welcome. "You are too generous."

Ria nodded and made sure to catch the eye of every person at the table. "I live to serve, piaron," she said, emphasizing the last word just slightly. Etiquette did not strictly require that she address him so formally, but as the game at this table had become one of statecraft, she felt that the relative stations of the players should be brought to the top of their minds.

A throat cleared behind her: Burqu, insisting on speaking to her before she sat. He brought her a few steps away from the table, which was now clinking with refreshed glasses and excitement. It was somewhere between a superstitious belief, and something of a tradition, that the players would do particularly well when the Gamesmaster joined the play.

"You must not do this, Dona," Burqu said, making sure to use body language which would make any onlooker think they were discussing some mundane matter. An over-attentive servant with some petty issue interrupting his dona.

"Do what, Juan?"

"You know full well," he replied, and looked directly at the deck of cards in Ria's slender hand. The rigged deck her brother the wiseman had enchanted for her. "You must not risk this. To even be accused of cheating..."

Ria let her eyes make the smallest roll. The annoyed dona. "There is no risk, my dear. I'm not using it the way you think. After all, I have you to protect me, don't I?"

Clearly recognizing he was dismissed both in appearance and in truth, Burqu bowed and walked away, off to scare the other tables.

A deck of cards enchanted by a Brother being used by a grandee to quash the devices of an uppity first-generation Don. The influence of the Séminaire could be found everywhere, it seemed. Even at Ria's own tables. They kept out of political matters themselves, by all accounts, but she wondered how much truth there was to that.

"Forgive me," Ria sighed, turning back to the carré game. "I will deal, if you would have me."

Don Vicenns applauded again, thin fingertips against the bowl of his palm. "You heap kindness on kindness, Dona."

She dismissed the croupier with a small nod. As the quiet fellow stepped away, he held his fingers to his right forearm in three quick movements. Ria was glad to see that her staff was keeping the secret signal language sharp. According to the flurry of small gestures, Vicenns had been winning all evening, but not by much. Sartian's patience was waning—he would start to play recklessly soon. The other three players were of no particular interest.

Sartian made a seated bow to Ria as she took her chair. "Dona, it is my pleasure to make your acquaintance," he said. His accent would have fit in at Corte without raising a single painted eyebrow, be he wood merchant or pedigreed don. "Your casino is the finest in the region, and I hope you would not think me too bold were I to commend you on the excellence of its management."

Ria smiled politely, but not too warmly. "Entertainment is a service I am all too happy to provide, Señor Sartian. And as the bulk of the house's earnings go to educational funds, you'll forgive me if I now try to win your money."

Pleasant laughter chimed over the table and Ria dealt the next hand.

Her brother's enchanted deck was of the standard style, no unusual card backs or flowery numbering. A common Fanzago deck, one of tens of thousands in Torreçon alone, easily found at any corner shop and the standard at most casinos in the country. Ria appreciated the simple beauty of the thing, and was something of a dilettante scholar on the history of the deck's design and production.

She had also made sure to learn the many interpretations that fortune-telling soothsayers made from the varied arrangements. She held no stock in such things herself; she was not one to allow hopes and fancies to clutter her mind. But her work was games, and she took it upon herself to learn all there was to know about them. Gamblers were a superstitious sort, putting great store into lucky talismans and winning streaks. The right card at the right moment could be a powerful tool for shaping a man's mind.

Within minutes of Ria joining the game, the truth of Vicenns's legendary skill became evident to her. Carré was her favorite distraction, and she knew the probabilities of a player holding three consecutive Acorns if he led a low Ribbon as well as she knew the hallways of her family home. Vicenns, though, seemed to know when an opponent held cards that were mathematically unlikely. He could have forced the game into a victory with ease. He held the bulk of the pot, and always knew which card to lay off and which to draw. A few times he pretended to be taking one of the row of cards simply to improve the picture they made.

"Hay forces me to sneeze," he said. "Let's get those farmers away from the city wall, shall we?"

The table chuckled, but Ria saw those farmers return soon enough.

She couldn't beat him. Even with her unreadable face. But she had time.

The game went back and forth between Ria, Sartian, and Vicenns for the first hour. The addition of Ria's skill to the table was enough to push out the other players fairly quickly. They left with the grace that suits a peer, and Vicenns went so far as to rise and clap when each left. This from the man who played with a paisan's future as if it were a child's bauble.

As he sat back down after the last of the other players bowed and walked off, Ria stilled her mind and used the deck as her brother had taught her. She asked the deck for a particular card, carving the detail of its image in her thoughts: *The two of stones.*

A lesser card. Of barely any use in the aggregation of any set, sequence, or royal. It depicted two men hoisting a pale cube of rock onto a cart. Even in the fortune-teller's trade it bore little interest. 'An ongoing endeavor.'

But Don Vicenns owned two marble quarries.

The first lie placed the two of stones between cards depicting a soldier and a weeping couple. In the next, adjacent to a blasted tree. Then to the right of a pillar, the position which was thought by fortune-tellers to represent a good thing soon to come to an end. So many combinations, and all of them seemed to spell trouble for the two, if one believed in that sort of thing.

Vicenns's friendly demeanor cooled a little as one hand followed another. His eyes watched the flip of each dealt card with a new intensity. Ria didn't need to beat him. She didn't need to use her rigged deck to give him a run of bad cards. She only needed to break his confidence.

Young Sartian did not hide his excitement as his stacks of gold grew taller.

A servant signaled to Ria as she refilled the wine glasses. The game was attracting some attention in the casino. Ria looked up for the first time in hours and noticed the many faces turned toward her. Coins and notes passed between hands: sidebets.

She could show them. She could let them see what happens when a peer acts unjustly in her establishment, especially some first-generation snob. A few sly looks would let her patrons know she was up to something.

But she could not risk it. Even the slightest wink would destroy her family's reputation, perhaps even their place in Corte. She kept her face frozen.

Sartian took the opportunity of Ria's momentary distraction to speak. "I can only credit Luck, Don Vicenns. She has been at my side all night, it seems."

The room went silent to hear Vicenns's response, but he made none. He sat straight-backed and waited for the next deal. Ria riffled the cards loudly to end the moment before any of the on-lookers decided to involve themselves.

She dealt a hand without the two of stones. She no longer needed it.

Three hands later Sartian placed a wild bet which went in his favor, contradicting every strategy Ria had ever read. He rose and clapped as Vicenns left the table. The Don bowed, but kept his eyes away from the other players.

She put herself out of the game shortly, though she made a decent run of it for show. A clutch of Sartian's friends—whether existing or newly-minted, Ria did not know—escorted him out under a hail of back-clapping.

As dishonorable as his behavior had been, Vicenns was still a guest and a peer. Ria slipped over to the quiet table where he was drinking one of the finer wines she offered and took a seat, uninvited.

He did not wait for coy allusions. "I suppose you have come to gloat on your victory."

"Sartian beat me as well, piaron," Ria said. The temptation to reveal her machinations was great, but she simply could not chance it.

"He has taken some of your money, yes," Vicenns grumbled. "But he has defeated me. You have ruined me. So much time in this place, some luck must have rubbed off on you; all was well until you graced us with your beneficent presence. If that boy doesn't toast to you with every glass he drinks tonight, then he is turning a blind eye on Luck herself."

The old man was drunk and angry. A single loss at the carré table and he had become a stomping child. This was no kind of behavior for a peer.

Ria flagged a glass from a servant and poured for herself from the Don's bottle. "Luck goes where she wishes. I would not take it too hard."

Vicenns gave her a sad smile. "No, *you* would not. You would not need to. If some rival set up a casino and took your business out from under you, then your grandee mother's treasury would see you to rights. She would buy you another peergild and you could continue to vote in a way which would protect your family. Not all of us have this boon."

An insult, now? "*Enough*, Vicenns," she hissed. "Enough of your howling. Your behavior at the table was unworthy, and now you insult me in my own building. Your dignity as a member of Corte should take precedence over your bruised pride. You lost a night's wagers to a paisan. Don't be angry he can no longer be your plaything."

Ria expected Vicenns to retaliate, to let his ire out at her in drunken rambling. A duel, even. Where was Juan, anyway?

But Don Vicenns sat straight in his chair and smiled again.

"Piaron, Lucas Sartian has been trying to gamble his way to quick money." His eyes went flat. "He plans to buy land in Valtiffe, the very country you yourself represent us to."

She blinked. Land in Valtiffe? Ria tried to make her face placid again to hide her confusion, but she had already let the mask break.

"The banks have stopped his credit," Vicenns continued. "And he has called in every favor he had. He was close to having enough to pay, but not quite. A decent man would simply let the matter go with some patience. But he has great ambitions, does Lucas. He has found some way through bribery, threats, theft, or what-have-you to gain some influence in that pagan place. I cannot say for sure what his ends are, but my play was the only thing keeping him from them."

"What is this to you?"

"If he owns land there, he gets a vote in their parliament."

"And?"

"Sartian has family in Cadogna, Dona. He has borrowed a great deal of money from the Cadois banks through them."

Ria's skin went cold. She should have been aware that someone with such close ties to Cadogna was spending so much time in her casino. It was not uncommon for people, especially those of the lower classes, to have some sort of family ties in the lands of the enemy empire. Soldiers, sailors, and diplomats had been plying their trades in those parts at the direction of the Corte for generations, and not all of them found their way home. But for one of her regulars to be in debt to the Cadois? She was spending too much time as a casino owner and not enough as an agent of the crown.

Don Vicenns kept drinking as he spoke. "Once he moves to Valtiffe, he will do all he can to ensure any stone comes from Cadois vendors in the future, to try to win favor. I ship stone to Valtiffe. One of my best customers will be lost to me.

"I am not of an old family, Dona Alodesal. I cannot weather this loss. If Sartian is as clever as I fear, I will likely have to sell one of my quarries. In a few years, I will be unable to keep up my peergild and will lose my status. Sartian has gained his ladder and lost a competitor in a single night, not through honest work and civic-mindedness but through luck, just as he hoped he would."

Was the old man lying to her? Was this some intricate bluff? How did this get away from her? She could not keep the frown from her face. She tried to guess what her mother's reaction would be.

"I am Ambassador," she reminded the old man. "I am empowered to enforce our treaty with Cadogna. I can use my influence to ensure that our mercantile relationship remains unchanged."

Vicenns took a deep breath and looked right into Ria's eyes. "How do you think Sartian will vote, Dona?"

It took her a moment to understand what he meant: the Tipping Point. The number of voters in Parliament who considered themselves citizens of Cadogna was nearing the majority. Once that took place, they would surely vote to become an arrondissement of the Empire in truth. The Empress was playing a long game.

Ria made some vague pleasantries and excused herself. She needed to find Juan. She would not be the one holding the cards when the Empress's intrigues got the better of Ombria. The Alodesal name would not be sullied by inaction.

* * *

Dona Ariadna de Alodesal y Juegon, grandee of Ombria, Gamesmaster of Torreçon, and Regal Ambassador to the Independent Country of Valtiffe, was on a ship the very next morning. The time had come for her to host another one of her famous Ambassador's Games in Saut-Leronne.

One need not limit wagers to money, of course. Not a few members of the Turquoise Club, where the more elegant set of the gentes of Soucisse gather, engineered their first invitations by winning one at a night of beaufils. Favors, introductions, trade deals, council votes—all have served as wagers in recent memory.

Among the greatest coups along this vein was won by the earliest Cadois émigrés to the cold little island of Valtiffe.

The Gente's Manual, etc.

Proper play might never have made it to Valtiffe were it not for the forbearance of our forbears.

Lord d'Alhambere
(attributed by de Tabanne in various sources)

V
VALEN

THE HEAVY STEPS of Hugues Arbelan's boots announced his arrival at Valen and Marguerite's rooms before he reached the door. His slow trip up the stairs to the third floor was accompanied by the jingling of metal: his infamous blade and belt.

Valen opened the door at the absurdly gentle knock—the knock of a man who knows he is expected—to find Arbelan dressed in his customary splendor. A salmon frock coat of a style too new for Valen to recognize over sea-green pants and vest, each trimmed with gold and dazzling with buttons which could certainly have had no practical function. The man smelled as if he had fallen into a vat of cologne, given himself over to his fate, and chosen to have a nice bathe while he was in there.

"Morning, Quinol," Arbelan said in his gruff, unpolished voice. He had the throat of a man who had grown up in the damp and frozen streets and now smoked as much of the harsh local tobacco as he could, not to mention the countless hours spent screaming at his little wards. "Let me in, would you?"

"Naturally, Monsieur Arbelan," Valen replied, turning his body and extending his arm in welcome. He hoped none of the other tenants had seen this rough character coming in. "You remember my wife."

"Your better half. Not that it takes too much in your case."

Marguerite rose from her sofa and bowed her head. "Good morning, Monsieur Arbelan. Shall I take your hat and sword?"

The hat, a massive felt bicorn adorned with a rosette of yellow and black—the colors of the Knaves—he gave, but not his sword. It remained at his side scabbardless and unwashed since the last time it drew blood. Valen wondered how long exactly that had been, which he imagined was the point of brandishing the thing like that in the first place.

"No tea?" Arbelan grumbled vaguely in Marguerite's direction.

"Refreshment is for invited guests, Arbelan," Valen said. "Say your piece and get your ridiculous boots off my carpet."

"I'll say what I like, and when I choose to," Arbelan growled, the hilt of that sword of his always a few inches from his doeskin glove. "And you'll be begging to lick these boots when you hear the job I have for you."

Valen sneered. "Save your breath. I have no interest whatsoever in any business with you or your pack of miscreants."

Arbelan took an unoffered seat on Valen's favorite chair. A puff of powder from his wig lingered in the air above him for a moment before settling on the upholstery, leaving a hideous residue. Valen consoled himself by watching the boor wiggle around to slide his sword through the chair's arm. Arbelan nearly knocked a small vase off the table in front of him as he tried to maintain his dignity.

"You will." He grinned cruelly. "Because I know how to make my people work."

Valen rolled his eyes. "Yes, yes. Your favorite boast. Ridiculous on its own, and more so as we happen to not be your people."

"But you are. You live in my district and I don't have my men toss you out of every barrel-top dice game in the city. You and your little crew fleece these idiots because I allow you to, and tomorrow night you are going to fleece a very specific idiot for me, because I asked you very nicely."

With this he lifted his toe and pushed the vase off the table. It fell to the floor, but did not shatter. Enchantments to keep pottery from breaking were among the first a student learned at Séminaire.

Still, it was no way to treat a host, especially one for whom the wrong noise meant eviction. Valen rose to object, equipped with some bons mots about a person's home and respect, but Arbelan let his fingers graze his sword's pommel and raised an eyebrow.

"You have heard of the Forbearance Game?"

Marguerite scoffed. "Is that all you want? For Valen to play a game for you? Just get him an invitation. No need to come here with your ne'er-do-well routine."

Arbelan didn't take his eyes off Valen.

"Everyone has heard of the Forbearance Game, Hugues," Valen said. "Even you."

It was true. Anyone who spent any time at the tables and clubs of Saut-Leronne could not go very long without hearing about the private, invitation only, one-night tournament that took place on every fourth full moon. The game where you could wager secrets.

Valen had tried to cheat his way in several times, as the the buy-in was substantial. He pretended to be rich, to get in on credit. He'd considered pretending to be poor, but in possession of a magnificent piece of information no one else knew—the waging of secrets was a great leveler—but to be caught in that lie would have been troublesome.

Some clever Cadois mayor in the distant past started the Forbearance Game as a way to learn the truths of his new citizens. Any secret would do, from a prided fishing spot to the contents of some unopened box. The old Hvallais families were poorer than the imperial transplants, of course, and some gave up their prize secrets for a seat at the table. These days, the value of a secret was determined by a single broker the night of the game, on a slip of paper sealed with wax with a single value written on it. Like a chip that could not be broken down to smaller values, and on which one player may place more value than another.

"So what is it you want, precisely?" Valen asked.

Arbelan smiled, an ugly thing. "I want you to play until you have beaten Clavis Dusmenil. Beat him so badly he has no money left at all and must pay in secrets. At the end of the night, you can keep your winnings, as long as the old codger is utterly out."

"You make it sound so easy. Just be sure to place in the city's highest-stakes game after having bankrupted one of its best players. First, I don't have the livres."

Arbelan snorted. "Better get playing, then. You put up half the entry in cash, I'll put up half in a secret: the location of the shipwreck of the *Victory Rose*."

The legendary *Victory Rose*, a merchant ship with full cargo that had disappeared due to the machinations of a ghost crew mutiny, or so it was said. This was valuable knowledge, and could be exchanged for quite a bit of credit.

Valen scoffed. "You know that?"

"It doesn't matter if I know it or not." Arbelan shrugged. "All that matters is if the Broker thinks you know it."

"If I go in there..." A quick look to Margo to make sure they were in agreement before he proceeded. She nodded very slightly. "...with a lie, whoever ends up with it is well within their rights to come after me."

"To come after who? The money-changer for the company in LaSalle? The bookkeeper for LaFayette? The speculator for that little place in Catin? You keep yourself hidden well enough."

"Do you know it or not, Hugues?"

Arbelan smirked at Valen's discomfort. "Heh. Now you see the good thing about this game: trust. People have to believe that they're betting for truths. That's why it's a game for the finer folk. Trust among gentlemen, and what."

"You're saying that the broker knows that you know."

"It's what he's for, then, isn't it?"

"Quit dodging," Valen snapped. "Problem the second: the game changes every time. How am I supposed to know what to prepare for?"

"You're the clever one. You figure it out."

"Which leads me problem the third: which of the events in our shared chronicle makes you think I would do a damned thing for you?"

"That's where I'm better than you, Quinol," Arbelan settled back into Valen's chair like a dotard father repeating his favorite story. "When I grab some kid from the street, or give one a warm bed when his dad's broken one too many bones, I start with food, clean water, rest, a bit of safety. Most of these kids, it takes them a while to stop jumping out of their skin at every loud noise. Where they're from that means a beating's coming, see, deserved or not.

"With their animal needs tended to, when they start getting treated as well as a dog, well, then you start to get to seeing what they *want*. Some try to run off, some steal. Leftovers from their old life of hand to mouth. Those take a little longer to appreciate what I give them. But each of them wants something.

"I had a girl just this week, seven or eight summers maybe, who volunteered for top watch on the bridge. Seven years old. In that cold and wind, up at that height. I figured her for a runner, trying to pull one over on an old man. If not, she didn't understand what she was getting into and would want down after the first shift. But here she comes grinning and skipping into my office, hands filled with scraps of paper with the trademarks of every cart that went over the bridge that day. I asked what she liked about being up there, and she said she liked the quiet.

"That girl, you see, she wants peace. Solitude. I won't be sending her to any festivals to cut purses and definitely not to the pits for fighting. She'll be my eyes in the sky. And because I give her what she wants, she'll do anything for me."

This preening fool's smugness astounded Valen; and Valen was a preening fool himself, to say nothing of being a cheat.

"You don't have anything I want, Hugues. Save your sanctimony for your shaving mirror. You're barely a step up from a slaver. I've seen what happens to the kids who try to leave. You don't have to make your teenagers wear those rosettes with your absurd colors; broken teeth are as much a badge of the Knaves as anything."

Arbelan's eyes iced over. "Imagine what I do to ingrates when they're full-grown. I'd like to see you shuffle a deck without thumbs."

"Don't threaten me, Hugues. I am not an enemy you would do well to make."

Valen knew the tricks of a good bluff. Part of it is the emotionless face. The bulk of it, though, is in the story, in the character you have built over the course of the game. Make them think they know you. Let them think they're smarter than you.

In Arbelan's eyes, Valen had unusual powers. He won at cards seemingly at will, and any digging into his past turned up nothing. Was he a witch? (Valen kept his abortive stint at the Séminaire a secret—who would sit down at the table across from someone who can enchant the deck? Not that enchanting a deck of cards did anything that would affect the game, but the laity had no way of knowing that.) Even a duelist who built a criminal empire by raising his recruits from nothing couldn't see through the story Valen had presented, of a man who couldn't be out-played.

Arbelan turned away. "I don't need to threaten you, Quinol. Especially since I'm going to give you a little secret of my own: they're giving up lifetime memberships for the three biggest winners."

Marguerite gasped, a tiny inhalation. Perhaps no-one else's ears would have picked up on the sound, and Arbelan certainly showed no signs of noticing. But a decade's marriage gives one a deep education into one's spouse's unspoken communications, if one was willing to listen. And Valen made a living interpreting unspoken communications.

For example, at that moment Arbelan sat tapping his sword belt. Not a threat, a nervous tic. That damned sword was his totem, his surest way of solving every major problem he had ever encountered. And here was Hugues Arbelan, the savage duelist, trying finesse. He held a decent hand, but not enough to ensure victory. He *needed* Valen to take this job. And Margo's gasp meant she wanted him to take it, too.

"I don't know, Margo," Valen said, turning to her. "It might be worth it."

"Don't be a fool, Valen. You're a fair player, and you don't need this powdered rat's help to get into that game. You don't owe him anything."

Marguerite always did play her role perfectly. They had run the Overcome-the-Shrewish-Wife con several times over the years. It was a great way to get a better deal on something you had already decided to purchase.

For the first time since he had handed off his hat, Arbelan turned to her. He opened his mouth as if to speak, but apparently thought better of it and turned back to Valen. His look darkened well past anger. "You do what I say, or I'll have your fingers. And maybe a few off your little crew's hands, too."

Valen cleared his throat. It was a tell and he knew it, but he needed to compose himself before responding. Margo was staring at him, willing him not to do anything foolish.

"Arbelan, do not threaten my... Don't threaten us," he said quietly, eyes hard. "There are more ways to hurt a man than with a sword."

"Fine," Arbelan quickly smiled away Valen's counter-threat. "I take back that last bit, if it makes you feel better."

"One codicil," Valen said. "You put up the money as well."

"I'm not here to negotiate."

Valen shrugged and walked to the door. "Then it would appear you are not here to convince me to join your little scheme. Good day, Hugues."

A rough smile rose on Arbelan's face as he stood up. The muscles in Valen's back snapped tight. Perhaps he had pushed this too far.

"You insult me," Arbelan rumbled. "I offer you partnership and you throw it aside. I won't stand for this indignity. I challenge you. Tonight. The Mark's Pier. Sunset."

Valen let out a laugh. "Don't be an idiot, Hugues. Who would do your gambling for you if I were dead?"

"...Three nights hence, then."

"So I am to dance for your pleasure and then be killed? Please, help a poor untutored fool to understand the intricacies of the opaque plot of a master criminal such as yourself."

"Coward!"

"This from the man who goes nowhere without ostentatiously displaying his sword."

"I will have satisfaction!"

Marguerite stepped forward, chin high. "You will have the satisfaction of retracting your challenge, and then the satisfaction of my husband's services at the Forbearance Game two nights hence. In that order, or not at all."

Emotions beat across Arbelan's face like a banner for all to see. Marguerite and Valen had outplayed him completely. He would not have come if he knew anyone who could take his place.

"Fine," Arbelan growled.

They waited as the man squirmed.

"I retract my challenge, you weasel." Arbelan's lips were uncomfortable around the words. "And I'll pay the entrance fee."

Valen smiled merrily, as if nothing had happened. "And I accept your retraction, Monsieur Arbelan. I will be there. And when the night is done, the last of Clavis Dusmenil's fortune will be dissipated among the populace. Shall we shake on it? Brothers in dishonesty, if only for a few days?"

Arbelan glowered as they shook, the doeskin of his gloves smooth and cold as porcelain.

"So, I must know," Valen said. "How will Dusmenil's shame help you beat Munnrais?"

Margo sighed, just as inaudibly as she had gasped before.

Arbelan stood up straight and squinted his eyes in what Valen assumed was meant to be the picture of condescension. "Don't trouble yourself with matters above you. What this has to do with Munnrais has nothing to do with you. The Knaves will have triumph over the Royals in time."

"I don't know if you know it, Hugues, but every time you try to sound clever, you sound even more like an idiot."

Marguerite delivered Arbelan's hat back to him and opened the door without a word.

"You just beat Dusmenil, and our business is concluded," he said. "If you don't get the job done... well, then the nature of our relationship will change."

* * *

As soon as Arbelan's clomping step—a little quieter on the way down—was gone, Marguerite smiled. "The Forbearance Game. It's time we had our chance there."

"I suppose we could have done much earlier, but my secrets are not for sale," Valen replied. "He is asking the impossible. If it weren't for the membership, I might have turned him down."

"Please tell me you are only lying to *me* with that nonsense, and not yourself."

"There isn't much time to prepare."

She had her coat and hat ready in the barest of moments. "Then we had better get to it. Let us go and find Ten."

"Ten?" Valen hadn't even considered including the others. "We don't need to bring her into this. Arbelan is a madman."

Margo put her hat on and checked it in the mirror by the door. "We will need a strategy. Ten's so contrary she'll point out any flaws."

"What, you don't trust my luck magic?" Valen pretended to be joking, but Marguerite frowned.

"I do trust it. I trust its future. But in two nights you are going to need something more than…"

"False hope?"

"Than experiments. We will rely on the sharp's arts, tried and true. Depending on the game, you may not even need to cheat at all."

"It will be a lot to negotiate, surely. But we mustn't have my new partner unhappy."

"We can use this," Margo said, pausing as she buttoned up her coat. "We can use this to get what we want."

Valen threw up his hands in affected despair. "And what is that again? To be the island's best cheat? To convince myself I can control probability? To open a foolish casino no one would want to attend?"

"Flop around as much as you like, husband. I know what I want."

So did Valen. He had known since the day they met, when his peculiar school friend Tenerève took him to a coffeehouse and introduced him to the woman whose parents had taken her in. Margo had scoffed at the Hoque family business and the role she was born to play in it. She would bend the world to her will, not the other way 'round.

"I wish we had met when we were younger." he said, avoiding the implied question. "A bookkeeper's son with ideas of cleverness. I needed the guidance of someone with your certainty. I didn't want to live my life trapped in a ledger, like my parents did."

"Do," Margo corrected. She had argued for years that Valen should contact his family. He had not. After his gambling had destroyed them, he could never bring himself to do so much as write a letter.

"I couldn't stay home in Verbichere. I went off to become a Brother and it didn't work out. So I adjusted and found something else. Same as you have done. I daresay you inspired me."

Margo laughed, but not without a hint of surprised anger. "I inspired you to become a cardsharp?"

"To do what I wanted, even if it made no sense," Valen retorted. "I will prove my accidental magic. I know every manner of false play there is, and can prove that when I call a card it comes to me because I will it, not because my hands are fast. By mastering sharping, I have eliminated the noise."

He did not say the reasons that came to him the nights when he sat alone with a bottle of wine and a candle, pretending to read.

"You would have done the same without me, Valen."

"I would not have. I would have given all this nonsense up long ago and actually been a clark." He shuddered comically. He had indulged himself with this line of conversation enough. "Can you imagine?"

"I can imagine you married to someone else if that was your path. I would never have stood for it."

"Well, if I don't manage to place in the Forbearance Game, I doubt the esteemed M. Arbelan will take it lightly. Perhaps I can fall back on clerkdom when he cuts off my fingers."

"But what of games of strategy?" is a cry I hear often. "What of games of board and piece?"

Diversions such as six-man-sessin and the eternal hagens certainly deserve their due in respect to the intelligence and focus required to play successfully. Many an argument has been made of the superiority of these games due to the elimination of the element of chance, which (in said arguments) pits mind against mind without intermediary. The players start with identical pieces, and no power outside of themselves can increase their opportunity for victory.

Yet it is in this triumph where games of strategy also find their tragedy. Given enough time and sufficient capacity for memorization, the "correct" move for any situation is always to be found. Were these to be written in a book—matter not how thick, so long as it is properly indexed—an idiot could beat a master if given access to it during play. A strategy game is as a mathematical problem with a single correct outcome.

These are cold, bloodless games which require solutions, not gamesmanship. As such, they lack the crucial element of the finer games of chance: they bear no relation to real life. Some people have better luck than others. Would that our life was as simple and ruled as a game of hagens!

Letter published in the *Soucisse Courant*,
de Tabannes

VI
OMER-GUY

OMER-GUY BENDINE, CADOIS Ambassador to Valtiffe and representative of Empress Oceane Caraliere de Flechard, was no stranger to hiding behind screens. He kept utterly still with no particular effort as he listened to Hugues Arbelan give his report to Lady De Loncryn. His breath moved his hateful beard, his badge of belonging here among these savages, only slightly. He had done substantially more active things silently behind screens than sit and listen; this was no trial.

The ever-present eyes and ears of the servants presented their own problem. Some wine-boy might be looking in through plaster cracks or around door jambs, anxious to bring some news back to whatever master had bought his meager espionage. He would report back to whoever was paying him for secrets of the Lady's private life, and talk about the Ambassador behind the screen. How to use this to one's advantage....

As the growling fop Arbelan cobbled together the tale of his success, his certainty that Clavis Dusmenil would be destroyed, his so-artful manipulation of some small-stakes gambler to do his bidding, Omer-Guy's mind wandered to the painted scene on the screen behind which he hid. A mighty chete tree shading a white stone fountain around which well-dressed people in the last century's fashions—wigs piled high, dresses cut low, shoes with tall heels reminiscent of riding boots, all the signifiers of wealth—courted and played instruments of gold. Every inch of the painting bore fauna or flora, all of which could be found in some region of the Cadois Empire. This screen, like all of Lady De Loncryn's décor, stated clearly that Imperial culture was the only culture of worth.

Omer-Guy allowed himself a jealous smirk. If only he could be so forthright. But thus is the life of an Ambassador.

Lady De Loncryn assured Arbelan that once Dusmenil—who she referred to as 'you know who'—was shamed, she would in return use the sizable powers at her disposal to weaken 'our mutual friend Munnrais,' who was apparently a rival of some sort to the man. There was some connection there, Dusmenil funding him or protecting him. The internecine dramas of the Saut-Leronnian crime world mattered little to Omer-Guy, but he did appreciate how easily De Loncryn hid her true intents from Arbelan. Of course, he had to assume she was doing the same to him—as, in turn, he was to her.

When the gang boss left, one of the subtler steps in Omer-Guy's dance with De Loncryn began. Would he wait for her to summon him from behind the screen, which would place him in the position of servant, or step out before she spoke, as would a master for whom the time and wishes of his lessers are a small matter if any at all?

He chose the former. As much as the Lady of Gabot Avenue had convinced the people of Saut-Leronne that she was a true noble in action as well as name, one who had their happiness squarely in her eye, Omer-Guy had spent enough time in her presence to see that she preferred control whenever possible. Hence her mastery of the arts of oratory and charm.

"Ambassador?" De Loncryn called, like a hopeful, innocent young lover. "Did you hear all of that?"

Omer-Guy's muscles eased at the movement as he slid out from behind the screen and into Lady De Loncryn's impossibly pleasing sight. To be looked on by Lady De Loncryn was like stepping into the warmth of a fire on an icy winter night: as much as your bones had adjusted to life without the heat, you could no longer imagine stepping back out into the cold. The plain affection in her gaze, the set of her smile which spoke of barely-contained joy at your presence, the open way she held her body, all of these mixed to form the best feeling in the world. Complete, welcoming acceptance and friendship.

But Omer-Guy did not gain his station by believing anyone cared for him. He set his heart against its natural desire to reflect back her warmth. His eyes, though, and his smile beneath his damned beard, he adjusted to give her precisely that. The false, cold light of the moon, which only a fool would confuse with the sun.

"I did, my lady," Omer-Guy said. "Though I cannot say I am sure I believe him."

"Oh, naturally not," De Loncryn laughed, as high and sweet as a silver flute. Her voice was nearly as impossible to resist as her gaze. "The man is a boor and a fool. Did you see...? No, you wouldn't have, being quite abandoned behind the screen. I can only presume you smelled his perfume?"

"I did," Omer-Guy said dryly. "Quite well."

"Eyes are watering from here to Soucisse, I am sure of it," she continued. "Well, you can imagine how much powder he must wear on his face, then... You must think me mad to depend on this painted idiot for a single thing."

Omer-Guy had to admit to himself that he did. "I am sure you have your reasons, my lady."

"Fear not, my dear. This scheme is only one of many. Your

friends in Court will have the information they so badly desire. Whatever that may be."

She raised a teasing eyebrow at that, and Omer-Guy favored her with a smile in return.

"With the rich and the mighty, always a little patience, as they say in L'Ombre." *Careful*, he warned himself. *Don't let yourself enjoy this.* "We poor servants of the Crown can only guess at the intentions of those who reside in the rarefied air of such heights. But I need not guess at this: Clavis Dusmenil's information is required by the Empire. Take what time you need to obtain it, but I would recommend against keeping us waiting for too long."

Most people would respond to an open threat such as this with obsequies and plaints of difficulty; some would sneer with rebellious scorn. But Lady Oceline De Loncryn laughed, as if he had just taken a complicated trick at a vivacious game of beaufils.

"I will have to state the obvious issue at hand here: once I have this exciting secret in my possession, I could do whatever I choose with it." Her eyes did not harden as she made her counter-move. "Surely your patrons in Soucisse would prefer it not go to their rivals."

"Which would not help your chances at receiving the backing of the Court in your attempt at the mayoralty. This was my promise, and be sure that I can retract it—or worse—if necessary."

"Oh, my dear Omer." De Loncryn placed a hand on the collar of her gown in mock astonishment. "You are letting the manners of these Valtivans take up residence within your own. If you insist on such nonsense, I might remind you that you are not the only person with the ability to curry favor and find interesting bits of information. Even the smallest rumor could have a deep effect on a man's career, wouldn't you say?"

Damn the woman and her impossible smile. She couldn't possibly know his secret. A half-rate gente scrabbling out a life in a minor estate in this nowhere country could not possibly have discovered...

"How is your son, Omer-Guy?" she asked, eyelids low.

The Ambassador's cheeks flushed and his hands shook. This was intentional; that he was estranged from his son, a failed social climber who had been forced to take the charity of a distant relation in the enemy queendom of L'Ombre to escape scandal, was hardly a secret at all. Indeed, most of the Court knew about it, and that was in large part due to his own machinations. If you make your opponent think he knows your weakness, he stops looking. And anyway, any member of the peerage who didn't come with some family disgrace would hardly be talked about, and not being talked about at all was far worse than being whispered about behind fans. A story involving illicit love—or at the very least, illicit coupling— and the possibility a boy is using his prowess to rise above his station, was far too fascinating to be ignored.

"My foolish Oscar. You wouldn't," Omer-Guy muttered. His hand rose to his head, beneath his wig, and pulled at a hank of his hair. *Let the servants report on* that.

De Loncryn frowned at his state. "My dear, please, do not upset yourself. We have an understanding, and a fine one at that. What can I tell you that will ease your nerves?"

She crossed the room to him and took his hands in hers. Her ungloved hands. Omer-Guy knew that any of the servants would whisper to their bribers that she and the Ambassador were becoming quite friendly indeed. This would attract far more attention than her discussions with a known criminal. Who of the gentry didn't make use of a rough-and-tumble sort now and again? And at least she had the foresight to make use of someone who kept the street urchin population at a minimum. It was almost a public service, really. But clutching hands with the imperial Ambassador? What could be meant by it?

By the Saints, she is a clever one.

"I... I would wish to know more of your plan." Omer-Guy made a show of deflecting emotions to return to the business at hand.

"My dear, you should have said so!" De Loncryn laughed. "Come, sit by me."

To any watching eyes, a flirtation. But clearly she felt it would allow them to speak more plainly. She explained that the Dusmenil fortune had all but disappeared. The same old story: Clavis had inherited a home of considerable pretension and ancestral farmlands that had never truly recovered from the long stretch of cold years after a season of violent volcanic eruptions. He failed to marry a well-heeled merchant's child, and thus had bled funds his entire life.

The old man would have to put up his secret—the family secret that the Court was so keen on learning—to stay in this Forbearance Game. And when he lost it, De Loncryn would simply have one of her night workers follow home whoever walked away with it and kill him. Frame it as a simple random mugging gone wrong, the time-honored standard. If that plan fell through—if Arbelan's crew could not actually do what he had said they could—she had a few other plans in play. A more traditional blackmail trap was developing, and she already had a maid looking through Dusmenil's private papers each night as the household slept. Omer-Guy had nothing to fear, she insisted.

When her speech was done, she looked pointedly at Omer-Guy's hand and then at her own knee, hidden somewhere beneath layers of shining fabric. He complied, reaching over to lay his hand lightly on his best approximation of that joint's location. She gasped and rose immediately, but allowed him to stay for a glass of Cadois wine.

He heard a light footstep on the other side of a wall. *Very clever.*

Patience games, those being games played solitaire, are a fine diversion for an idle hour, but one would do well not to be over-fond of them. They serve as excellent practice for counting up the cards in play, but little else. And those who say they can read one's future in the placement of the cards are swindlers of the worst type.

The Gente's Manual, etc.

VII
VALEN

THE COLD SEA air blew up the river and through the Hillside streets that morning, and Valen was glad to have it. The sharp smells of horse and night soil choked the streets on warmer days. A walk in the bracing autumn air would set his nerves to rights, perhaps.

Lifetime invitation to the Forbearance Game or no, Arbelan's request was troubling. So were his threats and knowing sneers. Valen shouldn't have accepted the offer. Or not caved to the thug's bullying; whichever. He should have taken more time to consider. He was so caught up in beating the idiot, in winning the hand, that he may have lost the rubber. Could that have been Arbelan's plan throughout? No. No, the man didn't have it in him.

Marguerite interrupted Valen's unquiet musings with a touch on his arm and a cold, calm smile. He knew he had a tell when his thoughts turned anxious, but he had yet to determine what it was, and Marguerite refused to tell him.

"Take comfort, Valen. You aren't alone in this. We're about to meet up with the two best gamesters you've ever seen."

He smiled at the thought. "They are, aren't they? I may not be the best person to associate with, but at least I have taught them a useful skill."

"And you have your ace in the hole—the best card-marker and dice-weighter in the known world."

"That you are, my love," Valen said with a fond frown. "I just can't get my mind around all this."

"We'll work through it with Jaq and Ten. You're useless when you get wrapped up in your own thoughts like this."

"Well, one does want to always be useful."

"Quite so."

Even here, walking through one of the better neighborhoods up in Hillside, the plastered stone walls bore layers of glued paper, palimpsests of advertisements and political treatises laid sheet by sheet over the decades. On the finest avenues in Saut-Leronne, one could see servants scraping the night's papers off the walls of their masters' gardens most mornings. That might do for the delicate imported-marble hulks of Gabot Avenue, but in the rest of the city the task was left to the wind and the rain.

They turned down Bjokker Street, its lively taverns dark at this early hour. These were mostly cold stone places of rubble masonry, converted from the homes of the fish driers and butchers who had lived in what were the outskirts of the river city back before the Cadois moved in. The imperial style of plaster and lath had never taken hold on Bjokker. The old road wasn't the fastest route to the coffeehouse, but the low basalt buildings reminded Valen of the rough miners' homes of his childhood in Verbichere, and Marguerite preferred the emptier streets for a morning walk. They made the decision to take the street without speaking.

Someone he thought he recognized ambled down the street with the nonchalance of a young man sent on an errand with no particular time-table. Valen stared for a moment, then felt himself flushing. It was one of the cook's serving boys from the Séminaire. Or no longer a boy now: it had been so long since Valen had seen him. Valen turned his head away and hoped not to be recognized. No good could come of reliving all that this morning. Bad enough he had to look at their damned tower floating above the city, aloof as a rich man's cat.

The view of the Pendent Tower was magnificent from Bjokker. The massive white column which served as home, workplace, and school for the Séminaire could be seen from nearly everywhere in the city, but here the cut of the street opened to show more of it than was usual. The top portion floated above the rest supported by only a thin staircase and scores of spells, swaying like a treetop in the wind. That impossible sight had given the Pendent Tower its name; before the top broke free it had simply been known as the Séminaire.

As much as he had hated his time there, Valen had to admit the architecture was quite stunning. The symbolism of the Tower looming over the city was not lost on him, though. The Brothers kept themselves apart from political affairs, but their power and presence could not be ignored.

A fair number of tradespeople and merchants, easily distinguished from one another by the feathers in the latter's hats and the general utility of the former's habiliments, moved through the street at the various speeds their business required. Some nodded, others proffered curt good-mornings, but for the most part they kept to themselves. Saut-Leronne was a city of industry at its heart, of shipping and trading, and being about of a morning for any other reason was questionable at best. This was not the imperial seat of Soucisse, where gentes and their hangers-on engaged in debate and debauchery day and night.

Marguerite pointed out some children engaged in a street game involving bits of barrel wood and a circle drawn in chalk on the cobbles. A boy of perhaps ten years, in clothes a bit too nice to be seen pitching chips in an alley, was arguing with a slightly older girl in similarly fine clothes about the precise measurements of a legal piece. Valen gathered that the girl came from another neighborhood, and that in hers they played with pieces no larger than the length between the first and second knuckles of the index finger (inclusive), whereas the remarkably local variant here on Bjokker Street used what was to her mind a far less just measurement.

"Do you know the game?" he asked.

Marguerite shrugged. "The variants of children's games are endless. For all we know, they invented this one at the last family gathering."

"I suppose you missed out on that sort of thing as a child. No siblings, no cousins for miles."

"Oh, the neighborhood children served well enough. And the sailors' kids."

Valen often wondered what Marguerite had been like when she was a little girl, growing up in the city with her gente parents. Had she been as proud and clever as she was now? Valen and she were adults when they met, with twenty winters each, and she had put any childishness aside before then. She worked diligently with her parents to learn their trade, and her father said rather often that she had a better head for being a merchant than either of them did.

Despite having spent every free moment with her for a decade, Valen still came across untold histories of Marguerite's young life from time to time: a place she had visited during her season in Cadogna or a friend she had never spoken of prior. The well of his own memories had run dry ages ago. All he could do now was retell the same stories, and hope Margo would indulge him.

She seemed to be in a talkative mood, and Valen took advantage of it. "What was your favorite game as a girl?"

"Games of accuracy were my best. Crow's cross." Margo smiled, her eyes distant. "You know, when Ten first came to live with us, she played exactly the same game, but called it 'flinks.' The rhyme had a different tune, but the same words. A Mistigris girl from an ocean away playing the same game as we did in Dockside. So strange."

Mistigris. The odd men out. He had never learned the full story of why Ten had left her clan, and didn't dare ask. He didn't much want to talk about why he'd left his family either. But he could blend in easily enough in any city in the Empire; Tenerième's sickly complexion and watery accent revealed her heritage to anyone who saw her. It often came up when she won against people with too few letters and too much wine, be they gentes or commoners. As difficult as Jacquemin could be, he never once stood for seeing Tenerième insulted, and Valen respected him for that, if little else.

He turned from the game and continued down the road. "Some things bind us all."

Upon their arrival at the coffeehouse, they found Jacquemin and Tenerième engaged in a small-stakes round of signaux with a pair of youths who, judging by the small stacks of books under their seats and uncut quills in their pockets, had nothing better to do with their time. Valen and Marguerite took a seat at an open booth and waited for their associates to finish. Valen sat where he could watch the game and had a good view of Tenerième's cards. He did take a sort of paternal pleasure in watching his friends play. He wasn't even all that much older than Ten, but still, he had taught both of them how to fool a player out of his money.

Jaq could barely bridge the cards before Val found him trying to palm a coin in a Dockside saloon and offered him a few pointers. The young salt hounded him for more until it became easier for Valen to simply bring him on as a partner.

His old friend Ten was a different story. She had hardly needed any instruction from Valen on anything but the rules of the games. She took to the social aspects of chicanery like she was born to it: the lies and false identities and playing on people's prejudices. Watching her in action was like taking in a magnificently-acted play. And unlike with Jaq, Valen felt he owed her. It was his pride that had gotten him kicked out of the Séminaire, and tarnished her reputation.

Setting his guilt aside, he pulled a small diary from his pocket and ran his finger over the pages as though focused on some financial matter, as a man of his alleged profession would be. Margo did the same, but her little book was genuine. Every kron and livre spent on ink for marking cards or won at tables around the city could be found noted in Margo's meticulous handwriting somewhere in that thin black book. Valen often worried about what would happen if someone found one of her volumes: she had the good sense to use terms from the ivory trade in place of the language of gambling, but codes can be broken.

Bending over books to fool onlookers seemed a silly ruse— they were here to meet up with a Mistigris and the worst-dressed sailor Valen had ever seen. Anyone who might recognize Valen would be far more surprised to see him in such company than at seeing him without a book in his hands. Still, it was good practice. Mastering the part of the shrewd clark of a financial firm was as crucial to his success as the scores of hours spent perfecting his bottom deal.

They ordered drinks and watched as Jacquemin and Tenerière finished their game.

The young students made their weaknesses evident without even touching their cards. One couldn't handle his wine, and the other fidgeted. Valen wondered if his friends would make use of them.

"If only I could know we were playing signaux in three nights," Valen muttered with a nod towards Ten and Jaq. "I dare say I might be able to pull this off then."

A response from Marguerite was interrupted by the arrival of two painted clay mugs of hot coffee. The waiter, a thin young man in a dark coat and an apron, served their steaming drinks, Marguerite first, and then stood motionless, eyes toward the wall. Valen dropped a five-kron on the table, and was startled by the speed with which the man grabbed it.

Marguerite smiled at her husband's surprise. "Perhaps you should offer that young fellow a job. He seems well-acquainted with the rapid tumble of coins. Hands like his could surely be put to better purpose."

"I'm sure his job carting coffee pays better, and suits his demeanor."

"Which may be an act, for all we know. He could be the life of every salon in Hillside once that apron comes off."

Valen took a long pull from his coffee. It was far too milky for his tastes, but it did its job, setting his nerves somewhat at ease. "You have spent too much time with rakes and gamesters. Some things are in fact precisely what they appear to be."

They drank chiroot coffee, the workman's drink. Coffee beans from the northern reaches of the Cadois Empire were far too expensive for ready consumption in Valtiffe, where they had to be shipped across a dangerous sea. The bark of the local chiroot bush was roasted, ground, and added to the coffee in most of the homes and restaurants, even in Saut-Leronne.

Valen preferred the bitter taste anyway; he hadn't touched real coffee until he was well into his majority, and was partial to the taste he had grown up with. Margo, though, had been accustomed to the original and had to develop a taste for chiroot. She let it slip once to her parents that she kept it in their kitchen, and Valen was sure that was yet another mark against him. The failed Brother who married their only child.

"And what of Arbelan?" Margo asked. "Why would he care about some old gente's secret? And this is the easiest way to get it?"

Valen stared into his coffee and sighed. "This entire affair is ham-fisted, even for my favorite orphan-corrupting swordsman. Who knows what he wants?" His eyes moved to Tenerève's cards. She held a few honours, but no suit strong enough to open with. He knew what he would do in this situation, but what about Ten?

"It must be something from his family's past. If the man had a secret worth anything, he would have used it to push off his debts."

"And what do we know about his family?"

"The Dusmenils? Surely you know their history."

"I do not," Valen said, frowning as Tenerève tried to finesse a low coin and lost the trick.

"You've heard the name Clotilde Deschamps?"

"The explorer?"

"Yes. Before the Dusmenils moved into shipping, they were Valtiffe's first real mapmakers. They hired Deschamps to survey the interior. They made a killing on a map of the unknown wildernesses away from the shores."

"That was three centuries ago," Valen said, distracted. Now Tenerève was running her hands. What was she planning? "We have all the maps we could ever want, and of far better quality than some pre-Cadois guesswork. It must be something else. Some scandal, perhaps. That would make sense, wouldn't it? He caught some gente with her hands in the wrong person's pantaloons and Arbelan wants to know who."

Marguerite frowned into her coffee. "This isn't for Arbelan. He has never once shown any interest in the clandestine. If he wanted something from Clavis Dusmenil, he would march up the man's walk and take it from him under threat of his blade. No, someone hired him."

"Hired Arbelan? You'd want to be desperate."

Jacquemin ended the game and the youths left in high spirits, clapping each other on the back as they walked out of the shop. The two cheats joined Valen and Margo at their table.

"What in the hells was that?" Valen asked Tenerième. "You gave a good half of those tricks away. If they were better players, they would have been keeping track of your hand and known something was up."

"What luck, then, that they are not better players," Tenerième said, unflappable. "I should say what a fine job Jacquemin did choosing these marks. They are university boys with an elevated sense of their cleverness, as well as a... liquidity of purse. Once they see our little game as a good investment, they will bring larger sums. I very much look forward to relieving them of most of it."

"Gods and fishes, you're right on with that." Jacquemin mumbled around a mouthful of buttered bread one of the boys had left behind. "Don't know how much longer I can bear their sniggering faces. Best part of the job, really, crushing those pretty little hearts beneath my heel."

Valen wanted to lash out at Jaq for taking such pleasure in others' pain, but contained himself. He wasn't angry at them, after all. Just being around them lifted his spirits a little. "It sounds as if your morning was more productive than ours, at least."

"What did Arbelan want from you?" Tenerième asked. "Did he come to bully you into paying a cut?"

"What? No." Valen hadn't even thought of that possibility. He could tell from Marguerite's look, though, that she had. "Nothing like that."

"He came to our rooms with a business proposal," Marguerite leaned close over the table and whispered. The waiter was in the kitchen and there were no other customers in the place, but Margo was always one for safety. "He has hired Valen to rig the Forbearance Game."

Valen expected the others to laugh, but Tenerève looked pensive and Jacquemin just kept eating.

"About damn time," Jacquemin said. "I'm sick of these ten-livre games."

Tenerève nodded sagely. "We should be presenting ourselves to the quality if we are to maintain our rate of success. We've taken the saloon games as far as we can. Yes. Perhaps we can purvey this into a membership in one of the finer clubs."

"We have memberships to some fine clubs," Valen said. How long had his associates felt this way without telling him? Damned gamblers and their unreadable faces.

Marguerite gave him a wry smile. "The Brunette and Blonde is hardly a place you can expect to see much of the gentry, Valen. We've broken into the bourgeoisie, but soon we'll have worked our way through their pockets as well."

"And here I thought I would have to convince you two. This will save some time. Which, to be blunt, is a resource we are not as flush with as I would prefer."

Jacquemin leaned back in his chair, folded his hands behind his head and looked at the ceiling with a long sigh. "Tough to rig a game when you don't know what you're playing. Any ideas?"

"It is my understanding that the game of the night is chosen out of a hat," Tenerève offered. "But there are a limited number of games. All are played with either cards or dice."

"Sneaking in a few weighted dice will be no problem," Valen said. "I don't dare hope there is any way for us to determine which printing house made the cards they're using."

"I'll ask around," Jacquemin offered. "I know the ones here in town. We've given them good enough business for the last few years they might let a hint slip about a big order."

Marguerite took Valen's hand and fidgeted with his wedding ring, running the tiny, sharp bump he kept facing his palm against her fingertip. "I'll sharpen your scorer when we get home. Get some practice in—we don't want you poking a hole in the card you're trying to mark."

Valen smiled and raised his coffee for a toast. "What a beautiful sight this is. Rogues and cardsharps pooling their efforts in the name of dishonesty."

Marguerite and Tenerième smiled. Jacquemin took the mug from Valen's hand, pulled a flask from a pocket, and poured in a liberal glug. "Bad luck to toast without a real drink, Valen," he said, and raised the mug himself. "To us, who make you think you're a king even as we turn you pauper."

They all clapped at that, and Jacquemin downed the drink in a single gulp. "So, what's got you so nervous, old man? You should be jumping at this. You think Arbelan's trying to play you at something?"

"He is certainly trying to play me." Valen glanced over at the waiter to see if their toast had attracted any attention, but found the slim fellow washing cups in silence. "The trouble is figuring out who's playing him."

He and Marguerite detailed Arbelan's particular request—the ruination of Clavis Dusmenil—and their suspicions.

"I see," Tenerième drummed her finger on the table. One of her more obvious tells, which Valen had trained her out of years ago. "Someone with the sort of sway to engineer an invitation to the Forbearance Game is using a criminal to get information of value. Yes. So aside from the dangers inherent in our line of trade, and aside from those involved in working with an unstable man like Hugues Arbelan, we are also concerned about whoever his mysterious employer might be, and what he might or might not do for Dusmenil's private knowledge. This is seeming less like a good plan now."

Jacquemin snorted at her. "Anyone fool enough to hire the Naughty Knaves is fool enough to be fooled by us."

"What sort of person would do that? It is like using a hammer to slice cheese. There is too much about this we do not know. I wouldn't do it."

"You don't need to, Ten," Valen said. "Sit this one out. I'll be on my own in there no matter what. I will play, and I will win. But it will be easier with your help. 'The work of the few, better living for all.'"

He smiled as he quoted the informal motto of the Séminaire, but she did not rise to the bait.

"What do we gain?" she asked.

"Well, I am fairly certain Arbelan will try to skewer me if I lose. He never has been one for disappointment."

"That's not it," Jacquemin said. "You want to get in with the rich sods and beat them. Show them your skill."

Marguerite countered with a phrase in Old Hvallais, which translated roughly to 'a humble lie is worse than a boast.'

"What's that?" Jacquemin's lips slowly curled into a scowl as he pulled his flask out again.

"Oh... It's from 'The Beggar's Bounty.'"

"I'll remind you that not all of us had the benefit of being raised among Saut-Leronne's mercantile élite."

"My tutor—"

"Us poor peasants who went to a public schoolhouse call them 'teachers.'"

"I didn't mean—"

"Forget it," Jacquemin snarled. "Whatever you said, it doesn't change the truth."

Valen stepped in before the spat could flare up again. "The

truth is, this is an opportunity. You have all been very tolerant of my experiments with this new school of magic, but it is time to take things further. Making a name at the Forbearance Game will provide access to more games, which means more opportunities to work on my chance magic, to say nothing of the depth of the pockets we will have the pleasure of tapping when we are invited to finer tables."

"The money I can see," Jacquemin said. "Your little tests, I'm not so sure on."

"We have been given a boon. We can do something different from what anyone ever has. Something new."

He produced a deck of cards from one of many concealed pockets, shuffled them with a few nice riffles, and dealt nine cards face up.

"Most of us plod through our days like it's a patience game. Like burny, where you're stuck with what you're given." He drew the seven of coins from the top of the deck, passed it over the dealt cards in a show of comparing them, then tossed it into the discard pile. "The order of the cards at the end of the shuffle determines whether you win. No choice in the matter."

Tenerière interrupted him as he went to gather up the cards, plucking the seven from the discard. "No. You might not get a choice about your draw, but you must be sharp enough to see the options when they come up and act on them." She placed her card on top of an eight on the table, the only legal move, and one Valen had missed.

"I'll allow that," Valen laughed, rearranging the cards into a cross, shuffling again, and adding a few more from the deck. "But our fates are not writ for us at the moment of our birth. It is more like atouts." He drew again, and this time held a knave of lamps over a five of the same suit, then the knave of hands, then back again. "Every choice you make sets up all the rest."

Jacquemin's chair creaked as he leaned forward and

vanished a card from the cross pattern. "Except in real life, other people screw with your cards. They don't respect your nice, lined-up plans. They take the ones they want and leave you to deal with it."

He passed a flat hand over the empty spot in the pattern. A new card was there now. "And they cheat."

"And that's what magic does," Valen said. He cut, then drew six cards in a row, each of them being exactly the card he needed. "Divination tries to see the next card. Enchantment makes you a better player. My magic stacks the deck."

He couldn't help but grin when he turned the seventh card.

Most of the trick was simple enough—when he riffled the deck, he memorized the card order, a skill he had honed in his years of boredom at the mines. A series of forces, false shuffles, and second-card deals over the course of his performance had set up most of what he needed. The last card, though, required his magic.

Valen's method had reduced the spell to a single phoneme, subvocalized. It meant 'bring' in old Hvallais, and was the crucial syllable in the word for 'find' in L'Ombrais. He accompanied it with the visualization of an image from his dream language—a simple wooden button, the currency with which he and his sister had played their child's games on the soot-stained floor by the fireplace. To Valen and Valen alone, a wooden button meant success over the odds.

But this little display was one of the few times it had worked in the presence of others.

Jacquemin took another swig from his bottle and passed it to Marguerite with a smirk. "Speaking of stacking the deck. Dusmenil won't give up his secret to someone, right? And that someone has found a way to get him to lose it—you come in and take all his money, and he has to play it. But what if *you* win the secret? They'll be at your door the next morning, cash in hand. And if the secret's worth buying from you, it must be worth more somewhere else. Please tell me we're keeping whatever Dusmenil's secret is."

Marguerite took a few long gulps and passed the bottle to Valen. "Jaq, we are definitely keeping whatever Dusmenil's secret is."

A false deal to yourself is a good thing. To a confederate is better.

Sharping Easy (rough pamphlet of unknown origin)

VIII
TENERIÈVE

THE MUSCLE UNDER Ten's right thumb ached, but she kept at her labors. The Flash Cut, which distracted her opponents with a nearly-dropped card as she manipulated the deck, did not come as easily to her as it did to the others. Her skin was too dry to slide the cards smoothly, and her hands were too small to split the deck without straining. She truly did not have the hands of a natural sharp. But she was used to making do with what she had.

The light in Margo's workroom was far better than in the close room Ten rented in the Warehouse District. At least she could see her failures a little better. Margo was oblivious to her efforts, hunched over her desk with her back toward her guest. She held a small knife with a pretty handle, and was in the process of trimming a three of coins along the long edge.

Margo was preparing a deck for cheating at oakey by making the odd cards slightly thinner and the evens shorter. This would allow the sharp to cut to either as would benefit his hand by taking up the deck along the sides or the ends. It was an effective cheat, and difficult to detect when the deck was rigged by Margo's magnificently careful hand. The deck the crew had used against de Niver had been similar, and the blustering fool hadn't noticed at all, even with his magnifying spectacles.

There was no guarantee oakey was to be played at the Forbearance Game, of course. Ten had been sitting in Margo's room for most of the day, watching as her host rigged fresh decks for every game possible. Valen was to smuggle these into the contest even though Jaq had not had any success at determining which printer's cards were to be used that night. To Ten, it seemed a foolish waste of time; but then, taking on the whole job was foolish.

A thread-thin curl of paper separated from the card on Margo's desk, and she leaned back in a stretch. "So are you going to tell me why you're here?"

Ten kept herself from smirking. Margo did love to be in charge. "Why would I not be?"

"Don't try to evade me," Margo sighed. "You didn't risk harassment by the neighbors just to practice mechanics in my workroom."

She was right, of course. Nearly every person Ten passed in the neighborhood of the Gouvernor Pole either gave her a wide berth or openly scowled at her. This was no place for a woman with skin as snow-pale as hers, no matter how much of it she tried to cover up.

"No. I did not."

"What, then?" Margo gave Ten the look she'd given her dozens of times when they'd shared a room in Margo's parents' home, one that expressed something between empathy and impatience. Ten had been reticent about many aspects of her life, but she learned very quickly that Margo would not abide anything less than full honesty. She gave it freely, and expected it in return.

Ten held a breath to bolster her nerve. "I want you to tell Valen to pull out of this job. The Knaves are too dangerous."

"I see." Margo turned back to her work, which hid whatever reaction she might have had, although Ten doubted she had much of any. "And why do you not tell him yourself?"

"I did. At the coffeehouse. The conversation rolled past as if I had said nothing."

There was a tiny barb at the end of her statement, which she had not intended. Ten was not in the habit of starting fights.

Margo did not respond right away. Ten waited until another thin curl of paper rolled down the desk. She had spoken her mind and saw no good in adding to it, as nervous as she was about Margo's answer. The small life she had here depended very much on being in Margo's good graces. As much as these people said they were her friends, she would ever be the outsider. Just like back in the caravan.

"I am sorry for that, Ten," She placed her knife on the desk calmly and turned around again, her face open and warm. "This little company of ours only works if we all ante in. But the element of risk is present in every game you play. Why is this one different? Not two days ago a hunter was shooting at you."

"One hunter, yes. Not a gang. Not an organized group who knows we are sharping, who knows where we'll be and with what."

"We all agree Arbelan is trying to play us, Ten."

"And what happens when a Knave calls the Guard?" She was getting animated now, but didn't care. Let Margo pout; it was better than facing this much danger, and would not last for long. "Valen can hide your fancy decks in his pockets for only so long when they grab him. No, it's not safe."

Margo held Ten's gaze for a long moment. Perhaps she was waiting for her to finish, or perhaps she was furious at being challenged. Ten reflected once again that Margo had a better face for bluffing than any sharp around.

"You can make it safer," Margo said with a sly smile. "You and Jaq can keep watch."

At least Margo had heard her. "We will not be at the game."

"Valen can handle himself once he's in the club, but you have to agree that his skills are not well-suited to the streets. Follow him. If any Knaves cause trouble...."

"I can't fight, Margo."

"But you can scream."

"Call for the Guard myself? You do know how that story ends for someone like me."

"It doesn't matter if the Guard comes or not," Margo's lips pursed. "Just causing an alarm will be enough to send the little cockroaches running for the dark. And if there happens to be a guard nearby, being seen with Jaq lends a person a sort of... negative credibility. They'll figure the two of you are up to no particular good, but not necessarily any harm, At least none they have any interest in pursuing."

So Margo did not see the risk of being a Mistigri on the streets at night when the guards are about. It was too much to expect her to, perhaps. "But for what? Why go through with all these silly machinations? Many things might go wrong. Anything. Why risk all this?"

"You know why, Ten," Margo's voice grew colder. "The opportunity is worth the danger."

Ten swallowed her frustration at the change in her friend's tone. She wanted to snap at her that it was easy to ignore the danger when one was sitting at home, but more anger would not serve her here.

"I do not know that I agree, Margo. We have come very far without involving the gangs, or any criminals at all."

"Save for ourselves," Margo teased.

"Yes. Only we evil bastards." Ten smiled. Time to hit Margo with that honesty she so treasured. "It feels at times as if all this is more risk for me than it is for the rest of you. Yes. Half of this city would see me sent back to the mainland whether I did wrong or not. And to have Valen entering this game without me even being there to help…"

"To secure your safety, you mean," Margo said brusquely. "I know just how that feels, Tenerève. I sit in these rooms, or walk about on my business in the city, knowing that my husband is out doing work that might get him stabbed. And when he is dead, where will the anger be turned next? Where will those we have cheated go for recompense? His rooms seem like a good place to start. And there isn't a thing I can do to ensure he doesn't take a little too much wine and miss a false deal. The greater portion of my life rides on you three and the speed of your hands."

"Why do you do this, then? Why be a cheat at all? What of your parents' trade?"

Margo sat back in her chair and smiled wrily. "Do you remember the time my uncle came to visit?"

Ten nodded. The man had been the most charming conversationalist she had ever met, and the gray at his temples had not detracted from his pleasing features. He stayed in the Hoque household for a fortnight, and every night had seemed like a feast day. It was one of Ten's fondest memories since she came to Saut-Leronne. For a while it felt like what she imagined a home to be.

"He had come to try to convince my father to borrow some money from him. Can you imagine? My father's pride would never allow such a thing, but Uncle Alain had no intention of letting his sister suffer when word got out that the Hoque fortune was gone.

"They said something had killed the walruses. That's all I could get from the whispers, anyway. My parents had invested too much in the season's hunts, and without mature tusks, they had little to trade. It was a roll of the dice, Ten. A year-long roll of the dice. After I pieced together that little crisis, I decided to rig every roll in my favor. Honest play had done my parents poorly, and I could no longer follow their lead. The world had cheated. I would cheat back.

"One might be a farmer, a miner, a priest. There are plenty of ways to survive which seem safe. But the world will play you as it sees fit, no matter how honest you are."

"Yes." Ten knew much more about the world's dishonest play than Margo did. "But why leave it in the hands of Val and Jaq and me?"

"I don't. I send you out with false cards and imperceptibly flawed dice. I don't have the mind for the mathematics Valen does, nor Jaq's dexterity, nor your knack for sounding exactly the way you want to. I know how to work hard and mind the details. I don't need to be there to watch over the games. All I can do is prepare as best I can against bad luck."

"And this is what you would have me do," Ten said. "Keep nearby in case of bad luck."

"I would. You know how to avoid trouble. If any comes, I know you can handle it."

Ten relented then, and the two of them laid out a few details. Later that afternoon, as she walked home, she found that while she had gone in those rooms to convince her friend to pull out of this job, she was now deeper into it than she had been when she started. Had Margo played her? Was the woman who was supposed to be her friend putting her at risk for her own gain?

These thoughts accompanied her as she walked up to her tiny attic room and prepared for an evening out.

No matter how cleverly one might manage his cards, the player who underestimates the careful attention the current state of the score requires will unnecessarily lose many a round.

Signaux Argot, Guillaume Salen

IX
RIA

THE SCURRYING OF rats in the dark corners of Ria's cabin had become so frequent that she hardly noticed the dry, anxious sound anymore. Like living by a waterfall. The perpetual creaking of rope and wood had long since become as imperceptible as the beating of her heart. Still, despite these weeks at sea en route to her embassy in Saut-Leronne, she had yet to get used to the dim light of the glowstones embedded in the ceiling.

One might think that when the Ambassador—a peer and a grandee, no less—requested permission to light a few tapers to help her read despite the edict that no flame be lit on board, the sailors would leap at the chance to win her favor. But the rules of nautical life have no regard for name or rank, and make equals of all. Ria appreciated the efforts at parity in concept, but found herself wondering if the captain kept a decent light in his own cabin for the nights he did his accounts and referred to his maps. Finding the dollop of land that was Valtiffe in the featureless expanse of the western ocean must have required better light than Ria was working with.

Her cabin was suitable, at least. A sizable table filled much of the space, for any dinners she might hold. Ria imagined it must have been built in the cabin, or else lowered in before the upper deck was installed. The legs were carved with intertwining hoodsnakes, one of the oldest symbols of Ombria. Ria found this comforting; as the centuries passed, the more gallant griffin had become the primary symbol of the queendom, but in the older cities one still saw graven snakes coiled around the pillars of public buildings. Ria's mother's arcada included a few of them among the more contemporary heraldry, a nod to the long history of Alodesal peerage. Ria generally identified with the hoodsnake, but she was feeling anything but fast and dangerous as she sat reading her mother's letter for the tenth time.

Ria had tried to leave Torreçon before her mother had time to intervene, and had been successful except for this one letter, carried down the hill and up the gangplank by a winded servant. Her mother had couched her message in some very maternal language about keeping safe on the ocean (meaning keep wary of any Cadois naval activity, and be sure to report back to those who value such knowledge), about her worries over her daughter's diet and health in the cold damp of Valtiffe (meaning don't be fool enough to think the Empress doesn't have assassins and spies in every shadow of Saut-Leronne), and about fearing that she will miss her quite terribly (meaning very plainly that Ria should not return until her job was done).

But Ria's mother was not the Ambassador. The senior Alodesal may be in the Corte, but her power in that arena extended only so far. Ria did not report to her in any way.

She was reminding herself of that when a quiet knock at the door—was she supposed to call it a 'hatch'?—interrupted her study of the missive, and Ria was thankful for it.

"Come in, Juan," she called. No one but her own man would disturb her, due to some mysterious shipboard etiquette which she was sure had been explained to her at some point. She tossed the letter onto the table, where it slid over her large map of Valtiffe to land on a sparse crook of coastline she had yet to learn the name of. Valtivan place-names made little sense, based in some long-dead language. She should have been practicing her pronunciation and testing her memory daily ever since she accepted the position as Ambassador, but she never did have a taste for the perfunctory.

The door, prettily painted in white and gold after the fashion of a Torreçon salon, swung open without a sound, and Juan maneuvered his massive frame into the cabin. He really wasn't built for belowdecks life, poor fellow, but he did manage to open the door without a creak, something Ria had yet to accomplish.

"Please pardon my interruption, Dona," he rumbled, eyes down. "There are ships nearby."

"This is the ocean, Juan. We must assume we will see many ships." She didn't bother to hide her boredom. Such games were unnecessary with her old servant, and he would have seen through them anyway.

"Yes, Dona. I had hoped, though, not to see ships of war."

Ria rose at that. At last, a little fun. "What banners?"

"Cadois mercantile, for now. But those are almost an insult— anyone can see what they are. There's a fat brigantine heavy with cannon and three nimble little cutters in attendance."

"A Cad patrol."

"Indeed, Dona. They could be pirates or sellships, but I doubt it. Too trim for anything but the Empress's navy."

Ria smiled bitterly. "Such as it is. Those idiots can't handle anything that doesn't have a flat bottom," she said, quoting her father. "Let's go watch them bob around."

Juan's lips pursed, but he said nothing as Ria walked past him and up the rough, unpainted stairs—or were they called 'ladders' here? The bulk of the interior of the ship did not receive the same treatment as the Ambassador's cabin, of course, but she had been led to understand that it was kept in better shape than one would see in any other vessel. This was a ship of statecraft—who knew who the Ambassador might lead down these steps?

The wet and cold of the air above deck slapped away any dullness of mind remaining after hours of reading in the close air and ill light of Ria's cabin. A spatter of droplets covered the deck, though she felt no rain. She looked to the sails to judge the wind, and for the first time wondered if the ten-foot golden griffins painted on them were the best choice in foreign waters. There would be no hiding who was on this ship, unlike the Cadois cowards.

The moon hid behind heavy clouds to the east, and the stars stared down unhindered in the westerly direction of the prow. A chain of man-made lights broke the horizon a few miles to the north.

Every seaman who saw her bowed and backed away, as was protocol. If the sailors were concerned, they did not show it. After the fashion of their trade, they kept busy with the rigging and called to each other in their inscrutable cant as if nothing were out of the ordinary.

The captain, a stooped man who kept his head shorn bald as if in defiance of the sun, stood at the rail with a farglass to his eye and muttered a constant burble of concern punctuated by the occasional curse.

Ria placed herself next to him and made her presence known with a deep breath. "What news?" she asked. She should have added a respectful 'Captain' at the end of her question—the omission was meant to communicate her expectation that the captain follow protocol as well as his crew did.

"Apologies, Dona," he growled. He had the smooth, deep

voice of a great singer, which made everything he said sound better than it was in fact. "I didn't hear your delicate step on the deck. Forgive an old tar for keeping his eyes on the approaching ships."

"No banners yet?"

"No. They're Caddies, though. No doubting that. Dona."

"Good," Ria said. "They will take no issue with an Ambassador's ship, or with its escort."

The captain turned away from the glass orb in his hand as if to face Ria, but he turned back before speaking.

Juan stepped up to rail at Ria's right and cleared his throat. "There have been cases when a diplomat's banner did not guarantee safety."

"We are not at war with the Empress. The treaty has stood for years. If some overzealous patrol captain were to fire upon us...."

"Yes, Dona. If news reached home of it, there would be difficulties. But if all our ships sank? The sea is a dangerous place. Who could say what happened?"

Ria's laugh carried far over the still water. "Three ships flying the griffin lost so close to the Empress's waters? Every port in Ombria would raise the war colors."

"Every port, perhaps," Juan agreed. "But would the capitol?"

Ria had never seen the war banners. There were some ports that would fly their vote over any small matter—a Cadois merchant spotted off the coast, or a handful of self-declared pirates in a couple of old tubs making noise in a tavern. Grand old Torreçon was not one of these; the Opal of the Coasts did not need to invent reasons to gain attention, nor had it yet forgotten what true war was like. Before the Culling of the Corsairs that Ria's father and Juan fought in, there had been the burning seas of the Fire War, when Ombria and Cadogna vied for the world.

Even if every port city in the Queendom flew for war, nothing would happen unless La Reina declared it. Ria considered what Her response would be to a missing Ambassador. An open declaration of hostilities over an assumption would never have the full support of the peers, only those who stood to profit financially from the demand in ships and guns. And the paisans always hated wartime; it was their children who died, of course. Ria doubted she was worth it.

"Well, then, Captain." She stifled a sigh. "What shall we be doing?"

"We'll be doing the sensible thing. We keep our attitude and wait until they've glassed us out to their satisfaction. Most likely they've no interest in bothering us."

"And if they do have interest? If they try and engage?"

"'Try' isn't the word, Dona." The man rubbed a rough palm over his scalp. "We're not fitted for serious action. They have longer range, more guns, and I'm guessing they've got every cannon 'chanted not to miss."

Numbers added up quickly in Ria's mind. "That seems a magnificent expense."

"Aye, Dona," Juan replied. "As you said yourself, the Cadois are no seafarers. What they lack in skill they counter with coin."

"You seem remarkably well-versed in the mind of a patrol captain who is considering breaking one of the principal rules of civilization. Did you spend much time firing upon diplomats in the war?"

Juan looked away at that, turning to the sea as if he were observing the nearing ships. "Pirates do not have diplomats, Dona."

"Then how was the peace achieved? Who attended the Treaty of the Pirate King?"

The captain coughed to cover a chuckle. Juan took a deep breath, a signal Ria knew well. He was battling with himself about his response. Perhaps she had pushed him too hard with her questioning. But how was she to act without information?

"Someone closer to those events could provide a better answer, Dona." Juan did not sound at all as if he were upset. "Perhaps your father."

This was not the sort of situation in which Ria preferred to find herself: unprepared, knowing less than everyone around her, waiting on someone else's move. Flying false banners. Murdering diplomats and blaming it on the weather. This was all very dishonest.

Ria raised her voice loud enough for the entire ship to hear. To every hell with the Caddics if they heard her too.

"Captain, signal our escort. One is to continue on course as vanguard. The other is to head away from those ships with full haste. We will regroup with the vanguard once this is over, so tell her to keep it slow."

The captain nearly dropped his farglass over the side. "Dona, I'm not sure what you're after—"

"I must apologize if my instructions were not in the proper naval jargon, Captain. Perhaps Juan can translate for me."

"That's not the issue…"

She raised one of her perfectly shaped eyebrows. "How may I assist, then?"

A naval captain is expected to be a little out of shape. Much of his time is spent in his cabin scribbling in his log, after all. This particular captain, though, must have spent more time with the crew than most; the muscles of his neck tensed when his teeth clenched. Unseemly for a man who was meant to be as able at the dinner table as at the helm.

"Ambassador Alodesal, I mean no disrespect to your or your family, but on this vessel, for the safety of you and your entourage, decisions on naval tactics fall to me."

"I see." She didn't bother with a false smile. "And what of

decisions of diplomatic strategy? Have you been burdened with those as well? Has La Reina poured the water over your hands and given you Her seal? What did you think of Her when you met Her?"

"Dona..."

Juan pulled himself to his full height and spoke quietly over Ria's head. "You gained this position through some excellent political maneuvering, Gianco. Captain of the Ambassador's Company is a plum job. Do you plan on keeping it?"

A name. Of course he had one, but Ria had not bothered to learn it. Trust Juan to have some gossip on the man.

The captain grimaced and stared at Juan for a long moment. This exchange had been won by Juan, one way or another. Ria hoped she wouldn't have to embarrass the captain by putting him in chains. She glanced at a few of the sailors, all of whom had stopped working to watch the exchange. Did they have their hands on their knives?

"With the rich and mighty..." Gianco muttered.

"My patience has limits, Captain Gianco."

He made a hand motion and looked to the rigging. The quiet clicking of a shuttered signal lantern began.

"And what of us, Dona?" Gianco was glaring at her now, but his voice was civil.

"Head straight for them. And roll out the cannons."

Gianco had the good sense not to hesitate. He gave a brusque bow and stomped off to shout at someone. Ria turned toward Juan, not waiting for him to clear his throat again. Better to force him to give his lecture to her face then to let him prattle on over her shoulder.

"Dona, we must not attack." His voice was tight. "Even if we were somehow to survive, the repercussions..."

"Do you think me that foolish, Juan? I have no interest in dying today. We will not shoot, but what do you think *they* will do? They cannot attack; unless they are fast enough to catch an Ombrian sloop, word would get out."

"Ramming is still considered an attack, Dona."

"What captain would confess to not being able to get out of the way of an Ambassador's ship? All the world knows the Cads can't sail. Surely a collision would do little to improve that opinion."

"And the cannons you are displaying?"

"We are practicing the salute we will raise when we approach Valtiffe. I can't imagine a seasoned veteran of the seas would be frightened by that."

The world rotated around them as the prow turned to face the patrol ships.

"I do not know, Dona. It seems an awful risk over a possibility. I do not know what they will do."

"They will do the only thing they can do, Juan. They will yield."

Naval events, in Ria's opinion, moved far too slowly. It was as if the passage of time itself had somehow slowed. She was certain she heard some men rolling bones belowdecks to pass the time. Over an hour creaked by before the Cadois patrol was close enough to prove her correct: the patrol broke formation to let her pass.

As they sailed on, Ria watched with the Captain's farglass. The concentric rings magically etched deep within the solid orb rotated and adjusted to keep her vision on what she wanted to see: the face of the Cadois patrol captain she had just outplayed. Either the Empress's navy had changed its uniform since last she had attended a diplomat party with Caddie veterans on the guest list, or her adversary had yet to show his face. Ria imagined he was in his cabin, penning a report on the event only to throw it away after a few lines and start again. That same dim yellow of glowstone light smoldered in the cabin windows and played on the dark water.

Another light streaked across the water in quick flashes, only barely visible and apparently coming from Ria's own ship. It looked like weak fireflies speeding toward one of the Cadois ships.

She lowered the glass to get a better look, but she couldn't find the odd green light until she raised it again.

"Juan," she called. She assumed he was nearby, though of course silent. "We are going belowdecks. I may need you to secure someone for me."

They walked down the steps and turned toward the bow, away from Ria's cabin and into the crew quarters. If Juan possessed the ability to enter a room unnoticed, Ria possessed its opposite. As soon as she stepped through the door, every eye was on her. She wasn't going to catch anyone this way.

She sent Juan ahead with instructions to find someone with an odd light of some kind. The process did not take long—the sailors did not even have time to resume their games before the big man dragged a woman through the tight quarters by the upper arm. He held a signal lantern in his hand.

The ship was utterly silent. Even on deck, no movement could be heard. No calls, no whistles, no bells. She knew what they were thinking. She had already shamed Captain Gianco in front of these people. What would she do with a spy found in their ranks? In the warren of shipboard life, surely the rest of the crew noticed when one went a deck lower than she needed to, or spent too much time at a particular port hole. These wiry brutes may not have been complicit per se, but they certainly knew something was afoot. And they chose to do nothing.

Ria would not do the same.

She let her gaze settle on the woman's defiant eyes. "Treason will face justice."

"I'm no traitor," the woman spat. "We're not at war."

A smirk tried to creep up Ria's face, but she resisted it. So the bilge rat was a legal scholar as well, apparently. A criminal is always well-versed in the precise details of the law she breaks.

"La Reina does not require your interpretation of Her laws, traitor."

Some of the sailors shifted in their musty corners. The paisan revolutions were ages past, but this was not the first time Ria had seen the effect speaking of La Reina had on some common folk. They had a long memory, it seemed. She had always found that holding firm worked best. But that was in Torreçon, in her mother's arcada, in her own casino. Not in the dark belly of a ship in the middle of an empty ocean. *The sea is a dangerous place...*

One of the men fidgeted with a knucklebone that even at this distance and in this light Ria could see was weighted to fall dog-side down. The man's stare showed not anger, but fear.

Ria had grown up in Torreçon, the greatest port city in the world. She knew something of sailors and their ways. These were people for whom luck was a real force, as invisible and as necessary as air. They lived and died by the accident of the weather, by the unknowable tossings of the desert ocean. When they scraped together enough money to play at her casino, they gambled as if the sun would not rise in the morning. In a life of rope and sailcloth and wood and pitch, every sunset might indeed be one's last.

That was what was happening here. Sailors were not sentimental with their crewmates, who would more often than not end up dead or run off. These people were not afraid of what Ria was going to do with their friend. They were not afraid of what she and the peerage might do to them for letting this espionage happen.

They were afraid she would do something that was bad luck.

"Take her to the captain," she snarled. "I can no longer bear to look at her. Leave her lantern with me."

The look in the woman's eyes stayed defiant, but a flash of fear was unmistakable. Ria didn't know what the standard punishment for this sort of thing was in the nautical world, but it had this woman nervous. She may have thought the port-living Ambassador wouldn't have the stomach for anything worse than chaining her up. She would have been right.

Juan did as he had been ordered, and all of the ship sounds had resumed by the time he reached the top step. Anxious eyes found their way back to their tasks; the fellow with the rigged knucklebone grinned like he'd been pardoned from the noose at the last moment. Ria's distaste for superstition was getting worse.

She took the lantern back to her cabin for a closer examination. It seemed like a regular signal lantern, though Ria wasn't basing that on any real knowledge. A switch opened and shut three metal flaps on the front of the thing. The glowstone inside was not working, though—it could have been a normal rock found on any beach. Signallers used glowstones of much greater power than the ones in Ria's cabin ceiling. Why wasn't this one blinding her when she looked at it?

The farglass was still in a pocket of her coat. She held it up to the dead stone and looked through, too curious to care if the burning rays of the sun itself were on the other side. A faint light, no brighter than an ember, now enveloped the glowstone. Had the damned thing been enchanted to only be seen by someone using a farglass? The light was so dim, though; maybe some other kind of enchanted lens was paired with it, and the farglass just caught a bit of the magic. She wished she could send word to her brother and get his advice—he was always curious about the strange reactions between magic and statecraft. She was starting to feel as if she didn't have a very good grasp of either.

Scuffling on the stairs, and two angry voices. Her door opened with a crash which only served to intensify the argument going on between Gianco and Juan as they entered the cabin.

"You are a damned fool, Ambassador!" Gianco was shouting as if he needed his voice heard at the top of the tallest mast in the center of a hailstorm. "A damned, damned fool!"

Ria held up a hand. The captain must have been strong indeed to get anywhere Juan didn't want him to. "Let him speak. But do close the door. We should at least pretend to some semblance of privacy."

"If you had some concern about a member of my crew, you should have brought it to me. Not sent this beast to manhandle whoever he chose. These are *my* people. You don't know what's going on here."

"Well, you certainly have my attention now," Ria said. "Educate me."

The man's voice quieted to a near whisper, but the veins in his bald head still throbbed. "Isenda."

"Who?"

"The woman you dragged through the whole fucking ship. Her name is Isenda. You should have let her be."

"She was sending a message to the Cadois, Gianco. Espionage is treason, and…"

"I know she was sending a message, you peacock! And she was getting one back!"

Ria glanced at Juan to see his reaction. Juan was looking right back at her, not bothering to hide his surprise.

After a long breath, Gianco continued at a more conversational volume. "You should stick to card games and dinner parties, Dona Alodesal. The beautiful game of nations does not suit you. Why do you think I allowed us to sail anywhere near a Cadois patrol? Do you think I don't know how to avoid one of those tubs? I am the captain of one of the most important ships in the peacetime fleet. As such, I have purchased some very nice 'chants from the Brothers, which you would know if you had ever bothered to set foot in my cabin instead of sulking in this fucking boudoir. I've a nice big ocean chart, and some nice little wooden boats that move around on it. I know where those fools are before they even crest the horizon."

"I know something of espionage, Gianco," Ria said flatly. "More than you might think."

It was bluff, but only a small one. She had been educated in some of the basics by a member of the Corte at the Empress's direction. Casinos were known to be a favorite playground for spies. There was even a coded language of cardplay, used to communicate during a game without anyone else noticing.

"Not enough to recognize a double agent at work," Gianco spat. "Isenda sends a message to the Cads, then reports back with whatever orders she receives. That goes up the ladder and I don't have a damned clue what happens to it, but she is a small but crucial piece in a very large and very complicated craft. You think the Corte gives a half a shit about you running off to Valtiffe to throw your weight around? All they care about is me making sure to run into the right ship so Isenda can do her fucking job, and your sudden decision to do yours for once has made mine a lot damn harder.

"Do you know how difficult it is to run a ship somewhere it's not supposed to be going without the crew realizing it? A gull can't shit in the ocean without my sailors swapping opinions about it for an hour. Tell them to tack an extra degree, and they'll have the whole plan figured. But I managed to fulfill my duty with you thinking I'm a paisan idiot the whole time."

Ria had nothing to say in response. She wasn't going to apologize, but if Gianco was telling the truth, she had misstepped greatly. "What will happen to her?"

"No clue about that either. She should get the knife for

treason and espionage, but I don't know if they would waste a resource like that. She won't be working on this ship again, no mistake. You set us back, Dona. Set us back quite a lot."

He stomped out of the cabin without another word. Juan followed; he always had a good sense of when Ria wanted to be left to herself. And considering how insignificant and puerile she felt in this new world of lies and death, she would want that for a long measure of time.

Her mother's letter was exactly where she had left it. Looking at the envelope now, it seemed the name 'Juegar' was penned thicker than the rest of the text. Juegar—her father's family name. Synonymous with naval prowess after the Culling. Impressive, but not much next to 'Alodesal'. A great grandee family, with generations of service to the crown as ambassadors, courtiers, and not a few spies. And now the scion of these great families had fouled up the affairs of both.

If Ria was going to unravel the web the Empress was spinning in Valtiffe, she was going to have to do much better than this.

Take a map of a city. Erase the names of the streets, the parks, the thoroughfares. Place a mark on the location of each of the city's clubs. Under each club, write the nature of the play there. Is it somber and focused? Lively and bright? Does a man howl when he loses? Does he treat his opponents to drinks when he wins?

From there, you might map the tenor of the neighborhoods. And from that, you will know the spirit of a city.

from de Tabanne's introduction to
Salen's History of Blots

X

VALEN

THE BUILDING WHICH housed Mme. Vabanque's Syncretic Club
jutted its marble staircase farther out into the street than its
more austere neighbors did, but did not stoop so low as to
display a sign. One was expected simply to know.

Valen did know, of course, having done a decent amount of
trade at the club's tables over the years. After spending far too
many nights proving himself an enjoyable companion around
the signaux table for a few well-heeled wool traders, he had
engineered a standing invitation to the club as a guest on casual
game nights. He had yet to be invited to tournament play, and
had given up all hope of being offered a membership.

The card he had received in invitation—a fresh six of lamps
written over in blue ink—declared quite proudly that this
season's Forbearance Game would be at the Syncretic Club
without providing an address or a time, leaving Valen to make
his best guess, knowing what he did of the social standards of
the city's élite. He chose to arrive a little earlier than was likely
fashionable.

As Valen crossed the street to the massive door a broad young man eyed him. He wore a round felt hat adorned with a black and gold cockade. One of the Knaves, of course; Arbelan's cronies making sure Valen was making good on his promise. He had to assume he had passed under the scrutiny of several top-watch kids as well.

Valen did not mind not being a member of the Syncretic; he didn't prefer the play there, anyway. The Syncretic Club's style was far more emotional than was necessary. The men and women who passed their hours there did not play to come out ahead so much as to have an exciting and memorable hand at some point in the evening. The club's internal mythology had made shining heroes out of players who played the perfect card when the chances of doing so were all but nil, but never spoke as to whether or not those heroes actually took home a decent pot that night.

In fact, the impression Valen had from hearing dozens of these tales over his months playing there was that when a hand like that came up, all play stopped and an impromptu parade started, with songs and wine overtaking the game completely. There was terrifying talk of a crown, always excitedly stage-whispered around Valen's uninitiated ears. He had made it his policy to keep the game from heading in such a direction through any means possible.

This, he mused as he climbed the pure white steps in the candlelight, was perhaps why he was never offered membership.

But he had managed an invite to tonight's Forbearance Game, which was no small feat. Even if it had been forced on him by a despicable fool and not offered out of respect for his ability, he would be a fool himself not to see it as good fortune.

Preparing himself for the night had been a savage affair of dressing and undressing in a bid to balance the propriety of his assumed character with the freedom of movement demanded by his sharping, to say nothing of the hidden pockets. In the

end, a man of finance must dress conservatively, and he chose
an unassuming form over the function he could have used.
Valen's costume included the very basics any man of quality
would be expected to wear: polished shoes, stockings without
a hint of a tear, vest, coat, neck stock. He wore no wig, though.
He kept his graying yellow hair in a neat queue tied with a
simple black ribbon. His persona was a servant of the élite,
after all, not one of them.

His toilette had included another round of the standing
debate between Margo and him as to whether or not it was
time to lose his mustache and grow out the beard, after the
fashion of men of a certain age in Valtiffe. Valen's argument
was that by the time a man stops shaving his chin he should be
farther along in his career than a clerk, and the change might
damage his cover story. Margo disagreed, and was kind enough
not to elaborate as to why.

Heat and light greeted him as he walked through the foyer.
The décor had not changed since the last time he had entertained
some bourgeois out of their money in Mme. Vabanque's. An
expanse of parquetry floors ran nearly the depth of the entire
building, ending in walls painted full length with pretty scenes
of blue-green chete trees swaying against a cloud-streaked
sunset. Had his view not been blocked by the crush of tables
and chairs, he could have seen the coy dramas of small fauna
acted out at ankle level on every wall. Gods knew he had spent
enough time examining them as he waited for these fops to quit
gossiping and lay a damned card down.

Before he could go more than a step or two, a severe young
woman in a simple powder blue dress and small wig placed
herself before him. She asked his name, paused a troubling
moment after she heard it, then smiled and moved aside without
another word. Valen laughed at himself—he was so anxious to
get into the game he had actually held his breath, wondering

if Arbelan had tricked him somehow despite his having very plainly received an invitation.

Valen recognized several of the men and women that filled the spaces between tables as they waited for the night's entertainments to begin. Some greeted him politely, but it was some time before he found a conversation open to receiving him. One M. Guillaume Gourdon Comines, a lean man with a ready, if empty, smile, recognized Valen from a mild night at the Club Maritime and introduced his companions: a cousin of some sort, and his children's first tutor. They made pleasant talk of their recent exploits at the tables, which Valen dodged for the most part, thankful that at least M. Comines's set didn't insist on any Syncretic histrionics.

The three-score players in the room hushed for a long moment. Valen turned in the direction of the door, as did everyone else. Stéphane Trouluc, the Secret Broker, had entered. Valen had never seen the man, a minor gente with an estate well outside of the city, but he could identify him easily enough from the snips and snatches he had collected about the secrets game. The old fellow was something of a celebrity to the gamesters of Saut-Leronne, and Valen found himself staring.

The Secret Broker of this generation did not seem to relish the position. On the far side of seventy with none of the lankness of old age, he was of the landholding set with connections in trade, finance, shipping, and the civil services of Valtiffe and Cadogna, as well as a known friendship with the Ambassador of Cadogna, Omer-Guy Bendine himself. He had been selected by the loose association of Valtiffe's moneyed scions that ran the Forbearance Game. As he passed through the gaming floor and to his chamber, anyone could tell from his sad glances that his preference would have been to be in the games. The affectionate touches he gave the felt might have seemed a bittersweet love gone wrong; but when he knocked a sizable knee painfully against a chair it became evident that age had taken his vision.

At least the old codger could still take part. The smell of smoke, the quiet whisper of cards and clatter of dice. Valen couldn't honestly say he didn't love the atmosphere.

Trouluc stopped at a doorway in the rear wall and turned to face the crowd. Next to him stood a woman in an emerald gown with a thin veil over her shoulders. Her round face held laughing eyes.

"A lovely night to all of you, my dears!" she beamed. "Welcome to the Forbearance Game, hosted this quarter by Mme. Vabanque!"

After some polite applause, which Valen contributed to in deference to an etiquette he had yet to learn, the woman laughed. "That being myself!" The crowd laughed along with her, and Valen feared the parade he had heard so much about might erupt at any moment.

The woman in blue who had greeted Valen at the door approached Mme. Vabanque with an upturned tricorn in her hands. Vabanque tittered as she reached in and pulled a single card from the hat. "Dieuroi!" she shouted.

An excited energy passed through the crowd as the tenor of the night was decided, but Valen's heart went cold.

Unlike most of the games played in Valtiffe, in dieuroi the players held no cards in their hands. A fabric square with numbers on it was laid before the players, and they placed bets of varying complexity on what the dealer's next card would be. Valen would have little opportunity to mark the cards with his scoring ring until it was his turn to deal. Without preparing ahead of time or having other players planted on his table to run a joint con, dieuroi was one of the more difficult games to cheat at, and also one of the more difficult to apply any skill to. There was no bluffing, no finessing, no interpretation of his rivals' plays.

He would have even preferred *dice* to this. At least then he could switch in his ringers.

Trouluc was approached by the woman in blue, who this time brought a wooden box lacquered in the old style. He opened its lid and produced a thin circle of metal. As the room began finding their tables and tittering about the game, Valen watched the old man ceremoniously place the diadem on his head.

Even from across the room, Valen could see the enchantment on the thing. This was the Couronne d'Oublie—the Forgetful Crown. Everything that transpired between the moment he placed the metal ring on his head and the moment he took it off would be completely forgotten. The crown was old, hundreds of years, but the enchantment had not faded. The Brothers of yore took their time with things. Probably because a few hundred years of entitlement and bureaucracy had yet to ruin their school.

The Secret Broker's chamber, a movable room which was taken apart and reconstructed in a new location for every Forbearance Game, hulked in a distant corner of the club's main hall. A line formed outside it, including a small, nervous man in a burgundy coat.

Clavis Dusmenil. The man Valen had come to destroy.

In my visits to Saut-Leronne, I met not a single Brother. Few will argue the wisemen of the Pendent Tower are the greatest practitioners of their craft in any nation, and as I navigated the cold streets of their river city, I hoped very much to see one of their number. Was not the great Naiibis himself schooled here? The man whose divinations predicted the eruption of Mt. Senecin, saving thousands of Cadois soldiers in the Fire War? He who dowsed the mighty springs of Soucisse in the center of the desert? What manner of men are these Valtivan brothers? And, of most interest to me, how do they pass their idle hours?

A Gamester Abroad, M. Jerôme de Tabanne

XI

MICHEL

IN A SMALL room between the Broker's chamber and the exterior wall of the Syncretic Club, two men sat on the floor in darkness broken only by some meager light from a single candle filtering through an enchanted window. The illumination was not much—the enchantment was not strong enough for a true picture, as anything stronger ran the risk of being visible from the other side, a shimmering heat wave at the edges of the wooden panel. So much of the art of Enchantment was like this, Michel Alcippe mused. The best solution was not always the best.

The Secret Broker's chamber, a temporary room which was moved to the location of every Forbearance Game, bore the strongest soundproofing enchantments anyone in Valtiffe had ever developed. Every part of the room was tested from outside the door, from the rooms at either side and above, and from the alleyway behind it. No amount of noise had ever broken through whatever magic had been inlaid in the honey-blond wood paneling or the deep cobalt wallpapers. The sparse, symmetrical pattern of golden flowers on the paper caught

Michel's eye, bored as he was. The small petals of the aergyn, the flower of silent promises.

Any promises made in the Secret Broker's room that night would not be as silent as all that—the enchanted window allowed sound to pass through the same as it did for vision.

A writing desk and two chairs upholstered in black whaleskin served as the only furniture; the Broker took no refreshments during his long night of service. A single taper in a simple iron candle holder lit the paper and pen with which the precious, hitherto-unheard knowledge of the people of Saut-Leronne would be preserved for use.

The old man who shared this little closet with Michel sighed and removed his periwig. He leaned to his side and reached for the bottle of wine on the stone floor to his right.

The younger man scowled at every grunt of effort and clink of glass during this entire process. How did he get stuck bringing Laciaume on this clandestine mission? The old drunk was quite unsuited to it.

"Relax, son," Laciaume said quietly, though not as quietly as Michel would have liked. "The room is sealed tighter than the Principe's purse strings. You should know this. It's not such an advanced enchantment. Or did they send me here with a diviner this time?"

Michel turned back to the ephemeral window and watched as yet another gente offered the location of his family's jewels. He was selected to lead this mission, and as trivial as listening to these secrets may have been, he did not need to answer to anyone.

Laciaume grunted and pulled a long draught from his bottle, not bothering to wipe the spare droplets from his bearded chin. "A diviner, then. You may wake me up if the voices in your head start telling you anything interesting."

"Keep quiet," Michel hissed. He may have been the younger

of the two, but both had attained Third Honors. The two men were equals in the eyes of the Séminaire. He had every right to hush the dotard.

"Have some faith in your elders, son," Laciaume rose from the dusty floor and began clapping his hands and shouting. "Halloo! Halloo there, you fat old goat! Turn around and give us a wink or I'll cast a curse that'll turn your cock green!"

When the broker made no response, Laciaume bent himself back into his seated position with a gloating grin. "You see? It's impossible. They can't hear us one bit."

"Perhaps I simply do not wish to listen to your relentless groans and gurgles." Michel refused to turn and face the old 'chanter. "It is not easy to concentrate with you harrumphing yourself into exhaustion."

"It's all a damned waste of time, anyway. We could set up a few Souvenirs in here and save ourselves the trouble."

Souvenirs were enchanted to make a record of a few seconds of time, retrieving a memory from the darkness below. The little orbs were quite banned now; Michel recalled a scrap of the history on the matter, the thrust of which was that a few powerful people had been embarrassed by their use in centuries past. Typical of the non-initiated.

The Séminaire was not truly bound by the laws of the laity, but in Cadogna and Valtiffe at least (he had no idea whether the L'Ombrais Brothers allowed them), the Brothers had decided it was better to comply with the ban than to fight. They were only memories, after all.

"Oh, very good," Michel sighed. "Let's pick an argument with the whole of the legal world because you are too lazy to do your job."

Laciaume responded with some bit of snark, but Michel wasn't listening. He had scryed for hours in preparation for this task, and the images had revealed that something unusual was going to take place. Unlike his associate, he would be vigilant. The assignment might be perfunctory—one might even consider it an insult to a Brother of his level—but it was an assignment nonetheless, and he would not do it poorly.

The two Brothers sat in near-silence for several hours, save for the occasional gulp from Laciaume's bottle, until a short man in an out-of-fashion pigeon-wing wig walked into the Secret Broker's chamber. He wore a burgundy coat that was leaning toward threadbare, and had a fearful, alarmed look.

A shard of an image. Michel remembered as he watched, something he had already seen in his scrying bowl: a single brass button amidst three gold ones. The same buttons were on the nervous man's cuff now.

"What is it?" Laciaume noticed when Michel sat up straighter. No quips when matters became serious, apparently.

The short man's voice, muddled by the multiple enchantments in play, sounded timid when he asked how confident the Secret Broker was that no one could hear them, that the Forgetful Crown worked. The Broker soothed the man's fears with patient condescension, like the tone Michel used with overly avid students.

When the man spoke his secret, Michel did not understand it. Laciaume, though, nearly dropped his bottle.

"Gods and spirits," the old man whispered.

"What is it? What does he mean?"

"He shouldn't know that. He can't."

Michel's voice rose despite his attempts to keep it quiet. He had seen something about this small man and the secret he was so loath to part with: blood and blades. "Well, it would appear that he does."

"We need to stop him. Stop all of this." Laciaume pulled a dark stone the size of his palm from a pocket. "This will do it."

"Do what, Laciaume?" The old enchanter's eyes spoke of

dark intent, and if there was anything Michel could not abide, it was not knowing what was going to happen.

Laciaume put the rock on the ground and it started to glow like an ember catching the wind. "We'll leave this here. When the job is done, it will look like any other cobble."

A rarefaction stone. Civilians might find a weak one in any winemakers shop, but this lozenge of rock and enchantment was not one of those.

"You want to pull the air out of the building? With everyone in it?" Michel grabbed Laciaume's bottle by its neck instinctively, a weapon if he needed one. Not that any Séminaire enchanter was likely to be going abroad without some protective charms on his person.

Laciaume rose with an ease Michel hadn't thought the old sot capable. "We need to tell the Principe. We'll use the Whisperwind."

"Laciaume, I am in charge of this mission. Stop this nonsense. Now."

The elder man did not acknowledge the order. The stone was making the hidden room uncomfortably close already. A building filled with blue-faced death would not be easily explained. Michel had seen no asphyxiation in his scryings. There had to be another way to handle this.

"Laciaume, we can't do this." He grabbed the old man by his arm. "Think. The Séminaire uses the information we learn from these games. A house of death the very night of the tournament is sure to attract suspicion, and we can't risk our little espionage being discovered by some witch who's seen a rarefaction stone before."

"This information—"

"—will be safe. We simply need to ensure this Clavis Dusmenil doesn't lose tonight. If you're half the enchanter you think you are, it should be easy enough. The rest we can handle later."

The enchanter didn't speak, but his rock cooled to an ashy glow.

"Good." Michel's heart calmed a bit. "Thank you. Now, we will have some work to attend to, but first—Why on earth is this information so dangerous?"

Laciaume looked like a man waking from a dream. When he explained what Dusmenil's secret meant, Michel agreed that the old gente who was gambling with it had seen his last sunrise.

The list of my loves is like a dieuroi night;
Give me time enow, and 'twill break even.

Barberaque, *The Faithful Scholars*, Act I, Scene iv

XII
VALEN

A MERCHANT PROVIDES goods where they are needed. Miners and farmers wrest necessary staples from the earth. Sailors help others make safe passage. All honest trades have an element of altruism to them, a benefit to one's fellow people.

Valen's trade involved *taking* from other people, no matter how he tried to frame it. There was no elevation to it, no dignity in the end when the night's winnings were tallied. He did feel some guilt about this, but he forgave himself with the knowledge that he did not cheat solely to take what he did not deserve. His attraction to the mental challenge and the excitement of the turn of the card notwithstanding, his true goal was to discover a new form of magic.

During his time at the Séminaire he had been taught—inculcated, more like—that Divination and Enchantment were the only two schools of proven, successful magic and any other inquiries showed a disrespect for the centuries of Brothers who had studied the bounds of the craft. *We've tried that, and it doesn't work, so listen to us and do your exercises.*

But Valen intended on finding more. He had lost much to the turn of a card, and he promised to never let that happen again.

He'd gambled with every kron to his name as a youth in Verbichere, winning more often than losing at the rough tables to be found in the few miners' taverns in town. His parents never spited him the enjoyment, though he was known to shirk his accounting work for his father in order to make a particular game when he had extra to spend. He was living as young people do: with other young people.

He knew he had a preternatural talent for cards. Too many times the exact card he needed would come to him, too many times to ignore or chalk up to chance. He mastered the mathematics of probability quickly enough, and his memory for which cards had been played by whom was a matter of local legend.

One time he played at a duplicate signaux contest at the mayor's daughter's home. In this version of the game, several tables are set with dealt cards, which remain in place between games. The players move from seat to seat, and at the end of the night a comparison is made as to how well people scored in the exact same games. The worst event that could happen at a duplicate tourney was for the hands to get mixed up— at that point the entire night is thrown, as a true comparison can no longer be made. Yet the mistress of the house herself absentmindedly gathered up the cards and shuffled them, a habit from her long hours of play.

Valen remembered all four hands in their totality, and saved the night.

These gifts, though, were not enough to account for his remarkable luck. It was easy enough for someone without his memory or his knack for calculation to think a soul with both was impossibly lucky. Valen, however, knew what the chances should be, and still he came out ahead. The only school of thought that allows for—indeed, often demands—the impossible is that of magic. He began to think of himself as a Brother, bending the laws of probability to his will.

He never cheated in earnest. Never once even looked at another player's poorly-held cards. He found the very idea of dishonest play despicable. What pleasure, what pride could be had from winning if the odds were not equal?

Still, too many lucky streaks can garner one some suspicion. Valen took pleasure in beating the people who accused him of false play, when he knew for a fact his hands were clean. He liked to push them farther and farther, baiting them into finding the sleight-of-hand he wasn't using. When drinks were thrown and fists raised, Valen laughed it off. He didn't cheat, and so he had nothing to hide. They might pull up his sleeves or tear at his waistcoat, but they would find no hidden cards, no intricate devices. He chose games, and opponents, he knew he would do well with, just as a hunter might have a favorite animal, one he has studied and mastered.

But even then he'd known, unlike mining, farming, or any of the other trades, he was making money by taking it out of the hands of other people. He did not grow things, he did not labor to make a thing of value and live off the sales. He beat people at games of chance, leaving their pockets empty of the fruits of the actual labor they did. He turned what should be a pleasant diversion into a trade, and dealt in other people's money as a fisherman deals in fish.

One day he came home from a night at the tables to find his parents lying on the floor, surrounded by broken furniture. Men had come in, beaten his father, and tossed the place, stealing anything of value. When his mother cursed them as cowards, they forced her to the ground and took a hammer to her hipbone until it broke. Valen's sister had hidden in a corner of the root cellar, terrified.

Valen did not speak. He ran into town, woke a doctor to tend to his mother, and left Verbichere never to return.

He gambled his way to Saut-Leronne, sleeping inside when he could afford to. It took him three weeks of walking to get from the icy mountains of Verbichere to the river city, and in that solitude he wrestled with his situation.

Up until the attack on his parents, his life had followed its tracks as well as one of the mine carts he had watched as a boy. He was the son of a bookkeeper for a small mining outfit, had learned that same trade, and would eventually either take his father's place or do similar work for a business in another town, with nothing to pass the long nights but his card-playing. He had supposed he would marry at some point. He was nearing his twentieth birthday, and when he imagined his sixtieth, very little was different.

Now everything he identified himself by was gone. The bookkeeper's son was now the bookkeeper's shame, and the quiet life he had expected had evaporated. If he could find a position as a clerk at a goldsmith's or moneylender's in Saut-Leronne he could reclaim some part of the stability he had known.

On the road, too cold to stop walking despite the height of the moon in the sky and the burning weariness of his eyes, he chose something else. He knew there was something more to his love of gambling than the game itself. He was altogether *too* lucky. Perhaps he had latent divination ability, and was predicting the cards. He knew little of magic, only what he saw in the enchanted tools of the best miners or the raving predictions of the witch who wandered the town square. Yet he knew there was *something* to his luck, and he determined then to find out what.

A game of stomach covered his admission to the Séminaire. He allowed a man whose cousin was, he claimed, in contention to be the next Principe to stake an introduction against a sizable pot. When the last card was turned, it was precisely the one Valen had hoped for. The one he'd willed it to be. Maybe.

It was at the Séminaire that he met Teneriève, the dour Mistigris migrant who had at least considered the possibility of his luck magic. And Teneriève was living with Monsieur and Madame de Hoque and their daughter Marguerite.

His life took a new tack, and he did his best to never think of the old one.

THE PLAYERS AT the Forbearance Game were either waiting for their turn with the Broker or just milling around. Valen wished Marguerite was with him; a look from her would be enough to calm his nerves, and even after their many years together he still wanted to impress her.

The game table was the only place in the world where he was impressive in the least, where he was an accomplished and respected man. Marguerite never gambled, and thus only ever heard about his successes second hand. She knew the man who came home tired or frustrated or drunk on victory, none of which were who Valen was at the table. The best side of himself was one his wife never saw.

His need for validation was going to have to wait until after the game, though. Best to keep his fingers from Arbelan's knife.

If he was going to live up to expectations, he was going to have to be one of the first dealers. He caught a look at the decks being used, and understood why Jacquemin had not been able to find any information; these green-backed cards were not of a pattern used by any of Saut-Leronne's printers. Most of the Leronnian decks were decorated designs of oldfolk, always riding on leaves or eating off toadstools and other such fae merriment. These cards had aergyn flowers and leaping dogs, a design Valen recognized from a small printer in Cadois Jaleaux.

They must have been imported for the night's game, which made sense. If you want to keep the locals from rigging the decks, don't give them time. The unusual cards set Valen to thinking—perhaps Arbelan's top-watch girl had seen the crates arrive and reported back to her master. If she had, Arbelan had not offered up the information. Arbelan wanted him to fail, maybe. Or perhaps he had not understood the logo the girl had drawn. Or perhaps he was in on it somehow, some kind of card-smuggling ring.

Valen shook his head to clear the paranoid thinking. He was here to play a game and to win against one of his contenders. Whatever foolishness he could dream up, the truth was laid plainly before him.

He considered drawing de Niver's spectacles from his coat pocket and balancing them on his nose. If he did succeed in marking the decks with his scoring ring during his deal—by no means guaranteed—the aid to his vision would certainly help. Scoring the finish on a deck made for a difficult cheat: unlike ink marks, spotting scoring depended on the angle the card was held and the tiniest difference in the light. With the enchanted lenses, he would have no problem discerning his handiwork.

Valen had played with these decks before, but only once. They were of a quality as fine as any found on Valtiffe, and those of Valtiffe were considered the best in the world. The paper resisted bent corners but shuffled easily, and the finish allowed the cards to slide across the baize. He would have to remember to tell Marguerite. She would spend the next week marking one up for him, just in case they became a new trend in town.

He stood in line and waited. The people around him chatted away, providing a mild cover to the unspoken question of why someone needed to risk a secret. His thoughts rested on one concern and would not leave it: if Arbelan's information wasn't valued high enough, Valen presumed he would be asked to leave, and perhaps not as politely as one would hope. Adieu to a few fingers in that case.

"Getting stuffy in here already," the man in front of him said by way of starting a conversation. He wore a fine ivory frock coat over a brocaded gold waistcoat which showed no sign of tightness over his belly. "They should start the fires earlier. Let the stones of the fireplace soak up the heat, then let the logs go down to embers. Between the wine and the people, I'll be sweating through my coat before the second round's done."

Valen smiled and tugged at his neck-cloth. "I daresay. Dieuroi requires so much movement as well. I wonder if we could convince them to open the door."

The man smiled sardonically. "I doubt that. What would be the point of a private event if anyone walking by could see who was in attendance?"

"I have to confess, I feel some eyes on me now." Valen sheepishly looked around at the milling crowd. "I hope none of these people holds it against me that I'm gambling with a secret."

"Ah, it will be fine. It's tradition. Most of us only visit the Broker for a lark, to keep the old ways going. We offer some secret which we could bear to lose."

"I see," Valen said, feeling a touch embarrassed. "A fun addition to the game."

Again the man smiled, and now he leaned in conspiratorially. "At least that's what we all say. A bit of mead with the medicine. No one wants to admit they actually need the credit. If it was a mark of shame to stand in the line, no one would do it. The game would be over. So, many of us make sure the line is filled, if only in case we need to use it in truth in the future."

Valen chuckled, making sure to speak loud enough for others to hear. "Ah, of course. A merry little contrivance. An excellent way to break up the monotony of regular play."

"Indeed," the man said. "A silly thing, some might say, but the old ways are the best ways, after all. How do you find the wine tonight?"

The two of them contributed to the steady burble of small talk as the line grew shorter. Some side games had started among those not waiting for the Broker, mostly the short variant of signaux, and the servants were kept rather busy with the wine casks. Those in line were treated to cooled firewine drinks as well, something to keep them refreshed through the physical ordeal of standing still.

Valen took account of what he was accomplishing here. He was going to push a man over the brink of failure in order to get a life membership to a card game. The Dusmenil's family legacy of successful shipping was all but gone, and how much of that was due to its current owner's personal failings was well outside of Valen's ken. He was well on his way to ruin already, and gambling away his last best secret was truly the action of a desperate man. And Valen would benefit from that desperation.

"There are some that call gambling a vice," Valen said.

There was now no trace of a smile in the other man's eyes. "Yes, and there are some who call leaving the fat on your meat the same, or an affinity for sweets, or tobacco, or sleeping in the same bed as your wife instead of in your own chamber. A person can lose himself in dice as easily as in the cask. There is nothing inherently evil in this. Look at the fraternal spirit here, the reduction of the social classes to those who win and those who do not."

Valen said nothing about the lack of peasantry in the room, nor about the several bright knots of gentry. "So it is a pastime in which merit prevails, not birth or wealth or beauty?" This was Valen's opinion, over all. The playing of games was the true equalizer. "Anyone who takes the time to learn the finer points can succeed."

"*Bof.* Perhaps," the other man said with a shrug. "But who can claim to have the most time to spare? Surely not the dockworkers who labor through all weather to get wealthy men's ships out to sea as quickly as possible. Nor sailors with their daily six hours for sleep and leisure. I am a warehouse holder, and even my time is more dear than that of a landholding gente. No, card-play is a luxury, not a vice, though some may conflate the two. And though it may be a way to lose your family's fortune, it is by no means the only one, nor even the fastest."

Valen tried to stop himself from looking ahead in line to Dusmenil, but was not successful. "But you speak only of losing. What of taking another person's money over the turn of a card? Is that not taking advantage of another person's loss for your own gain, and offering nothing in exchange? No goods, no services?"

"It is not for one gentilhomme to decide what another person can afford to lose. It is hard enough to guess at a man's cards without having also to guess at the morality of taking his money."

This line of conversation was clearly becoming too serious for Valen's companion in line, and he let it drop. He moved instead to the Tipping Point, the city's favorite political topic. How soon before the number of Cadois subjects who owned land in Valtiffe outnumbered the Hvallais? And what would they do when they reached their presumed majority? Vote the island over to the Empress? Among polite society who did not know each other well, this topic met with examples from history and a practiced indifference, both of which were perfectly safe for a night of gambling.

*   *   *

AT LAST VALEN was ushered into the Secret Broker's chamber and offered a seat across from the man at a small desk. He looked around the room at the ancient décor, and was surprised to see a sigil carved into one of the panels, small and almost hidden by the grain of the wood. The rune itself would have been from long before Cadogna arrived, and possibly even before the Hvallais; there were rumors of a peripatetic tribe that settled on Valtiffe for a season or two in the time before history. Perhaps this oddity had been carved to add to the mystique of the room.

The crown was indeed powerfully magicked, and the sound-blocking enchantment was in full effect. Valen imagined the Séminaire shored it up from time to time; it seemed unlikely it could have held this long without some attention, especially seeing how it was taken down and reconstructed for every new locale.

Did this explain the game of choice? The house's take was always a little higher at dieuroi than others. Maybe the association needed funds for the expense of maintaining the silent room, in paying off the enchanter and the workmen. Everyone trusted that Mme. Vabanque had chosen at random, but what confirmation had been made of the sanctity of the slips of paper? It had the air of a party game, but at least two men's livelihoods were at stake here. Perhaps this was an elaborate con to get Valen to reveal something. But what did he have of value? That a man about town who no one actually did any business with was cheating at cards was hardly worth all of this. Could it be his private pursuit of accidental magic? Was the Séminaire trying to force him to show his hand so they could destroy him?

*   *   *

A MILD APPROBATION from the Secret Broker distracted him from his nervous reverie. "Your secret, then?"

"Ah, yes, monsieur." He took the quill from the inkwell in front of him and drew a small map of a spit of land which extended off of the northern coastline. He added a square inland and wrote 'La Ruse,' a distant fishing village. He then wrote 'one and three-eighths miles north-north-east' next to the tip of the finger of land, then drew a small 'x.'

The Secret Broker examined this rough map through a monocle. "The wreck of the *Victory Rose*."

Valen nearly tipped over the inkwell as he put the quill back. Was this common knowledge? If he didn't get a decent value for the secret, he might not be able to buy into the game.

Sweat pooled in the hollow at the base of his throat. Arbelan would not be very forgiving.

"You knew it already?"

"I did not know it already," Trouluc said mildly. "I deduced it. A secret off the shore was most likely to be a shipwreck. The *Victory Rose* is one of the more famous, as its casks of oil and wine were sealed by Séminaire enchantment. Anyone who could get to them would likely find them intact. There is a fortune to be made there, as you are no doubt aware."

"I am." What was the broker up to? There was something of a game here. Did he have anything the broker might value? Any chip to bargain with?

Trouluc pursed his lips. "The seabed is not so deep off of La Ruse. The fishermen there keep traps along sea floor and pull them in with ropes no longer than fifty feet, which you would know if you kept tabs on the particulars of the trade records in the periodicals, those dull tables you can find on the very bottom of the back of your regular broadsheet. Rope-makers send these lengths up with some regularity, as the grasses required to make the rope do not grow in any abundance out near La Ruse, which abuts miles of useless lava fields.

"This is no secret, of course. It is only of interest when applied to other bits and pieces of knowledge. And when you know the port the *Victory Rose* left, that being Jaïs-de-Trèzel, and the port to which it was headed, that being Iquem, our easternmost found just north of La Ruse, it becomes clear what your little 'x' is meant to reveal."

By the Saints, Valen thought. this was how the old man found enjoyment in his duty. He had made a guessing game out of it. He did indeed appear to have the comprehensive knowledge which the rumours had attributed to him, and which made him so suited to determining the value of each offered secret. If he could deduce so much from a small map, he must surely do the same with just a person's name, attire, and bearing. How many secrets came into this room that he found too easy to guess, and therefore of less value? And, of a more pressing matter, how would he value the one in front of him?

"Seven hundred and fifty livres." Trouluc frowned dramatically. "This figure estimates the profit from the reported holdings, assuming no more than a quarter of the jars were damaged in the wreck or by the merciless sea, and that any wine on board has gained in value at the same rate of similar wines on land of the same vintage. It allows for the cost to hire a ship and crew as well as to pick up a few of the deep-lunged pearl divers of the southern shore. It neither takes into account the extra premium a collector might pay for a wine from the infamous *Victory Rose*, nor the reputational value a scavenger ship might gain. Are any of the casks unbroken? And what could a person be convinced to pay for them? That we will have to leave to chance. But then these are gamblers, are they not?"

Seven fifty. This and the money Arbelan had given him to buy in would be enough to get him in the game and keep him in it for a while. The powdered fool had come through.

The Broker wrote the number on an envelope and put Valen's secret inside. On this night, this little envelope was as steady as actual livres.

Valen rose and bowed to the Broker, who responded with a curt nod. It was nearly a shame that the old man didn't get to remember any of it.

HE FOUND HIS seat with the help of a black-suited servant and greeted the other players with a smile. Just another player here to enjoy himself. The first deal was selected by a low card cut, and the honor went to a woman with silver hair and bright blue, dancing eyes. He had been tempted to try some magic to get himself the first deal, but had decided against it. Better to save it for when he needed it. Or perhaps he was too nervous to try.

Dieuroi was essentially a guessing tournament; a chart of the card value from Ace to Empress was placed before each player, and before the turn of each card they placed a token with their bet on one of the numbers, or in the upper left corner if they were betting the card drawn would be higher, or the upper right if lower. Additional bets could be placed odd or even, honors or no, a pair or run, all designated by the arrangement of tokens.

This was little more than a child's game, reducing the educated predictions found in other card games to blind guessing. Dieuroi was no game for a serious player, but it was popular for its ease of learning and the potential for exciting bets. Just like The Syncretic Club preferred. Another suggestion that the choice of game was not so accidental as had been presented.

Valen's ability to make use of his practiced skills was reduced by not being able to touch the cards until his deal. Cheating at dieuroi was not a skill Valen had cultivated; he had spent tedious years mastering the manipulation of cards during shuffle, cut, and deal, and had spent less time on the sleight of hand vanishings Jacquemin prided himself on. Being able to palm a token would come in handy.

All he could safely do was move his counters after the card was flipped and hope no one was paying close enough attention to remember where he had placed them. This was accomplished most easily by attaching a long hair to a token and relying on the relative dark of the candlelit room to keep it from sight, or so he had read. The ratty old pamphlet that recommended it had been sadly silent on how one would stick a hair to something unnoticed.

Some players considered cheating of this sort to be part of the game. If you could fool the dealer with a dishonest play, it was thought to be even better than winning honestly. If you dared to do it, it was yours to try.

Pulling tokens with a hair was a tad amateurish in Valen's opinion, but as he watched the dealer's fingers he imagined Arbelan's threats. His pride no longer seemed such an important consideration.

He had not prepared anything for this. Indeed, he could not have; the tokens handed out had been minted for the event, and bore the date, location, and the representation of the Couronne d'Oublie that served as the symbol of the Forbearance Game. Even if he had brought a suitable strand of hair, he doubted he would have a chance to attach it to a counter.

Without being able to depend on artifice, Valen would have to depend on skill, and hope for success with his accidental magic. He knew he could keep track of the cards better than anyone, and run the probabilities in his head. Still, dieuroi was a game of guts, not brains. Fortunately for him, he knew that most everyone he was playing would favor boldness, in the style of the club. He planned to make every use of that weakness.

Valen managed to win at his table without much trouble.

He fell behind at first, more due to a practiced caution and some unlikely turns than any bad plays on his part. Once he started applying his skills at counting cards, it only took a few rounds before his victory became all but assured. He took the opportunity to practice his magic a little. For all he knew, he was going to need it very soon.

The dealer drew a three, then a five, and Valen placed a side-bet on a four. Nine fours had already been played this round, so the likelihood was low. A garrulous fellow two seats down from him, a man of the kind that insists on providing commentary on every single turn, raised his eyebrows and declared that the rest of the players had a chance after all. Valen chuckled politely as his mind's eye drew the edges of the four of hands in shining light and he mouthed his magic syllable. The table erupted in surprise and laughter when the four turned, attracting jealous eyes from the other tables in the room.

A success for his accidental magic, and in actual play. This was almost worth a few fingers.

As the winner of his table, he was now placed with other first-round winners. After this, only the final contest remained. Dusmenil had made his way to the second round, fortunately, and was now at Valen's side.

Card table gossip had it that Clavis Dusmenil was one of the finest card players in the city, but Valen had no clue whether or not the fellow had any talent for dieuroi. When he caught a look at the man, he was surprised to see neither nervousness nor pride, but utter astonishment. The old ruin looked like he was having visions and didn't have the courage to ask if anyone else was seeing the same thing.

A few duels broke out over accusations of cheating, as was to be expected. Tables were cleared to make room, but the dieuroi game was not interrupted. Oaths were made, followed by insults to each other's names, families, faces, choices of mistress, aptitude for coitus, and dedication to the whims of fashion. Then swords were drawn, and after a single touch of the smallsword these fights ended and wine was shared, in accordance with custom.

The second table went much like the first for Valen, with one exception. Before Valen took his turn as the dealer, he memorized the position of each player's tokens before each card. He was positive that Dusmenil was moving his tokens, but the old man never rested his hands above the table. Three of the other players had pipes, which they smoked with their right hands and emptied into ash trays at their left, as was tradition for cheaters at all manner of games. Valen had seen several tokens moved by players' sleeves as they reached across to ash, and had paid no heed. But how was Dusmenil moving his? The table was far too solid for him to jog it with a knee and hope for a jump.

Just as he took his turn to deal, Valen noticed the invisible shimmer around Dusmenil's tokens. Someone had enchanted them. Whoever it was had done it too quickly if they were hoping to avoid notice—anyone with any training at the Séminaire would be able to see the enchantment, as presumably would most witches, if they were provided with enough bugs to munch on.

Valen lost himself in his thoughts as he shuffled. Who would do this? Was Dusmenil a witch? Unlikely; he wouldn't look startled by the tokens' dance. Could someone have done it ahead of time and made sure the servants gave Dusmenil the ones they had enchanted? Possible, but then the magic would have been cleaner, less visible. No, there was clearly an enchanter nearby. Would they have had to see the tokens to work an enchantment on them? Valen's own courses had focused on his specialization in Divination. Perhaps Jacquemin or Tenerieve might have known. Who was trying to keep Dusmenil from losing?

The other six players were staring at him. He had gotten himself caught up in his own anxieties again, trying to figure out every possible lie he was being told and every possible outcome as if he were counting cards.

As he dealt, he noticed that he had absentmindedly marked a number of the cards as he shuffled. Hours of practice had made the action a habit, like walking a street you have been down a thousand times. His personal marks which signified the honours, lightly scored in the finish of the card backs. He'd also placed at least seven twos and threes at the bottom of the deck during his shuffle. All it had taken was a sharp eye, some dishonest cutting, and very fast hands.

Between the packet of bad cards at the bottom of the deck and his marking of the honours, Valen had no problem wiping out several of the other players. He simply dealt from the bottom when it suited him.

A bottom deal was one of the baser forms of manipulation, and among the first Valen had learned. It was a matter of placing a thumb on either side of the deck, as one would for an honest deal, and sliding the bottom card out too quickly for notice. No serious sharp uses the bottom deal often; a small difference in the sound of the cards gives the method away if one knows what to listen for.

To resort to bottom-dealing...! Valen vowed to tell only Marguerite.

Despite the chicanery, Dusmenil with his rigged tokens was still in play when Valen reached the back card—the end of the deal which left a dozen cards left in the deck to eliminate the possibility of anyone memorizing the whole thing and betting it all on the last few. The old man had the next deal.

Dusmenil shook as he shuffled, and more than once sent cards flying across the table in a loud flop. He made no table talk, and looked no one in the eye.

It soon became evident that whatever enchantments were protecting Dusmenil didn't apply to the cards themselves. Having marked the cards, Valen was well on his way to taking the game in less than half the deck. It could have been sooner if he pushed his advantage a little more, but with the stakes as high as they were, he didn't want to risk it.

Once his last chip was claimed, Dusmenil placed his secret on the table. The packet had *15,000* written on it in Trouluc's hand. Valen heard several people gasp. The chatter behind him made it clear this was the largest single sum at which a secret had ever been valued.

He made a show of his surprise, to keep his intent from being noticed. Dusmenil looked as if he might weep.

A ruling was called for by someone in the gathering crowd. Valen covered his shock at the suggestion by leaning back from the table and smiling at a few of the excited onlookers. A ruling? On what? It might not go his way. His plan for gaining Dusmenil's secret might have been for nought. Arbelan would not be very understanding, he was sure.

Mme. Vabanque tottered over with a few other elders of the community. "Ah, now this *is* fun. I know we have something for this in the by-laws, don't we?"

A worn document was removed from a fine étuis, and the elders chattered over it too quietly for Valen to hear. A few of the other players happily wondered aloud if the Forbearance Game had by-laws at all, and if they would supercede.

Dusmenil would not look at him, eyes trained on his hands folded in his lap. Was there a thin gleam of hope in those eyes? Valen spun a token on the table idly and shook his head, as if the whole matter was just so very funny.

It was determined by Vabanque and her friends that in this case, all of the opponent's chips and secrets were to be put up against the value of the larger secret. If the holder of the larger won, he took the other player's pot in its entirety and no additional debt was to be incurred against the loser. If not, the opponent simply took the secret at its full value. If both bet correctly, whoever was closer would win the hand.

So this was to be it, then. The crowd made approving noises and Dusmenil lifted his head. The old man placed his token, betting that the next card would be lower than nine. Given the cards that had already been played, this was the safest bet possible, a fact repeated by many of the people watching.

Valen looked at the deck and saw one of his dim marks.

The crowd fell to silence and waited for his bet. Valen decided to give them what they wanted.

He tossed his token into the air above the table. It landed flat on its face on a bet that the next card would be an empress. The crowd gasped. Valen shrugged in likely defeat.

There was a great deal of shouting when the dealer turned up the empress of hands, but Valen heard none of it.

He laughed and cheered and accepted the congratulations, but his mind was completely occupied with trying to guess who might have tried to rig the game with enchantment. Was the Séminaire involved somehow in Dusmenil's secret? Or were they finally going to have their revenge on Valen for his impudence?

Those were his thoughts as the others applauded. Those, and the look on Dusmenil's thin face as the final card turned and he lost the last of his fortune.

Valen took Dusmenil's tokens and handed them to the old fool. They felt fuzzy with enchantment magic.

"You should keep these as a memento. The little bastards did everything they could to help you win."

A small toast was raised at that among the people near enough to hear it, but Valen's eyes were on Dusmenil. The old man shook his head, refusing the offered tokens. He exited the building without bothering to get his hat and coat. Some boos at his unrefined behavior followed him, but these were mainly to keep the spirit in the room light and ignore any empathetic feelings for the man who had clearly lost something very important to him.

Taking third place was easy after that. Valen stayed through the celebratory drinks at the end of the night to make a good show of it, despite the dangerous secret in his pocket.

For a brief period, the playing of cards and dice was disallowed by the mayor of the arrondissement of Jaleaux. In a fashion typical of the people of that area, they put in place this draconian law out of concern for the public health. A spate of deaths (some suicides, some from overdrink, and a handful from fights and duels) attracted the well-meaning attention of the civic leaders who did as the Jaleaux have always done: they took personal dignity and responsibility away from the citizenry and made their decisions for them. Is it any wonder that a populace treated as children would not have the capacity to govern their own passions?

transcription of de Tabannes' speech to the council of Voet, reprinted in the *Courant* as "Against the Proposed Law"

As careful as they were, the Worryback Crew soon found need to leave Jaleaux for greener pastures*; games of chance were banned after their exploits ruined many good people.

———

translation of the L'Ombrais idiom "unfished seas"

Notes on the Disease of Sharp Play, Grandee Ariadna de Alodesal y Juegon, Trans. Salen

XIII
TENERIÈVE

"A KRON FOR the gods of chance," Jaq announced. A coin winked into his hand from somewhere and he tossed it into the rubblework fountain gurgling to itself a few streets up from the Syncretic Club.

Ten did not remember seeing this particular fountain before. Long plates of dark gray rock had been stacked knee-high in a circle in the center of the intersection, which had been empty not six months prior. Warm water ran through pipes under the ground to burst out of the center of the thing in an ugly little spout.

A fountain in Saut-Leronne. The locals were becoming more Cadois year by year.

There was little to do but wander and wait for Valen's game to be done. That would be hours from now. She did not feel all that prepared for any sort of Knave-related excitement, but this at least was better than pacing Margo's sitting room.

"And which are those?" Ten might as well get Jaq talking to pass the time.

Jaq screwed up his face as he always did when he wanted to look like he was thinking. "Well, there's St. Anrix that the

Caddies love so much. Rashain, she's more of a queen of the oldfolk than a god, but those ones never mind the promotion. If you have a mind to see the more weathered ports of L'Ombre, you'd find wee statues to gap-toothed Tonpietra all over. I knew a girl in Jaleaux who introduced me to Mellivan, a personal god of her own. She called him the Shaded Man, and he always brought her good fortune."

"Many to choose from."

"Aye. But what of you? Never met a Mistigri who'd discuss it until now, so you're stuck with my questions. Who do your people pray to?"

Ten saw no reason to lie. "We do not."

"Never?"

She remembered her great-aunt muttering a strange word from time to time, a word that seemed like a name.

"My family is angry at the gods."

"I can believe that, no mistake. And what of you?"

"I have paid worship to many gods," she said with a shrug. "It was always a good way to convince the locals not to come after the caravan for a night or two. I've sung hymns to more saints than you can name. Yes."

"I doubt that, my friend. A volsaeti is a…"

Ten held up a hand to stop him. Damn these Hvallais and their odd old words. "A what?"

"A volsaeti? Aye, well that's a temple," Jaq explained, surprised. "A place to pray. And those are good fine places to sober up out of the sun without the captain being able to haze you for it. Stop into the vol… the temple of Ste. Lourde in Dockside some morning and you'll see last night's plankrats mumbling in devotion. I've spent plenty of time sitting among them myself."

"Then, Jaq, you and I have chosen the wrong trade. We should be scholars on the religions of the world. We will write a book and sell it to all the people sitting by their fires."

"Aye, that'd be a sight better than slogging around in the cold waiting for Valen to lose. Jacquemin Erdannes and Tenerième Cassel, here to expound on the nature of man's devotion to all the fine folk of wherever we are! We'll take pay in coin or wine, as the only difference between the two is time."

"Perhaps Valen would be better at talking to the crowds," Ten laughed. Jaq did have a way of making things light when he chose.

"Valen?" Jaq's mismatched eyes bulged in mock disbelief. "He'd have them falling asleep before he finished his first sentence."

Their laughter echoed down the quiet roads.

Three youths, all boys, came into sight. They stumbled out of an alley where, Ten guessed, they had just relieved themselves of some of their night's ale. Had she seen them in a scry? Perhaps not, but she tensed anyway. A group of young men is dangerous enough sober. Their clothes were new and not soiled, which meant they had money. Not gentes, perhaps, but boys with parents who could afford to dress them well. They could likely get away with whatever they chose to do.

Jawing at each other and laughing rudely, they walked right toward the fountain. Ten made to step aside.

One of the boys noticed the movement, cocked his head, and smiled cruelly.

"Yeah?" Jaq walked up to the sneering boy and shoved him hard in the chest. The boy was easily half a foot taller than him—and was the shortest of the three revelers—but Jaq didn't seem to notice or care.

Ten sighed to herself. This was hardly the first time this had happened.

Wide-eyed, the boy lost his balance and fell on his back on the cobbles. Jaq didn't stop moving forward. "Go ahead, lovely," he growled. "Call her something. You just say the word 'blue.'"

The boy crabwalked backwards on his elbows, his eyes on Jaq's solid boots.

Ten had come to understand that Jaq fought like a sailor. That was not to say that sailors have some particular style of fisticuffs, the way a swordsman of Valtiffe favoured a different stance from one of L'Ombre. Rather, Jaq fought as if a whole crew of shipmates would soon be by to pull him out of the worst of it, and that he wouldn't be back to this port for months if ever.

The other two boys regained themselves enough to grab Jaq from behind, one on each arm. Ten moved to help, but Jaq pulled himself free before she'd even taken a step, tearing his shirt in the process.

"That's my very best frock, pretty," he said, affecting outrage. "My only shirt, in fact. My boss is going to be quite displeased."

He pounced like a cornered fox on the boy with a scrap of cloth in his hands. Two seconds later the boy's coat was pulled down around his biceps. A quick shove landed him in the fountain.

Jaq turned to the third, but Ten stepped between them. She raised an eyebrow at her friend. He stopped, but shifted his weight from foot to foot like a boxer and kept his eyes over Ten's shoulder on the last boy standing.

All three of the youths pulled themselves together and ran off toward Hillside.

Ten wanted to fight Jaq herself. "They'll bring the Guard."

He sniffed loudly and walked to the fountain to wash his hands. "They won't. I hardly touched them. Who'd admit to losing three on one?"

"Three on two." Ten wasn't ready to let this go so easily. "We're supposed to be watching for trouble, not causing it."

"And if the Guard hears the mewling of three drunk fops and jump into action to defend their poor hurt pride, well then you can just put on one of your voices and talk us out of it. We'll be gone in a minute anyway."

"Don't defend me, Jacquemin. Not ever again. Yes. You don't make matters any easier. All you do is make it even harder for me. People will use any excuse to kick out a Mistigri, and getting thrashed in the street just for looking at me is a pretty good one."

"Well, the way they fight, they'd better not look at *anyone*," Jaq said with a chuckle. "You'd think I was old Reali come to life the way they shivered."

Ten's anger faded at the joke. She imagined Jaq in the carved whalebone armor of Reali the Tidebreaker, the legendary hero who stepped across the waters and cleared Valtiffe of serpents so that his people could make a home there.

"We should get you some whalebone," she said. "And stilts. Yes." Reali was seven feet tall.

A look into the fountain stopped her laughing abruptly. An image. Bright steel. Fire.

She could not be sure. She had never 'keened,' never scryed without intent before. Some diviners had a difficult relationship with standing water, and were plagued by visions which came to them unbidden. A snatch of spellcraft could be formed accidentally, especially by experienced diviners with well-developed dream language. The language never truly *stopped;* one might as well try to stop consciousness itself. The mix of phonemes in any living language contained many from the dead ones. The recipe was there.

The linguistics of divination were of less interest to her at that moment, though, than the images of violence and what they might mean. They could be a future not her own, or one decades away. Without having cast the spell herself, there was no way to tell. But considering the madness Ten's crew had entered into, sooner seemed much more likely than later.

"Jacquemin. We must get Valen. Come."

Jaq's face fell, and he did not question her. A fellow

practitioner, even an unlettered witch like himself, knew better than to doubt a diviner when she took action. Doubt was for a quiet room, a scrying bowl, and a complicated question, not for a scrap of terror in dark city streets.

She kept her pace rather less quick than a run. Tearing down the cobblestones at this hour was a good way to attract whatever danger she was trying to avoid. A brisk pace would get her to the Syncretic Club's building soon enough, and she could keep her eyes to the shadows and corners for any menace.

"There will be trouble this night," she said, as emotionless as a shepherd killing a lamb.

"What did you see?" Jaq sounded concerned, but not as much as Ten would have wished.

"Weapons and fire."

"We knew this might happen, Ten. We've a plan for it. When the Knaves make their move, we cry foul. Just stick to the main streets and we'll be fine."

Ten let her face tighten with anger. She never let her emotions show unless she had a purpose for it, and getting Jaq in line was purpose enough. "Do not try to stop me, Jacquemin. I warned against this idiocy. Yes. Allying with Arbelan…"

"No one's allying with anyone. It's just a job."

"I never agreed to doing jobs for evil men. I will take their money in play, and that is all."

Jaq nearly tripped over a loose cobble trying to keep up with Ten's long stride. "You'll take *anyone's* money, be they good or less so. Don't go and start pretending we're not evil folk ourselves. Growing a conscience just when we've found a way into higher society is damned poor timing, Ten."

"It is not my conscience which protests." Her patience was quickly thinning. "Hugues Arbelan is dangerous. Working with a man like him is dangerous. What do you think the Guard will do when they follow my shouts and see a blue-skinned woman arguing with a local boy? And when they put me in front of a magister, how could I claim innocence when I am working with a known gang?"

Jaq slowed his pace. "That's what's vexing you about those boys? Never mind getting pistoled by a Knave, you don't want to get in trouble with the Guard? I might say you've chosen the wrong line of work."

Ten let him lag behind and ramble. He was more manageable when he had his chance to bleat for a while.

Perhaps she had indeed chosen the wrong line of work. Or perhaps the wrong line of work had been chosen for her. She had not asked for any of this—it was the Brothers that forced her into it. It took all she had to trust these people, these friends of hers. Her great-aunt had always said to never trust a man who slept under the same roof four nights in a row.

A shorter man walked towards them from the direction of the Syncretic Club. The silhouette of a long coat and tricorn was all she could see—he could have been anyone. There was no need to be nervous just yet.

"Well, that's a good sign." Ten could hear the smile in Jaq's voice. "That's Clavis Dusmenil there. Old Val must have beaten him already."

Her tension quieted for a moment, but only barely. "He does not appear to be armed."

"Armed? The man's practically a dotard, Ten. He's more likely to piss himself than...."

Jaq trailed off as Dusmenil slowed to a stop and bent over. The gente suddenly looked as if he had just run up a mountainside.

Ten hesitated, but Jaq only said "Hurry," and ran toward the ailing man.

The last thing Clavis Dusmenil, the end of the Dusmenil line, saw was a small fellow in a torn shirt biting the head off a rat and shouting something about trying to save him.

Up until his victory at the Forbearance Game, Quinol was a near-unknown in the finer circles of Saut-Leronne play. He came to prominence just as that city made its violent and momentous entry on to the world stage. Indeed, when one interviews the players who were present for those events, they often speak of Quinol in the same breath.

De Tabannes' *Lives of Gamesters*

XIV
VALEN

FRUSTRATION SET VALEN'S teeth grinding. All he felt as he made his exit was the undeniable, unavoidable pressure of not knowing just what in all the hells was going on. He stepped out of Mme. Vabanque's and into the quiet street, relieved to finally be away from the happy crowd and able to let his anger show on his face. If only he knew at what he should direct this rage.

Fifteen thousand livres! If he sold the secret, he would have his choice of buildings for his casino. He could practice his luck magic all day and with no risk. He would even have a vote.

But Marguerite was right. Whatever this all-important secret was, no money would be worth losing it.

The boy wearing the Naughty Knaves colors was still in the same spot as when Valen entered, though now two empty wine bottles accompanied him, as did a urine stain on the wall a few feet down. Valen scowled at him and saluted. The inebriated boy took a long bow, nearly toppled over, and ran off into the alleyway.

He stomped down the lamp-lit avenue toward the tavern which was to serve as rendezvous with Tenerième and

Jacquemin. At least Arbelan would be happy. Clavis Dusmenil was most certainly destroyed, so whatever villainous nonsense Arbelan had in store now had the table laid for it quite nicely. All Valen earned was a standing invitation of the Forbearance Game and a small envelope containing a secret worth all this trouble. Trouble that likely included the Séminaire, or at the very least someone trained in the Brothers' arts.

He was deep in a brown study when the silhouettes of his friends, Tenerieve's tall frame a step in front of Jacquemin's wiry form, passed below one of the candlelight lamps. They were coming to meet him, which was not the plan. Perhaps they had grown tired of waiting, or perhaps they were excited to hear of his victory. It didn't matter. Valen's heart had sunk deep enough that the thought of seeing his friends at all brought no pleasure. He would be unable to engage in the jollity and would sour his mood even further.

But Valen prided himself on his ability to hide his emotions; his choice of career depended on it. He put on a merry face and smiled at his approaching companions. Tenerieve wore a dark green riding habit, tan breeches, and her ever-present tricorn, while Jaq wore his typical rags. Something seemed a little off, though.

"By the gods, Jaq. What happened to your shirt?

A single ray of light across Ten's worried face was enough to douse Valen's smile. Something had gone wrong.

"We must hurry," Tenerieve said without greeting. "You should be out of the light. Yes."

Jacquemin took his forearm in a pincer grip and pushed him toward an alley. "Saints, could you be any slower, Valen? The woman can see the damned future and you stand there like a broken buoy."

"My apologies," said Valen. "Must be the soporific effect of all that fine society. It does cloy one a bit."

"I'll cloy your ears if you don't shut up."

Once they were out of the light and well into the damp darkness between two long buildings, Tenerìeve stopped abruptly and spun to face the two men.

"Valen, Dusmenil is dead. We came across him just down the hill from his home." Her accent was as strong as Valen had ever heard it.

He did not allow himself to react. "How?"

Jacquemin mumbled around a toothpick, nervous. "It looked like exhaustion to me. Like the old bugger's heart just gave out on him. He was in the middle of the damned street, no less. But Ten says otherwise."

"I say it may not be as it seems." Tenerìeve rose a hand in quiet protest. "A man's heart bursting when he has lost his last coin is not improbable, yes, but my keening spoke of more. I cannot say what, but there is something dark afoot. Of that I am sure."

A question in need of a solution. Something to focus on. Valen's mind turned to the new problem like a shark at seal blood. "You had a keening?"

"I did." Tenerìeve's eyes narrowed. "And good that I did, perhaps."

Valen nodded agreement. He pulled poor old Dusmenil's secret from his pocket and held it up for his friends to see. "There was enchantment at play tonight, and I don't think it was Dusmenil's. Someone didn't want him to lose this."

He explained the enchanted tokens. Jacquemin had a few guesses, but Tenerìeve did not respond.

Jacquemin gnawed at his whalebone with renewed vigor. "Someone could rig those things to move?"

"Most certainly." Tenerìeve nodded slowly. "Enchantments to make an object move on command are very well established. The question is who could do it so quickly, possibly without seeing the items themselves. Yes. And of course, how was the caster working his will on the artifacts without being present?"

Jacquemin spat his bone to the ground and fished a new one from a pocket of his ragged coat. "And were they standing on their damned heads and singing Le Colonnade? I don't care about the tokens. I care about some elitist Séminarian killing a man with a few words. I've heard of curses that will do a bit of work like that, but never seen one used, and I plan to keep it that way."

"It doesn't matter," Valen said. "We need to get home and lie low. Whatever is going on here, we're not going to resolve anything standing in this muck." *And I need to get you two to safety*, he thought.

He made to leave, but where there had been nothing but candlelight a moment before, there were now two figures in his way.

The two men did not seem to mind being outnumbered. Both wore dark clothing and had the brims of their round caps pulled low over their faces. One held a pirate's boarding axe, small and fierce, and the other what might have at one point been a butcher's knife. A cruel-faced child entered the alleyway behind them.

Valen idly wondered what Marguerite would say when she saw his dead body.

"Perhaps heading back into the light might be preferable," Tenerière rasped. "No fights this time, Jaq,"

"No argument here," Jaq said. "These lads are armed."

The three of them moved steadily back toward the avenue, Jacquemin at the rear. The pursuers walked more quickly, but did not break into a full run. Assassins are known for their patience.

One of the great failings of contemporary magic, to hear it told at the taverns and coffeehouses in most districts of Saut-

Leronne, was its complete uselessness in combat. The old sagas told of powerful Brothers who could turn arrows away with a thought and bring armies to their knees with no more than a book and the knowledge to apply it.

The accuracy of these tales was naturally subject to skepticism, especially from the Séminaire. Stories of men pouring fire from their hands might be metaphor, propaganda, or simple storycrafting for the entertainment of drunk warriors, but certainly could not be seriously considered of any historical value.

All interest in history aside, Valen wished his knowledge of the ways of magic could be of any assistance at all against two men with sharp objects.

His stomach lurched suddenly, as if he were on a small ship in a particularly angry storm. The last time he had felt the like was in one of his classes. A demonstration of a very powerful spell; the one which kept the upper floors of the Séminaire's Pendent Tower floating above the city, tethered only by a thin wooden staircase stretching through empty air.

He stopped and looked to Tenerième. The woman's eyes were frantic.

The grim men with weapons jumped into a savage run. Valen's hands wouldn't stop moving. He shook them to try to regain control, but they felt like lightning was striking them. He took a step forward, past Jacquemin's protection.

He drew the envelope from his pocket. As he did, he heard a whisper of old Hvallais and the unintelligible language of other people's magic.

The casting of magic spells of the Séminaire fashion, the clean kind which did not require anything as unseemly as blood, required three languages: a living language, a dead language, and the personal dream-language of our most private thoughts. Much of the study requisite for becoming a Brother was learning one's unique language, the combination of phonemes, rhythms, and pitches that speak to you and you alone. Valen had always thought Tenerième's sounded ranging and distant, like horses given free rein over a vast field. His was crisp and sibilant with long pauses punctuated by sudden rushes of syllables in steady beats.

The language Valen heard from somewhere above him in the alley was refined and intricate, complicated enough to be a true language of its own, with a history, dialects, etymologies, long-standing scholarly arguments. It was spoken with native fluidity.

He had to get rid of this damned envelope before whoever was casting nearby did anything drastic.

"Very well, you filthy cheats. Let's not pretend this is some accidental attack. Here; you may take what it is you seek."

The toughs sneered at Valen, but slowed their approach.

"Val," Jacquemin whispered.

"It's not worth it, Jaq. Let them choke on it."

The taller of the assailants snapped the envelope from his hand and passed it to the child—not one of Arbelan's, judging by the simple clothing. The kid tore off, but the ruffians didn't move.

"Sorry, friend." The tall one licked his teeth. "Contract's for lives."

The voice just out of Valen's hearing stopped and all was silence for a long moment. Then the alley ignited into dark blue flames.

The mortar between the bricks of the walls dripped cobalt fire. The cobbles started to glow red.

The assassins froze, which Valen felt was the incorrect thing to do upon having sprung a magical trap. The shorter one had the sense to run, but soon tripped over his own feet. He caught fire as soon as he hit the ground and was ash in an eye-blink.

The other man's boots lit fire as he ran, and he shortly went the same way as his co-conspirator. Smoke rose from their corpses in thick chains.

The child tripped violently, but whatever was happening hadn't reached him yet. Would they really kill a child?

Surely whatever enchantment this was wouldn't be possible to control without line of sight—the speaker must have been very near. Valen whipped out de Niver's glasses, pressed them on to his nose, and scanned the building tops and windows above the alley.

His jacket had started to smoke. The nice one, with the flowering vines embroidered at the seams. The bastards.

Jacquemin pushed Teneriève back in the direction they had come in and grabbed Valen by the wrist, shoving them down the alley without a word.

Valen pulled back. "Wait, Jaq. If they want us dead, running won't help."

"Who?" Jacquemin barked, the blue fire glistening in his eyes. He looked around wildly, as if he could punch his way through the blazing walls to whoever was about to burn them alive. "How are they doing this?"

Valen spotted two silhouettes in a high window, dark clothes against an unlit room. One was pointing down the alley toward the stumbling boy, and the other faced Valen and his friends.

Two Brothers, and remarkably good ones. There wasn't time for warding enchantments, and who knew if two half-trained amateurs like Ten and Val could even work something strong enough to stop the fire from devouring them. A tense look from Teneriève told him she didn't think so. Jacquemin seethed with frustration, but did not move.

Despite the terror of the moment, Valen choked back a sob at seeing them like that. Frightened. In danger. Because of him.

No one is hurting my friends. Not tonight.

The key to a good bluff is telling a story, especially if it's mostly true.

"We didn't read it!" Valen shouted. "We don't even know what it is!"

The shorter of the two Brothers spoke, and the flames crept toward Valen's feet. The other man grabbed his arm. They were arguing.

That hesitation was enough. The three gamesters darted toward the street, convinced with each step that the fire was going to engulf them.

Something loud snapped from a direction Valen couldn't identify. The fires abruptly stopped.

He slid to the still-smoldering ground and looked back to see a small, round hole in the window, and a splotch of red on one of the Brothers' waistcoats. Valen saw the boy run out of the other end of the alley as Jacquemin pulled him to his feet and shoved him out into the dimming light of the main avenue.

Low's the man who sought to beat the odds
'Neath the shadow of the Pendent Tower

traditional skáld song

XV
MICHEL

To Sæmunder Magnús Handar,
Principe of the Séminaire of Saut-Leronne
From Brother Michel Alcippe,
Third-Honor Faculty, Order of the Sjónleysi

*Want of time to attend to the matter with the appropriate
etiquette will excuse me addressing you directly, and with
this, a letter quickly encrypted and even more quickly penned.
I currently stand in a foreign room without the guidance of a
candle to assist my vision and no desire to stand closer to the
windows. Three persons lie dead in this room, two of them by
my hand, and the other of our own number.*

*Laciaume, Third-Honor faculty member and a talented
enchanter, was shot in the chest by an as-yet-unknown assailant
from some distance, and died immediately. The briefest of scrys
returned no information of use, and I considered the time better
spent ensuring this report reached you with the utmost expediency
than in wrestling further with the spellcasting. I shall return to the
problem as soon as I have dealt with the more immediate issues.*

We discovered that the secret of Skyndiferth was known by one Clavis Dusmenil. Despite our efforts to prevent it, our secret was written on a piece of paper which has been taken by some child to a location I do not yet know.

Unless I hear otherwise, I will pursue this matter exclusively, in complete neglect of any other. I myself, a dedicated Sjónleysi who has provided much intelligence for our order with the greatest discretion, was not even aware of the existence of Skyndiferth until mere hours ago. If a member of an order dedicated to preserving our secrets through subterfuge was not allowed to know of it, I must assume it to be of the utmost importance, and will act accordingly. I have killed an innocent family, two hired ruffians, as well as Dusmenil himself, and would have done the same to the other witnesses as well as the running boy had I been able. I know the Order would expect nothing less for so dangerous a secret, and will be sure to complete the task shortly.

I must ask for particular instruction on what actions to take regarding the witnesses.

There is not time for a messenger boy, so I shall risk using the Whisperwind to ensure this news reaches you. It is past middlenight, so the darkness is on our side.

With the deepest honor and esteem, I am, Principe, etc. etc.

M. Alcippe

MICHEL RAN A shaky hand through his tangled hair. The paper bearing his message hovered in the air before him. He spoke the necessary words, and the edges of it caught fire, the same blue as in the alley below. It lit the room, but Michel did not dare look at his handiwork. Five dead. His first time in charge of a mission for the Sjónleysi, and five dead.

The response came before he had even moved from his spot by the window, an uncomfortable buzzing in his mind.

The Tower. Now. Leave them.

MICHEL TORE THROUGH the moonless streets at a full sprint. His simple necklace bore an enchantment to keep him from losing his breath. His cloak would make all but the most curious look away. He would reach the Tower before dawn's light, and anyone who might see him at this hour was likely too drunk to be credited. The Principe wanted Michel's help, and the Principe would have it.

The upper roofs of the Pendent Tower could be seen from most places in the Saut-Leronne, not that Michel needed directions. He was born in the city, and had rarely ventured past the mountains that rose to either side of the river valley. His was a family of glaziers who had a hand in the construction and repair of a large percentage of the city's buildings. Michel learned the city's streets as his father's delivery boy, carting delicate panels of tinted glass.

It had been this deep knowledge of Saut-Leronne that had first led to his assignment to the Sjónleysi. The old men of the Séminaire knew that divination alone would never provide all of the information they needed to keep themselves safe; the Sjónleysi served as the watching eyes of the wisemen when magic alone would not do.

Michel had accepted the assignment with pride. There could be no better measure of the Séminaire's esteem for a young faculty member than to be put in charge of their secrets. It was well known that most of the seventh-honor faculty had served in this capacity. And Michel had not come as far as he had to stop at the third tier.

Michel did not slow himself as he reached his destination. Most visitors to the Pendent Tower looked up as they approached, even those who came to purchase enchanted goods on a weekly basis. His wonder at the craftsmanship never lost its luster. A pillar of perfect white marble, not a single vein to be seen in the whole of the building. Never marred by weather or dirtied in the least. No seams between the individual bricks. A masterpiece in the application of Séminairian magic. Even the Glassed Castle of Soucisse, constructed by the best wisemen of the continental Empire, could not rival it for purity of design. Perhaps there was something greater in L'Ombre, but Michel doubted it.

The building's one flaw was its greatest credit. Several smaller towers shot up from the main pillar at the higher levels, leaving only the tallest at the center. When Mount Eldad's eruption shook the ground of the entire island, that tallest tower cracked and fell away. The enchantments which kept the building aloft, though, were engineered well enough to keep the tower from plummeting to the ground: it glided away from the center, the spiral staircase at its core unwinding like a spool of thread. It had taken some very quick casting on the part of the Brothers of old to keep that staircase from splintering, and the results of their labor were now legend. If anyone doubted the superiority of the Brothers of Valtiffe, they need only look up to see a few stories of marble tower held aloft by the Loose Stair.

Michel loved the building. His marvelling at it, at the vast difference between the staid houses he worked on and the miracle which floated above them, had set his mind to the life of the Séminaire before he was big enough for his feet to reach the floor when he sat at the dinner table. It continued to be a source of great pride for him to call it his home. Even when he learned the enchantments that made up this wonder, he never lost his adoration of it.

To lose his place there was unthinkable.

The interior of the building did not match the pristine fascia to be seen from the streets. A dense labyrinth of corridors and oddly-shaped rooms had developed organically over the years, in a way which no single mind could ever hope to understand. The original massive lecture halls had been separated by walls of plaster over lath to provide private study chambers for the faculty. Most were dark, dusty places, but highly prized despite their lack of comforts. In most cases the only time one was granted to a Brother was when another Brother died, and even then only after a complex algebra of tenure, rank, and favor was taken into consideration.

As a third-honor, Michel had an odd wedge of space well above the ground floor. The path to it required several flights of stairs—both up and down—a turn down a small hallway which looked very much like a closet, and not a little faith that a certain plank walkway across a corner of the atrium wouldn't fall through. Michel had never had to explain the wending path, as he never had any visitors. He was no diviner-for-hire, loaning himself to anyone with the livres and the sense to eschew the rattling company of witches. He was of too much import for such tawdriness. His contributions to the body of criticism relating to the divination spells of the pre-Cadois Brothers had seen to that.

When he reached the Loose Stair, he took the steps two at a time. They always said not to look down, but he did. He wasn't afraid. The enchantments which held the structure were sound, far more sound than the timbers that held up the roofs of the buildings that clung to the riverside below him. He had seen the enchanters shoring up the spells, as regular as the tides. *The work of the few, better living for all.*

Repairing the Skyndiferth matter would be done the same way. Somehow a closely held secret of the Séminaire's had been known by some Cadois gente. This was no different than the icy storm winds that buffeted the upper tower: unpredicted, and dangerous if left alone. Careful preparation, the will to act and practiced skill would see it all to rights, just as they had allowed him to incinerate an alley with a word.

The years of hodge-podge redesign that had crabbed up the lower tower had never reached higher than The Loose Stair. Michel's footfalls echoed in a round chamber ringed by that pure white stone. Basins of rock and metal dotted the room, casting long shadows in the light of the new dawn. He had been this high only once: his initiation to the Sjónleysi.

This is where the best of the diviners worked. Enchanters always had their eyes down, on their work tables and along the thin lines of their charts and tables. Divination was the purer art, looking ever outward and upward. An enchanter might live in his own mind, but a diviner lived in the abstractions of truth and time.

The Principe was a diviner, as Michel was.

No guard watched the final stair up to the Principe's hall. None was needed; no one unwanted could climb those ancient steps. Michel composed himself, straightened his hair, and prepared to offer his solution, Brother to Brother. Diviner to diviner.

The icy winds of the skies above Saut-Leronne did not enter the glassless windows of the Principe's chambers. The morning sun was melting the coat of rime that had formed against the wards overnight, casting its light across the receiving hall in heavy bands of orange that caught the floating dust.

Michel had never been in this room. From the Principe's bearing he had assumed he would find desks piled high with the papers that business dealings breed, adjacent to the fading spellbooks of the greatest Brothers ever to cast their eyes upon the world. But no furniture cluttered the massive space save two simple wooden chairs, a small table, and a glass scrying basin on a marble pedestal.

Sæmunder Magnús Handar stood in the shadow between the stripes of dawn, his hands folded behind his back. The old man had dressed in a workaday outfit, but left his head uncovered, revealing short hair with no color left to it. Michel had seen it before, in a scry. There had been no way for him to identify it at the time. He had seen this coming.

"What have you seen, Brother?" Handar's high voice was as clear as if he were standing next to him.

"Opportunity, Principe."

A small cough was the only reply. A chuckle perhaps? Or a scoff?

Michel was prepared for both. "This Skyndiferth is a masterpiece of the art. Dusmenil..."

"What have you seen, Brother?"

"I... we can use this. Tracking down a criminal will take..."

"I did not command you to me for your counsel, Brother. Answer the question."

The frost was all but gone from the empty windows now. Michel's moment was slipping away from him.

"I have not yet scryed in any seriousness, Principe. I came here directly."

"Directly. Indeed you did. Brother Laciaume's blood is just now starting to dry on your sleeve. Have you ever tried scrying a puddle of a Brother's blood?"

Perhaps the question was rhetorical. But the old man had just insisted on his questions being answered. "No, Principe."

"It is not unheard of. I have seen no credible citation of that liquid being any better for the craft than water. This does not surprise me. Does it you?"

"No, Principe. Blood is for witches."

"I have never seen a Brother's blood. I have never seen one die of violence. Now I see many."

No amount of sunlight could warm Michel's skin now. The

Principe had scryed—perhaps he was ever scrying—and had seen something terrible.

"How shall we proceed, Principe?"

Handar still did not turn. "You shall return to your chamber and get your eyes on some water. We all of us shall. The other Sjónleysi will handle the muck work. We will need information in the days to come. The years."

My chamber? "Principe, I am the closest to this affair. I can...."

"What are you working toward, Brother? What drives you to this lonely life of ours?"

Michel did not need to search for this answer. He had known it as a boy, and reaffirmed it every time he set to his labors. He would do more than build houses for people to live their little lives in. He would change the way people lived.

"I am here to contribute to the improvement of the Séminaire's arts, and thus to the betterment of all mankind."

"And I am here to help you and your Brothers do just that. It does not require a clear bowl and decades of study to have the foresight necessary to sit you down in your rooms before you do any more damage."

The rebuke silenced Michel for a long moment. Never once had he been spoken to in this manner, since entering the Séminaire. He was the most talented diviner of his generation.

"Principe, Laciaume was..."

"First you try to claim your error is in fact an opportunity. Now you blame a good man who died in our service. Your office, Brother."

Michel left the room without another word. Frigid wind nearly knocked him off the Loose Stair.

His failure was so complete they no longer trusted him in the field.

He would have to show them.

"O, to be a cardsharp!" one might say. Surely this would be the gambler's life brought to perfection, to finedraw sharp play and get away with it. The cleverness, the risk, the romance of it!

But remember this: where the honest gambler might bask in the regard of his fellows, the sharp must ever hide his talents. This lonesomeness is anathema to the easy companionship which has ever been the greatest boon of gaming.

Dishonest Play and Players

XVI
VALEN

Tenerıève and Jacquemin kept quiet as they walked back to the Gouvernor Pole building, which gave Valen some much needed time to weigh his options. He was halfway up the stairs to his rooms when he broke out of another one of his anxious fugues and realized his friends were going to look to him for answers. His friends, whose lives he had risked with all this.

This life of gambling and sharping was one of Valen's creation; all of the members of his small circle—even, and perhaps especially, Marguerite—could very easily have gone a different direction than the one that Valen had sold them on. With his history of piracy and witchcraft, Jacquemin would have no trouble finding work with any of a number of lucrative ships of fortune. Tenerıève had a refugee's tenacity, and could carve a life out of less than nothing wherever she chose. And Marguerite's parents would like nothing better than to get her back into the family business.

They had all followed him into this life. Anything that happened to them because of it— say, being burned alive by murderous wisemen—was his fault. Once again, the people he cared about would suffer because of his stupidity. Like Ten getting kicked out of the Séminaire. Like his parents. His sister.

He needed to solve this puzzle.

Two DIM OIL lamps lit the drawing room. Marguerite sat reading the evening's paper for what Valen guessed was the third or fourth time. Valen smiled at her as they entered, but let his eyes show her there was something wrong.

She rose, placed her paper on the table primly, and went around the room turning the lamps up. She never once met Valen's eyes. "No bullet holes tonight, I see."

"Not in us, no." His chair looked comfortable, but he was in no mood to sit. Jacquemin sprawled out on the couch as Tenerière took the small seat by the window and sat with her back straight.

Marguerite went to the sideboard and began pouring firewine. "So am I to assume that Monsieur Arbelan will be claiming a few of your fingers?"

"Nah," Jacquemin drawled. "He's about the least of our problems, I'd say. Our lad Valen did what he was asked. Third place, and Dusmenil's ruined."

Valen was about to restate Jacquemin's summary with a bit more style when Tenerière interrupted. "He is much more than that. The poor old fellow's heart failed right in the street."

Marguerite distributed the tumblers of clear wine in silence. When at last she faced Valen, her eyes were troubled. "So you killed him."

"Not hardly," Jacquemin sat up eagerly to take his glass. "I'm still spitting out rat hair after trying to save him."

Tenerière was holding her hands on her lap a little tightly, which was as much of a tell as Valen had ever seen from her; he thought she might scream. "I'm not sure his heart went of its own volition," she said.

"We think there was some 'chantry at work." Jacquemin downed his glass in a quick gulp. "Considering the damned kiln they turned George Alley into, seems like they've got a vested interest."

"A... kiln?" Marguerite turned again to face Valen. "There was a fire in George Alley? Set by... whom? The Brothers? What in all the hells happened out there, Valen?"

The look in Marguerite's eyes drove Valen's fears home. "Margo's right, Jaq. I did kill the man. Whether he died from the strain or through some kind of murder spell, I'm sure he would have survived the night if I had stayed home. I killed him the moment I accepted Arbelan's offer."

"His threat, you mean," Margo's voice was hard. "We knew he was up to something larger than his regular scams, but I didn't expect him to be dabbling in magic. The Knaves and the Séminaire? Ridiculous. Arbelan must have double-crossed us. He must have killed Dusmenil to increase the value of the secret. Poison, perhaps. But a fire? What would that gain him?" Her eyes flicked back and forth as they did when she was working out some particularly esoteric financial equation. Valen had never seen it applied outside of her ledgers.

"I will explain," Tenerième said. "It is as bad as I warned, and worse."

Tenerième laid out the events of the entire evening: Dusmenil's jumping tokens, the ruffians, the errand boy, the dark fire, the gunshot. Valen's mind tore off after each possibility, but there were too many cards in play. Marguerite listened patiently, but did not show any reaction. She really would have been a remarkable bluffer, Valen thought.

"I didn't know you people could light the streets on fire with a word," Marguerite said at last.

"They shouldn't have been able to." Valen said. "There are enchantments that will do such a thing, but only if the item in question has been magicked ahead of time. Like a hearthstone. There's no doubt that fire was unnatural, though. The Brothers were involved, one way or the other."

The room sat in silence for a moment, uneasy. Valen was well aware there was much about magic he would never know since he left the Séminaire, and even more about enchantment.

Everyone turned to Tenerieve, the other authority on Séminaire magic. Her brow was deeply furrowed. "A powerful divination may have shown them something they could have used."

"Something as specific as what alley three people they had never heard of might turn down?" Valen countered. "At their best they might have seen an image of a paving stone, or a bit of garbage."

"We do not know what the upper echelons might or might not be able to manage. We never learned their secrets, nor would we know of any new advances in the art since we left."

Valen stifled a disgusted laugh. "New advances? I left because they refused to even consider new advances."

"As I recall, you left because they refused to consider *your* new advances."

"Yes, and I was the only one trying," Valen barked. He knew he was getting angry, but couldn't prevent it. Perhaps he felt a bit self-indulgent, considering his evening. "So much of our so-called training was stewarding these old bastards so they could get high and guess at the future. It's all part of their game. Learning humility before learning the truth. Letting go of the self to see the oneness of something or other. I might have thought they could foresee a well-aimed bullet, at the very least."

Tenerieve's face softened, and she smiled. "I also recall you saying something very similar when you decided to leave."

Marguerite chuckled at that, which took some of the fire out of Valen's belly. He needed to keep his head. He had been in scrapes before and worked his way through them. He would do it again.

Jacquemin frowned. Valen had come to learn that the sailor hated being left out of the inevitable inside jokes and funny memories the rest of them shared. Tenerière apparently had not learned, or didn't care.

"I was furious," Valen explained to him apologetically. "These men, they have so much power in the city. People bow to them when they walk by, and the bastards never deign to look back. I came to resent them. When I first came to my master with some real progress with luck magic, he barely raised his head. I pulled out my yard, pissed in his scrying bowl, and told him he didn't see that coming."

He smiled, expecting a laugh; Jacquemin's humor tended toward the ribald. Instead, the smaller man swallowed the last of his wine and stood.

"And what are you saying then?" Jaq stormed across the room to the window. "The old pricks have stores of enchanted supplies all over, just in case they decide to fry a person up?"

"I have no idea. But I do know we aren't going to solve anything tonight. Except perhaps this."

He passed a hand over the low table and produced three envelopes without moving a finger. Each had a number written on it in the Secret Broker's thin hand. One of those numbers was *15,000*. Jacquemin wasn't the only one who could pull a card from his sleeve.

"You bastard," Jacquemin laughed, his stern face creasing. "You switched it."

Valen gave him a smug grin. "It may come as a surprise, Jaq, but this is not my first time cheating at games of chance."

Tenerière's brow knitted again as she walked over to examine the secrets. "I saw the one you gave them. It said fifteen thousand livres."

He ran the tip of a finger lightly along his hairline at the temple, the sort of casual movement one would completely ignore, and showed them a pen nib and a tiny vial of ink. "One does not marry the known world's greatest forger without picking up a few tips. After seeing Dusmenil's tokens slide around like butter on a skillet, I had to assume something was afoot, something too clever for Arbelan to have been behind it. I marked up another envelope as soon as the game was over, just in case. It took some skill to turn *750* into *15,000*; I wonder at your skills even more now, Margo."

Jacquemin graced Valen with a powerful slap in the middle of his back, which the older man weathered as well as he could. "Can't tell if I'm more impressed with the forethought or with that bit of palming you just showed off. So what'd that poor boy end up with?"

"The location of the wreck of the *Victory Rose*, if Arbelan and Trouluc are to be believed. And I wish his employer well with it. Now, what do you say we see what poor old Clavis Dusmenil had to die for?"

He turned to the table, but the envelope was gone. It was in Marguerite's hands, opened.

"One doesn't marry a cardsharp, et cetera," she said, unfolding the paper within. She read to herself in silence, much to Valen's frustration. He wouldn't interrupt, though. She had staked just as much as he had on the contents of that envelope, and had had to sit home and wait, trusting to him. Let her read.

"Have you heard of something called the Skyndiferth?" she asked. "There's a map of the interior, then an inset of some valley with an 'X' labeled 'Skyndiferth.'"

Valen looked to his partners, who looked as nonplussed as he was. "Is there anything else?"

Marguerite shook her head. "That's it. I suppose it must be worth a great deal to someone who knows what it is."

"Aye, and useless to us, then," Jacquemin grumbled. "Here I was hoping it might help us against the Séminaire, who are surely after us now, and against whoever that lad ran off to, who will be soon as they figure out they got took."

"Too many unknowns." Valen nodded. "All we have is the knowledge that someone who knows magic wanted to make sure this information stayed secret and that someone with enough money or influence to hire men to kill us wants the opposite. And they may both know who we are."

"Valen, you are a fool," Tenerieve spat, her eyes hard. "We did not agree to this."

Valen realized she hadn't spoken since he had revealed the switch. The last trace of his smile died. "We said we were going to keep the secret, Ten."

"We did not say we were going to switch out something false."

"I was only keeping our winnings safe," Valen said. He looked to Jaq and Margo, neither of whom showed any sign of helping. "It only made sense that someone would try to take it from us."

"There were killers there, Valen. And Brothers. And someone else shooting a rifle from somewhere. This could be over. You could have let them have it, but you have kept us in it."

"Well, there was the small matter of the alleyway being on fire."

"Not when you wrote '15,000 livres'!" Ten was shouting now, something Valen had never seen. "You did that alone, without anyone making you. Whoever sent those men will learn of the deceit. He will come for us now. For all of us."

"He won't," Valen struggled to keep his voice calm. He wasn't so sure, but having a woman screaming in his apartments in the middle of the night wasn't going to help matters with the downstairs neighbor. "If it wasn't the secret our mystery attacker thought it would be, then it's his loss. Who could say what secret Dusmenil was going to bring?"

"And the *Victory Rose*? That is worth *fifteen thousand livres*? Who would believe such a thing? No, Valen, you are reckless. You have endangered all of us to impress yourself."

The knock at the door was expected. Marguerite and Valen both went to intercept the downstairs neighbor, but Margo did most of the talking. Valen tried to keep an ear open to what Jaq and Ten were saying to each other, but couldn't make out their whispers. In all the years he had known Ten, in all the bad situations they had faced, she had never reacted like that. He hoped he hadn't damaged things with her too badly.

Whatever it was Jaq said, Ten was no longer spitting fire when Valen closed the door.

"We should go and look upon whatever it is that may end up being our deaths," Tenerième said, any hint of anger gone. "I leave at first light."

"Alone?" Valen asked.

Marguerite clucked her tongue at him. "Tenerième grew up in lands like the interior. You know that."

"Aye, but a guide wouldn't hurt," Jacquemin said. "I'll travel with you to my parents' home. They'll know someone who's familiar with those lands. La Ruse's got plenty of folk who know their way around a lava field."

"And perhaps it's time for me to go back to the scrying bowl." Valen was glad to be headed away from an argument and towards something he could actually manage. "Our little escapade surely did not go unnoticed by the good people of Saut-Leronne, and I would be armed with as much foreknowledge as possible."

It wasn't much of a plan, but at least it would get his friends out of town and safe until he could learn what was happening. He would learn what he could through divination and over the card tables until he found a name. After that, he would have to play it as best he could.

They finished the wine and read the remaining secrets, which were of no particular consequence considering the situation. After the guests left, Marguerite went to bed in silence. Valen stayed up and enchanted his cloak to ward off fire.

Corte of Torreçon and Surrounding Regions
Proclamation

As a hub of culture and equality, Torreçon has maintained a long and storied tradition of the betterment of society through games of skill. The title of Gamesmaster has been granted to the keepers of this tradition for three hundred years, and embodies the Corte's dedication to this grand history.

As follows are the duties of the Gamesmaster of Torreçon:

The Gamesmaster must oversee any formal games at the Corte.

The Gamesmaster must act as final arbiter on disputes on gaming matters, to include decisions on the official rules of games as well as the determination of fair and equitable treatment in matters of debt between players.

The Gamesmaster uses her discretion to ensure honest play.

The Gamesmaster maintains records and histories of important matches.

[...]

It is the honor of this Corte to appoint Dona Ariadna de Alodesal y Juegon as Gamesmaster.

[etc.]

The proclamation of Dona Alodesal y Juegon's appointment (trans. Salen)

XVII
OMER-GUY

THE PENDING ARRIVAL of a L'Ombrais ship of state turned the Dockside district into an all-day festival, complete with the sort of drunken foolishness Omer-Guy had come to detest in the people of Valtiffe. These savages took any opportunity they had to drink beer in the sun, even the ones of Cadois heritage. But these were the people he was stationed to deal with, and he made a good show of joining in the fun. He and Lady De Loncryn sat in one of the watching booths used by the Saut-Leronne élite for taking in the water traffic, and the two of them passed the morning watching the heavily-laden flat-bottomed boats from the farms and mines further inland and the pretty skiffs that shuttled merchants and bored travelers upriver.

This was the magic that had taken Cadogna from a wealthy agricultural country to an Empire too large for most maps; without having to row against the current or disembark and pull one's boat upstream by rope, the Cadois quickly made footholds in every upstream region they could reach. The L'Ombrais had the shoreline, but the rest of the world was decidedly Cadois. Omer-Guy found himself wondering if the enchanter who first magicked a prow into pulling a boat upstream envisioned the effect his creativity would have on the world stage.

He imagined that he did not. The thin creatures of the Séminaire rarely saw past their own books and bowls. It was better that way, all considered. A wiseman with political aspirations would be a problem indeed.

These musings could not be credited to the bitter Valtivan beer Omer-Guy had been sipping at all morning. How did these people tolerate the stuff? Unlike any decent Cadois red, such as the one Lady De Loncryn was enjoying between flirting and winking at him, the local drink was barely strong enough to have any effect in any quantity under a gallon, and by then you had to piss so badly you were of no use to anyone, either in conversation or in bed. He felt like a cow chewing its cud, though his experience with animal husbandry was blessedly limited.

"Ambassador Bendine," De Loncryn cooed. "What a grace it is that Ambassador Juegon has decided to come to our little home so early in the season. The balls have been so dreary of late, and a lady of L'Ombre is sure to provide some spice."

Bendine smiled, but did not take his eyes from the river. "We should endeavor to address her as 'Ambassador Alodesal,' I believe. Dona Ariadna de Alodesal y Juegon is her full name, and as a general rule in L'Ombrais names, whichever name is listed first is the one we are meant to use."

He knew this was a dodge to her unstated question—why was the L'Ombrais Ambassador showing up unannounced? Precisely at the apex of De Loncryn's schemes for power, no less. She had come through with Dusmenil's secret, and now expected to be rewarded by the Crown with the mayoralty, or at the very least the Crown's support in her bid for the position. This was a coup for her, one for which she had thrown her adopted home of Saut-Leronne into complete disarray. If

Bendine understood the machinations, De Loncryn had caused an imbalance in the détente between the two major gangs in Saut-Leronne for her own ends.

This Dusmenil fellow had been using his influence to protect one of the local gangs for some tawdry reason, the one called Les Royaux, headed up by one Munnrais. Munnrais's rival was the powdered fool Arbelan that Bendine had spied on from behind the screen in Oceline's—in De Loncryn's, that is—drawing room. By bankrupting the man, Arbelan was doing for himself the very thing De Loncryn had promised in payment for his service. She got something for nothing. She was so unusually clever, in truth.

Rumor had it Dusmenil died of a burst heart walking home from the Forbearance Game. As if bankrupting him wasn't enough, now the poor old gente was dead. The end of Dusmenil's protection for Munnrais meant the time had come for Arbelan to make his move, and he had apparently done so with vigor. The carriage ride through the Dockside district had been a tour of the after-effects of street fighting and gang violence; Omer-Guy had seen at least three puddles of dried blood on the cobbles as he drove past.

Was her plan simply to endure upsetting the balance of criminal powers in order to get what she wanted? Or was the violence in the streets in some way beneficial to her bid for the mayoralty? He would have to think on that.

All these strings were being tuned very carefully by De Loncryn, and she must have been very nervous indeed at the unannounced arrival of the L'Ombrian Ambassador just as her work was at its most delicate. Omer-Guy had no intention of assuaging her fears. Until the Dusmenil information was safely at Court, he would hoard every modicum of influence he could muster.

Safely at Court, and safely in the hands of his connections

in L'Ombre, of course. Let the dueling thrones do what they would with the knowledge, just as long as they let his son be.

"It does seem odd, though," he offered. Best not to let Lady de Loncryn think he was intentionally keeping her in her state of concern. "The woman has shown no interest in our society whatsoever. The Empress sent me to be in permanent residence, much to my delight. Does La Reina think so little of Valtiffe that she only sends her Ambassador to host her little games from time to time?"

"Perhaps it is the air of the season she desires. She is but five and twenty, I hear say. Just old enough to begin to be concerned about her age and its effects on her health."

Omer-Guy shrugged. "*Bof*. Perhaps so. And perhaps she has heard tell of the untouched beauty of Lady Oceline de Loncryn and felt her first pangs of jealousy, though I daresay that my lady could live in the smoke of Soucisse and still look as stunning. Quality of character reveals itself in the visage, and that would be unchanged no matter what the location."

Oceline actually blushed—what an artist!—and turned away to whisper something to her servant. The young woman dutifully giggled, completing the false tableau of silly women playing at statecraft. Omer-Guy rarely spoke to his manservant, doing his own part to affect the serious gentilhomme. This was all part of the intricate language of politics, where one spoke a single word of import in a thousand of appearance and posturing.

"And what of Empress Oceane Caraliere de Flechard, long may She reign?" Oceline asked coyly. "What does Her visage reveal about Her quality of character?"

Omer-Guy smiled, an honest smile. "Ah, but that would be telling."

He had met the Empress but once, when She touched his head with Her scepter in the ancient ceremony of binding to which all ranking servants of the throne yielded. If She had been dressed in rags and begging for cheese rinds in the gutter, still men would have genuflected at Her feet.

If he could, he would tell De Loncryn that Alodesal ˙had somehow learned that the balance of power was soon to change in Valtiffe, and had come to ensure that L'Ombre had a seat at the table. L'Ombre had little trade with the island country, and had never shown the slightest interest in adding to their collection of conquered lands. The only reason to come was to take a pawn or two from the Empress, all part of the long game of world domination. A point for the Cadois, no matter how small, was a point against L'Ombre. Either La Reina or Alodesal herself had heard something that led her to believe that the Empress was making a move in Valtiffe. The surprise visit was meant to show that they knew.

That, at least, was the most likely reason Omer-Guy had come up with. His handler had not sent him any information about Alodesal's visit. Did that mean it was of too little importance to risk a message, or was it part of a scheme so secret that even La Reina's man in Saut-Leronne was kept from knowing?

Omer-Guy did not enjoy not knowing things. This Alodesal dilettante's secrets would not be kept from him for long.

A thrum of excitement ripped through the drunken crowd and Omer-Guy looked downriver. A fair craft, its unnecessarily unfurled sails painted with the rampant griffin of the Queen of L'Ombre, had made the turn and showed itself. The crowd began cheering, but the gentes withheld their applause. The Ambassador's vessel had yet to arrive.

They did not have to wait long; a ship of magnificent luxury came into view a few moments after. It was a cutter, an oceanfaring ship with no good cause to be floating in a river as shallow as the Magdalene. The sides had been painted—no, inlaid with gold leaf. Three sails bloated with nonexistent wind strained against the rigid masts, each a full tapestry of what

Omer-Guy recognized as the history of L'Ombre. The sailors wore red uniforms far too complicated to be effective at their jobs. Dona Ariadna de Alodesal y Juegon had arrived in state.

The woman herself did not appear until her ship was firmly docked and her functionaries had jumped into the crowd, tossing gold pieces and small jewels. A smaller ship held a thirty-piece orchestra, playing complicated arrangements of three L'Ombrian folk songs from their perches on the halyards. Once they were silent, Alodesal appeared from below-decks.

She wore a simple dress, but in crimson, and her hair had none of the architectural excitements popular in Cadogna. She waved at the common folk first, then curtsied to the boxes. Lady De Loncryn raised a hand in greeting, which Omer-Guy silently thanked her for. He was so caught up in trying to read Ambassador Alodesal's movements that he forgot to respond himself.

The fat little mayor of Saut-Leronne met her first, accompanied by some well-heeled members of Parliament. A formal announcement was made as to the date and location of the Ambassador's Games. Omer-Guy ignored all of this, left his seat, and made his way through the crowd to the captain, a bald old salt with a scowling mien. He asked the quiet man to deliver a letter for him to Oscar Bendine.

Oscar would eventually receive the letter, but not all of the contents of the envelope. Omer-Guy's L'Ombrais handler would intercept the message and ensure the Skyndiferth map, whatever that was, reached the correct people in La Reina's espionage organization. Omer-Guy had opened the 15,000-livre envelope using a Lover's File, a small blade enchanted to remove a wax seal without breaking it, and made a copy of its contents before sending the original to the Empress' Court in Soucisse.

Losing the two bladesmen in that alley fire was a shame, but such was the price of statecraft. Munnrais's organization was rife with upstart would-be street commanders, easily bribed, who thought a little action on the side would be a boon to their careers in violence. Omer-Guy kept a handful in his pocket for just such an occasion, which he offered to use for De Loncryn's purpose. He wished he could have spoken with the boy who delivered the envelope, but clandestine drops in dockside barrels were not conducive to conversation.

The walk back to the street to meet the Ambassador could have been shortened with some elbow work, but such conduct did not suit a man of Omer-Guy's standing, even if it might earn him some respect with the Valtivans. He used the time to reposition his mind to the task at hand. He had done his espionage for L'Ombre. Now he needed to do his job for Cadogna.

A fight broke out at the edge of the crowd of commoners. At first Omer-Guy assumed it was some puerile grandstanding over a spilled beer, but the push of the crowd—away from the combatants, instead of toward them to cheer—spoke of something more serious. There were seven men fighting, swords drawn. Three wore the white and blue of Munnrais's gang, while the other four wore cockades of yellow and black on their hats: the Naughty Knaves, Arbelan's men.

Ah, so it is true, Bendine thought. Most of the stories he had heard of the uptick in violence were clearly hyperbole; Bendine's rumors came from over-drunk gentes who had in turn learned them from servants or lovers, and a second-hand tale never shrunk in the telling. But here was a swordfight in the middle of the day, and in full public view. Matters were indeed getting worse.

The town guard placed themselves between the clutch of gentes around Ambassador Alodesal and the fighting. None of them seemed likely to try to break up the fight. One had to assume at least some of them were on the payroll of one of the gangs. The cleverer ones would be on both.

The Knaves fought well, all with the smallsword and the moves that spoke of some level of training. Omer-Guy remembered hearing something about that ridiculous Arbelan being accomplished with the blade; perhaps he offered hirelings instruction. Les Royaux used rough knives and clubs, making up for their opponents' speed and reach with ferocity and strength. They pushed to get close, which in turn forced the Knaves back, but the ruffians didn't have the organization to encircle Les Royaux. Amateurish. Les Royaux were outnumbered, but still managed to control the engagement. There was a reason Munnrais had ruled the streets so long.

Two more Knaves came sprinting down the avenue and joined the fray, which effectively ended it. Les Royaux tried to run, but the town guard provided a well-armed wall for the Knaves to back them against. The three men died quickly, each with two blades in him.

The oldest of the Knaves, who to Omer-Guy's assessment had seen no more than twenty years, bowed in the direction of Ambassador Alodesal.

"The Naughty Knaves welcome the Ambassador to our humble city. We hope our gifts are to your liking. Don't let the fuckers in the nice clothes tell you they can do anything for you; Saut-Leronne has only one government, and that's us."

Dona Ariadna Alodesal y Juegon walked through the wall of guards, their momentary protests quieted by the slightest look from her. She walked over to one of the bodies, bent down to take the dead man's sword, and rose with it pointed at the Knave. Blood seeped into her dress where she had knelt in the puddle spreading from the man's wounds. The tip of her blade did not move in the least.

"Face me," she said calmly. "Draw your silly little sword and see how you fare, you barbarian."

Any hint of color left the Knave's face. Omer-Guy thought

the idiot might faint. What a play!—Arbelan wanted to scare the swells, and Alodesal robbed him of the chance by facing his lieutenant down. The terrifying thugs were now foolish boys, long overdue for a lesson.

The Knaves ran off with a few mumbled threats. Ambassador Alodesal handed the sword to one of her servants and asked that it be sharpened and cleaned, as it seemed she might need it.

Omer-Guy would have to tread unusually carefully with this one.

Sailors have diversions all their own. Dice do poorly on rolling seas; games of strategy take too long for men looking to gamble their pay before stumbling off to sleep. With watches and chores, finding a foursome to play a full rubber of signaux is unlikely. It is no surprise, then, that oakey was born belowdecks: a counting card game which can last minutes or hours, which requires only two players, which provides many opportunities for wagers, and is scored with a board of holes and pegs.

Despite its low beginnings, oakey has made its way to some of the more reputable clubs of late, and has surprised some of the greater minds with the potential for scientific play. But one would do well not to bring up the game's history in decent society.

Table Talk, de Tabannes' column in the *Voet Charger*

XVIII
TENERIÈVE

THE WIDE TRADER'S road along the coast took only a few days on horseback. Teneriève had expected longer; sailors made remarkably poor riders in her experience, and she assumed that she would be spending much of the journey teaching Jacquemin the language of touches and sounds that would convince his mount to do what he wanted. He surprised her, though, and while still unsteady, he picked up enough to keep from being a bother.

His insistence on joining her on the trip to the interior proved annoying enough.

"You know the dangers, woman," he nagged. "You're no good to anyone dead."

"Thus the guide you are so sure your family will be introducing to me."

"It's not just the land, Ten. Hells, you've seen lava plains more than most."

He was correct about that, though she did not enjoy being reminded. Before long she would be picking her way across miles of untouched basalt, the remnants of the giant eruption of Mount Eldad centuries prior. She imagined it would feel like a sort of homecoming; the mountainous Mistigris region of Cadogna had been the native soil of her people before Mount Senecin exploded and bathed their land in its hot blood.

Whenever the caravan road took the wandering Mistigri far enough north, Tenerième's great-aunt would pack her off to see the old mountains. "To get a taste," she would say. Tenerième had been glad to get away from the grinding monotony of life among the traders' carts, but the trips were not a fond memory for her. It was the only time she had seen Lucie weep.

The old woman had pointed to a break in the peaks and called it 'home,' where her own grandmother had played with foxes, cribbed sweets, and fussed over the endless small injustices of a happy child's life. Tenerième had seen no remnant of a town; just pocked black rock.

She hoped she had grown capable enough to avoid the skinned palms and twisted ankles of those trips. More than that, she hoped the persistent ache of missing Aunt Lucie would not worsen as she saw a place so similar to her lost country.

The dream of a life outside of the caravan, any true home, had been her private wish for most of her childhood. She learned the arts of trading as she was told to, as well as the refugee's skills of belonging while never belonging. Keep away from the locals, unless you're selling or working. Never stray from the camp; these people do not see you as a full human. Make them feel safe and superior. If a crime is committed, pull up stakes and leave in the night: they will blame us anyway. Smile. Always smile.

"I will be quite at home in the interior, Jaq," she said. "With the Royals and the Knaves warring in the alleyways it will probably be safer in the wilderness. I will see what lies at the spot marked on the map and return directly home."

"The wiseman bastards tried to burn us alive to keep their

secret. Tried to burn a child alive. You'd better think on what kind of defenses they're like to have."

"I stayed at the Séminaire longer than did Valen. They may have denied me my Brotherhood, but I am a peer in divination to many."

"And have you seen anything that might come in handy?"

Ten frowned. "My scrys have shown me naught."

"Aye, we can agree on that at least." Jacquemin gnawed at his toothpick with frustration. "I went to Corned Mary, and her bones spoke the same."

Tenerième wasn't pleased to have some muddy-kneed witch's prognostications measured against hers as equal, but she held her tongue. She had seen enough to Jacquemin's practices to know that the witches of the world did possess some skill, if not to the level of Séminaire-trained wisemen. His way with the weather was difficult to argue against; no atmospheric enchantments she had ever seen worked so well as what he managed with a strangled rooster.

She had seen very little indeed in her scrys: Mist, mostly. Rainbows. Ice. Nothing important.

In the end, as the dim lights of the town grew in the horizon, Jacquemin gave up arguing. She could credit the man with this, at least; he knew when words had failed. She had told him she didn't want him slowing her down, but in truth she did not want to risk him. As contentious as their friendship could be, it was one of the very few she had ever had.

Let him go back to town and hunt for information there. The wilderness was hers.

Jacquemin's nervousness grew as they neared the rough stables that marked the town's unofficial limits. He flicked the reins too often and tapped his heels against the horse's flank as if intending to annoy the poor beast to death.

"For a career gambler, you are terrible at hiding your tells," she joked. But as always, her attempt at levity came across differently than she intended.

"Well, I'm not gambling now, am I?" Jaq snapped. He quickly sighed, abashed. "A visit to the family's not always a relaxer, is it? Just try not to react to my brother, right? He's... well, he's sickly."

"You need not fear me, Jaq," Ten said, as assuringly as she could. "I know of your brother's troubles."

A flash of surprise, completely unhidden. "What, you did some scrying or something?"

"No. As I said: your tells."

"Oh." Jaq leaned back in his saddle. "So you've made some guesses. That's fine. Almost natural, that is."

"We're business partners, Jaq, and in a business in which partners very often become rivals or worse. You're a pirate and a cheat. You'll allow that I've been a little curious. Yes."

"Aye, I'm a fascinating fellow, and no mistake," Jaq said mirthlessly. "So what is it you think you know about my brother?"

"I know he is either sick or injured—likely injured—and that's why you became a pirate."

"Hah. Close. But you have the order swapped."

"Well, enlighten me then. I would have your story."

Jacquemin gave her a long appraising look, then smiled. "My story? Not so different from everyone else's. Born to a fishing family here in La Ruse. Could have stayed with the family's boat, but struck out on my own. Fourth child, no real hopes of a future there. Left without a fight, which is a rare thing. Did a season on a crabber, got picked up by pirates for a few months, on account of my off-colored eyes. The sailor's tales say mismatched eyes means good for magic.

"So I learned the witchcraft of the seas. It's called different stuff: wavetalker, Captain's Favor. But it's witchcraft, same as those you'll find scraping by in the lava fields. Blood and secrets. Captain made a special trip to the island of Alcippe so I could learn the craft from an old goat too weak to sleep belowdecks anymore. There's not much to it, all things told. A few basics, then you build your own ways from there.

"Learned how to lose all my money at every port you've ever heard of. They never let me fight so as to protect their investment, but they let me take a share of the earnings from every attack, and I just couldn't get my mind together to win.

"One night the wine was a tad too strong, and one of my shipmates, a topman called Craggy, beat a man to death over a loss. Said he was cheating. Everyone always says the winner's cheating, but Craggy's victim exploded with cards every time the old bastard landed a punch. He had 'em in his neck stock, his stockings, his sleeves, everywhere. How did they get there? Had he managed to slip them out from the table while I was watching?

"You're not gonna learn something as fancy as card cheating from pirates, so my education on that topic went slowly. I caught a woman making like to shuffle but leaving the top card untouched. A fellow holding a card to the bottom of the table with his knee. Bits here and there.

"With a few coins in my pocket, I jumped ship at a port and made my way back to the loving bosom of my family. They were glad to see me, sure, but weren't so happy to tell me about my brother. He'd caught the valor, and decided to follow his fool brother Jaq out into the world. Had no trouble getting a job on the coast patrol. Got himself in a fight over dice and had an eye put out by some puffed up Caddy gente. The bastard never saw a tribunal, no jury. A man without land's got no claim against a gente, no matter what the scribblers say. My brother got a decade at the oars, and the Gente Gringolleur got nothing.

"Maybe you would say convincing a pirate crew to attack a prison scow might not be easy, what with all the armed guards and lack of plunder. Well, that's until you remind those of them what have been on one that the guards on board make a good living taking bribes from families for decent treatment. Some work it the other way, hazing the tar out of any prisoner whose family doesn't ante up. There's money on those tubs, no mistake, and plenty of men who'd take a pirate's bunk over a prisoner's any day.

"We sprung my brother, but he's been a broken man ever since. I don't know what they did to him on that hell-ship, but he's hardly a person I know anymore."

A loved one hurt. Damaged permanently. Ten tried to imagine it. Her youth had known its share of loss, but not among those closest to her. She made a guess as to how old her cousins might be. They were forever children in her memory, but they'd be adults now, same as she. How many had married? Had left the clan, like she had? Had died? What pain had they known, in the home she had left?

Jaq rode in silence for a moment, then smiled again. "That'll teach you to think twice before asking a sailor for his story, I'll wager."

"I can see why you took up the life of a sharp," Ten said. "Much more relaxing."

"Hah! That it is. Though the last few weeks have been a taste of the old days."

"Let us hope we shall not be assaulting any floating prisons."

"Oh, no. I'm sure whatever the Séminaire has hidden in the middle of an impassable lava plain is gentle as a kitten."

TENERIÈVE HAD NEVER gone home. She paid merchants to get letters to her family from time to time, but found she had very little news to tell them. She had worked so long to find a place away from the caravan, somewhere stable where she could sleep in the same bed under the same skies every night, that her image of a homecoming was surely warped by time. Her parents and siblings would smile and clasp her arms, perhaps, or perhaps she would have lost too much of her accent for them to understand her easily.

She imagined sitting on a blanket on the damp ground around an open fire and watching as the caravan drank wine she could not stomach and gossiped about matters she knew nothing of. And always the press of people. How could a group that lived in the open insist on being so *close* to each other all the time? Her father would hector her to get married, and her mother would do nothing to stop him.

The entrance to Jacquemin's family home was of a different kind. His mother embraced him wordlessly, a hank of sewing still in her hand. His brother sat wrapped in a rough blanket and stared at the fire with his one good eye. He did not move when Jaq put a hand on his shoulder and greeted him. When Jaq introduced Tenerième, there were no pressing hands, no knowing winks. Nothing but an offer of some firewine to hold her over until the men returned with her guide.

Ten had prepared a persona for the event, a surly woman who kept to herself, but found she didn't need it. It was not a cold welcome, exactly, but very different from what Ten had imagined from the brash, vital Jacquemin. She found that her friend was a completely different person in the space of his family's drawing room. He was not unlike a dog who, having been up and barking at some noise or jumping to play with some newcomer, finally curled up into himself and rested. He pulled a clay pipe from a drawer without looking and asked his mother very little as he smoked.

Mrs. Erdannes introduced herself as Jeannette and made

the requisite polite conversation, asking Tenerìève about the weather during their ride, if they had stopped in Nares for refreshment, if they had seen the schooner that had docked that morning. Never once did she ask a question about Tenerìève herself, her plans, her past.

If this was what a home was like, perhaps she didn't need one after all.

All throughout, the brother stared at the burning logs. Ten had thought it might be an awkwardness to have a stone-silent man living in the room, but as with Jeannette's easy politesse, she found no such thing.

Smoke from Jacquemin's third pipe fairly clouded the room by the time the noise of people on the steps brought an end to the wait. The father and eldest brother were easy to identify by their great beards and woolen sweaters. The woman who came with them might have been Jacquemin's older sister, but this was no fisherwoman. Her face had been weathered not by salty storm air, but by long days in the cold sun, and her eyes were set deep in wrinkles that spoke of hours looking over far distances. She wore heavy boots up to the knees, and a short jacket lined in coarse wool. Her hair, streaked with gray and kept wild, might never have seen a hat. This was the guide, surely.

Tenerìève felt at ease as soon as she saw the woman. A week or so in the wilds with a lone man meant being ever on her guard and ever bearing the small iniquities she had come to expect from the company of men—if not worse. With a woman, Tenerìève would have to be cautious against theft or other deceits, but these were her trade. Also, the Erdannes did not seem to be the sort of people who were easily snowed, especially if they were at all like Jaq. Their trust of this woman, then, was excellent commendation.

Jeanette rose to greet her guest, whom she called 'Maddie,' and introduced her to Jacquemin and Tenerìève. Her husband did not wait for the pleasantries to be done before he continued what was evidently an ongoing argument.

"You tell me, magic woman." The older man directed his attention to Tenerième as he removed his oilcloth coat and set it to dry on a peg by the door. Jaq must have told his parents about her. "If you were to see a L'Ombrais frigate not ten miles off shore, what would you think might be a good reaction?"

The brother, a broad man with his mother's stillness, interrupted. "Welcome, friend. I'm Gilles. This is my father, Guy Erdannes. And this is the person you came to meet: Madeleine Ekrurum."

"Yes, forgive me." Guy nodded his head in an approximation of civility. "I've had a bit of a shock is all. Let us sit."

They all retired to the drawing room, which Jacquemin had never left. He rose to greet Madeleine, spoke a brief syllable of salutation to the other arrivals, and resumed smoking in his chair.

Guy took a bentwood rocker and placed it across from Tenerième's seat. "You've come on business of your own, and I won't keep you from it. Maddie is the best person you'll find for an excursion into the interior."

Madeleine smiled. "I'll get you where you need to go, and back again if that's what you want."

"It is," Tenerième replied. "I would leave as soon as is convenient for you."

"Any entourage?"

"None," she said, quick to respond before Jacquemin could. "I will carry my own supplies, if that suits you."

"It surely does," Madeleine said, still smiling. "No reason to take up these fine people's time, then. We can talk price once we're on the road."

This seemed odd to Tenerième at first, but she saw her guide glance at Jaq with a touch of hauteur. She must have known that the destination was secret, and had given Tenerième an out to avoid speaking of it in front of the family.

Jaq noisily exhaled a gout of smoke. "A moment. Let's hear about this L'Ombrais vessel first."

"It wasn't L'Ombrais," Gilles scoffed. "They'd never send a ship out of the harbor without golden paint or some such fluff."

"Never mind the ship, look at the sailors," Guy insisted. "Look at the rigging. If that foreline was any tighter, the mast would have punched through the damned hull when a proper wester came up. Those fools have never tried a Valtivan sea in their lives.

Jeannette looked back to Gilles. "What were they doing out there?"

"It looked like they were trawling," her son said. "They had divers. They stayed in one place and worked the ocean floor."

Tenerième shared a long look with Jacquemin. If that ship was L'Ombrais and they were searching for the *Victory Rose*, that meant that the ruffians who had attacked them in the alley were L'Ombrais, or working for them.

She walked through the steps in her mind. Dusmenil bets his secret. Valen wins it, then gives it to the thugs. After that, it must have made its way somehow to L'Ombre. Someone there must have received Valen's false secret and acted on it. Perhaps these sailors off the coast were La Reina's agents.

They were looking for Dusmenil's secret. Why?

Jaq dumped the burned tobacco out of his pipe and tucked the rough clay thing back into the drawer. "I know a good way to see for certain if they're L'Ombrais or not. Best wait till morning to set out on your journey, ladies. I've a feeling a wicked storm comes tonight."

TENERIÈVE STOOD WITH Jaq on the shore as he swallowed the head of a fish and summoned up an ice storm from the east. Of all of the ships at sea in these waters, only a lone frigate needed rescue—they were not very experienced with frozen lines and stays.

The tavern talk later that night was of the accented speech and over-warm clothing of these alleged fishermen. All in the small town agreed by morning that these were L'Ombrais.

Jacquemin and Tenerième wished each other luck and set out at dawn, she to the west and he riding south to tell Valen what they had learned. The sky was cloudless.

Carambol holds a unique place among the diversions of Man. Of the sedentary games, it is certainly the most active, but it is played in the smoke and lamplight of a room rather than the out-of-doors. It is a favorite of those with keen eyes and steady hands, and of those for whom a night seated is an anguish. Wherever the vigorous people of Cadogna are to be found, carambol is not far behind.

The Gente's Manual, etc.

XIX
VALEN

PERHAPS IT WAS the tense walk through the Dockside streets that had him nervous, but Valen started when Floret Hoque crashed through the front door of his home, desperate to get out of the sheeting rain and into a bottle of cognac. It no longer seemed impossible for some Knave to decide to give forcible entry a try. Black-and-yellow cockades were being brandished in broad daylight now, as were swords and the occasional pistol.

The hallway candles—not so many as to be ostentatious, but enough to befit the Hoques' station—danced precipitously in their sconces as the wind from the door cut through the house. After depositing his overcoat and hat on their appropriate hooks to dry, Valen's father-in-law rushed into the sitting room where the fireplace glowed merrily, his decanter awaited, and his wife, Cécile, sat reading the day's papers and entertaining her guests with some mild conversation about the impending Ambassador's Games. Valen watched the man's eyes go from worry to delight at seeing Margo, and finally to disappointment at seeing him.

"Ah, I didn't expect you," he said, turning back to Margo and smiling. The man had bright red cheeks when he smiled.

The Knave of Secrets

Valen had compared them to brandied apples on more than one occasion, but he soon found it wasn't worth the joke to raise Margo's ire. "I might have returned sooner!"

Cécile folded her paper quietly and placed in her lap. "Well, you're in a state, husband," she said mildly. "I hope this doesn't mean you've lost it all on a scratch."

"Not tonight, I fear." Floret poured two glasses of cognac a finger or two higher than one might expect from two gentlefolk nearing seventy winters. He placed one in his wife's hand with a smile and sat in the upholstered chair across from her. Valen looked at his own glass, nearly empty, but said nothing.

Cécile raised an eyebrow as she took a small sip. "And you're in the mood to talk, I see. To think I just cut the papers. What gossip from the club, then? Did Gente Lauvergne finally call it off?"

"Yes," Valen said. "What's the news in society? I keep hearing that I *won* the Forbearance Game, which is simply not the case. I…"

"I'm afraid there is no gossip to speak of, my love," Floret said, eyes dancing gleefully. If he heard Valen's question, he showed no sign of it. "Something much more serious."

Again, Valen watched Floret's eyes change. It was good the man played carambol and not cards. Any attempt to bluff, or even to hide excitement at a good hand, would have been an utter failure unless he played in the pitch dark. Even then, his breathing would probably give him away. At this moment, he looked as if he was unsure how to proceed. His mouth opened more than once without a word coming out of it, and he attended to his cognac more frequently than strictly required.

"Come, Father," Margo chided. Valen had seen her do this dozens of times. He had even noticed her doing it to him once or twice. "Tell us what happened."

"Perhaps I shall give you a preview of an account which is likely to appear in those papers of yours tomorrow morning."

"Well, have out with it, then," Cécile teased. "I still have tonight's to get through."

"Fighting in the streets, my dear! These very streets! Lauvergne heard tell of three distinct scuffles in the neighborhood last night, and is given to understand that all three were between two rival gangs."

Valen and Margo shared a glance. The Naughty Knaves were gaining power in the streets. They assumed that whatever Arbelan was up to with the Forbearance Game had landed him money, power, or both. That would mean the detente between the gangs of the city was threatened, and that it was Valen's fault.

"Gangs?" Cécile shook her head, disbelieving. "As in, bands of criminals?"

Floret leaned forward in his chair and nearly spilled his drink. This was part of the dance he and his wife had kept going since they were youths, as Margo told it: Cécile withheld her belief in Floret's tales until he could overcome her doubt. A modicum of vigor and drama did the trick most nights, and Valen was sure Cécile did it simply to improve her husband's production. A pleasant little game, but not one Valen was interested in listening to right then.

"What did you hear?" he asked.

Floret ignored him again and kept speaking to his wife. "Very much so, my love. And violent ones. Apparently we have been living in unknowing safety under the aegis of a group which calls themselves The Royal Family, or more casually Les Royaux. Smuggling, theft, all manner of outlawry can be attributed to them."

"And yet we have suffered none of these evils."

"None that we know of, and thank each god for that! But have we not seen the occasional crate of goods carried off by men who did not appear to work for the warehouses? Right across this very street? And did Gente Locuillet ever recover that ivory-headed cane she misplaced? Hmm?"

A long sip of cognac, and Cécile nodded—very slightly—for Floret to continue.

"Another one of these bands, who call themselves the 'Naughty Knaves' of all the ridiculous things, have decided to break down the time-honored secret borders of the criminal element's various claims to our city. And we are now caught in the very middle! Three fights in a single night!" Floret looked into his drink with a heavy sigh. "We shall have to leave, my love. Leave the house my family has owned for these generations. Leave the house where we raised our child!"

Floret waved an arm at Margo. Cécile's smile fell to a pale line. The fun was gone from Floret's performance. This was not his regular report on the harmless tribulations of the city's gentry. Valen wondered if, after so many happy nights spent in this way, he didn't know how else to tell a story.

"It can't be as bad as all that, husband," Cécile said. Her words were consoling, but her tone betrayed her fears. "Let us see. We will see what the papers say. Who knows if we would be able to find another suitable home? We have our work, after all, and if we could avoid the expense of a carriage it would be preferable. No, we need not sell. We will wait. It would be so very much of a change."

She did not say what Valen knew was foremost in her mind: the vote. If they sold in a hurry, they would likely have to rent, and thus lose their place in Parliament. Margo's proper place in society was at risk, even more so than it was already.

Valen's in-laws had always claimed to be against unification, but he had his doubts. They were gentes, after all, members of an old Cadois family. The point was moot if they sold their old house, anyway. Margo would be the first Hoque in generations to not have a vote in Parliament.

Floret smiled, made a few pleasant statements, and lit himself a pipe. Just a half-bowl; it appeared he was in no mood for either conversation or contemplation for very long.

They sat in silence for some time, Cécile devouring the evening's papers, Margo writing in her ledger, Valen practicing sharping while playing a patience game, and Floret nursing his cognac and pipe. The only words spoken for the better part of an hour were a mutual decision to not put another log on the fire.

Floret broke the silence when his drink was empty. "I should not put such fears in your minds. These are groups of youths playing at war-princes. A few scuffles exaggerated for effect by the wine-soaked gentes of the Herringbone Carambol Club. A taste of youthful exuberance to sharpen the flavors of mild tobacco and imported liquor!"

"Of course." Valen smiled winningly. "Clubs are always like that, are they not? An idle sin for idle players."

Floret did not take the statement in the spirit it was offered, clearly. He gave Valen a pointed look accented by draining the very last drops of cognac in his glass. "At least at carambol we are not seated the whole night through, like your card-playing clubs. A night at the Herringbone might do that belly of yours some good, dear boy. If you could get in, that is."

Valen did not remind Floret that any member might invite a guest. Might even sponsor a person for membership. Floret had never offered, and Valen had never asked.

Floret was rising to take Cécile's nearly-untouched cognac and do her the service of finishing it for her when the window behind him made a startling *pop*. A small hole had appeared in the glass.

Cécile was prostrate on the carpeting in a moment, her paper still gripped in her hand. "Get down!" she yelled.

Valen ran to Margo, who had done as her mother had recommended and lowered herself to the ground. He knelt next to her and guessed which way would be the safest to get out of the house. Up the stairs, out the master bedroom window, on to the low roof of the neighbor's shed, and into the tangle of alleys.

Ten had been right: the Knaves had come for him. Something had gone wrong.

Floret stormed over to the window. Cécile shouted again for him to hide, but he took no heed.

"Come to the pier, will they? Come to my *home?*"

Another pop, and the window adjacent shattered. Valen let out a yelp, but Floret did not react. He just looked out to the street.

"A good thrashing will do these children well. I probably know their parents."

Margo rose, eyes on her father. Valen joined her as she ran to the window and pulled Floret to the ground. He stayed standing just long enough to see what was going on.

A man lay on the cobblestones, the rain pattering off his coat in splashes lit only by the dimming candlelight from a street lamp. He was not moving. Two other figures stood just outside the pool of light. Valen recognized the shape of pistols in their hands as one of them raised theirs to point at him.

The other figure said something, and the both of them ran off, leaving the third to soak in the unabating rain.

Valen forced his lips not to tremble. "They're gone. It's over."

"Yes, it's over." Floret shuffled to his feet angrily. "The Guard will surely have heard the noise, and will be by soon. I am going to go out and see to that man in the street."

"You will not," Cécile said, her voice cracking.

"I will, my dear. Perhaps he can be helped. He may be a rogue, but there is no decency in watching a man die alone. Come, Valen."

Valen helped Margo off the floor, then moved to assist Floret as he tried to do the same for Cécile. The old man shoved him off.

They walked across the street in the rain without their coats. Valen could not feel the cold. His mind had detached from the event, and he walked through it as distant as a ghost. This was his fault, of course. Once again, his foolishness had destroyed a home.

Floret bent down without a groan and shut the dead man's eyes. Valen and he stood over the stranger in what felt like a vigil. A vigil for a man they had never met, who may even have been the one to shoot at them.

"We will have to leave," Floret said quietly. "I cannot let Cécile live like this."

"You will stay with Margo and me. As long as you need to."

"Yes. My Marguerite. Her mother does not always see it, but my daughter has more good sense than anyone I have ever known."

Valen had no idea how to respond to that. Marrying him had been a lapse of judgment, from any sensible point of view. And even if Floret had such faith in his daughter, why say so just then?

The Guard did come eventually. Valen and Floret left them to it.

When they entered the house, Floret told his wife all would be well and shuffled off to the pantry to find some tarpaulin to cover the broken window. Valen couldn't bring himself to meet Margo's eyes.

A single cheat can ruin an inn. Two can destroy a club. Three, a city.

Dishonest Play and Players

XX
VALEN

Valen sat at his dining room table, a dozen candles casting light down on him. He was about to tell the future; this was no time to skimp on lighting. Margo and her parents were all fast asleep, and he hoped they would stay that way so he wouldn't have to explain what he was up to. He was supposed to have given up magic and become a clerk, after all; he didn't relish the idea of another conversation about knowing your skills and sticking with your choices.

He slid his Fanzago deck out of its worn paper box and rifled through it for the spell he needed.

At the Séminaire the very first task for any would-be Brother, outside of taking instruction on the care and feeding of the elder Brothers, was the selection of a spell book. The magic used by the faculty was far too complicated for any but the freakish to remember in one's mind. Too many variables, references, and wheels of logic, to say nothing of requiring three languages. Most students used simple black notebooks, the kind used for diaries and recipe books, but those only lasted so long before becoming utterly filled with writing. Wisemen often had the pages of their spellbooks rebound several times over the years as they grew in their art, both to keep their notes together and to show off finer cloth and more delicate binding as their wealth grew.

Valen, though, had no use for the empty pages to be found in either a small notebook or a thick tome. They reminded him far too much of the ledgers he had snored over back in Verbichere. When he learned his first divination spell, he wrote it on the face of a faded old Fanzago deck.

The L'Ombrais cards were larger than the Satique deck used in the empire, nearly as large as the pocket pamphlets some of his classmates started with. The odd approach was dismissed as a puerile affectation by his mentors, but soon it became clear that Valen's spelldeck had a benefit that a regular book in the codex format did not—when he needed to reference a stanza from another spell, he could do so easily by pulling the requisite card. No indices, no bookmarks, and certainly no keeping one's thumb wedged between pages.

A spellbook in the hands of a novice could be dangerous, to say nothing of the ownership of the ideas within. Thus any paper book of spells bore some sort of encryption, normally hidden.

Most spellbooks had large blocks of the current language and snatches of the wiseman's dreamtongue in plain text for anyone to see. The text was difficult enough to ward off nearly anyone. The third required language, the dead one, was hidden. Valen used subtly different shapes on certain letters to hide his code— an elongated 'h,' or a tilted 'o,' for example. Simple enough to read when you know. In the rare cases in which a great Brother's book was committed to print, a special type was used to the same effect.

Here in his rooms, a soup bowl served Valen as his scrying glass. The great basins of the Séminaire were no more effective, and he kept his pageantry for the card table. After selecting the base spell, he shuffled the deck nine times and drew the top three cards: A spell from the Remonde Cycle, built to limit the time range of the prognostication. An incantation for clear vision. A skáld's song in the symbol code of Valen's personal magic language.

This language was the true key to magic. The dialect of dreams. As personal as a face, or the lines on one's hand. Unknowable by any but the holder and created without his counsel. These were the symbols of the self below the self, the illogical, inexplicable part of a person's mind that moved without his bidding.

In Valen's dreamspeak, a dark tunnel meant safety, a sharpened axe meant friendship, a drop of milk meant disaster. He knew—guessed, really—that each of these could be tied back to some experience in his childhood.

Of the few wisemen who debated such things in the Pendent Tower, there were some who said that a person's language was created in its whole between birth and four years of age, when the mind is growing, and that if a record could be made of every image and every feeling in that child's life, one could find a primer to his dreamspeak.

Others believed that many symbols sprang from within, rather than being formed by one's experiences. They held that the deepest, stillest parts of ourselves were not akin to carambol orbs, only moving when moved, but acted on their own logic, not bound by the rules of the waking world. Valen was of these latter men.

Gazing into a soup bowl on his kitchen table, he thought once again of how far he was from the Tower.

He used his divination so rarely these days. From time to time, always when completely alone in his rooms, he would cast something to try and see his family. He had never found much success on that front, but was at least fairly sure they were all alive. His guilt never improved after those sessions.

The images were the most difficult aspect of casting. They moved through his mind without his control, like bad dreams. A man's mind should be his own. But to divine what one can about the future requires opening those doors, the doors of unnatural perception. Valen might close his eyes, cover his ears, but the visions could not be stopped once called.

They came in a tumble, some moving, others still. In some he could not see colors, a world of grays and halftones like a lithograph. He was tiny as an ant, or massive as a stormcloud. All were of a size useless for learning anything. He saw a hem of green thread thick as cable, a lava plain the size of a handkerchief. Snatches of the language of song, of tears, rarely matching whatever image the magic placed before him.

Focus and desire. These were the traits which drove magic, and Valen made use of both. It felt like trying to memorize an entire deck of cards at once, thrown in the air.

Pushing the discomfort of his sweating neck and aching forehead aside, he kept casting. Eventually, he saw the corner of a book. Bound in blue leather which had faded pale on the spine. Marbled page edges and gold-leaf embossed text that would be easy to remember. It sat in a pile of similarly beautiful books. He heard a voice—numbers being called.

THE IMAGES HELD little meaning until days later, when he saw a flyer advertising an auction for the library of Dusmenil. All of this business had begun with the old secrets of the Dusmenil family; perhaps there was something else in the stacks that could help him.

He brought the question to Margo that night at dinner. Her parents had dined early, and were engaged in their hobbies of reading the news and drinking in the drawing room.

"An auction? Seems very un-magical," she said.

He broke a hunk off of the loaf of bread and shrugged. "I must agree. If it were a lottery I might have a chance, but an auction? I could play like mad for months without having enough money to buy that collection. I suppose we don't need the whole thing, though. Maybe I could find some way to sneak into where it is being held. Surely a well-respected and harmless man of finance could find a reason to take a look. Not that they would want me digging through the collection unsupervised. A distraction of some kind, perhaps."

Margo chuckled over her wine. "Why go through all that trouble? We can simply rig the auction."

"Rig... that's possible?" In years of cheating, Valen had never once heard of fixing an auction in one's favor.

"Oh, quite possible. I've never done it myself, mind you. We Hoques buy our materiel honestly. But that does not mean we don't know how the thing is done. Just as an honest player might learn the tricks of a cheat to protect himself against them."

"Yes," Valen said dryly. "I've read plenty of books on the strategy of play that include that sort of advice. More than one included the address of a shop where one might buy the kinds of devices used for false play. So that one might know to avoid them and anyone seen there, of course. Which is why the prices are included in the books as well."

Marguerite grinned and turned away. "I suppose there are different levels of dishonesty."

"Let us put aside which of these levels you engaged in for the moment," Valen said with a flirting grin. "Your parents are in the next room after all. The question is: to which level are we headed?"

"Oh, the very utmost."

*　　*　　*

As Valen came to learn, bid rigging was easy to accomplish with any auction not closely monitored by large people with an affinity for weapons. The investment of a few punchbowls at some of his haunts and some clever inquiries in trading circles by Margo quickly revealed where the action was for interested parties.

Valen and Marguerite met with a half-dozen like-minded individuals over a game of signaux one afternoon. The location was a spacious old storage closet in the back of a theater; the room had been converted to a bar to keep the actors from leaving the premises with their pay in their pockets. The owner of the gaudy old pile was the master of this little scheme, a pinched fellow in black who looked as if he had never attended a comedy in his life, or if he had, he had not favored the actors with a single chuckle.

The rules of the game were simple: all of them wanted to grab this collection wholesale and sell the antique books off one at a time. Instead of competing with each other, they were to send a single representative to buy the lot, split the cost, and divide the library evenly. This would keep the price low, and everyone involved would make at least some profit.

It was all very formal, as befitted any archetypally smoke-filled back room. Signatures were penned, copies made, oaths taken. Valen had managed to avoid any gambling rings in his time, and found himself enjoying the camaraderie despite himself. Everything between he and his crew was verbal, with little thought put into the intricacies of winnings distribution in case of accident etc. Did he need to follow suit here? Was this how such matters were handled by swindlers of a certain caste?

Valen was concerned for a moment about how he could

ensure he got the book his visions had shown him, but the right of first choice was to be determined by lots. Margo gave him a little wink, and he pulled the shortest without any difficulty. His magic worked.

"What can I say?" she laughed. "He's always been lucky."

AFTER THE AUCTION, the group reconvened in a drafty warehouse owned by another member of the ring, a stout woman with a quiet voice who never had to raise it.

Seven unopened boxes for seven sets of conspirators, Valen and Margo being considered a pair. They had made what they had called a 'back-up' plan, though they expected to need it: they would keep track of who won the book they sought and find a way to take it from him. Valen thought a game of clips would do the trick, but Margo suggested simply buying it.

As it was, the luck spell Valen had prepared for the occasion went off with no issues, requiring only some sub-vocal muttering. He picked first, and the box he chose at random held, among many other fine volumes, a book bound in blue leather with mottle marbling on the paper edges.

His magic had worked again.

THE BOOK WAS a journal of an early Dusmenil explorer reprinted in rough text. It claimed to be the sole copy. Valen and Marguerite read the book together over wine at the table in their kitchen, trading passages to read aloud and generally annoying each other with questions and theories.

By dawn, Valen began to doubt the accuracy of his vision, or at least his interpretation of it. Marguerite had done so hours before, and had said so plainly. But she did love the paper and ink of an old tome, and didn't seem to mind spending a long night and too many candles running her fingers over the deliciously textured old pages.

Sleep and wine had nearly overtaken him when he saw the encryption. The old trick, not of explorers, but of the Séminaire.

But this was not a Brother's spellbook. This was a lesser explorer's travelogue. Why would there be a message encoded into its text?

Valen and Margo took turns sleeping for four days, each waking to find the other newly terrified by some detail in what they had decrypted in the past hours. The ink stains from their transcriptions never fully came off the kitchen table.

After suffering these indignities, I was more than glad to enter the jewel city of Soucisse. The air no longer caught in my throat as it had in these last days of desert travel; the fair fountains cast their divined waters skyward and cooled every corner and alleyway.

Keeping a mind to my task, I watched for clutches of children at play, the hour being too early for most folk to take up card or die. Before long I spied a few mud-kneed boys playing what seemed to be a type of skiptop, tossing a knucklebone in the air and gathering others from a puddle before it landed. In Soucisse, water is a part of all things.

A Gamester Abroad

XXI
TENERIÈVE

ALL THE TRUEST secrets come out on the road. Tenerieve knew
this from her youth among the ponies and rattling caravan
carts. Any town they stopped in was likely to result in a hanger-
on or two, most often people who did not care to travel on
the road alone: women, elders, and men smart enough not to
risk themselves for bravura. Tenerieve had watched as her older
cousins made friendly conversation to pass the time or pick up
interesting news. Time and again those people, those strangers,
revealed more about their inner thoughts than she had ever
seen any member of her clan do. The road was temporary,
quiet, and lonely, which made people pensive. A journey of any
length meant change of some kind, to people who didn't live as
nomads. Hopes, fears, imagined disasters, choices. There is a
tacit pact of silence to any conversation on the road.

She met a boy once who took a shine to her, probably because
he never shut up and Tenerieve rarely spoke. His family were
potters, and they were moving to a town in the southern half
of the Rushed Road in pursuit of the finer clay of the rivers
of those lands. The parents were far too engaged in worrying

about things they could not control to bother keeping track of how their son was spending his time.

He spent four days telling her all he had ever seen and everything he had ever thought. She prompted him with nods and questions, enjoying the easy company of a new friend on a long trip, to say nothing of the food he gave her after his meals. When his family said their goodbyes to the caravan, she was surprised at how much she didn't want to see him go.

It was only six months before Ten and the boy saw each other again on the caravan's trip back north. By then, they had moved on with their lives and interests, and barely said 'hello' to each other.

This was how friendship was on the road: brief, intense, and most of all finite.

The road with Maddie did not offer the same camaraderie. The guide walked several paces ahead at all times, often charging up a grassy rise to look for a blaze. Tenerière fell into the steady pace she had developed as a youth, and was glad to find it did not wind her too badly. There were no trails to speak of, only miles of moss-covered rock. No animals grazed here. Birds were few. Still, Maddie found the easiest paths through the unforgiving land, and never crowed about it once.

They clambered over the hardscrabble stone for two days before reaching the mountains. Ten was relieved; at least there they could get above the knotty mosslands. The lava of Mount Eldad had poured around these peaks and left great emptinesses of black rock through the uninhabited plains. Unlike Mt. Senecin, where people burned.

A strand of white against the black rock caught Ten's eye one morning as they picked their way towards a cleft in some far off hills. She attracted Maddie's attention and pointed to it.

Maddie's wrinkles deepened as she smiled. "Maybe you do have a touch of magic about you. Let's have a look. It's not far out of our way. But if I tell you to run, we run."

She hunched her bag up on her shoulders and walked off without further explanation.

A boulder began to take shape as they neared it. It stood taller than either of them by several feet, and was as wide as the fountain Ten had seen on the street near the Syncretic Club. Pale rock was shot through with bits of a gleaming red mineral Ten could not identify.

"This was what you thought we might run from?" Ten thumped the rock with a closed hand. "I do not think it will chase us."

Maddie's eyes were hard. "It won't. But others may. Look around, girl. This is no lava rock. The volcano himself couldn't touch it. This boulder is detached from the rest. Ancient. You are knocking on an oldfolk stone. Sacred to them."

"The oldfolk?" Ten was so surprised she couldn't help but laugh. Was her guide as superstitious as that? "That's what you're so afraid of? Will they dance after us and lure us back to their sunless lands with fruits and jewels?"

Maddie's serious look didn't change. "I hope not. But that's not what I thought we might have to run from. We are not the only people out on these rocks, girl."

Ten's shoulders tensed. A few quick glances at the land around them didn't reveal anything.

"That's right," Maddie said. "You won't have noticed the signs. At no point on this little trek have we been more than a shout away from somebody who lives out here."

She had heard of witches hiding in the lava fields, but hadn't expected to find anyone so far from a town. How could anyone survive in this wasteland?

"And they love this rock?" she asked.

Maddie's look softened again. "Oh, yes. Very much. The people out here have made a kind of peace with the oldfolk, they say. True or no, if you go near one of their sacred stones and they don't want you to..."

The landscape which had seemed so barren now appeared to Ten to be hiding any number of wild-eyed hermits. "We should go then, yes?"

"Yes. But not until we pay our respects."

Maddie reached into a pocket and produced a worn kron. She placed the coin on the black ground and whispered something. Ten looked to the sky. Though the sun hid the stars, she still said a prayer in the native tongue she had not used in years.

As THEY SAT by the fire after the night's meal and before bed, Maddie surprised Ten with her stillness. Every other night the guide had found something to do with herself, sharpening a knife or repacking her bag. Now she sat and poked at the moss fire with her walking stick.

Ten was used to being the one not speaking. This silence bothered her more than any other had.

As the fire was starting its slow journey to dying, Maddie spoke at last.

"Why don't you just ask me what you want to ask me, girl?"

Ten wanted to ask what she meant, but she knew where that conversation would lead. Ten *did* want to ask the guide something; she just hadn't realized it until right then.

"The people out here. How do they live without others? How do they eat? Who protects them when they sleep?"

Maddie's eyes stayed on the fire. "That's not what you want to ask. It's close. But not quite."

Ten took a breath and nodded. "How do *you* live alone like this, Madeleine?"

Alleged witches in the black rock might as well have been oldfolk themselves for as much as Ten was likely to understand them. They were probably mad or hateful of people or both. But the Erdannes family smiled when Maddie arrived. People respected her. She didn't need to live out here in the wastes.

The woman did not smile. "Closer. You want to know where I make my home."

"Yes."

"You grew up without a home. Why am I so strange?"

"I... had a home," Ten said, trying to work her feelings into words. "It moved always. Yes. But it was a home."

"And what made it so?"

She thought of her parents' wagon, where she slept on winter nights. But that was not it. The wagon had burned once, and they simply made another. She remembered her mother's eyes.

Maddie looked up, her face still unreadable. "There is another word for what you mean by 'home': community. I may not have a house, but I have a home—it is in myself. La Ruse, people like your friends the Erdannes, they are my community. I am not there often, but neither are the shipping sailors or the shepherds. I may live by myself and sleep under whatever sky I choose, but those people are mine."

Ten did not ask any more questions that night. As she lay under her tarpaulin, she thought of all the homes she had tried. The Rushed Road. Voet. The Hoque household. The Séminaire. Her rooms by the river. Not since she left her clan had she had a community.

Not until Valen. Margo and Jaq and he were all the people she knew, in truth. They were close, tied to one another by their choice of trade, their history, their shared secrets, just as Ten's clan had been. But still she felt alone. These were friends, not blood. Did they truly think of her as one of their own, or was she simply a hanger-on of Val's and Margo's marriage, like one of the children who would follow after her caravan? Pleasant for a while, but who would one day tire and go home?

Were it not for the long hours of walking, she likely would not have slept that night.

THE NEXT TIME Maddie set up camp, they were within five miles of the Skyndiferth location.

"The rest of the way is for you," she said gruffly. "You're not paying me enough to be burdened with whatever secret you find up there."

It was the middle of the day. Tenerieve could make it close enough to see what was there and back before nightfall. She nodded brusquely and moved on. They had not spoken much since their conversation by the fire. Ten had not seen a need to.

She followed a dry river bed through a sickened valley and tried to prepare herself for… what? She had been pushing the mystery out of her mind for days, not wanting to lose herself in foolish fears. Now she was at the very moment. It could be a Brother treasure trove, which they most certainly would be guarding. Perhaps a site of some magical power, like the aquifers below Soucisse which Naiibis had summoned to the surface. Or perhaps some terrible secret, given the lengths the Brothers went to to keep it a secret from the world.

Perhaps Jaq had been right, and coming alone was foolish.

Walking down a riverbed in plain sight now seemed like idiocy. Anyone on the high ground to either side of her would be able to watch her every move. She was dealing with people who could explode a person's heart—tromping along through the loud gravel was no way to be safe.

She climbed the sunnier of the two slopes next to the riverbed to try to find a way to creep up out of sight. When she reached the top, the throaty rush of water spoke of a cataract, and a sizable one. She thought it must have emptied on to the other side, away from the cracked land she was walking.

After a few miles she saw a great falls yawning across the valley, easily a quarter-mile wide. But where was the river?

And then she climbed closer, and saw the falls disappear into nothing.

She didn't believe it at first. Some trick of the light. It was as if something *ate* the water, in a straight line two feet above the ground.

Losing her footing often, she clambered back down into the valley, keeping her eyes on the base of the falls. It became more and more apparent as she approached that this was no illusion. No enchantment could simply devour that much water. Light, maybe, or heat. But not water.

The clean smell of a mountain river welcomed her as she walked toward the impossible waterfall. As a child it would have meant clean clothes, newly-filled canteens, and a long rest from the road. But it did not calm her now. This was an aberration.

She was a quarter mile from the dry base of the falls when she saw a building, a rough shack teetering against the rock just to the right of the water. Someone lived here.

A building was something she could understand. She decided to investigate it before she took a closer look at the troubling waterfall.

Empty. Recently used, though, to gauge by the coals in the fire pit. The shack was mostly books—under a table leg, jammed into a crack between the roof and the wall, stacked next to a chair with winestains on the top cover. An old sigil marred the front of the chimney.

"At last."

Tenerième spun on her heel to face a frowning man in worn breeches and an open shirt. The hair on his chest was coarse and gray. He wore no beard, nor any hair atop his head save two weak tufts above his ears. The man stood in the doorway, blocking her exit.

"Yes, I am here." Tenerième built the lie for herself in moments. It is always the same lie: *I belong here. I know exactly what I am doing. I am open and honest and here without motive.* This was the lie she learned in the fat towns of Cadogna as a girl, and the one she kept up at the gambling tables. "I apologize for the delay."

The man's frown didn't change. "Not your fault, I'm sure."

Tenerième beamed a smile at him. "A little, perhaps."

"Never met a woman Brother before."

"Perhaps that is why it took me so long."

He motioned for her to sit on the one chair in the room. "Please. You have travelled far."

"I thank you." Ten took the seat and watched as the man slowly entered. He took a place on the rough cot and folded his hands between his knees.

She knew she was being sized up. Without more information, she couldn't come up with a good story. She needed to get him talking.

"It's bigger than I imagined," she said, motioning to the door and the cataract outside. A puddle was forming on the floor from the mist.

"Hm."

"When do we start?"

The man finally looked away from her, but his deep frown didn't change. "We are not going to start anything. I don't know why you are here. Whatever your reason, it doesn't matter in the end. It's a shame—you must be a talented diviner indeed to find this place."

The man spoke a triple-word. Pain raced out from her chest, down her arm, up to her jaw. Her breaths would not come to her. Her back burned like molten iron.

Tenerième swore at herself. She had seen this done once already, to Dusmenil, and instead of learning how it was done and how to counteract it, she had run off to find the Séminaire's secrets assuming the worst she would face would be memories of her homeland. She would never know what it was to live in peace, to find a place in the world, to be her own. She would die in pain at the hands of a man she did not know.

A keening. In the pool of still water on the floor of the room. A design of a griffin in gold.

"L'Ombre," she croaked. "L'Ombre."

The pain did not stop, but it abated enough for her to look the murderer in the face.

"What are you on about?"

Her mind raced. What could she say that would give her time? Why would the Brother stop at the mere mention of a country?

"You... you do not know what they can do," she bluffed. "The Brothers there, they have discovered so much."

Curiosity. Always the bane of a true wiseman. Since the schism of L'Ombre and Cadogna, their Séminaires rarely spoke.

The man's eyes flashed with anger. Not at her, she thought. At the injustice of it. "What have you seen?"

"The time will come right quick when you will see for yourself. They sent me. Yes, a woman. They allow women to learn the wisemen's arts there." She started to layer a L'Ombrais accent over her Mistigri. "You were right: I am a very good diviner. Good enough to find your Skyndiferth despite your best attempts to shield it from us. Yet I am nowhere near as talented as others. Dozens of us, all Ombrian.

"They have sent us as a warning. We will end this Skyndiferth of yours. Others will topple your proud tower. All the great magical works of the Valtivan Séminaire will be undone by Ombrian disenchantments."

"Dis... *dis*enchantments?'" The Brother looked at her in confusion. "You have a method to undo the enchantments of others?"

Ten pulled her lips into an evil smile. "Your works will die. Even those of that novice Naiibis. Try to kill me if you must, but we will not be stopped. We are innumerable."

The Brother stood and walked to the door. "Naiibis. You would kill Soucisse. You would let the desert take it."

"We would, and we will." His back was to her now. A few steps out that door and she might charge past him and get away. If she could keep him confused, she might even live. "But you will not see it."

SHE SPOKE NONSENSE as menacingly as she could and stared at the man's heart.

He did not fight her. He simply frowned once again and disappeared from sight.

Startled, she walked to where he had stood and felt nothing. She walked outside into the cool mist and looked all around, but saw no sign of the man.

Tenerième was alone. It felt wonderful.

Now, again, Tenerième had seen something impossible. There were enchantments which would make a person more difficult to see, but none that would make him invisible altogether.

This was why she had left home. She herself was so strange that she had wanted to find the other strangenesses in the world. She walked right up to the behemoth falls, right up to the edge of where it disappeared. Waterfalls have a powerful tug on people. That's what she told herself when she stepped into the falling water.

She did not fall far before her feet hit the bottom. The sun was gone, and no light replaced it. She held her breath as the water pushed her up against a wall. A stone wall, made by human hands. She swam up, broke the surface of the roiling water and gulped the breath she hadn't been sure she was ever going to have again.

The light sliced through a large room. The wall had a top, and she pulled herself up. This was a pool of some kind; an aquifer. A quarter-mile sheet of water gushed from nowhere against the far wall, toward a row of great pipes.

A window. The flat heat of a desert sun, cut by mists from many fountains that towered above her. She recognized imperial symbolry on the walls. This was Soucisse, the capitol city of the Cadois empire. The Empress's home.

The rush of water in a closed space. A memory of her childhood crept up unannounced: she and Aunt Lucie in a hollowed out cave behind a waterfall. A little outcropping, only barely big enough to stand on, doused with freezing water for a few seconds every several minutes. Lucie had joked that to stand on it and face the spray was to be as strong as the old heroes. Ten had been ready to step out and try her luck, but the old woman held her arm. "Brave is good. Smart enough to know when *not* to be brave is better," she had said.

This foolishness had gone on long enough. Ten could no longer compete against powers such as these, powers which could fling a river across the world. She could either make peace with them or run, but she could not stand against them. She had to go to the Brothers and confess everything.

The idea of going back to the Tower made her stomach churn, but the shame of it would be a small price for her safety, and that of her friends—her idiot friends who chased this nonsense and pulled her right along into it. They would never agree to her asking the Brothers for help. Jaq hated them, Margo didn't trust them, and Valen was far too proud. She might even lose them. Lose their friendship, and the closest thing to a home she had.

She had lost homes before. Better to lose their regard than to have them murdered by the wisemen. Valen wasn't going to understand.

CREPIN: You cheat because you are lazy.

AVI: I cheat because it is difficult.

CREPIN: You cheat because you think yourself too
smart for the world.

AVI: I cheat to make the world as I wish it.

The Rake's Price, Barberaque

XXII

VALEN

THERE COMES A moment in many games at which a sensible gambler knows he has pushed his luck farther than he ought. The cards were falling so well, the opponents could not match his skill. An off hand or two, surely, but nothing in the face of the successes early on. A minor setback. Not a slump, of course; not enough to stop playing. Yet the gambler knows where this road ends, and if he has any wits about him at all, he cuts his losses, bows graciously, and departs before matters become worse. It is a sense an experienced gambler develops, and often means the difference between a successful gambler and one killed by his debts.

This sense was telling Valen in no uncertain terms that he had taken this game of secrets too far.

Just how many turns of the drawing room he had taken, he could not be sure. The Dusmenil book and some related research papers had been stacked very neatly on his sideboard, though he couldn't fully remember doing it. The decanter teetered on the arm of his divan for reasons at which he could only guess. Margo and Jaq stood at the windows, awaiting Tenerève's arrival. If they had any opinions whatsoever on Valen's fretting, they did not communicate them.

Here, at least, he could loosen his guard. With so much of his life spent dead-facing his opponents across the card table, something as natural as a frown was a luxury. In his own home, though, and with friends, he could pace around madly and wring his hands with freedom. His wife's parents had the decency to be out at coffee shops most of the time.

Jaq's news about the L'Ombrais ship searching off the coast had not helped to ease his mind. There was no way to guess what information Tenerième was returning with, but it was sure to put everyone in greater danger from the Séminaire. And the secret he and Margo had discovered, the second Dusmenil secret, involved powers even greater than those. They were higher stakes than any he had played for.

But with all that, he dreaded telling Ten that he had found more.

"That'd be her," Jaq said.

Margo moved to stand next to him, a disbelieving look on her face. "Where? I don't see her."

"Just past those horses. Down there."

"I still don't... oh, yes," Margo replied with relief. "A sailor's eyes are better than most, I imagine."

"Better than a forger's, at any rate. You might try your husband's close-up spectacles. Let your eyes rest a bit when you're marking cards."

"You shouldn't mock an older woman for her eyesight, Jaq."

Jaq grunted a short laugh. "Maybe not. Or maybe you shouldn't assume that everything a younger man says is a joke."

"But it is. Jokes are all young men have."

"Don't be forgetting my rugged good looks."

They chuckled at that together, their enmity put aside for once. Valen smiled to himself. At least they had found something better to do than tromp around the room.

Tenerième entered after an abrupt knock on the door. Valen tried to guess from her eyes what she had found, but she had the most natural deadface he had ever encountered, utterly unreadable. They all greeted her: Margo with an embrace, Valen with a touch on the shoulder, and Jaq with a silent wave. They sat without refreshment.

"Ten, there is something you need to hear," Valen began.

Tenerième nearly laughed. "I cannot imagine you have any news that would supersede mine."

"Perhaps not, but I must beg to go first. Consider it a rare favor."

"Hardly 'rare,' Valen," Marguerite chided. "You ask for favors all the time."

"Still."

A long moment of quiet passed before Tenerième nodded assent.

Valen took a long breath. "I have no skill for stories, so I will simply out with it. The volcanic eruption which destroyed your homeland was caused by a Brother at the behest of the Empire."

When Tenerième did not react, he continued. "They tell us the Fire War was effectively ended when Mount Senecin exploded and covered the land in its lava and ash. The greatest tragedy in the last three hundred years. The Cadois force was..."

"Was regrouping," Tenerième said, her face cold. "Had pulled back to Tymere in preparation for the winter, having made insufficient advances in the north to weather the season. They had a head-start when the mountain blew. They helped—"

She broke then, just slightly. A catch in her voice accompanied by the smallest dip of her eyebrows. It did not last long. "They helped the Mistigris evacuate. The people on the borders. Those of us near the mountain burned."

"Yes," Valen said. "As did much of the L'Ombrais force. Ten,

I found a book. A book from Dusmenil's library. A simple travel journal of no value. Encoded within it was this allegation."

"Encoded?"

"As you or I might. As a Brother does. It was the personal account of Naiibis."

"The diviner?"

Valen was sure she held her breath.

"The same. It would appear, if this story is true, that he was not a diviner at all, but rather had invented a new discipline. One of... I don't know what to call it."

"'Magic of the deeps,'" Marguerite offered. "He did not locate the desert fountain beneath Soucisse, Ten. He *caused* it. He caused the destruction of the interior by Mount Eldad's eruption as well. And likewise the eruption of Senecin."

Jacquemin stood suddenly and moved to within a pace of Tenerième's seat. "The bastards did it on purpose, Ten. Do you not see it? They found a man who could summon the earth's fire and used it to lay waste to your homeland. You've never known a home because of them. They could have told the Mistigris. They were supposed to be defending you from the damned L'Ombrais, and they murdered you."

No one moved. Valen held his breath, preparing as best he could for Tenerième's reaction. Even someone as composed as she, as hardened against life's tribulations by a life of struggle and unbelonging, would be crippled by this news. She was the friend he had known the longest. It was his doing that brought her to this life of crime. And his was the voice that told her the secret of the betrayal of her people.

"May I tell you of my news now?" Tenerième asked. "I believe I have been more than patient."

"I... of course." Valen still couldn't understand how she wasn't throwing the furniture through the windows in anger.

As she told her story, a story in which yet another kind of

magic was shown to exist, it was all Valen could do to keep himself from running to her side and holding her close to him. She revealed no anger, nor any sadness at hearing of the lie that killed her people and doomed her to a life of wandering. She was not a graven statue, after all. She must have felt *something*.

Her story dovetailed well with the Naiibis account. The springs below Soucisse were not natural—they were stolen from a waterfall in Valtiffe. Stolen and sent across the world.

"So our volcano was the same trick, then," Jacquemin said. "Naiibis destroys miles of land for the Empire, just so they can hide the fact that they're doing some madness with one of our waterfalls."

Marguerite shook her head. "Not madness. The founding of Soucisse was fate. A miracle. Water in the desert, brought forth as proof of the Empire's rightful domination of all the lands of the world."

"A lovely story," Valen said. "But let us not forget the very mechanic that allows this miracle to occur. A door was opened in the air. And as Ten was so kind as to prove, people can pass through it unharmed. If the Empress wanted to, she could throw an army through that gate and take us unawares. This is the secret that Dusmenil lost at the game."

"Aye." Jacquemin smirked. "And your broker set it at too low a price, by my count."

"Well, let us take a full accounting of our situation," Valen said. "Dusmenil knew what the Skyndiferth was, the poor old fellow. The men in the alley gave what they thought was this information to the L'Ombrais somehow, and the Séminaire tried to stop them, but someone—and we have no idea who— shot them. We are now in possession of this knowledge, but still have no clue as to who set all of this in motion. Oh, and let us not forget that our fair city is now plagued by war between rival gangs, after the remarkably-timed weakening of

Munnrais. The question now becomes, what we do about it?"

Tenerième looked Valen directly in the eye. "We do nothing. Secrets of state are no business of ours."

"Don't quail on us now, Ten," Jaq said. "This is an opportunity. The gentry has done this to us."

Marguerite clucked her tongue. "The gentry has nothing to do with this."

"The common folk suffering so a few that own land might benefit? Who do you think is buying up all of the property by the docks?'

"I'm from the docks. My parents are from the docks. They fled their home to get away from the violence. If the gentry stood to gain, why did my father nearly get shot?"

"*Who gains,* then?" Jacquemin nearly shouted. "Not us regular people, I can tell you *that.*"

"We're on the brink of losing everything. Our home, our vote. And all because some of these commoners you're so proud to call yourself a part of would rather steal than…"

Valen raised a hand to break into the debate. "You have it there, Margo. It's the vote. The Tipping Point. People like your parents, people who want Valtiffe to stay independent, are forced from their homes. And who will buy them but the monied gentes of the Empire? And how will they vote? This has all been a play for Valtiffe."

When Tenerième broke her silence, all other sound in the room ceased. Valen was still waiting for her to blow up at the news.

"To what end?" she asked. "The Empire practically runs our lives even now."

"Yes, but we have something they need," Valen said. "We have the Skyndiferth. Our Brothers keep the water in their precious capitol city flowing through its fountains. If the Séminaire decided, they could destroy Soucisse with a word."

"The man I met," Ten said. "The man at the waterfall. I told him I had a way to undo enchantments. Dis-enchant. It was a quick lie off the cuff, but it scared him. He must have been afraid there were Brothers out there who could undo their work. Could drought Soucisse without them knowing how. Their power over the Empress would be weakened."

Marguerite spoke to her husband and Tenerième, but not to Jacquemin. "They have more immediate things to fear than that. The Empress wants the Séminaire. Our Séminaire. If Valtiffe becomes an imperial state, the Pendent Tower will be an island surrounded by her lands."

"Aye," Jacquemin spat. "It's not enough they've taken nearly all that makes us *us*. They want *us*, too."

Tenerième's eyes turned downcast. "And be glad they do. Yes. It is certainly better than what they do to those they do *not* want."

The explosion Valen had predicted did not take place. Instead, his friend collapsed in on herself, a cold fire.

"The Brothers," she whispered. "They are not so neutral in the end. They say they are. Yes. But they hold a power over the Empress herself with this Skyndiferth of theirs."

Margo nodded. "And She over L'Ombre. Just knowing that they have magic that pulls water from the ground must give Her an edge against them."

"So my erstwhile brothers have chosen a side in the long game of nations after all," Valen said. "Whether they meant to or not."

Jaq spat on the rug, and Valen found himself too distracted to care. "The old bastards only care about themselves. Doesn't matter to them who's wearing the crown so long as She leaves them in peace to overcharge for 'chants and flounce about like they're royalty."

"Two new disciplines of magic in a matter of weeks," Valen said. "This is becoming something of a trend."

Two new disciplines, and at least three dead men. Why did they keep these powers hidden? The Brothers had thrown Valen out for daring to even imagine a new kind of magic. What would they do to keep their secret magics from becoming known?

"Ten, do you remember learning anything about how Naiibis died?" Val asked. He thought he knew the answer, but hoped he was wrong.

She thought for a moment, then frowned. "Found dead in his rooms on the route back from Soucisse. L'Ombrais assassin."

Jaq laughed at that. "All the brains in that tower, and you believe that? Someone sneaking into a hotel filled with Brothers and stabbing someone who calls water from the earth like a god?"

"I know, Jaq," Valen said. "I encourage you to remember that at the time we were taught this, we didn't know they would burn people alive over a piece of paper."

"So what do we do?" Jacquemin was failing to hide his anger.

A constellation of possibilities played out in Valen's mind, each with its own risks and chances. The world had broken, and the best thing to do was to adjust. He needed to back off, back away from this conflict of crowns. Find a way to placate the Brothers, and hope the Empire and Queendom alike ignored him.

A memory of his childhood home on the day he left. The grimaces of his family in pain. The labored creak of the door as he closed it behind him for the last time.

No one he cared about was going to get hurt by his carelessness again.

"If all of this is true—by all the gods, if *any* of it is—I will put an end to it." Valen looked at each of his associates for a long moment. "I will not allow them to sacrifice us as they see fit. We all of us know the truth of this life. No matter what any of us do, death finds us in the end. The house always wins. Knowing that is hard enough, but when those with crowns stack the deck for their own gain, it becomes intolerable."

"Yet that is what *you* do," Marguerite said. "You have made a career of stacking every deck you can lay hands on."

"I don't hurt people. I don't ruin lives."

"You ruined Dusmenil's."

Valen's breath caught at that. He wondered if anyone noticed. He had indeed killed Dusmenil, and had done irreparable damage to his own family long before. He felt his jaw muscle tighten, and could do nothing to stop it. Not a good sign for a cardsharp.

"I did. I cannot deny it, and if I could reverse the matter I would go back and face Arbelan some other way, and let the poor man keep his secret. I don't suppose you came across any kind of time-wandering magic with the others, Ten?

"Sadly, no."

"Then I am going to use what little useful skill I have to put an end to this. The Empress wants to play this maddening game for our country. She wasn't prepared for the best gamesters the world has ever seen. The Cadois can't buy houses if they have no money. We can control the flow of coin at every table in this city, right into the pockets of the Hvallais. Let Her Majesty try to stop us. My friends, if you will join me, I would embark on a cardsharping spree for the good of the land."

Jaq grinned like a shark. "About time you fools came around. Especially after winning the Forbearance Game."

"I didn't *win* the…" The tension in Valen's jaw eased, and he nearly laughed. He looked to Margo, hoping for a smile or at very least a nod. She rose without looking at him, went to the sideboard, and rummaged through the bottles to find the best firewine they had.

"No point in saving this," she declared, brandishing it in the air. "Whoever takes our rooms when the Empress imprisons us doesn't deserve it." She caught Valen's eyes and smiled.

He smiled back. She always did love a good gamble.

When they toasted to their success, Tenerième did not speak. Valen guessed she was still reeling from the truth about Naiibis, but something in her bearing, something too subtle to be noticed with only one's eyes, told him she had a different matter on her mind. And this was no time for secrets between conspirators.

The thrill of the combat! Growls mingled with cheers, sweat with blood newly-spilt! A sudden turn of events when a fast bite lands! Take all the time you wish to evaluate the health and ferocity of one combatant, but no mathematics can predict the events of the ring. These sports are the most passionate, the most apt to bring out that desirable flush of the spirits. Truly a fitting pastime for people of quality everywhere.

The Gente's Manual, etc.

XXIII
OMER-GUY

THE ENTIRE POINT of a hedge maze, in Omer-Guy's estimation, was that one should find it difficult to find the center. This night, though, any time he lost his orientation around a cunning bend or hidden break, he simply listened for the violent cheers or looked to the sky to find the glow of torches. Getting in and out of this savage festival without missing his contact was going to be much more of a challenge then keeping his sense of direction in this little labyrinth

Oceline—*the Lady De Loncryn*, Omer-Guy had to remind himself—had a remarkable talent for disguise at the least. The roughspun clothes had been easy enough to procure from the closets of her servants, of course. She and Omer-Guy had made a game of even that, crouching and sneaking meekly through the staff quarters in the small hours as if they would be punished for being somewhere they did not belong.

But it was her demeanor that polished the counterfeit. Gone was her natural lightness, the perfect carriage which made her appear a thing weightless, floating while others walked. Her expression changed constantly after the fashion of commoners, who seem incapable of experiencing the slightest emotion without showing it on their faces. One moment she gasped in open-mouthed wonder at a pretty flower in the hedge, the next she screeched at a shadow and pulled him close. She was a true artist.

As much as he hated the feel of his untailored peasant clothing, and had yet to figure out how he was going to get away from De Loncryn long enough to meet with his contact, he had to admit to himself he was having fun. It had been a very long space of time since he had indulged in anything resembling that.

The notification that a L'Ombrais spyhandler had an assignment for him had come in the regular fashion, that being a particular arrangement of pieces left on the hagensboard in the coffee shop he frequented. Among the other pieces was a wiseman in Red's left corner, two white chevaliers adjacent to each other, and a red ship facing White's empress. It was a position which could legally come about in play, but was uncommon enough to be unusual, especially in a game left unfinished. In another city—Torreçon perhaps, or Jaleaux, where one might find some decent hagens players—it would have been considered too much of a risk to leave something like this lying about, but the people of Saut-Leronne didn't have the mental force to see past three moves, let alone recognize such a rare arrangement.

He had been expecting the summons. With Ambassador Alodesal's gold-foiled coterie entertaining themselves about the city, it seemed only likely that one of them would be engaged in some sort of espionage. Omer-Guy would report that he had delivered the Forbearance Game's secret—without describing how, of course; the individual hands of La Reina's network of dark workers rarely knew what the others were doing, and he had no interest in ruining the system he had developed with his handler by blabbing it to a double agent. He was a double agent himself, after all, and had his pride to consider. He would provide his report and do whatever was required of him next.

The system of leaving secrets in missives to his son turned his mind once again to the lad he had not seen in so many long cold years. What would Oscar think of his father dodging uninvited around a hedge maze with a pretty woman as if he were a man of nineteen or twenty? Omer-Guy's wife had died some twenty years past, shortly after Oscar had fled to L'Ombre, but a son does not always understand such matters when his own mother is involved. Would Oscar hate him if he knew?

Oscar hated him already, if a decade's silence was to be believed. Still, Omer-Guy had sent his letters year after year, their questions never once answered, their offers of affection never echoed. He had utterly forgotten Oscar's voice now, save for the lisping lilt he had had as a boy too small to be left alone with a candle. The face he remembered, much good might it do him. His son would be coming on thirty now, and surely looked little like the pale-eyed, smiling debauchee he'd last seen. His years in exile amongst those severe L'Ombrians would have hardened him. Perhaps he had married. Perhaps Omer-Guy might recognize himself in the face of a grandchild.

An animal shriek and a round of shouts rose from the center of the maze. Another winner had been decided, apparently.

"Ooo, sounds like we missed a good one," De Loncryn whined. "I might have brought my little boy along. He's so clever! Don't you think he's clever, Manny? He'd have us through this maze in seconds. I don't want to miss much more. Did you say there was food, Manny? How much do they charge, you think?"

Omer-Guy slurred his speech and made a show of stumbling a little. "It's all the sweeties you want, my sweetie. Everything you can fit in your mouth." He made his best approximation of a lewd gesture and favored her with a lecherous stare, causing a titter between a young couple passing the other way. "All the firewine, too. I know you've little head for it!"

"Oh, don't you go on about your little head," she brayed. "I've done my part to keep it secret!"

He feigned outrage and tickle-chased her past a half-dozen sloshed youths into a narrow dead end where no moonlight reached the ground. A stone bench with a low back rested in the gloom, its purpose clear.

Oceline's squeal was by far the loudest sound for miles as they flounced down on the cold bench in a mess of limbs and coarse fabric. She nuzzled under his arm and giggled until none of the other attendees were in sight.

"Such a strange event," she said, her peasant accent gone. "I have never seen the point in betting on animals. How does it all work, do you think? Why do they do it?"

"It excites a seemly stimulation in the blood. And there is money to be made, surely."

"It seems like a risky venture."

"Ah, and here enters what is called the Penaux Book," Omer-Guy brightened at the opportunity to share some knowledge with her. He spent so much time hiding things. "It's how bookkeepers make their money on events like this. Regattas. Horse-races. The mathematics of the payouts is such that they are guaranteed to return some winnings, regardless of the outcome."

Oceline chuckled. Omer-Guy could feel her breathing. "A clever investment, then."

"For the bookkeepers, yes."

A shadow crossed the light. Omer-Guy guffawed like a boor and jostled Oceline a bit until the person was gone. They fell back onto one another.

"Ah, Omer, you play your part well." She didn't move away.

So she was pleased with him and his odd suggestion of attending a fox fight in the country. How to use this to his advantage? "People of the Court must play many parts. Is it not so?"

"Ah, it has been so long since I have been at Court, I barely remember."

"Are you... dissatisfied with your life here?"

"No," she sighed. The note of hesitation in her voice would have been unmistakable even if Omer-Guy had not attuned himself to read her every syllable. "This is the home of my childhood. Of my family and my heritage. There has been a Lady of Gabot Avenue for over a century. I have traveled, I have seen Soucisse—all of those silly fountains of theirs—yet always I returned here."

"It is a pretty place."

She tensed a little. He might not have noticed, were she not so close. "Don't lie to me, Omer," she said defensively. "You detest everything about Valtiffe, try as you might to hide it."

"I suppose I do, at that," he admitted with a quiet smirk. "But having met you has softened my opinions. I hardly feel homesick at all."

That was a risk, perhaps. The game of coy flirtation they put on for the listening servants was a deception. Having said such a thing when it seemed no one was there to overhear put him in a position of weakness, a position she could exploit. But he guessed that she would not. The correct move would be to let the lapse go unanswered in order to encourage more such risks in the future. De Loncryn had a remarkable talent for the long play. He knew she would wait.

He was surprised, though, to realize it was also true.

"You are kind, you preening sycophant," she teased. "I am doing my best to make my small corner of this island as much like the Empress's Cadogna as one can. It pleases me to hear my efforts acknowledged."

So she intentionally misinterpreted. That was fine. A good play.

"Of course," she continued. "This will be easier once I am mayor."

"I do not doubt it," Omer-Guy said quickly. He had no intention of letting the unasked question hang in the air between them for longer than it had to.

Not a word had come back from Cadogna yet on the Empress's backing of Oceline's candidacy. She had delivered Dusmenil's secret as promised; now the Crown had to fulfill its half of the clandestine bargain. He could only keep her waiting so long before matters became more urgent. Oceline's opinion was highly valued by the quality people of the city; she could delay the Tipping Point for some time if she chose, and undo what he understood to be the Empress's plan. The long game once again, and Omer-Guy was feeling less like the strategist than the pawn.

"That is why I wanted to come here tonight, you see," he stalled. "I am meant to meet a contact who may have new information on this very topic."

Another risk. Never mind the fact that he was lying; she could very easily attack him on the use of the word 'may.' There would be little point—one would not expect an agent of the Crown to know the specifics of what his handler was going to tell him in a secret meeting—but she could express her impatience. She could start to make threats.

"Oh, but my dear Omer! I thought this night was for pleasure, not statecraft!"

She jumped up from her seat and ran down the shadowed lane, her impossibly sweet laugh trailing behind her. Omer-Guy followed, unable to contain his smile.

Fox-fighting held its own against the many diversions to be found on Valtiffe, both for excitement and the opportunity for gain. It had, Omer-Guy was proud to remember, come to this island along with the Cadois settlers centuries past.

As indigenous mammals were few and sheep could hardly be convinced to fight at all, let alone to the death, the job fell to the foxes. Back home there would be proper dog-fights, but one could hardly justify the expense here. None but the most ostentatious gentes kept dogs on Valtiffe, and those with a powerful dedication to hunting—no one would waste a fine hound on bloodsport.

Omer-Guy blinked at the brightness as he turned an overgrown corner into the crush of people at the main event. At least twenty torches lit the fountain square carved in the center of M. Echouaf's hedge maze, no small expense. The old gente lived utterly alone and was far too deaf to hear the excitement taking place a good half-mile from the pale blue stucco walls of his mansion; trespassing was half the fun.

He fancied for a second that he might find Oceline by her perfume, but was disabused of the notion immediately. M. Echouaf's fountain was not of the normal sort, with clear water in soaring crystalline arcs—it was a geyser, one of the foul-smelling hot springs that pitted Valtiffe. A fifteen-foot cauldron of natural rock scarred the ground, the boiling water within interrupted by a few old marble statues, quite misshapen and yellowed by the decades of endless scald.

A sort of bridge of rotting logs had been lashed together just above the heads of the statuary. Omer-Guy could not see it easily through the laughing crowd, but it was no more than a foot wide, certainly. Two foxes snarled and barked in the steam, high above the men and women who had bet on their deaths.

He had been to this event before, and with similar purpose. Something troubled him this time, though. Was the crowd a touch more violent? Or was the Crown's silence simply making him nervous? And where was Oceline?

The fountain hissed as a plume rose. A fox yelped. There was coin for the winners and wine to succor the rest.

"All is as the gods wish it," a small voice muttered behind him. One of the standard phrases La Reina's spies used.

The man was taller than Omer-Guy, and younger by half, but lacked a certain sophistication in his bearing. He wore the clothes of a merchant, or perhaps a lesser gente's fourth son: conservative, after the fashion of someone who does not buy clothes often and dares not invest in a style which might change. His tricorn flopped a degree or two on the right side, which threw his entire appearance into asymmetry when he half-smiled.

Omer-Guy smiled back. There was no need to rush things. "The fox's gods must not have cared for him, then."

"Will the water hurt him?"

"Hurt him? My boy, if you were to look into that pool even now, you would see no fox, no fur, no bones. The water has burned him away into mist."

The spy's eyes widened. So he was playing the ingenue, the golden boy out for a bit of sport with the peasants. "A dangerous thing to have open on one's estate, is it not?"

"I would presume that is what the maze is for," Omer-Guy chuckled. "I was just about to search out some wine. Can I offer you one?"

"Ah, no. I left a few bottles back in the maze." His smile appeared again, this time like an imp of the oldfolk. "I left them with a friend of mine. And her friend."

"Well, don't let me distract you from your plans, my boy."

"Certainly not. I needed a moment's respite. They are rather healthful, my friend and her friend. I wonder if another man might help me entertain them."

Omer-Guy took the young man's arm and led him back into the cool dark of the hedges. "Anything for a gente in need, surely. You did say you had wine?"

They walked for several minutes in silence before the spy

unhooked his arm and slunk into the shadow of a trellis. Omer-Guy had to stifle a laugh at the cliché.

"What orders, then?"

"None, Monsieur Bendine." A hardness replaced the foolishness in the spy's mien. "You will no longer be receiving any orders."

Omer-Guy did not react. He knew enough to wait. Spies did love to play their little games.

When it became clear Omer-Guy was not going to respond, the younger man continued. "The Empress thanks you for your dedicated service, but your term as Her Ambassador has come to its end."

The *Empress?* This was supposed to be a meeting with his L'Ombrais handler. "What do you play at, boy?"

"I play at nothing. But if I were free to speak my mind, I might tell you to ask yourself what it is you played at to get yourself in this situation. An Ambassadorship is a lovely position. It is a shame to see you lose it."

He had been fooled. The summons had been made by one of the Empress's agents, not one of La Reina's. They had found him out somehow, and sent this child to sever his ties with the Empire.

"I will not have this," Omer-Guy barked. "I will speak with Mme. Silhou, or M. Danican...."

"You will speak with no one. You are a free man, but you will have no contact with the Court. I wish you good luck."

The young man bowed brusquely and headed off toward the tangle of paths leading to the entrance.

"Was it my son?" Omer-Guy asked.

The young man walked off without answering, leaving Omer-Guy with no companionship but his own thoughts.

The worst had come to pass. His treason had been found out, and he had been cut off. Not killed, surprisingly. Why?

What move was the Empress making? How had he slipped and revealed his secret? And what was he to do now?

These questions filled his mind as his feet took him back to the fountain square. He needed to find Oceline. She could help. But how could he tell her?

The bridge above the steaming geyser creaked more loudly than it had before, and an impassioned scream rose from the crowd as one. Two men sparred on the slippery logs above the fountain.

This was not meant to be part of the event.

The competitors were a well-dressed, neatly-bearded Hvallais in his prime and a wiry young Cadois with black teeth. There were no weapons, though the older man had a pistol at his hip. It was like watching an experienced hunting dog of pedigree squaring off against a scrappy, scarred whelp used to killing rats by the barrelful.

Money changed hands. Even if it wasn't planned, the event was dedicated to greed.

Omer-Guy shoved his way through the bloodthirsty crowd. He had no interest in gambling. He needed to get to Oceline. He could manipulate her into getting as much time as possible with the L'Ombrais Ambassador. He would have to be even more clever than usual to keep from revealing that he had been playing Empire and Queendom against each other. Cadogna had abandoned him, and his other master was now his only option.

He found Oceline stuck in a knot of screeching men, unable to push her way past their tightened arms. A splash and a scream exploded behind him as he caught her frightened eye.

No great game has ever been played solitaire.

Lord d'Alhambere

XXIV
MICHEL

MICHEL DID NOT throw his silver scrying bowl across his office, although he had imagined doing so for days. Perhaps then the fool thing would know he was serious about his endeavor, and would show him some images he could use. He needed the sort of answers he would have found through straightforward espionage had he not been confined to the Pendent Tower.

His divinations showed him little more than odd glances. He needed to know what was happening with the secret of the great waterfall that fed Soucisse across an ocean. All he knew was that the man who won the Forbearance Game was named Quinol—the gossip of the event had reached even the Séminaire's aloof ears.

I must have seen him. I must have seen him when he was in the Secret Chamber, Michel thought. Not only there, but in the alleyway. Aside from the woman in the tricorn, he couldn't remember what the clutch of people he had set on fire had looked like. So much for a scryer's head for images.

Two men walked past his door, heads low in private conversation. There was more and more of that sort of thing in recent days: the Sjónleysi had learned something. One of their members in the field had returned, and had brought frightening news. Michel had seen his brethren gathered in anxious knots of conversation in the halls. Yet still his bowl told him nothing.

He resolved himself to approaching the Principe in his lonely chamber once again. He would feign some small progress for a chance to speak with him. If only he could get outside of the walls of the Tower, he could fix this problem. In a year's time, all anyone would remember was him saving the Séminaire further embarrassment, or worse. But to do that, he needed permission from the man who had imprisoned him.

The very day he had planned to mount the Loose Stair and be heard, a woman walked into the atrium. She was Mistigri, which only added to the surprise on the faces of the Brothers at seeing a woman in these halls. She was dirty from travel and clearly exhausted, but Michel recognized her immediately. He had tried to kill her.

This was the woman who had been with Quinol on the night of the Forbearance Game.

HE APPROACHED HER before anyone else had the opportunity and ushered her up to his office.

She was a quiet person by nature, clearly. She took no effort to fill the air with idle conversation as he poured her a glass of beer and offered her some bread. She sat at his desk—the one chair in the room—after only a few prompts to assuage any fears of impoliteness.

The woman looked around the room as if afraid she might break something. Surely having an audience with a ranking wiseman of the Séminaire would inspire reverential wonder in someone like her, but she seemed even more nervous than that.

"And what brings you here, demoiselle?"

"I have not been in this tower for years," she said. "I expected it to have changed more."

She had been here before? "You were a servant here?"

"I was a student."

Michel blinked at the very concept, but then remembered hearing some oblique mention of a female having studied at some point. It would appear this was she. Her agitation was not due to meeting a Brother, then; what troubled her?

"Then you know we are very slow to change."

"I do. And it is to *prevent* a change that I come to you."

She explained that she had seen the Skyndiferth. That she had even stepped through it and climbed back out. That a Brother had tried to stop her, but disappeared. She had lied to him to stay alive.

"I see." Michel struggled to hide his surprise. The deferential frankness with which she spoke was startling. States could be toppled—*would* be toppled—if this information were made public. If these secrets were a chip with which she meant to bargain, she should have kept them quiet, only alluded to them until she knew she could get something in return.

He knew he needed to be delicate here. He could use this woman. As long as he kept her convinced he had power over her, he could use her.

She continued. "The problem is, I have been caught up in these matters without it being my intention. My team and I..."

"Team?"

"Yes. I work with two men. One of them won your secret."

"Valen Quinol."

Her eyes widened slightly at that. "Yes. Valen Quinol and one other and myself. And his wife, in a way. We didn't mean for this to happen, you see. We want to help."

And that was it. This woman wanted to be forgiven. She wanted an assurance that no harm would come to her.

Michel let his voice raise and curled his mouth into a sneer. "After all that you have done, you claim to want to *help* us now? Lies and threats to a Brother? Our treasure unguarded?" He took a long breath before dropping the façade of anger for one of mere frustration. "But I suppose you can help, after all."

She held his eyes for a long moment. "I would help. Please."

"Who knows about the Skyndiferth?"

"Aside from us, I'm not sure. I think the information may have reached L'Ombre somehow, but only in part. But I don't know for certain. It's only a rumor."

His fingers twitched. A few gamblers, he could handle easily enough. If L'Ombre knew, this was far worse than he had feared. He needed information, and eyes outside of the Tower walls.

"Here is what you are going to do," he said grimly. "You are going to stay close to these friends of yours. If you studied here, you know of the Whisperwind?"

"Yes."

"I will need you to keep me apprised of what is going on. If you have any reason to think the secret of the Skyndiferth is going to be communicated, I need to know immediately. You and your friends are in far over your heads, and I want to give you the opportunity to prove yourselves. Not all of the Brothers would feel this way, you understand. It would be for the best if we kept our communication private."

"It would. Yes," the woman said quietly. "There's only one thing I can say for now. We'll be playing hard. Taking as much money as we can from those who serve Cadogna's interests and losing it to those who do not."

"I see." Not very interesting, and not related to the Skyndiferth in any way he understood. Another tack was needed. "This friend of yours. Quinol..."

"He was a student here. He... he departed shortly before I did."

Michel did not care for rivals. The Mistigri was clearly no threat, but what of this friend? "Tell me about him."

The woman hesitated for a moment, doubts showing clearly on her face. "He's a cardsharp."

"A wiseman turned common cheat?"

"That's right. Just like I did. We're very good. At the Forbearance Game, he worked the best players in town like it was nothing."

"Describe his appearance."

She leaned forward in the chair and put her chin on her hands. "I'm sorry, but that's a problem with Valen. He does a lot to ensure he doesn't look like much of anything. He's got yellowish hair and a small mustache, though he's old enough he should be wearing a beard. Somewhat of a paunch. His dress is unremarkable."

"How did he win?"

"He didn't. He wanted one of the secrets and got it. He got another secret recently, too." She gnawed her lip, frightened. "He learned the truth about Naiibis."

Michel couldn't help a small gasp. "Naiibis... the Enchanter? From centuries ago?"

"Yes."

By every hell.

How much did Quinol know? The man had outwitted poor old Laciaume and Michel long enough to keep from burning in the alley. He had learned about the Skyndiferth, and now about Naiibis's legacy as well? He took what he wanted from the Forbearance Game right under Michel's nose.

Michel would have to play his cards right, so to speak. This woman came to the Pendent Tower for protection. He would have to make sure she earned it, if he offered it at all.

"This is a very unfortunate business, demoiselle. You see it, do you not?"

"I do," she replied, shame in her weird Mistigri eyes.

He let the tension drag for a few moments before giving her a small smile. "You did the right thing by coming to us. We are secretive, of course, but we are not tyrants with our knowledge. You remember this from your studies here, I'm sure. The work of the few…"

"Better living for all," she said with a shy smile. The Séminaire had managed to never descend into clubbishness so far as to adopt a formal motto, but that phrase was as good as one. It came up in nearly every argument on policy.

"Just so. I will talk with the Principe, and we will determine how to proceed."

"Perhaps… no. Well, would it help if I talked to him?"

"I would caution against it. We wisemen do love our strata of authority. Running up the Loose Stair to face the Principe would very nearly be seen as an attack on our institution. You know this."

She sighed in relief. Michel thought that she must have been a terrible gambler indeed, with a face as open as hers.

"Just keep me informed, and I will do the same," he said, ending the matter.

The woman rose and gave him a polite bow. "I will, Brother."

Their conversation done, the Mistigris woman—Teneriève Cassell was her name—left as quietly as she had arrived, though she was perhaps not quite as frightened.

He now had a spy of his own, and knew that L'Ombre might be up to something. The time had come to break the Principe's foolish rule and get back in the field.

EVERY MEETING OF the Sjónleysi took place in a sealed room well below the first floor of the tower, supplied with air via cunningly devised enchantments. There were no stairs leading to it: the only way in was to use the sigil carved in the wall and step through nothing. The magic of sudden movements; the Skyndiferth method.

Sigils had been placed in hundreds of locations around the known world, and all a practitioner of the art needed to do was envision the correct sigil, speak the languages, and take a step to get to any of them.

This was complicated magic, practiced only by the most talented of the wisemen and kept secret from all but those who needed it. When Michel was tapped to serve in the Sjónleysi, he was granted access to the single piece of paper which held the method, and then only under the supervision of the Principe in a small room tucked away in the section of the Tower above the Loose Stair. He learned it immediately, and applied his own languages to it with ease.

Everything had come easily in his early years. His mind held the abstractions of magic like flies in a web. Finding his dream language was as simple as breathing. He rarely erred, and if he did he learned readily from the mistake.

It was matters outside of the Tower that he had yet to master. He was of no great family, was not schooled as the wealthy children were in protocol and treachery. Nor was he a rough case up from the cruel alleys, street-smart and knot-hard. Michel often felt he was still the errand boy even now, running around at an older man's orders.

His intellect had brought him this far. It would serve to bring him farther.

He grabbed a few items from his table, envisioned the Sjónleysi sigil, and spoke the triple-tongue word.

Cold air, much colder than that of his rooms, filled his lungs. His eyes adjusted slowly to the pale light of glowstones. The room was just as he had seen it last, its long table nearly covered with maps and papers, a handful of men arguing over something. The smells of spilled wine and loam suffused the place.

One of the men stopped speaking as soon as he saw Michel: Handar, the Principe, with his short, grayed hair and distant eyes.

"You came," the old man said, his high voice betraying no anger.

The half-dozen other Sjónleysi stopped their bickering as soon as the Principe spoke. Every eye in the room was carefully trained on Michel. He knew what they were thinking—he could have come to hurt them in a fit of rage, or maybe he was going to make a passioned argument for reinstatement, or some other embarrassing display. That is what he would have been thinking, in their place.

He chose to ignore the coming argument and act as if nothing were the matter at all. "I assume you have been busy."

"We have," Handar replied.

"I am glad of it. I am here to offer my assistance."

"It is not welcome."

"Nonetheless, I offer it."

Handar took a long breath before responding. Michel considered that a win.

"Go back to your chambers, Brother," Handar said. "If we need you, we will call upon you."

"Principe, I am at your service. I remind you of my lineage."

Another pause from Handar. Truly this would be a day remembered.

"Your lineage?"

"Yes, Principe. Not my family lineage, of course. Such things matter not here among the wise. My educational lineage."

Handar's eyes flashed with anger, or so it looked to Michel for the briefest of moments. The other men continued to stare, nonplussed.

"There are so very few of us, considering how old Didier was when he began teaching. I believe I was one of less than five who studied with him before he passed. Didier studied Divination under Roysat. Roysat under Scalamand. He under Ressu, he under Hollan, and Hollan apprenticed directly under Naiibis himself."

The tenor of the room changed. The other wisemen broke their stares at Michel and looked to each other in surprise. Handar, though, was as fixed as stone.

Michel continued. "I am one of very few in the world who can say their education came in a direct line from the greatest of our number."

"Not all see him as the greatest," Handar countered, his eyes showing the slightest hint of irritability. "Many see him as the cause of our woes. They say his rashness took us away from the worlds of study and service and into those of politics. They say he changed history for the worse."

"Yes, but he changed it." Michel waved a hand casually. "When you have decided that you can look past your pride and take the assistance of the only Sjónleysi who is of a direct line from the one who started all this, please send for me. I wish only to be of use."

He left then, using the sigil in the hidden room of the upper tower. As he left that closet and made his way back toward his chamber, the air was even colder than before.

They would not listen, of course. Michel was cast out from that body, and no amount of grandstanding would gain him entry again. But that was not what he needed.

Counterintuitively, the Loose Stair was an excellent place to avoid being seen. The noise of either the upper or lower doors opening was enough to warn of any unwelcome eyes, and no one on the ground had vision sharp enough to see what a lone man was up to at that height. There wasn't a soul in the world who could see Michel take the small glass globe from his pocket and hold it up to his eye. A Souvenir.

The glass showed him the first few seconds he was in the Sjonleysi meeting room, before he had been noticed and when the men were still speaking freely. He had hoped that it would be enough to give him something to work from. He couldn't go back out into the world without some direction, something at which to aim.

One of the Brothers had said a name; Omer-Guy Bendine. A man who knew the secret of the Skyndiferth.

A name. But how would he find the person attached to it? All his time in the Sjónleysi had been about watching and reporting, not seeking. And what would he do if he found this person?

He needed help. And after the day's events, he knew just who to go to for it.

Michel pocketed the Souvenir and walked down the Loose Stair, not feeling the wind at all.

One would do well to keep a wary eye open for those who act as confederates in sharp play. If you find yourself at a merry little inn and are approached by two people who claim to never have met, take caution. If a few friends say they happened to find some knucklebones laying around as you journey across the seas, avoid their impromptu game. Perhaps only one is a rascal, but they are both your enemies.

Dishonest Play and Players

XXV
VALEN

VALEN DROPPED A card. The five other players at the table groaned, cursed, or kept silent in accordance with the personae they had chosen for this night's game. Jaq was one of the silent ones, pretending to be too much of an awkward country fellow to fully understand the etiquette of the situation. He played the role well, as Valen saw it. He had caught the young man several times looking in awe at the cut glass chandeliers as he held his cards a few degrees farther out from his chest than he should have. The fine Cadois gentleman seated to Jaq's left had shown no shame when he looked at the poor rube's hand. Valen let him—entitled snobbery was an excellent weakness to exploit.

The café was not an exclusive one, but had done well enough in recent years that white cloth now covered the tables. Valen credited himself with contributing to the establishment's recent success; he played there frequently, and always kept the punchbowl filled for his opponents. These players were as likely to be of old Hvallais shepherd families as from the mercantile Cadois, a mix which Valen found to his liking. All were equals at the table, after all.

All except for the sharps.

Apologizing repeatedly with his speech slurring around the edges, Valen re-dealt, slipping the dropped card to the bottom of the deck. The ability to hold one's drink was one both the Hvallais and the Cadois held in great regard—a sign of strength for the working folk and of being accustomed to luxury for the wealthy. Valen often presented himself as having neither, being a man of finance who made his living with papers and ink. Pride makes a player act a fool more than drink ever could, so Valen gave his adversaries every opportunity to feel superior.

The night's entertainment was fornal, a six-hand partner game in which the trump suit changed mid-hand when an eight wins a trick. Some idle chatter had revealed that three of the players were Cadois citizens and the other—after Valen and Jaq—was not. The full-bearded man owned a home in Hillside, which made him the target of Valen's efforts. The stack of counters in front of the man had grown steadily.

Valen wanted him to leave with a full purse. More money for non-Caddies meant better fences around their homes and better lights on their streets, which in turn meant less reason to be afraid of the dangers of the fighting between the Naughty Knaves and Les Royaux. Less likely to move, less likely to sell. Less opportunity for the Cadois to buy more land and get more votes in the Parliament. And more of a chance that the Empress's long play for Valtiffe would be stopped, or at the very least slowed for now. The forces at play were far beyond Valen's understanding, but he could do some small part to influence life on his little island.

He had nearly finished dealing, with that dropped card going to the bearded man, when he heard a familiar sound coming from the doorway. The jingling of a thin sword on an ostentatious belt, accompanied by heavy boots tromping on the rug. The night's breeze hissed through the open door and the smell of perfume reached Valen's nose, even where he sat at the far side of the room.

Hugues Arbelan wore a frock coat tailored in the contemporary style and dyed yellow with black trim. The three young men who entered with him had not seen the need to dress for the occasion, although Valen doubted their muscular frames would have fit well in coats anyway.

Valen had wondered how long it was going to be before he crossed Arbelan over the tables again. With the hours he was spending in play, it was a simple matter of probability, which increased with every hour.

Arbelan spotted Valen, grinned, and stomped over to his table. Glasses and ashtrays had to be grabbed as he jostled the tables en route.

"Quinol," he sneered, affecting a bow. "May we cut in?"

Whatever clever retort Valen had planned for this moment refused to come to his mind when called. "Of course. This is a public table, after all. The pot is fairly even, though. I'm sure someone at one of the other tables would be happy to give up her seat."

Arbelan's men stood directly behind each of the other players, too close for politeness. Valen and Jaq soon found themselves accepting the excuses of their erstwhile tablemates, who quite suddenly found they no longer had a stomach for play and rose mid-hand.

"We've been playing for some fair stakes, Hugues." Valen shuffled the deck with a disinterested look, but moved all of the eights to the top of the deck by carefully cutting and riffling in ways that looked and sounded like genuine shuffles. His palms sweated as he worked his trickery; he had to confess to himself that Arbelan and his blade scared him. "Everyone's been playing hard in preparation for the Ambassador's Games. Are you sure these children can play?"

Arbelan chuckled and dropped his purse on the table with a loud thud. Assuming it wasn't filled with falses, there was enough in that little bag to buy drinks for the whole bar for weeks. "I'm here to raise the stakes, Quinol. Business has been good recently."

"I'm glad to hear it. I could use a little extra cash."

Arbelan's eyes darkened, and he slapped the purse off the table violently. Coins chimed across the floor in an explosion of wealth. Every game in the room stopped as the players turned to watch.

"No cash." Arbelan's voice was as rough as a surly dog's.

Valen and Jaq exchanged a worried look. There could be no doubt what Arbelan was after.

"I did my part, Hugues," Valen said calmly. He hoped to get people looking back to their own games, or at very least their drinks, without any further commotion. "I did exactly as you asked."

"That you did. I admit it: that you did." Arbelan sat back in his chair and laid a gloved hand on the hilt of his sword. "You did just as you were told, like the good little boy you are."

"And you got what you wanted?"

"And more."

"Then what do you want from me?"

Arbelan's hideous smile revealed pristine white teeth. "You owe me a duel."

The three Knaves chuckled in unison like the chorus in some old play.

Valen shrugged, his eyes on the cards in his hands. "I have heard no challenge."

"Shut your fool mouth or you'll see it slapped across the floor like my money," Arbelan said, not raising his voice. "Here's how this is going to work. We play. If I win, we duel. Tonight at Mark's Pier."

"A stimulating wager. And what if you lose?"

Arbelan's smile stayed frozen in place, but his hand stopped stroking his sword-hilt. "What?"

"If you lose, Hugues. That's how gambling works. If I beat you, I get something I want. Otherwise why would I play?"

The Knave chorus looked at each other, confused. None of them looked at Arbelan. Valen guessed that making eye contact with the boss when he was being embarrassed is a good way to get cuffed, hard.

"By each and every god, Hugues," Valen said with false exasperation. "Did you actually stumble in here to threaten me without thinking past 'If I beat you, I kill you?' No wonder you're not getting anywhere against Les Royaux." He turned to the youths, who had lost most of their self-possession by this point and were all but running out of the room. "Why do you follow this idiot? Hale young men like yourselves would do well on the docks, or even aboard ships. And you'd probably get to keep all your teeth."

The whine of steel attracted a few looks again. Arbelan had half-drawn his sword.

"In truth, though," Valen continued, still cutting and shuffling. "How many weeks' worth of food do you think that pretty coat of his cost? At least enough to buy the three of you nice boots in your own sizes."

The boys looked as if they might faint. Arbelan was breathing so heavily his wig was losing its grip on his scalp. Valen made to get up, but all four of the Knaves stood.

In the brief silence that followed, Jaq cleared his throat. "Think I'll sit this one out, boys."

"You're damned right about that," Arbelan burst. "I know you're one of his. You didn't think I knew, but I know. I know all about your little crew."

Valen nodded a goodbye to his friend. "Goodnight, then. I'm

afraid we won't be able to play fornal now without a sixth, Hugues, and I doubt anyone here would be interested in your company. After all, if they wanted your money they could just pick it up off the floor."

Jaq left without so much as a glance at Valen. Arbelan looked at one of the boys and jerked his head in the direction of his purse. The boy just looked at him in confused fright.

"Pick up the damned coins!"

The boy jumped up and began kicking the coins into piles. Not the most efficient method, Valen thought, but Arbelan's wards weren't known for their mental fortitude.

"There," Arbelan said. "Now we're four. Signaux."

"You still haven't told me what I get if I win."

"Fine. What do you want?"

"I want you to stop the fighting. Keep the territorial lines between you and Les Royaux as they are right now, and pull out of any contested areas. That and keep your ridiculous face out of my sight."

"Then you are a fool indeed, Quinol," Arbelan said. "I could leave this shit café promising all sorts of things, but you would have no way to make me do them."

Valen shrugged again, as if this was all so much childishness. "Perhaps not. But your orphans do." He turned again to the remaining boys. "He tells you he's a gentilhomme, doesn't he? And he tells you he can make you just like him as long as you do as he says. But if he breaks an oath to me, what is to keep him from breaking his oaths to you? He promised you a better life, and all he has given you is enough gruel to survive on and some pretty harsh lessons. Why stay loyal to someone who risks your lives in petty street fights for his own gain?"

"Enough of that." Arbelan let his sword fall back into its sheath. "It won't matter. We'll beat you. I accept the wager."

"And you lads?" Valen asked the muscle-bound boys. "You

will play for these stakes as well? Looks to me like you win either way. Either you get to watch your boss actually use that sword of his for once, or you can stop risking your necks every day."

"They accept too. Deal the cards."

Valen smiled at the boys, who both stared at the table in silence, and gave the deck one last cut.

"Not that one," Arbelan said. He called to the bartender for a fresh deck and tossed a coin across the room. It landed squarely in the bartender's hand—Arbelan may have been an idiot and a brute, but he did have good aim.

PLAYING AGAINST THREE confederates for stakes including one's own life proved remarkably stimulating. Arbelan played as if he had never once thought Valen was as unbeatable as all that. The two boys knew the game well enough to play into their boss's hands, laying down low when an honour would have trumped Arbelan's lead and that sort of thing. A lifetime of avoiding the back of his hand had probably taught them this brand of play.

When the deal came to the taller of the two boys, Valen took notice of the way he held the deck. There existed only a few ways to grip a deck of cards in order to deal from the bottom without being caught, and this boy was using one of the better ones. Valen had to give the boy credit for making it look natural. Even the sound of the cards didn't reveal the sharp play, a common error for people new to the art, and one it took scores of hours of practice to adjust for. If Valen hadn't been looking, he wouldn't have even guessed.

Arbelan had brought his own cheat along. And he thought it would ensure his victory. Ridiculous.

The game had now become a battle between two cardsharps. If the hands being dealt were any indication, Valen was far better than the boy was. Even when a run of truly outlandish hands had been dealt to Arbelan, Valen managed to keep things even. He had the advantage of knowing the game well, of knowing exactly how the boys would have to play to keep Arbelan winning, and his uncanny memory for the cards.

Despite all that, it was only a matter of time before three versus one caught up with him. Arbelan was a terrible player, but the sharp and the other boy played well enough for youths. The addition of someone skilled with false play tilted the scales against Valen, and he knew it.

He began to make mistakes. A small one at first: a finesse gone wrong that cost him a trick he'd planned on taking. Then he miscounted where he had placed the queen of hands in the deck and ended up dealing it to Arbelan instead of himself. He lost his grip at one point and dropped the deck in two messy packets, completely ruining his stocking and forcing him to play the hand without knowing what the other three had.

His magic was of no use to him. He tried hand after hand to summon the cards he needed, but as had so often been the case, he did not succeed. He could sit in his rooms and pull this off all day, but as soon as any stakes were laid he was useless. Perhaps the whole concept was some delusion, some trick he was playing on himself.

This line of thought did not improve his performance. Cursing himself, he used some truly rudimentary cheats. He crimped the top of one of the honours in hopes of spotting it more easily. At one point he slipped a card in his sleeve and held it there until he could put it where he wanted it. Arbelan's noxious smile only grew as the counters stacked up in front of him.

When Valen was down to his last counter, the deal went to the sharp. The bastard gave him a hand which looked like it might have won and then kept the two crucial honours which would undo it to himself. The kid was toying with him.

Valen Quinol, the best sharp in Valtiffe and a very capable signaux player, bested by an amateurish card-bender and two idiots. He was slipping at exactly the wrong time.

Arbelan frowned as Valen rose from his seat. "We'll accompany you to the pier. Too bad you won't get a chance to say goodbye to your wife."

The racing tracks of Penaux were built by a peer of L'Ombre before the Fire War, when that city was not yet a part of Cadogna. Such public works are commonplace now in the time of peergilds, but in that era little value was placed on such public-mindedness. The man who funded the installation, though, managed to pay off the entire place in three years with the earnings from the races. Any peer today would be maligned for such success.

Of Corte and Courtship, Salen

XXVI
TENERIÈVE

THE MARK'S PIER was hardly a pier at all any more, from what little Ten knew of such matters. A few mossy poles stubbing up from the water, criss-crossed with the grayed remains of wooden platforms. Most of the wood had been salvaged long ago, and what was left was hardly enough to support a few people, to say nothing of any freight. The place was a known favorite of the types of criminals who made their deals by moonlight. Romantic types, who saw their degeneracy as freedom from the strictures of society and were all too proud to boast about it. People like Hugues Arbelan.

She had met Jacquemin just outside the café where she had intended on joining him and Valen in their game. This business of pushing money around to prevent the Tipping Point was more than a little on the silly side, considering the powers they were up against, but it did keep the others in public and busy. Hiding and bored would have led to something terrible. When Jaq hailed her in the street and explained that Val was now likely to duel Arbelan, the idea seemed so small. A threat from Arbelan had been what started this entire nonsense. Now the gang leader seemed as insignificant as an ant under a wagon's wheel.

Jaq explained that he was running home to find a sword for Valen and left her in the empty street to figure out for herself what she was going to do. It seemed the Mark's Pier was where the action was going to be, so she headed there. Her new patron in the Pendent Tower would be interested to hear what happened. He seemed interested in just about everything, especially when it came to Valen.

The guilt of passing on information about her friends had kept her awake nights since she first agreed to it. They would be more hurt than she dared imagine if they found out. But if she kept the Brothers happy, she could keep them safe. They were all in well over their heads and too stubborn to be reasoned with. This deceit was painful, but it was the best she could do.

At least the Brother she was dealing with bought the 'scared commoner' routine she ran on him. In all likelihood, she was going to be reporting to him that Valen was dead. He had been so plainly, intensely curious about Valen she feared telling him almost more than telling Margo.

Ten looked up to the clear sky. She called the names of the stars to herself in the language she had grown up with. No matter where she travelled, the stars were ever the same. This season's sky held Ouajen, the Oarsman, whose oars dragged the firmament in its course above the world. She had made something of a personal god of him, and if there was any figure she prayed to it was the silent man who did his lonely job in peace every night.

She would not let Valen die. Not for this. Not for some aging street fighter's pride. She didn't know if she would ever really forgive Valen for taking that damned secret and putting her in this much danger, but she wouldn't see him dead on Arbelan's sword if she could help it. She would kill the rogue first. The

Brothers, the Guard, Parliament, the Empress—none of them would give half a damn what happened to Hugues Arbelan.

Many years had passed since she had learned to use the Whisperwind. It had come back to her with little effort.

She told this Brother what was going to happen. She asked him to teach her the spell that burned hearts, the one that had been used on her outside the Skyndiferth. The one that killed Dusmenil.

The moon had moved several degrees through the sky when five men turned from the street and started the walk down the rickety pier. The Brother had yet to respond. Had she cast the spell incorrectly? Or was the death of Valen Quinol something he was happy to let take place?

Valen looked surprised to see her, but said nothing. Arbelan was accompanied by three young roughs. He didn't spare her more than a glance.

One of the boys knelt by the edge of the pier and drew a sword from beneath the planks. This he handed to Valen with a cruel smirk.

"I hope you have another down there," Ten said, allowing her Mistigri accent to come out in full. All of the men turned to face her. "Yes. Unless you are afraid to fight two novices at once."

Arbelan laughed. "A duel is between two in these lands, woman. No would-be rescuers."

"Yet you bring these three mules."

"I'm not here to debate. Stand aside or be drowned."

Valen took a step between Ten and Arbelan. "There must be some forms to be observed in a situation such as this, Hugues. You know more of dueling than I; how is this sort of situation handled? Surely you have had more than one person trying to kill you at a time before."

"If there's more than one challenger, then they can form a

fucking queue," Arbelan seethed. "So which of you wants to die first?"

Ten pushed Valen out of the way and walked right up to Arbelan. "I'm not waiting. Arm me."

She was close enough to see the stubble under his face powder. He could draw that sword of his and slice her in half before she would be able to react. The danger felt like cold ocean air after a day belowdecks. Shocking and uncomfortable, but bringing a delicious flow to the blood.

"Let's consider this, though," Valen said, one finger in the air. "This challenge was not of the normal type, Hugues, and perhaps the queue rule does not apply. I accepted only because I lost at cards. You did not insult me, nor I you. Neither is the aggrieved party, and neither truly proffered the challenge. I suppose perhaps you did...."

Ten didn't release Arbelan's merciless eyes from her stare. Valen was stalling. Why?

Arbelan turned and looked up the pier, then, and his face fell. Ten followed his gaze and saw several people—dozens, maybe—walking toward them through the dark. Even in the moonlight she could see the white and blue of Les Royaux.

She looked to Valen. He didn't seem surprised. He knew. He had planned this, and hadn't told her. She had been ready to risk her life to fight Arbelan, and he hadn't stopped her. The bastard.

Arbelan and his boys didn't bother putting up a fight as the rival gang swarmed around them. Hands were tied and swords taken with quiet, dispassionate efficiency. As the throng walked back toward the street with their captives, one of the Knaves was left behind with orders to tell Arbelan's second-in-command she would be contacted with terms.

* * *

VALEN AND TENERIÈVE stood alone on the Mark's Pier, with nothing to listen to but the lapping of the river. The entire affair had taken no more than three minutes.

"Ten, do you remember when I got kicked out?"

She frowned at the question. What did that matter now? "Yes."

"I've always remembered what you told me."

"I don't recall." Maybe it would hurt him that she had forgotten. She didn't care.

"I had just pissed in Handar's scrying bowl, and had to get out before they got serious about forcing me to leave. I went back to my room, threw my stuff in a few bags, and headed down the stairs. You were on your way up."

"Yes. I had heard what happened."

"Of course. Of all the vices in that Tower, gossip is the greatest," Valen said with a smirk. "You ran up to see me, and I could barely face you. I knew that being my friend was only going to make things worse for you there. They hardly acknowledged the work you did already, and sent up dozens of others to their honors that were less worthy than you. Now you were going to be associated with a boy who insulted the entire institution.

"I hadn't thought of that when I did it. I expected you to be furious with me for putting you in that situation. You weren't. All you said to me was 'But this is your home.'"

She remembered. She hadn't been able to understand how anyone could intentionally risk the safety of home and hearth. He would be out in the world alone; he had put himself in the situation she feared the most. She should have known better than to fall in with someone who made such poor decisions. She wouldn't be dealing with wisemen and nations now.

"Ten, you weren't supposed to come down here." Valen's voice was barely louder than a whisper. He didn't look at her.

She stared down to the river. "And where would I have been?"

"Anywhere but here. I thought you'd go to Margo."

Back to safety. Back to the sister figure who had taken her in. Was that what Valen thought of her? Always hiding from the world behind the kindness of others?

"I did not even think of it," she said. "I came to help."

"And I thank you, Ten. They would have killed us both. You needn't have risked yourself for me."

Ten drove the heel of her boot down on the rotting edge of a plank, sending a shard of it into the water. "He would not have killed us. He would have fought you first, and I would have tripped him up."

"Not exactly fair play." Valen looked up at last, his eyes sad. "You've been around me too long."

She didn't laugh at the joke. Another splinter cracked off the board and floated away.

Valen sighed. "You've heard of a Penaux Book?"

"No."

He had the good sense not to sound didactic. "It's a maths game, really. Horse races set the odds for each contestant in such a way that the house profits no matter which rider wins."

Ten thought of the Rushed Road, and of the carnival games she saw in the little towns on their festival days. "I have seen such things."

"Well, I set up a little Penaux Book against my dear friend Hugues. When he walked in and made his little wager, I knew I had him. If I won, he would have to stop the fighting—or would at least have some trouble explaining things to his followers if he didn't. If he won...."

"If he won, then Jaq would go and tell the Royaux that he knew where to find the man all but alone," Ten said. "You planned this."

"We did," Valen said. "We didn't want to involve you. We're all carrying around enough secrets these days."

"You were not protecting me. You knew I would tell you not to do it. Yes. You truly are a magnificently bad liar, Valen."

She left him then. Her walk back to her rooms in the damp night air gave her plenty of time to go over the things she might have said differently.

In the end, Valen had been dishonest with her. Who was to know what else he was hiding from her? She had thrown herself into danger for a man who lied. For her *friend*.

So much for community.

When the Whisperwind brought a rote response back from the Brother she was working with, she replied with a great deal of information.

In the months which followed the Forbearance Game, Quinol was celebrated at every table in the city. Oddly, the folklore has it—and the wager logs of the clubs show—that he rarely won. He played constantly, but seemed to only ever break even.

Lives of Gamesters

XXVII
RIA

THREE WEEKS HAD lumbered by since Ria's arrival in Saut-Leronne, and all she had to show for her labors there were a cheap sword, a thousand unasked-for opinions on how she should run her tournament, and a persistent stomachache from eating under-salted lamb for most of her meals. The sun had all but forsaken the city. Her laundress had the temerity to suggest that Ria may not have brought a sufficient number of wet weather coats. News from home arrived regularly, but none of it contained answers to her questions. Scolding letters from her mother came with some frequency. The price of bringing shame to the name of 'Alodesal' had been mentioned.

She was, in short, disinclined to accept an invitation to another foolish dinner party.

The letter was on the whitest paper she had seen since leaving Torreçon, and easily noticeable among the stack of Ambassador's-Games-related mail she had tossed on her desk. A corner of it stuck out from the pile, a blade of white that caught her eye again and again as she tried to focus on the morning's papers and their listings of homes that were coming up for sale, her research on the Tipping Point. The reading was as boring as any Ria had ever done, especially as she knew few of the names of the sellers. She looked up from it several times a minute. Each time, that invitation distracted her.

Lady Oceline de Loncryn—a wealthy Cadois pawn who was rumored to be the front-runner for the mayoralty of Saut-Leronne come the next election, as well as being involved with the Cadois Ambassador—certainly knew how to entice her; her letter had promised a night of card games after the dinner hour had passed. Most invitations she had received had included similar promises, begging the honor of having the Gamesmaster of Torreçon grace their carré tables et cetera, but De Loncryn had stated that the party would leave her home and descend upon a nearby tavern for the night's entertainments.

Playing with the city's well-to-do had left Ria impossibly bored. They all acted as if every turn of the card was fraught with some political meaning, and she had long since exhausted any pleasure she took in manipulating their precious opinions of themselves. It was dreary work, really. She had to be sure to make at least one casual double-entendre insulting the Cadois Empress, or her hosts would be disappointed. She had to tease merchants with an openness to trade, succor the gentry with acknowledgment of their superiority, suffer flirtations from well-meaning eligibles, and all in the language of the game.

At first she had taken some enjoyment in the intellectual challenge of using the cards of the Satique deck for her bon mots, but even that small pleasure had waned. The limited suits and repetitive court cards offered less opportunity for witty improvisation than the Fanzago, and one can only call so many drunk noblemen 'knavish' before coming to detest the joke and oneself for making it.

A night out among the paisans, though, sounded like a warm breeze. And perhaps she could learn something about this alleged Ombrian ship trolling the waters off La Ruse. The Corte had not seen fit to inform their Ambassador about the matter despite her repeated inquiries, and had in fact told her in no uncertain terms to stop asking. Naturally Ria's plan to involve herself, and thus L'Ombre, in the matter of the Tipping Point was not the only iron the Corte had in the fire, and she would never expect to be made fully aware of the more clandestine endeavors. Still, she would have preferred to have known.

She called her manservant and responded to the invitation. Ria knew full well De Loncryn had some design to the offer, but she could not bring herself to care. Let the woman try whatever she had planned. If Ria spent one more night engulfed in the scent of overpriced wig powder, she would go mad.

THE ONE BUILDING on Gabot Avenue not built from stone was a tavern which shared its name with the street. This was the destination to which Lady De Loncryn paraded her guests after they had dined, a three-story building of wood and plaster with a single window of very old glass.

Ria walked alongside Omer-Guy Bendine, with whom she had taken up a pleasant acquaintance in the weeks since her arrival. As Ambassadors, they had naturally been thrown together at many soirees and official meetings of introduction. He was a pleasant-enough fellow, with the impeccable manners and talent for conversation that one would expect from anyone in their line of work, but it was his status as an outsider that drew her to his company so readily. At least she had someone with whom she could complain about the wine.

"The tavern takes its name from the street?" she asked, gesturing to the cracked paint of the sign above the door.

"The opposite, in fact, Dona," Bendine replied in his languorous Cadois accent. "This tavern is one of several that claim to be the oldest in Saut-Leronne. It was here on the hill before the avenue was more than a sheep path. The local legend is that the avenue was built to manage the traffic. Very good beer, they say. Brewed in the same vats they've been using since before we Cadois started to emigrate here."

"Before? The name certainly sounds Cadois."

Omer-Guy smiled at that and leaned in close to speak quietly. "As with so many names here, it changed over time. It was *gabbathi* in Hvallais: 'The Trickster.' A very rough haunt that boasted freely about its unscrupulous rigging of the games played there. The last few generations of owners have done their best to let that particular pearl of local legend fade into obscurity, as you might imagine."

"A true piece of local history, then," Ria laughed. Not too loudly; it wouldn't do for her host to think she was overly charmed by the man. "How lovely of Lady de Loncryn to bring us here. I would have thought she would have preferred something more in line with her tastes."

"Oh, they carry a very capable selection of Cadois reds here. One does not keep a tavern open for hundreds of years without keeping up with one's patrons."

The smells of tobacco and cooking meat—beef, not lamb—filled the dark tavern, and Ria took a long, appreciative breath. At last, somewhere she could play in peace.

Ria and Bendine cut in at a signaux table and made to introduce themselves, but were met with friendly laughter before they could begin.

"There's not a bar in Saut-Leronne that doesn't know you two," a plump old gente in a lovely brocaded gold waistcoat declared. "We're honored to play you. It will be like your Games are here a few weeks early!"

The players rose and offered their names, which Ria was disappointed to learn all had titles in front of them. All but one, the last to speak: a quiet-voiced paisan who gave his name as Valen Quinol.

Ria did not hide her interest at meeting a fellow player. "Quinol? You are the man who won the last Forbearance Game, correct?"

"Dona Alodesal, it will ever be a source of shame to me that the very first words I spoke to you are to beg your forgiveness," he said. "Yet beg I must. Forgive me, but I believe you may have received some incorrect information. I did not win the game. I had the good fortune to take third place."

The first man who had spoken laughed again. "Don't be coy, Quinol. You won the most valuable secret ever played for. In a season, no one will remember who won that night, but we'll all still be talking about your twenty-thousand livre piece of paper."

"It was *fifteen* thousand," Quinol replied, exasperated. "And I assure you, it will be surpassed soon enough."

Ria noticed a tiny change in Bendine's bearing. He was sitting nearly motionless, and had been since she'd mentioned the Forbearance Game. It was a small tell, but a tell nonetheless.

"I see." She smiled at Quinol and motioned generally to the room. "And I thought The Gabot was the only local legend with which I would become acquainted tonight."

The players all laughed at that, Quinol shyly and Bendine perhaps a touch too loud, and got to the business of play.

Ria had made a study of signaux in an effort to better understand the character of the odd island nation to which she was Ambassador. Finding people to play in Torreçon had been no challenge—her casino entertained its fair share of enthusiasts who took interest in the history of games. This was a game without partners, a rarity in the trick-taking family, and no extra points were given for holding honours. Some of the Cadois affectations, like dealing four cards at once instead of one at a time, had made their way into the game over the centuries, but the core game was practically untouched. Signaux favored skill, memorization, and interpretation over getting a fortunate deal. This was a game for people who hated luck.

Before the years of Cadois immigration turned the nation mercantile, Valtiffe was a land of fishermen and shepherds living under the constant threat of volcanic activity. Bad weather could kill, either by drowning or by the slow starvation of a year's bad crop; disease could turn a lucrative herd to naught. Luck was more likely to be bad than good in Valtiffe. Their favorite pastime reflected their distrust of it, and rewarded a player clever enough to do without it.

They played for over an hour before two of the players decided they had lost enough for the night and left the table. Ria allowed herself the luxury of good play and lost her frustrations in the cards. Bendine played well enough, but had not won much. Most of the winnings had gone to the other woman at the table, a garrulous young Hvallais who owned a home in the dock district. Quinol had broken even.

She thought she saw Quinol holding the deck in an odd way when he dealt. The difference was subtle, but after a while there was no mistaking he had his small finger pressed against the bottom on certain cuts. This was one of the grips that cheats used, and only the *best* cheats.

A flush of warmth rose from her neck. Even mired in espionage and statecraft as she was, there was still nothing she hated more than a cheat.

"I wonder," Quinol said. "Do you prefer to play carré, Dona Alodesal?"

"I am happy to continue with signaux," she replied. What was this dastard up to? Did he truly think he could cheat her at carré?

"And you are very kind, Dona. But as your hosts, we Valtivans should take care not to force our ways upon you, especially when you are meant to be taking your pleasure. If I had known we would meet, I would have brought a Fanzago deck."

"What luck, then," Ria said with a warm grin. *To the hells with it.* "I have one on me."

"Would you do us the honor?"

Ria gave a brief refresher of the rules as she shuffled her brother's enchanted deck and dealt the first hand. Her opponents' play was unsurprisingly weak, and they took several hands to remember some of the more obscure rules. Still, it was indeed enjoyable to get back to her favorite game. She even risked calling a card or two, using the secret thoughts her brother had taught her to request a specific card from the deck. She did this sparingly, of course, but enough to make the game more interesting.

She must have been distracted, though; several times when she called a card, it didn't come. That had never once happened before. Had she had too much decent wine? She had not, but still the cards rejected her. Was the magic wearing thin? Was that even possible?

This unusual problem occupied her until the fifth hand of the third game, when Bendine played oddly. He placed the Sailor next to the three of Acorns, and let the corners overlap. An unremarkable play, but the placement stood out. In the Ombrian language of espionage, letting the Sailor touch another card was a declaration: it meant that the player was part of the great game of nations. A spy.

Presumably this was just chance. Cards touching was not uncommon, especially in fast play. Ria played the standard verification response, sliding her next card into position with her first two fingers. On his next turn, Bendine confirmed by placing the tip of his finger on the first card in his hand before he played.

So the Cadois Ambassador was a spy for L'Ombre. That was a well-placed pawn, certainly. Unless Bendine had learned the Ombrian card language somehow and was reeling her in. At this point, she had no choice but to play along.

Over the course of the next several hands, a silent conversation took place beneath the regular table talk.

Danger.

What kind?

Physical danger.

Immediate?

Unknown.

Have you been made?

No.

Other player is dangerous.

Other player has information.

I can protect you.

No.

Yes.

No.

Am I at risk?

The exchange took longer than it should have, since Ria's deck wasn't listening to her. The card language was meant to take hours, to fit seamlessly into a night's games without becoming obvious, but a man was begging for her help, and she couldn't respond as quickly as her enchanted deck should have allowed her to. What was going on?

She was in the middle of asking her next question when a stir rose in the place. Someone outside ran by the window at a sprint, bellowing a single syllable: "Fire!"

Everyone in the tavern jumped up, looking around fearfully for signs of disaster. There was no smoke, and no glow of flames. Ria saw an odd purple light through the cracks in the floorboards overhead, presumably tinted by a thin carpet of some kind. Bendine froze in his chair and closed his eyes.

"Omer, we must go!" Ria shouted. She shook his shoulder, but he did not move.

"Don't run," he muttered. "It won't matter."

Most of the patrons were doing just that, scrambling for the door. Quinol stepped up to stand on the table and yelled to them.

"Not the street! Get out of the street! Go to the back of the building!"

One of the waitstaff screeched back at him. "There's no door back there!"

"Then we'll break down a wall! Go now! The alley is safer!"

No one listened. There was smoke now, and heat from above. Ria scooped her cards off the table, swearing when they stuck on the felt.

"Forget the deck, Dona," Quinol jumped down next to her. "I know someone who can mark you up a new one."

"It's... it's a family heirloom."

"It's three years old, starting to show some wear, and certainly not worth your life. Come with me."

Bendine had just warned her about this man. He was dangerous. This was an assassination attempt, or perhaps a kidnapping, for an Alodesal's ransom. "To die in the larder?"

"No. This way will be better than the street. You must believe me."

"Goodbye, Monsieur Quinol. I hope you burn."

With the last of her magic cards now in hand, she darted for the door and out into the street. Flames lashed up the outside of the east wall, an unnatural blue fire which started on the bricks of the avenue and poured unhindered up the walls. The top floor was in flames.

She stayed and watched. No bucket brigade came. A witch woman called for rain, but it took too long. The fire consumed the entire building in less than a quarter of an hour.

There was no way to know if the assassin Quinol made it out through whatever back passage he had planned on. Perhaps Bendine had come to his senses. More likely Quinol murdered him. Lady de Loncryn was in tears, her story-high wig on the ashen ground.

Ria had no allies, no support, and no information. But she had a name.

Take care which of the players at the table you ally yourself with, even for a single hand. Signaux is a game of all against all.

Signaux Argot, Salen

XXVIII
VALEN

ANY CITY—LIKE any person—that reaches a certain age has its share of stories written on its body. The sun-cracked posts along the river bank just to the north of town told of the old docks, before the new bridge. A fashion for yellow cobblestones marked the streets built in a particular ten-year period. Limestone lumps, most no larger than a cat, found at odd points along the main thoroughfare were once street markers carved in dedication to the many gods for a festival whose meaning was all but lost to history, any semblance of the once-stern faces and gaily dancing bodies long worn away by rain and wind.

The alley behind The Gabot was well-known to be haunted. A witch had left the city proper to live in a bower in a small stand of trees. She'd kept a benevolent eye on Saut-Leronne and cast weather spells to keep the river healthy. Once every few years she'd returned to town on some errand known only to her, and on one of these visits she'd died in the alley. Tales vary as to the cause, be it hatred of witchcraft, general lawlessness, or some dreadful misunderstanding, but they all agree in one detail: she was trampled by a horse. Anyone who had the bad luck to encounter the Gabot Ghost would die of a horse-related accident within three seasons.

Valen, singed at the edges and exhausted from kicking his way through the plaster and lath of the tavern's kitchen wall and all but carrying a willful Cadois Ambassador out into the damp night air, would have been happy to see the poor old specter. Let him be trampled six months hence—at least he'd live longer than the next few minutes.

The fire-ward he had placed on his cloak after George Alley had kept the worst of the flames off him and the Ambassador. After having seen some Séminaire bastard pull blue fire from the ground, he had thought it best to be prepared. If only he knew some enchantment that might increase the size of his lungs, he might have a better chance of escape. At least the muddy, unpaved alley wasn't on fire. His guess had been correct—the Brothers' enchantment was related to the brick roads somehow.

The heat of the blue fire was still bearing on his neck when Bendine collapsed, this time showing every indication of never moving again.

"She'll win," he groaned. "It doesn't matter. She'll win."

Valen congratulated himself on not kicking the man. "Ambassador, we really must be going."

"The secret. The one you won. Do you know what it is?"

"Do you?"

"I wish I did," Bendine gave him a small smile. "It wouldn't matter in the end, perhaps, but I would know what it is I'm going to die for."

"If you would quit lounging on the ground like a mongrel, you might live yet."

"No. I have angered the Séminaire. You remember what they did after the Forbearance Game, yes?"

Valen's head spun for a moment. This was unexpected. "You were there?"

"I heard."

"From the boy?"

"The rifleman."

"So you killed one of theirs," Valen stated. "That's why they want you dead."

Bendine shook his head. "The spice in the cake, perhaps. No, I stole their secret. I am the only one who knows it, or so they think. I gave their secret to L'Ombre. Do you hate me for it?"

"No," Valen said. "I hate you for making me stay here."

"I make you do nothing. Go."

"I'm not leaving any more people to get hurt by this affair. Gods, you Cadois really do love to whine. Get on your feet and we'll discuss this all over some warm punch back in my rooms."

"And your rooms will be destroyed by the anger of the wisemen. No. I stay. I would have stayed in the Gabot. It will make no difference. She will have her way."

"Dona Alodesal?"

"Ha! No, friend. The Empress. Empress Oceane Caraliere de Flechard, long may She reign!"

Valen's heart lurched and sank deep into his stomach. Then this game was for even greater stakes than he'd feared.

The Ambassador straightened his cuffs, frowned at the result of his efforts, and sighed heavily. "The house always wins, is it not so? Like they do at the horse races, where the house makes a profit no matter which nag comes in first.

Valen nodded. "A Penaux Book."

"Ah, not so savage as your countrymen, I see. A pity we meet so late. The Empress, she had made a Penaux Book of this secret of the Séminaire, and I was too much of a fool to see it. They said nothing to me of this secret which was so important. They are not impatient for it. They do not seem to care about it at all.

"You see, she knew. The Empress must have known I am a

spy for L'Ombre. She did not want the secret for herself. She wanted L'Ombre to have it."

Here was someone with the answers Valen had been doing without. It was clear he wouldn't be leaving without delivering his lecture, anyway. "Why?"

"Power, for one thing, and no surprise there. Power over the Séminaire. They are too strong to be kept outside of the Empire. The long game of buying up the property, and thus the votes, may work or may not; she needed another plan. This secret in the seas outside of La Ruse, it must be related to the Brothers. Nothing else in Valtiffe has such value. The Séminaire has some power over her, and this secret is the source of it. This much I have guessed, and some little of it I have been told."

He was right about that, the clever fellow, but Valen did not correct him. "The secret isn't in the seas, but it is water. Séminaire magic allows the fountains of Soucisse to flow."

"Ah! Of course! Yes, this fits. Such a public display. Yes, this is just her game. And now I see the truth of it. Of what she really wants from all this."

"Which is?"

"War, M. Quinol. A justifiable war. A war for which her citizens would die happily. The crown has wanted a reason to attack L'Ombre for generations, but they are far too canny to provoke us. So she has set a trap for them, and I, idiot that I am, have sprung it.

"Let us say L'Ombre finds whatever is on this map, then tells the world what they have found. Very good. Proof the Séminaire has too much power over the throne. She has justification to take over Valtiffe for the good of all. And L'Ombre has broken the treaty, and has opened themselves up for retaliation. And with the wisemen under her control, who could oppose her?

"Or let us say L'Ombre simply steals it, or destroys it, but does so in silence. Now the fountains dry up. The fountains discovered by Naiibis! The Séminaire must have done this, yes? So she takes over Valtiffe and the Brothers. And just place the right idea in the right mind, and a connection with L'Ombre will be made. The people, hearing this over wine at their taverns, will think they know the truth and will back the war.

"And if they destroy it publicly? Well, then, L'Ombre has drawn first blood. We must defend ourselves. You see, she wins no matter the outcome. There is no course of action we can attempt. She will have Valtiffe, she will have her war, and many, many people will die."

Ignoring the wrenching pain in his knee, Valen leaned down and forced the man to some approximation of his feet once again. "Let us leave the prognostication to the wisemen and witches, Ambassador. I am quite sure death will find us right quick if we do not leave the Hill."

Bendine did not respond with more fatalism, much to Valen's surprise. Instead the man began to scream and clutch his breast. He wriggled out of Valen's grasp and fell to the ground to writhe in breathless agony.

"My boy." Bendine was trying to speak, but could only manage screams. "Oscar. Please. Please."

The man was dying of exhaustion right at Valen's feet, just as Dusmenil had done. Whatever Brother was involved in this madness was killing him. And Valen was likely next. Bendine was gone—perhaps the death spell could only be used on one person at a time. He might escape if he moved quickly.

But only for now.

"I would see you, Brother," Valen called to the air. "We are fellow Séminarians after all. Perhaps we suffered the same courses together at some point. Consider it a reunion of alumni."

The man who stepped out from a shadowed rear doorway some twenty feet away appeared far too young to have been a student at the same time Valen was. Considering the many impossible things Valen had been witness to recently, though, he had abandoned any reliance on his senses. This mop-haired young fellow muttering his evil spell might have been a thousand years old for all he apparently knew about the workings of magic.

Bendine's suffering ended quickly, which Valen had to count as a blessing. Now the boy looked at him. The wiseman did not speak, or make to move. He simply regarded Valen with obvious anger.

"You've killed enough, son," Valen said. "We never took any oaths for this."

The young man sneered. "*You* did not, no."

"How does this further the study of magic? A man dead in an alley. The L'Ombrais Ambassador put at risk. Lady de Loncryn. To say nothing of the rest of us. A piece of Leronnian history burned..."

"I do not answer to you, Valen Quinol," the man said, growling like a beaten dog let loose. "A man too stupid to learn from the masters. A gambler. A popinjay. You would have done well to pay heed to your betters; you might have seen the wisdom in steering clear of their affairs."

"Why haven't you killed me, then? You appear to have mastered the art of assassination via ventriloquism. Why delay?"

The Brother grimaced and looked away. Valen watched the muscles in his hands tense, the movement of his chest quicken as he drew shorter breaths. If he was at the card table, he would push now, as hard as he could.

"What is it you need from me, boy?"

The wiseman looked up at him, some of the hatred gone from his icy eyes. "You are a rogue."

"I do not bear insult easily, friend. Not unless there's a wager involved."

"No, you have *gone* rogue. You left the Séminaire."

"I did. Quite willingly."

"All that knowledge. All of the secrets of the ages. You threw it away for pride."

"I threw it away because those old men are hypocritical fools," he said. It felt good. Valen had not known how much he had wanted to explain himself to a fully-vested Brother before. "They resisted any true advancement of the art. The only ideas which were given any credence were their own. I wanted to do something new. Something unique and untried. They forbade it."

A look of desperate frustration crossed the Brother's face. "Do you not now see why? The Skyndiferth is a liability, Quinol. Look at Naiibis, who turned his knowledge of the earth's hot blood into a weapon more powerful than any other ever known. Every new school of magic ends in danger and death. We are not diplomats. We are scholars, and men of politics manipulate us so very easily."

"Men like this one?" Valen nodded to Bendine's dead eyes. "I'm afraid there is a fairly glaring error in your argument."

"You know what is happening here."

"I do. And considering your moves so far, I am still lost as to why I haven't joined Bendine in death just yet."

"You won the Forbearance Game."

"I did not win..."

"Laciaume and I both tried to stop you. Two wisemen of no small ability. But you won Dusmenil's secret. Then you fooled your attackers. You escaped our fires."

"And my address is easily found by asking around. You could have muttered your death spell from the street and killed me in my sleep. Why didn't you?"

"I... I thought you could aid me."

This Valen did not expect. "Aid you in murdering the innocent?"

"You know this world. The world outside of the Séminaire. You have out-thought everyone with whom you have matched wits."

"Not everyone, apparently. I'm standing here getting cold waiting for you to murder me." He emphasized the word 'murder.' The boy was having some crisis of conscience, of how he viewed himself. If Valen could exploit that...

"The Principe. The Corte of L'Ombre. Parliament. The Empress herself. The great powers of the world. I cannot discover how to do this. I must keep the secret from reaching... I am not even sure who, now. I do not know who knows it. All I can do is stem the flood where I can."

"By killing men like rats in the streets."

"I have had no choice."

"Again, we differ," Valen stepped closer. He wasn't going to be able to run. The only way out was to outplay him. "Do you know how I learned about Naiibis? I read a book from Dusmenil's library. I had seen it in a scry, and I bought it at auction. And I didn't kill a single man. You didn't even consider the rest of Dusmenil's library, did you? If you were cleverer, perhaps you could have found solutions that don't involve burning messenger boys alive."

"The boy lived," Michel was shaking his head, eyes widening. "He lived, did he not?"

"Because you failed."

"And who might he have told? He could have copied it down himself and... or did he have time enough?"

"You can't even keep that straight, can you? How did the Séminaire ever allow you to get involved in such things?"

"I didn't know..."

"You didn't know, and you *don't* know. You have no idea who knows about the Skyndiferth. You might as well just incinerate the entire city. Did you ever pick up Naiibis's methods? You're a dab hand at lighting streets on fire."

At the mention of Naiibis's name, the wiseman gathered his wits. He stood straighter and faced Valen with a glare. "I am at that. But I don't need to kill everyone. You can help me. Help me to stop the secret getting out. You've made a life of deceptions and trickery. You must be able to find a way."

At last: an out. "I will need time to think on it," Valen said. "But I can help. If it will stop the killing, I will help. It doesn't have to be this way."

"Think quickly, Valen Quinol," the Brother said darkly. "You are a liar and a sharp wit. But I will destroy you, your wife, everyone you know if you try to play me."

Valen thought better of leaving with some sly quip this time. As he turned his back on the murderous wiseman, he thought Jaq would be proud of him.

Even when the game seems to be lost, you may find the card you need in your partner's hand.

Llewell, J., *Beaufils Wisdom*

XXIX
VALEN

"It comes down to this," Margo stated. "Are we clever, or are we violent?"

Valen and Margo sat at the ink-stained table in their kitchen with a bottle of wine and a single taper flickering against the dark. Another late night, with Valen having once again avoided death by a very narrow margin. His clothes still reeked of the Gabot fire, and his injured shoulder felt as if it might have been further damaged by the night's exertions. If he had not chosen such an idle occupation, he might have understood the workings of the human form better.

His understanding of the workings of the human mind and heart were faring similarly.

"We are not violent, Margo. At least, we do not want to be."

"And yet."

Valen frowned. "Aye. And yet."

"I find myself thinking we should bring the fight to them," Margo said. "Jaq has a chip on his shoulder; I'm sure he could be convinced. One good windstorm could topple their damned Tower."

"The 'chants are too strong for that. But..." Valen caught himself following her line of thought and stopped himself.

Margo frowned. "Do you see? Look what has become of us. I hate myself for it, but how else can I react? You can't stop a fire with a marked card."

"The bastards," Valen muttered. "They enchanted the whole city to burn at their command. It's something in the bricks of the roads. Sickening. Gods, who knows if they've done it to other cities, too? Every grain of sand in Soucisse might be magicked, for all we know. And we don't know a damned thing about what the Brothers in L'Ombre are up to. They could be enchanting people's fucking *teeth*."

The candle flickered at Valen's outburst. He sighed heavily and gave Margo an apologetic look; her parents were asleep in the next room, after all. Her parents, who had left their home because the Empress was making small moves to win her large play.

"It's all too much." He put his forehead in his hand. "Damn Arbelan. We may have ended his war, but damn him nonetheless. Damn him for getting us involved in this."

"Damn him for many things." Margo poured the last of the wine as she spoke, equal amounts in both glasses. "But how could he have known? How could any of us? There is only one action which bears any blame, and it is mine."

"Yours?"

"Aye, Valen. I told you to keep Dusmenil's secret. If you hadn't, if you had just let those brigands steal it, our involvement would have ended. The Brothers would have no reason to come after us. We would have known nothing. We would have been no threat. But I wanted more. More information is always better—so I have always said. This is the first case where I think I was wrong about that. Saints, I don't even know what I was thinking of *doing* with the damned secret when I had it. I just wanted it."

Valen waited for her to finish, as much as it pained him. How long had Margo been suffering this way, blaming herself for these ills?

"They still would have come after us," he said. "This Brother: he is a cornered fox, lashing out in any direction he can find. He actually asked me for help."

"You? Why?"

"He said something about not understanding the world. Not understanding how it works. The maniac is feeling the same way we are, it seems."

Margo looked at him doubtfully. "What did you tell him?"

"I played for time. I told him I would consider it."

"And will you?"

"I don't know. Make peace with the Séminaire when every time I look they are trying to kill me? Knowing what we know now?"

"I doubt it would matter," Margo said. "Our problems are bigger than the intellectualists in the Tower. You know, I don't think anyone in my family has ever even seen an Empress. Generations of gentes, and not one has had the honor. Now we're at our kitchen table trying to guess at what She'll do."

Valen chuckled. "And perhaps She is doing the same right now. Sitting on a floating palanquin, rubbing Her temples as She and Her consort puzzle out our next move."

"Well, if She has any ideas, I would welcome them," Margo threw up her hands in mock despair. "Can't you Skyndiferth your way over there and ask?"

"Would that I could, my dear, but there does appear to be a fairly substantial gap in the education with which I was furnished at Séminaire."

"Useless man," she teased. "I should have married a clark."

"Aye, at least your parents might have been happy then."

"Oh, I doubt that. Father hates clarks. 'Too much ink, not enough spine,' he says."

"And here we are, as much spine as you please and no idea how to proceed," Valen said, ruining the moment's mirth. He didn't have as much spirit for it as he had thought. "You mustn't blame yourself, Margo. We all wanted that secret."

"All but Ten," Margo sighed.

"Aye."

They sat in quiet for a while, and Valen thought about Tenerière. Had she been right after all? The poor woman would do anything to avoid getting in trouble, and now she was in as much danger as the rest of them. All her fears about these matters had come to pass. She was going to lose a home all over again if this continued, or worse.

Naiibis. Valen's mind wandered to the old wonder-worker. The liar. How many had he killed with his damned volcano? How long would the tragedy go on? How could the Mistigri, without a home and reviled everywhere, ever rebuild? The bastard had killed an entire people.

It was easy to think of the Mistigri as separate, as other from himself. With a tragedy so great, distancing oneself seemed the only way to be able to understand it without going mad. But Ten didn't have that choice. She lived it every moment, and was made to suffer for it by the very people who had benefited from the end of the war.

By knowing Ten, Valen had stopped letting the language decide his thoughts—the very term 'Mistigri' obscured the truth: that these were *people*. When a terrible thing happened to the citizens of Valtiffe, or even of Cadogna, there was no separate term used for them. When a sudden storm overwhelmed a dozen fishing ships off the coast, everyone said 'those poor people.' But when discussing the Fire War, the phrase was always 'the poor Mistigri.' Always a step removed.

Had that distinction allowed Naiibis to see his action as noble? He was saving people from the advancing Ombrian army at the expense of a few thousand *Mistigri*. Could he have done the same if it were a few thousand 'citizens?' 'Cadois?' 'Allies?' 'People?'

Valen was a wiseman. A fallen Brother, but a Brother just the same. He knew the power of language better than most. Words had power. Words could kill. And secret words all the more.

"We have to fight them, Margo," he insisted, hardly above a whisper. "There is no running from this. No tricking my way out. My selfishness, my focus on my own idiotic plans, has brought only pain. That's what got my family hurt. And now, whether we should have or not, we have learned frightening things. Things I can't live with knowing if I don't act."

Margo's eyes were steely in the waning candlelight. "Nor I. But we must do this as we have done all else: with preparation, with a plan, and by being many shades smarter about things than anyone else."

"Bendine thought the Empress could not be beaten. She had made a Penaux Book, and would get her way no matter the outcome."

"Bendine is dead. We are not."

"Aye, poor soul," Valen said. "Dead because a single Brother wished it. Caught in this maze the mighty of the world have laid out for us."

Margo reached across the table and took Valen's hand, not in affection but in earnest. "They would kill us, too, my love. Be it burned by the Brothers or tried and hanged by one nation or another, they will try to kill us. The information we have is too valuable. It was bad luck that brought it to us. And we are luck's masters."

"Aye," Valen agreed. He knew the forces he was playing against would win in the end. The house always wins. But he would deal them a blow before they had the chance. "I have the beginnings of a plan. There is only one way to take away a word's power, and if we are careful, we might do just that. If we can afford another taper, I would stay up and put our strategy together."

Margo smiled; a sad smile, but not completely without mirth. "I suppose one more won't be the end of us. Let's see if the game is worth the candle."

"I miss the days when we would sit up drinking wine and planning for our casino," Valen said wistfully. "You always had such fine ideas for bringing people in."

"And your thoughts on the décor were inspired, Valen. But first, let us face off with the great powers of this world."

"Always the practical one, my love."

Knowing the statistics, working out the numbers, reading the board—all of these are valuable skills for success at blots, but none as much as learning to discern what your opponent is trying to do.

The History of Blots, Salen

XXX
RIA

THE LIGHT FROM the candles on Ria's desk cast shadows across the face of the messenger girl Juan had escorted into the chamber. The hand he had gripped around her upper arm looked like the talons of some beast of folklore. The girl's lips were quivering, and her eyes darted around the room wildly.

Ria smiled, but did not tell Juan to release her. "Please forgive me. This is not the sort of greeting one should expect when coming to my rooms, but my man here is very ardent when it comes to security, and he tells me he hasn't seen you running messages before tonight."

After the attempt on her life at the Gabot, Ria had directed Juan to bring any visitors directly to her for interrogation. She had not needed to tell him that she preferred they be afraid when they got to her.

The girl made a tiny whimper. "I just bring 'em, milady. I mean, Dona!"

"Of course. And who sent this one?" Ria held a magnificently white envelope between her fingers.

"I don't rightly know, my... Dona. She looked fancy. I was up on Gabot and she gave it to me herself."

Ria widened her eyes and looked at Juan. The servant smiled, a rare thing.

"The Lady de Loncryn," she gasped. "How I have hoped for this letter! We have not spoken since we survived that terrible fire. I do hope she is well. How did she look?"

"She looked well, Dona," the girl managed.

"A little overdone, I imagine," Ria chuckled cruelly. "Too much makeup, not enough bodice?"

"I..."

"Would you say she looked like a girl of fifteen? And was she dressed like a street urchin? And did she affect a ridiculous peasant accent?"

The girl's terrified demeanor melted away, replaced by a bitter grin. Lady de Loncryn stood to her full height. Juan released her arm immediately and left the room.

Ria gestured for her to sit in the high-backed chair by the fire, the one with the legs carved like hoodsnakes. "Don't feel too badly, Lady. Juan and I have seen all manner of disguises in the casino. So many people trying to appear to be things they are not."

De Loncryn eased herself into the chair with all of her famous poise. "Perhaps that girl is the real me. Perhaps the Lady of Gabot Avenue is the disguise."

"Tell me you didn't come here to open your heart to me about the tribulations of nobility," Ria said flatly. She poured two glasses of wine—Ombrian red—from her decanter, gave one to her guest, and sat in her desk chair.

"I did not," De Loncryn said. "The act was silly, I admit. But I can't trust any of my staff, can I? Not for a good long while."

Ria nodded over her glass. "Always a risk. I'm fortunate to have Juan."

"I'm jealous. But a bear following me around wouldn't match my style, I think."

"You should give it a try sometime. I'd loan him out, but I have him a little tied up preventing my assassination."

De Loncryn took a very long drink. She wasn't faking, either; Ria watched as more than half of the glass disappeared. The Valtivan set her glass on the sidetable and looked into the fire. "Which of us do you think he was after, really?"

"He was after me," Ria said, her fingers tight on her glass. "I am sure of it. Bendine told me surreptitiously that he was dangerous. And then the bastard tried to convince me to go into the back alley with him. To save me, he said."

"And yet Omer-Guy is the one who died." De Loncryn turned her eyes to meet Ria's. They were unreadable.

Ria looked away. She had liked Bendine. Perhaps hardened agents of La Reina were used to losing their associates, but Ria was most decidedly not. She almost told de Loncryn about Bendine being a spy, just to ease the woman's pain a little.

If she was feeling any pain at all. Ria couldn't tell.

De Loncryn sighed and took up her glass again. "I suppose it doesn't matter, in the end. Maybe he was after Omer in truth. Maybe Omer had learned something about the man, and that's all there is to it. The gods know my sad little network of informers has turned up very little. He may have been involved in rigging an auction recently." She shrugged and finished her glass. "Nothing to make him seem like an Ombrais assassin."

"Nor a Cadois one," Ria said. There was no rancor in the statement. She felt as if she were complaining about the price of sugar with a fellow business owner. There could be no doubt that the assassin had come for Ria, not after Bendine's warning. But de Loncryn would have had nothing to do with that.

De Loncryn's eyes went distant. "If he hadn't disappeared when the fire started, and if Omer-Guy hadn't... hadn't died, I never would have guessed he was more than a lucky clerk. I am going to need to improve my intelligence operation if I'm going to be any good at being Mayor."

Ria looked down and noticed her own wine was gone as well. She reached across and poured de Loncryn's glass nearly to the rim, and then did the same to her own. "You'll be fine. Just keep letting the Cadois buy up land and the Empress will make sure everything works out. You can put a fountain at every intersection."

"Aye, maybe," de Loncryn said with a smile. An actual smile that disappeared as quickly as it had come. "But I doubt it. Her own ambassador dead in an alley. Foolish, sweet Omer-Guy: murdered. I haven't heard anything about the Imperial fleet descending upon Valtiffe to declare martial law until this affront to Her name is paid for in full. His own servants are just cleaning up his offices to get them ready for the next idiot She sends. She doesn't care as much about our little island as we all thought, it seems."

The firelight was dimming, and Ria couldn't get a good read on de Loncryn's face. "The Empire will respond," she said, not quite consolingly. "They can't do something that public, as I'm sure you know."

De Loncryn's smile returned, now with a bit of mischief in it. "Of course. It would be fun, though."

Ria laughed quietly and smiled back in earnest. "That it would."

They watched the fire fall to embers before speaking again. Ria tried to remember a time when she had felt as calm and companionable. Some time with her brother, maybe, at the family's winter palacio. Long before the complexities this life had brought. Back when she knew what she had to do all the time.

Ria sipped at the last of the wine. "So, will you be killing Quinol, or shall I?"

A Hvallais, a L'Ombrais, and a Mistigri enter a signaux club...

> Common opening for Cadois jokes

XXXI
TENERIÈVE

THE DAYTIME WAITER at the Syncretic Club had given up on taking the bottle back to the bar after Jacquemin's third blustering rant that he just leave the damned thing, and Tenerième was glad to see the battle end. If Jaq was even remotely aware of the startled looks he was getting from the club members, he wasn't showing it.

A woman in a blue dress had invited her and Jacquemin to enjoy a drink as they waited to see if Mme. Vabanque would accept Valen's message and meet with them. She probably had not imagined that Jaq would request a sheaf of cigars and proceed to light them from the lamp's flame with little regard for the fine glass shade.

The Syncretic Club kept oil lamps burning even in the full light of day. *A marvelous waste*, Tenerième thought. Jaq lit his fourth cigar and spilled a sizable measure of the oil on the delicate lace tablecloth. Tenerième chuckled sadly. *Time was I might have killed for that much oil. Enough to trade for a nice handful of turnips, or even a brace of rabbits too old for anyone else. Now I must act so refined as to not even notice its loss.*

Jacquemin caught her eye and scowled. "I'd expect *these* bastards to laugh at me, Ten, not you."

"Oh, it's not you, Jaq," she said with a grin. A false one. Her deal with Brother Michel—no, she could not call him that. They had not made a Brother of her. Her deal with the wiseman required her to keep her thoughts to herself.

"What is it, then?"

"This odd situation in which we find ourselves. A fisherman's son and a Mistigri spending an idle hour at a club like this one."

Jaq nodded approvingly. "Aye. I can barely wait to get out of here. If that Vabanque doesn't see fit to grace us poor souls with her so-fine presence some time soon, I'm going to have to pick a fight with one of these gentes to keep myself entertained."

"No fights," Ten insisted. "We need your hands at full strength if Valen's plan is to work." Not that she knew the plan in full detail. It had something to do with the Secret Broker's chamber, which was why they were here in this ridiculous club.

Jaq grimaced at the mention of Valen. "He already won that blighted Forbearance Game. And look at all the shit we've had to deal with since. Now he wants to take the Ambassador's Cup too? And in the same season?"

Perhaps Jaq would understand. Valen had met with them a day prior and outlined a ridiculous scheme, one which required him winning the tournament to be held by the L'Ombrais Ambassador, the main prize for which was a boon from the Ambassador herself. He did not offer up any details on precisely how this victory would end the danger all of them had inherited along with Dusmenil's secret. When pressed, he only said he needed to get to Ambassador Alodesal, and it would be safer for his friends if they didn't know, as failure was the most likely result.

This was foolishness. But she would play along and use her new role as spy for the Séminaire to save herself, and if she was very lucky she might save the others.

But did she *want* to save them? She had thought she was building a community for herself, but she had been lied to and had her fears ignored. The thought of these people being hurt stung her, but was that only foolishness? Had they duped her like they duped everyone else they met?

"I will agree it's bold. Yes."

"Bold? It's a feat fit for a legend. That man's self-importance is beyond my reckoning."

"It's not self-importance. He needs access to Dona Alodesal, who has said in no uncertain terms that she would prefer him dead."

"I can't say your intuition for people is anywhere near average, Ten, even for a gambler. You've known him longer than I, and by a long while. You've not seen how he sets himself apart? Chasing some nonsense about luck magic, as if a man who never even finished the Séminaire could create a new way of doing magic out of whole cloth."

"Now is not the time for us to criticize each other. Think of it as..."

Jaq cut her off with an angry stabbing motion with his finger. "If you tell me to think of us as a ship's crew, I'll challenge you to a duel right here on the carpet. You've never seen the life. Sailors are beholden to a captain and the officers. We sleep when they allow it, eat what they provide, and suffer any hazing they choose just to try and minimize the amount of our contract wages they skim off. You've no idea."

Ten bit back an oath. "No idea? I? Consider yourself lucky to even know the word 'wages.' Every town I ever saw spat on me more often than they paid up, and I could work thrice as hard as any of the others, but who do you think was last to elbow her way to the soup bowl come mealtime? And that is 'mealtime' in the singular, Erdannes. One per day, and a few dozen older kids muscling their way ahead of me in line. I went months eating naught but broth, scraping my bowl's bottom in desperation for a dab of marrow. I've seen your childhood home. I never once saw a fireplace until I was twelve years old. Save your woeful tales of the sea for someone who's slept in a bed for more than a third of her life."

Jaq took a long pull off his cigar and glared at her, but his mouth turned up in a crooked smile around the noxious thing before he exhaled. "Let's not reveal all too much of our sad, sad lives at this table. The great Madame might have her lads throw us back out in the gutter where we belong."

She knew he was dodging, but she allowed it. She had not reached this point in her life by moaning about her past, though she had always kept it in reserve, a hidden weapon to quell others' self-pity. Jaq was smiling it off because he did not dare pursue the matter further. But he had heard her; that, she did not doubt. Still, she would be sure to avoid any nautical metaphors in the future.

He would forgive her. She was certain that when Jacquemin knew that she was working with Michel to secure their safety, he would forgive her deceptions.

Margo would be another matter.

"We each of us have our reasons for this life," Ten said.

"Aye. And what's yours?"

"My what?"

"Your reason. Your reason for sharping cards instead of telling fortunes or any of the other things you'd do well at."

"Ah. Yes." With the argument past, she was feeling as if she could be open. Or perhaps she was just covering her lies. "I agree with Valen, you see. Games such as the ones we play, they have an equalizing effect on society. Even a barely-civilized refugee like myself is measured by the quality of my play, not by my accent or my eyes or whatever else."

"I've heard folk call you a 'filthy Mistigris.' Broken a few jaws over it."

"Yes, 'tis true," Ten said with a wicked grin. "But I still took their money."

"That you did, Ten. That you did. Mad old Valen. As ridiculous as the fool is, he never disrespects me. He'll take a jab at my clothes now and then, but that's nothing compared to what I give him."

"He's been that way always. When we were at school, he was the only one who treated me, a woman and a foreigner, fairly. He saw my work, and respected me based on that alone."

And now I betray him.

"Best we keep our skills up, then," Jaq said. "Wouldn't want him replacing us with some fast-handed kids."

"You *are* the fast-handed kid, Jaq. I was positive he was going to send me away when he found you."

"Nah. His best plays wouldn't work without the two of us taking the hits for him."

WHEN MME. VABANQUE at last greeted them—having spent a minute or two with each and every one of the club members first—she took to Tenerième immediately. When Ten requested the use of the Broker's Room, she was all too happy to do a favor for her very dear friend Valen. Tenerième caught her staring at the pile of ash Jaq had left on the floor beside him, and thought perhaps the woman was simply trying to get them to leave.

Tenerième did as Valen had asked, and evaluated the room for any manner of magical oddity. Jaq stood off to the side and gnawed at his toothpick.

The silencing enchantments were obvious, of course; but after several minutes she found a window enchant. Anyone on the other side of the wall would be able to look right into the room where players told their secrets.

What was Valen about, here? He must have suspected. But what good would this information do him? Was it another bargaining chip? How many Valtivan secrets was he planning on giving away?

They left without bothering to find Vabanque again.

"Right, then," Jaq slurred. "See you at the show."

"The Gamesmaster uses her discretion to ensure honest play." And not a word as to how she'll do it, you see. I hope I am never subject to the business end of her 'discretion.'

Lord D'Alhambere, as quoted in *Table Talk*

XXXII
VALEN

IF MONTMORENCY STREET, the main thoroughfare of Saut-Leronne, was a river of humanity on most days, then on the morning of the Ambassador's Games it was a bulging cataract at snow's first melt. As Valen maneuvered through the crush he feared he might lose Jaq and Ten behind him. If they were to separate, he might not know which games they started at. He wouldn't know which games to lose and which to win in order for the first stage of his plan to succeed. He might still be able to pull off the rest in that case, but it would rely on chance far more than he would prefer. And if he lost, he would face the continued rancor of the Séminaire, the L'Ombrais Ambassador, and perhaps the Empress herself. What would Margo say when he returned home, if he did at all? What would they do?

A sharp elbow in his stomach woke him from his paranoid reverie. Some young fellow, the owner of said elbow, rushed past with an angry word.

Valen smiled. It was good to see some of the old traditions of cutpursery were still to be found in crowded streets. He was meant to challenge the offending elbower, and another lad was to steal his money during the ensuing argument.

That other lad himself was presumably the one Jacquemin was in the act of tripping up at that very moment. A smaller boy in a coat and hose befitting the younger child of a respectable, if not wealthy, merchant family let out a surprised yelp and slid across the cobbles in an explosion of coinage. He didn't even bother to pick them up as he clambered up and ran off.

Valen turned to his friends with a frown. "That boy's master will not be kind to him if he returns *sans* lucre, Jaq."

"Maybe a good thrashing will give him pause as to his choice of career," Jaq countered gruffly. What little good humor he had been in before the walk down to Montmorency had completely run off, leaving the man with a scowl that showed little sign of abating.

"I hope so," Valen said. "He'd do much better as a gambler. One does hope to see the youth of today taking up one of the honest trades."

Tenerieve chuckled at that, breaking her customary severity. Valen thought she must have been nervous. Either that, or so completely independent as to not care a jot about the end of freedom in Valtiffe, to say nothing of the fiery death of at least one of her friends.

Games were everywhere: dice games against the curbs of the cobbled walkways, cards played on makeshift tables where they could be found—and the grass where they could not—games with sticks, with marbles, with tiles. So many here for the chance to win the Ambassador's boon, or just to be a part of the fun.

Valen caught the briefest of glimpses of a game on a board which was popular in the far south of the empire, rarely played if ever in Valtiffe. He watched as a woman dealt a seven-handed variant of signaux he had only ever read about, and Jacquemin had to nudge him to keep from stopping to watch a hand or two.

Their challenge, though, was the tournament itself. The noon-to-dawn event was to be a matchup of players in several different games, all of which Valen was prepared to win. Margo had outfitted him with at least one rigged deck of each of the currently popular styles and several sets of loaded, shaved, or otherwise dishonest dice. He wore a simple holdout clip in each sleeve and had several hidden pockets at the ready. Jaq and Ten had their own favorites on hand as well, but the plan required Valen to win the grand prize. Considering the crowd, he would need everything at his disposal.

They approached a woman in a plain dress and a vest of L'Ombrais yellow who looked as if she were perfectly delightful in most situations but was beginning to lose her patience. Her smile seemed completely natural if you ignored the movement of the muscles of her jaw as she ground her teeth and the labored breaths she was taking through her nose. To Valen, she might as well have been shouting.

She held a long paper and a quill as if they were sword and shield against the throng of people putting their names on the list for the tournament. When Valen and his friends reached her, she took down their names with the same forced 'good luck' she had given the dozen people before them.

In the hour that passed before the tournament began, the three cardsharps sat and played a few rounds of joccas as they went over their plan one last time. Valen practiced switching out the straight dice for loaded ones to keep his fingers nimble. Tenerième's steely assertions of her ability to do her part and Jacquemin's casual air about the entire matter left Valen confident they would succeed, which left only his performance to worry about.

Getting on the list was easy enough. After his success at The Gabot, he was never more confident in his luck magic. The bell rang, names were called at random, and among them were the ones he chose.

Jacquemin snorted. "Well that makes it easy. Looks like I won't be knocking anyone out this morning."

"I had planned on bribing mine," Tenerève scolded. "You would have had to hit a person rather hard to put them out for the duration of the event without killing him, and I am quite sure we have yet to become common murderers."

Valen packed up his dice—his clean dice—and rose. Enough chatter. "Common or uncommon, we remain as bloodless as always."

"'Bloodless' means 'weak,' you know," Tenerève said, an eyebrow raised. "Pale and anemic. Not the most reassuring boast before a trial such as this."

"If I had known you were expecting some stirring speech, I would have had someone write one for me and pretended it was my own work. As I stand here today, I have no plans to deceive anyone."

They both looked at him in surprise at that.

"Ah," he stammered, realizing his mistake. "Not you two, anyway. Many other people, I suppose. Just... good luck."

With that over, they split up and found their tables without another word.

THE FIRST GAME of the tournament was fornal, which he had not played since his altercation with Arbelan. He was partnered with a grinning young Hvallais woman who was giving every indication of having started the day with a solid breakfast of wine, but who played quite shrewdly. Valen kept one Empress and one eight in his sleeve holdouts at all times for safety's sake, but had little trouble advancing to the next round without using them.

As the winners of the first tier gathered at a smaller group of tables, Valen was glad to see both Jaq and Ten had made it. As per plan.

At some point during that second round, a man at one of the tables started shouting. Valen did his best to ignore him, but as the play at his table stopped—which, he hoped, would give his new partner time to get his mind back into the game from whatever holiday it appeared to have taken—he had little choice but to turn and watch the commotion unfold.

A ruddy-faced gentleman in a fine coat sparkling with silver buttons was standing at his table and jabbing his finger at his opponent. He was well into a repetitive argument, the main thrust of which was that a woman sitting across from him was a cheat.

The woman in question, a stony-eyed Mistigris in men's glasses, was Tenerième.

A muscular man in a surprisingly well-fitting crimson vest came to the table. "What's the accusation?" he asked, not bothering to hide his heavy L'Ombrais accent.

"That woman there," the accuser bellowed. "She is a cheat of the worst kind."

"And what proof do you offer, *piaron*?"

The accuser had apparently not thought this line of reasoning all the way through; he scowled deeply at the man, presumably with the haughty face he kept for servants who had done some unconscionable wrong like opening the wrong wine or being in the way as the young master barreled around a corner in his father's manse. Upon finding that his scowl was not producing the desired effect on the massive L'Ombrian, he huffed and resumed his odd pointing.

"Those glasses! They are trickery!"

Tenerième did not react in any way that Valen could see, not even when the imposing man in the vest paced around the table toward her. Not though everyone who could see her was looking at her. She was like a graven idol.

The whole park was utterly silent, which made the Ambassador's voice all the easier to hear from her seat on the platform. "What is it, Juan?"

"Nothing to trouble you, Dona," the man called back. Then, almost gently, to Ten: "I would see those spectacles, if I may."

Ten frowned angrily, but placed them in Juan's hand. As the man investigated them, another voice was heard.

"Aye, and what would make you be so very confident of that, de Niver? They familiar to you?"

This from Jacquemin, now standing at his own table.

Valen caught himself smiling. It was the same fool hunter from the roadside game the night before Arbelan came to Valen's rooms.

"Take a look, Juan," Jaq continued. "Note the fine details on the thing. A wonder of craftsmanship, it truly is. You can even see a tiny de Niver crest on the right arm of it: a stag rampant and some of those chevron things."

De Niver stood on his chair and resumed jabbing his finger in both Jaq's and Ten's directions, silver buttons chiming on his cuff. "Another cheat! These two are a team, I swear it!"

Juan shoved de Niver off his ersatz rostrum without looking up from the glasses. "I'll have all three of you quiet."

"I would ask that you do not malign me simply because you lost a game against me once," Tenerième said primly. "It's not my fault you dropped your lucky glasses."

"They aren't just lucky, you know that!" de Niver howled from his spot on the trampled grass.

"Juan!" the Ambassador shouted. "All three of them, out, now. They are a disturbance to this merry event."

Every member of the gathering, Valen included, looked to Ten, Jaq, and de Niver to see if any of them were going to be foolish enough to challenge their expulsion. When it became evident that none of them were, everyone returned to their games.

After the excellent distraction, the marked deck Valen had switched in assured his victory. He would need one—with his friends out of the game, he could count on no support from this point forward.

The play of a weak hand reveals the quality of the player.

Signaux Argot, Salen

XXXIII
TENERIÈVE

"I will be sending a formal complaint to the Ambassador, of course," Tenerième said, reciting the lines Valen had given her. She and Jaq had taken their time leaving the plaza, and even more time sharing a bottle of wine as they sat on a bench looking forlorn. A sizable crowd had gathered as they stood in the road outside of the game area, all doing their very best to look as if they weren't listening.

She was playing one of her favorite roles: the offended gente. "Removed from her games without so much as a chance to defend myself? Is this how things are handled in L'Ombre? That de Niver was about to lose. I suppose he thought he might as well take a rival with him. I cannot believe I managed to be stuck at a table with him again."

"Aye," Jacquemin grunted. His character was always the same, regardless of situation: ever the rude, rankless one. "And thrown out today of all days."

"What I would not have given for a shot at that preening, gold-plated fool. She may be Gamesmaster in her Corte, but she has much to learn of the social graces required for a game of quality here in Valtiffe."

"Never mind the game. I wanted to hear Quinol's secret."

Ten's breath caught in her throat. This was not in the script. "What?"

"The winner of the Forbearance Game. Rumor has it he's going to share that forty-thousand livre secret with the world. Going to take Alodesal right to the Secret Broker's room and tell her, give her an hour to get back to her ship out of respect, then tell the rest of us. Whatever it is, it must be damned dangerous."

Her heart was racing. She had to tell Michel about this. "Nonsense," she muttered. "Why would anyone do that?"

Jaq shrugged. "*Bof*. Who cares? Whatever is it, I wanted to hear it from the man himself before it gets sullied from retelling. The news in this city's one big game of pass-the-word. Any story's unrecognizable after long."

They walked together for some time, then parted ways as per the plan. The eavesdroppers did not follow as Ten ducked into a coffeeshop and sat at a table in a dark corner.

The bastards had kept their plan secret from her again. Valen was going to get the entire city burned down, or unleash open war between the great powers of the world. Whatever he thought he could gain from this was madness. She had been right to go to the Brothers.

No one saw TenerÈve write something on a piece of paper and burn it.

The greatest game of all, the one which balances strategy and chance most purely, is in fact one of the oldest games known to us: blots. That the people of Cadogna play it far less than L'Ombrais speaks more to a disappointing bias against that culture than to the quality of the game itself. We could learn much about our rivals by studying it.

Salen's introduction to *Corte and Courtship;*
this line is to be found in the original draft,
but was never in a printed edition.

XXXIV

VALEN

T HE MOON HAD risen, cast its light on hours of game play, and fallen beneath the tips of the trees lining the park by the time Valen correctly called out his opponent's bluff and won the final round of the tournament. He had burned through several decks of marked cards and much of his mental stamina, but he had won.

Perhaps it was the will of the crowd. Perhaps they were casting luck magic in their own way. Once he was recognized as the local legend he had become, the tension in the crowd around each of his games increased. People gasped when he played boldly, and he was sure he heard coins changing hands after each of his plays. Everyone wanted him to win. A record win at the Forbearance Game and a victory at the Ambassador's Games in the same season? The onlookers would tell their great-grandchildren about this day.

This was assuming, of course, that no one caught him cheating. That giant Juan Burqu, the Ambassador's personal pit boss, kept a close eye on every game. Valen did not dwell on what would happen if he was caught with something up his sleeve. The real skill was to win by just enough, and slowly. Knocking someone out of a game with a ludicrously unlikely hand was sure to blow him in. Even a steady progression of mildly unlikely hands would be seen as suspect. He had to give himself luck at—or even below—the average and still win.

After the first few hours of signaux, most of the crowd had become a little bored. Feet shuffled. Empty drinks were filled. The best of the onlookers, people who he had seen at the clubs and knew to be experienced players, were rapt. These were the people who taught courses on the best opening hands in signaux, or wrote essays on what to play when the dealer's second lead is an off-suit nine. These would be his champions in the months to come. Whenever anyone cast any doubts on the honesty of his success, they would shake their heads and offer examples of brilliant plays with poor cards that kept him in the game until the honours came his way, as of course they eventually must do.

Even if he ended up on a L'Ombrais prison ship or incinerated by a mad Brother, at the very least his reputation would be intact.

The crowd cheered as Valen stood, some with polite claps and some with wantonly crude language regarding the Ambassador. Had Valtiffe changed so completely that the sentiment against Cadogna's old rival had taken such a hold? Was this how this game would be seen by history? A contest between the Empire and the Queendom? He imagined what the woodcuts would look like.

Burqu led him up to the Ambassador's stage without a word. Smiles and words of encouragement flanked him as he walked behind the giant's impressive back. They meant nothing. In truth, his reputation meant nothing. He wasn't doing this for the acclaim, and never was. He was doing this because women and men should not die in wars initiated for the benefit of the rich and mighty. He was doing this because he believed life should be fair.

He just needed to keep the game going long enough to prove it.

Dona Alodesal stood by a chair and clapped along with the rest as he ascended the stairs. As her eyes met his, though, she hesitated. Only slightly, but it was enough. Much of Valen's plan depended on this moment, and as the Ambassador's eyes flicked to her pit boss, he thought he may have miscalculated.

She smiled even more warmly and approached Valen as if she were marrying her child to him. Valen smiled back, meeting the steel in her eyes with coyness in his own.

"A greeting, friend," she said, turned to the crowd. "So you would try to win my boon?"

Valen bowed. "It is an honor to play at all, Dona. But I will certainly try."

The final game was to be blots, an ancient game involving three dice, checkers, and a board with painted columns. The variants were surprisingly few for a game so old, and Valen had come prepared with dice which would turn the way he chose for all of them. Blots was notoriously difficult to cheat at, as the same roll could be useless or essential in different situations. He would have to switch his rigged dice in when he needed them and back out just as quickly. No mean feat with a crowd of thousands watching, to say nothing of the professional cheat-breaker sitting across from him.

"This board has been in my family for over a thousand years," Alodesal declared. She allowed the crowd a moment to cheer. "You are one of fewer than a hundred people who have played on it in the last few centuries. Every game is logged in our family records, with illustrations of each move in gold and silver leaf. An analysis of every game is provided by whoever is considered to be the best player in Ombria at the time. This little match of ours will be preserved for as long as my country stands. May it serve as proof of the loving friendship between our two nations."

Valen clapped awkwardly and made a show of being nervous. It didn't take much acting, if he was being honest with himself.

"Tonight, the old meets the new," Alodesal continued. "A game from before our time of empires, in a city on the brink of change." She provided no detail about what she meant by that, but held a pause long enough for the crowd to wonder. "And what better way to commemorate that than in the combination of the storied board of the Juegar family and the latest change to games of chance?"

She grabbed the dice from the table and held them high. They didn't look like ordinary dice to Valen. Were they shining?

"I have had these dice custom made by the magnificent glaziers of Anillar. They are perfectly balanced, and completely clear. The very first of their kind, and my gift to you, Valen Quinol, no matter which of us wins tonight!"

Glass dice. This would mean the downfall of loaded dice altogether. How does one hide a weight in a clear die? Alodesal certainly knew how to make a cheat nervous.

As they sat to play, a curtain was pulled back to reveal a giant version of a blots board with each of the checkers on a peg. Three large squares ran down the side, each numbered. A young fellow in livery stood nearby. The game was to be mirrored for all to see.

A servant poured wine from a crystal decanter, a luscious deep red. Valen took a small sip from the fine glass tumbler the servant offered him. He thought he might propose a toast, but stifled the idea immediately. The Ambassador seemed to enjoy center stage too much to be flattered by someone else raising a glass, even to honor her.

Not being able to depend on his rigged dice was a problem, but not an insurmountable one. Valen knew a few trick throws that would let him control the outcome somewhat. On the third throw, he tried one. He hooked his middle finger around one of the three dice—the all-important "drip," which replaced the lower of the regular dice on evens and the higher on odds—and whipped it in such a way that it spun instead of tumbling. The other two fell normally, but his trick ensured he would replace the lower.

"Higher."

The voice was Burqu, who Valen had not realized was standing right behind him. Unusually quiet fellow.

"I'm sorry, what do you mean?"

"Hold your hand higher as you throw."

A chorus of offended cries from the crowd was silenced by a look from Burqu. Offended they may be, but the pit boss was right—in order for the whip to work, Valen needed to keep his hand near the board.

"You might as well just let them bounce off the backboard, Monsieur Quinol," the Ambassador chuckled. "My employée will never be satisfied otherwise. Years of keeping my casino patrons honest has made him jaded, poor man."

Valen covered a sudden onset of sweat by speaking sideways to the crowd. "Of course, Dona. I was simply afraid I would shatter the glass."

The crowd laughed, and the tension passed. Valen was still sweating. None of his throws, not a single one of them, would work when the dice were bounced off of something. It was a simple request to cover any sort of cheating and a polite standard for many games, not unlike offering a cut of the cards. Unnecessary among people who trust each other, but embedded in enough tradition to raise no eyebrows when requested.

Valen was good, but the Ambassador was better. He knew the percentages for each roll, weighed them, and played the best move possible, but somehow Alodesal was ahead. Not by much, but enough that if his luck didn't change, he would lose.

He had to risk his luck magic. The dice were clear, after all. Even if he rolled seven perfect rolls in a row, no one could discredit him. And after The Gabot, he had reached a new tier in his self-imposed hierarchy.

A few rolls here and there. A six when one was useful. A four-two-one, normally a terrible roll, right in the rare situation when he needed it. With each throw he cut the dice in his mind and envisioned success.

Alodesal whispered just barely loud enough for Valen to hear as she sipped wine from her glass. "What do you keep saying to yourself?"

"Nothing," Valen whispered back, turning away from the crowd as if to check that the display board matched reality.

"Best be careful, murderer. Juan would love to gut you. He'll wait until the end of the game, if you're lucky."

"I am that."

"I'll make you a wager. Win this game, and I'll let you run off to Cadogna. Lose, and Juan crushes you before you reach your home."

So that was how it was going to be. Surely she was bluffing. She was trying to get him to make a mistake.

It would very likely work. He needed to go on the offensive.

"I am so very happy to have the opportunity to play you again," Valen said loudly. "We didn't get to finish our game the night The Gabot burned." *Roll. Clack, clack.*

"It is true, Monsieur. Perhaps when you have lost tonight, we can try again." *Roll. Three clacks, one to the side of the board.*

A hoot from the crowd.

"Tell me, Ambassador, what is the nature of that Fanzago deck you had with you that night?" *Roll. Clack, clack, clack.*

"Oh, a silly old thing. Another family heirloom. Or it will be some day. A gift from my brother." *Roll. A long drag of a checker from one end of the board to the other.*

"Ah. And what is his position at the Corte? Forgive me for not knowing." *Roll. Clack.*

"You have in no way offended, Monsieur. My brother is not very much known to society. He is a member of the Séminaire." *Roll. Four clacks.*

Valen's next toss ended up on the ground.

"The Séminaire?"

"Yes. All words and mysteries, that one. He is quite accomplished, in his way."

She whispered once again. "He put a good luck charm on that deck. I use it to suss out cheats."

Cold sweat ran down his back. A 'good luck charm'? What could that mean?

Was she trying to confuse him? No enchantments worked like that. He had tried for years. Or was she telling the truth, or some part of it? If someone else was working in luck magic, was that why his cards came so easily that night? And if that were so, would his magic work without it? But if someone else was using it, wouldn't that make it real? Even if he didn't invent it? Isn't that what he wanted?

"Roll, Monsieur," Burqu said.

He had lost himself in an anxious reverie again. The crowd was silent.

Alodesal was smiling at him.

He rolled and moved defensively, eschewing an opportunity to knock a few of the Ambassador's pieces off the board. If all the actors in his plan were performing their parts, he wouldn't have to hold out much longer. He knew he could count on Margo and Jaq, but Ten was a risk. He told himself he knew her well enough to guess her next move, but he had been wrong about the Mark's Pier. What if he was wrong now?

The change in Alodesal's tactics was immediate. She pounced on the opportunity provided by his move, and the statistics of the game changed. He ran the numbers in his head. The balance was in her favor, even more than it had been.

If he didn't regain control of the game, she would beat him before his scheme had time to unfold. Burqu would carry him off, and this whole matter would come to an unpleasant end.

This plan was idiocy. It depended on him playing against a famous cheat-breaker who wanted him dead. He didn't even know anything about her. Their game at The Gabot had revealed no weaknesses.

But surely she had one. He had been foolish not to look for it. Valen had been so caught up in politics and magic and danger he had forgotten how to win.

Why would she be here? Why would L'Ombre send her now? They had practically no interest in Valtiffe, if the frequency of her visits was any indicator.

"How wonderful it is to have you here with us in Saut-Leronne, Ambassador." He didn't have to raise his voice at all for the crowd to hear him now; the plaza had gone silent after his change in strategy. "I hope we have entertained you enough to make the assignment less taxing."

"Oh, I am not on assignment." Her eyes didn't leave the board as she spoke. "I decided it was time to visit the dear place."

She gave him information just like that. Not even a hint of suspiciousness about it. Surprising for a courtier, and even more so for an Ambassador.

A roll of the dice by Alodesal and the perfect play. Valen hadn't even seen the possibility of the move. She was truly a master player.

But she was too focused on winning this game, right now.

Her play was perfect, but her behavior was ever rash and impulsive. She had threatened Valen at the Gabot, when keeping her intentions silent would have been wiser. She had done the same when he had walked on stage. Her visit to Saut-Leronne seemed as if were taken up on a whim.

She knew games, yes. But she didn't know the long game of living.

Valen focused as much of his mind as he could spare on guessing her weakness. How had someone so impetuous stumbled into the Ambassadorship? What did she have that others did not?

Family. She had a name, and the expectations that went along with it. And if anyone knew about disappointing one's family, it was Valen.

"Tell me, Ambassador," Valen said. "What does that term in front of your name mean? 'Grandee'?"

The slightest hesitation as she rolled the dice. He had her.

"It is a title granted to families of a certain history and stature."

"Stature?" *Roll. Clack.* "You mean wealth?"

Roll. Clack, clack. Still her eyes were on the table. "Not precisely."

"You'll have to explain it to me sometime," Valen said. He let the dice dribble from his fingers, just grazing the backboard. "We do not make such distinctions here."

"Surely you do. You have old families."

Valen nodded. "Yes, but we do not grant them pretty titles." He rolled, selected a piece to capture, and held it up between his finger and thumb as if appraising it. "Here on Valtiffe, we are not like hagensmen: empresses and chevaliers, some powerful and some not. Here we are like blots. None above another."

A few chuckles from the crowd. Alodesal's eyes darkened, though her face didn't change.

Roll, clack, clack, clack. She ran one of her pieces along the board and captured three that Valen had left unprotected. He couldn't have asked for her to get a better roll.

The Ambassador put the pieces to the side with a sneer. "Then it must be by chance alone that a person lives or dies, succeeds or fails."

Valen sat back and took a long pause, shaking the dice in his hand. He glanced up at Burqu, who was frowning. Even the boy tending the display board was shaking his head. The Ambassador had fallen into a trap. Capturing the three pieces made perfect sense, but only if the player didn't think about the following moves. Now she would likely have to break up her defenses in the middle game and risk more pieces than had been necessary.

"No, Ambassador," Valen said, leaning back in to the game. "Not chance alone."

Dig a hole with false leads. Disguise it with underplay. Bait the trap with finesses. Perform these at every opportunity against your opponents.

Signaux Argot, Salen

XXXV
MICHEL

THE WHISPERWIND MESSAGE stung like a wasp in Michel's ear. He nearly fell over in the street for the surprise and sudden pain, but long years of practice at self-control kept him walking toward Montmorency Street.

If only his self-control had been enough to keep him from this rapidly degenerating state of affairs.

He's telling her everything. In the Secret Broker's room.

The bastard. Selling the Skyndiferth to L'Ombre. He would see war and suffering, and for what? Money? Influence? By the Saints, for sex?

Michel turned into a doorway and closed his eyes.

He would walk into the Secrets Room through a door which did not exist. He would wait there in his hidden chamber and kill them both. He would kill their families, their friends. Anyone he could link to them. This was worth a few cold Valtivan lives.

Step.

There was more noise than he expected. A crowd in the streets on the other side of the wall perhaps? And how was there a breeze?

Michel opened his eyes and discovered he was standing on a stage lit by torches. Two people stood near a table, a man and a woman. They were shaking hands. A remarkably large man stood to the side. Thousands of faces were looking at him from the crowd below.

He was sure he had the sigil correct. But he was not where he should have been. How did this happen?

The big man darted toward him with the speed of an angry bull.

"Juan, wait! He'll..."

It was Quinol speaking. The bastard himself.

The beast man tried to grab Michel, but could not get a grip on him. His clothing was enchanted to be as slippery as a cold fish to anyone but its owner. Should he run? No, he would stand his ground here. He allowed the man to engulf him in a bear hug and lift him off the ground. He could always burn the man's heart if he needed to.

How many people was Michel going to have to kill?

"Dona, we have just witnessed something which I would explain to you," Quinol said, in the sudden silence. It was as if the whole city of Saut-Leronne was holding its breath, waiting for his explanation.

The Ambassador's face was unreadable. "A mountebank's trick? Who is this fool?"

"I am no mountebank, woman," Michel growled. "I am a fully-vested member of the Séminaire of Saut-Leronne. Tell this clod to stand down or I will..."

Hells. This was no way to handle this. Michel was lost.

Quinol stepped forward. "Please, just listen to me for a half-minute, Dona. I knew you would not believe me if I simply told you, so I had to show you. The secret of the Forbearance Game, that famous fifteen-thousand livre secret, is why I came here today. I would give it to you freely, if you would have it."

The bodyguard was holding Michel away from the Ambassador. He could not see her response. Perhaps she nodded; perhaps she did nothing at all. Michel was so far from understanding how an instrument of state might conduct herself, he could not guess.

Quinol continued regardless. "The secret of the Forbearance Game is that the Séminaire—possibly just the Séminaire of Saut-Leronne, possibly all of them—has kept a very unusual sort of magic to themselves. They can open a hole in the air and walk through it, to end up wherever they like."

"Foolishness."

"You just witnessed it yourself, Dona."

"The man clearly has no desire to be here."

"Of course not," Valen said. "Think what you like, but thousands of people just saw a man walk from nowhere on to a well-lit stage at dawn. I had to trick him to come."

Michel struggled to keep still. His lips moved, the muscle memory of a thousand spells.

The Ambassador walked downstage until she could see Michel, but spoke to Quinol. "What are you playing at?"

"I am not playing at anything, Dona. You needed to see this. Your people needed to see this. Think what you like, but you can't deny something unusual happened just now."

"It matters not. You won your game and did... whatever this was supposed to be. Now get off my stage."

"I will, Dona. But I know you would not send me off without granting me my boon."

The Ambassador took a long time to respond to that. Michel's hands were starting to lose feeling. "And what is that?"

"When you tell the Corte about this, they are going to be very confused. The cleverer ones will have their people look around the city for sigils like that one."

Quinol pointed at a symbol on one of the draperies decorating the stage. It was the sigil from the Secrets Room, painted over an embroidered pattern of simple shapes. It was no bigger than a hand, and nearly invisible from where Michel stood. The bastard had switched it somehow. He must have ruined the one in the Secrets Room and put its like here.

"They will very likely find them," Quinol continued. "And they may make a few connections between unexplained stories and the locations of these symbols. A ghost in the larder. A man in black where none should have been.

"My boon is this—do not retaliate. Valtiffe is too close to Cadogna. We are the same, in the eyes of most of the Corte, I assume? Yes. Mysterious Cadois wisemen with access to whatever they like? This will be cause for war. Don't let it be. Toss the sigil-scrawled boards and stones into the sea. Let the bastards step into the briny dark if they want.

"Think about it, Dona. Who is truly sitting on the other side of the table? You've revealed one of her strategies—don't lose your advantage."

Another long moment passed, and the Ambassador said nothing. The woman was as inscrutable as stone.

Quinol turned to face Michel. He spoke just loud enough for Michel to hear. "And you. You are going to walk back to the Séminaire without doing a damn thing, or I'll tell everyone that you fuckers have the masonry in every road in the city rigged to light on fire at your words."

Michel wanted to kill him. He might have torched the entire place if it would have helped. But it was too late.

He had succeeded at everything he ever tried until that moment on the stage. Whatever the Principe had in store for him was nothing compared to that.

Three, one, three. 21-18, X. 21-20, X. Red W.

Note: An unusual event occurred just as the game ended. The event is outside the purview of these records. Consult historical sources.

The Rolls of Blots on the Juegon board,
trans. Salen

While this missive carries information of great import, I offer a strategy for response which may seem unusual.

An open letter from
Ambassador Alodesal to the Corte

Of the few notable games of blots played outside of L'Ombre, the victory of Quinol at the Ambassador's Cup of Saut-Leronne remains the most important, not only for its long-reaching effect on our history, but for the unusual combination of plays Quinol used to win after a poor showing in the early game. This ability to come back from near defeat, as we shall see in the following pages, came to be a trademark of his greatest victories.

Lives of Gamesters

XXXVI
VALEN

VALEN SAT WITH his wife and his two associates in a small boat which rocked savagely on the shale-gray sea. Between the spray and the waves, any notion of getting a game of cards in was well outside the bounds of likelihood. It was a shame—the fourth hand in the seventh round of signaux from his night at the Ambassador's contest was still puzzling him and he wanted some help understanding it. Why would anyone play the five at that point? The other player, that falsely-drunk blonde woman, had made no mistakes at all until that point, but was it truly a mistake?

This was a distraction, of course. The Ambassador's admission about her brother and the enchanted deck had filled his mind completely in the days following the event. It would appear that Valen's accidental magic had been developed already and was in use in L'Ombre, hidden from him by hundreds of years of a rivalry he had nothing to do with. The one thing that distinguished him in this world was already being done by others, and better.

Margo and Ten sat side-by-side at the bow and were discussing some matter he couldn't hear anything about. From the way Margo was laughing, it was probably nothing to do at all with him. He was glad of it. The entire point of being a cardsharp is to be invisible, and he had spent far too long at the very front of too many crowds recently. Let these poor people have some time off from Valen and his nonsense.

The single sail was filled with more wind than Valen thought was truly blowing. He looked at Jacquemin, but there was no sign of him swallowing a pigeon or anything like that. Rope and cloth and wind were a mystery he simply did not understand.

The Ambassador had left shortly after her contest, without a word to Valen about what she planned to do. In the end, it didn't matter. The secret, or at least some small part of it, was out. The Séminaire would gain nothing by killing over it now, and the Empress could not act on it in any of the ways Bendine had described if it was public knowledge. She was playing a game far above Valen's understanding, but he was fairly sure he had at least taken one trick.

He would likely never be able to play in Saut-Leronne again. He was too famous among the players now, and he had managed to pull a Brother out of thin air, which left his credibility as an honest player in tatters. But there were other venues. A long vacation to the continent might be just the thing. Margo's parents could take care of his rooms while they were away. Financing would be a bit of a problem, now that his only source of income had gone dry. But, with any luck, that was about to take care of itself.

Ten had forgiven him, he thought. When the Ambassador's Games broke up, he had found her walking toward the docks.

"You knew," she'd said, eyes low. "Yes. You planted the story of the Secret Broker's room knowing I would pass the information on. Is that what Jaq was doing at Mme. Vabanque's? You had him deface the sigil there and memorize it."

"That's correct," he had admitted. There was no need for pretense. "Margo painted a copy on the backdrop before the event began. All I needed was for that firehappy maniac to think his way into the trap."

"This is why you said nothing about your plan for Arbelan. You did not trust me with your secrets. You knew I would betray you and Margo and go to the wisemen."

Valen conceded that he had guessed as much, and that he knew her tells well enough to know she'd been hiding something from him. She hadn't looked angry at his deceit, but confused.

"Ten, you wouldn't have believed me otherwise, but you have a home here. With me and Margo. I knew you would try to make amends with the Séminaire, to prove you were no threat to them; those are the skills that have kept you alive. We wanted to show you that we understand. If we had told you about our suspicions, you would have run off."

"So you tricked me."

"I did. You tried to undo my plan, which would have caused who knows what damage."

"And this does not anger you?"

He had smiled at that. "I'm your friend, Ten, not your father. You were trying to do what seemed the best way out of the problem. So was I. But my way worked."

He hoped he was right about that.

Margo had told him that she had spoken with her as well. She told her that this was what a home meant. That you were always forgiven.

"This is it, old man." Jaq was in the middle of some strange behavior with the rudder and ropes which slowed them to what seemed to be a stop. "Don't be scared now."

"My thanks," Valen said, rising unsteadily from his seat. "I'm sure there's nothing to be concerned about. Ten, you are quite sure about this enchantment?"

"I am not at all sure, Valen. Need I remind you I studied Divination along with you?"

"A hat that lets you breathe underwater." Margo laughed. "You didn't have a vision of him dying, did you?"

"The images are hard to read sometimes."

"I'm more concerned he won't be able to lift anything," Jaq said. "How can a fellow with such a big gut have such skinny arms?"

"Just another of life's mysteries, Jaq. Now hand me my chapeau."

Valen took a deep breath and let himself fall over the side, completely trusting of Ten's skills with enchantment, and Jaq's with navigation. There was no doubt in his mind he was directly over the wreck of the *Victory Rose*.

END

APPENDIX I
MAJOR PLAYERS

Excerpted From *The Voet Charger's Compendium of Notables:*

Dona Ariadna de Alodesal y Juegon. Grandee of L'Ombre, Gamesmaster of Torreçon, and Regal Ambassador to the Independent Country of Valtiffe. Called "Ria" in familiar circles. The daughter of two peers. The Alodesal family is one of the oldest grandee lines in history, while the Juegons have been known mainly for military service. Noted for bringing a tournament of games to Valtiffe as part of her ambassadorial duties there. An expert carré player. The Juegon family's historical catalog of their blots games is legendary.

Omer-Guy Bendine. Cadois Ambassador to Valtiffe. Known for a scandal at Court relating to his son, who now lives in exile in L'Ombre. Has written smaller essays on hagens strategy for the *Charger*.

Juan Burqu. Pit boss at the casino in Torreçon. Personal valet to Dona Ariadna de Alodesal y Juegon. Military history. Has been seen playing oakey.

Empress Oceane Caraliere de Flechard. Empress of Cadogna. The de Flechard family rose to prominence at Court in the century prior to the Fire War between Cadogna and L'Ombre by serving as advisors on matters of trade and economics. Trade was seen as an unsuitable topic for the gentry at the time, and the de Flechards filled the gap in Court left by that prejudice. A complicated series of marriages over the course of several generations put a young Oceane de Flechard in the line of succession. She was installed after the death of her mother, the Empress Argine Bonneteau de Caraliere. Her critics find fault in her hesitation to expand the borders of the empire and reclaim contested regions, but the popular opinion is that her hesitance to use military force is an improvement over some of the more bellicose rulers of the past. Plays some carambol publicly, but little is known of her personal gameroom.

Lady Oceline de Loncryn. 'The Lady of Gabot Avenue.' A gente of a Cadois family old enough to still take the honorifics 'lord' and 'lady.' Owns the Loncryn manor on the well-heeled Gabot Avenue of Saut-Leronne in Valtiffe. Socialite. A lover of beaufils.

From the personal notes of Hannes Arginson, Chief Guard of Saut-Leronne:

Michel Alcippe. Séminaire Brother. Spends a lot of time outside of the Tower. Family in the city.

Hugues Arbelan. Leader of the Naughty Knaves, the major Hillside gang. Showy. Good with a sword.

Teneriève Cassell. Mistigri. What is she doing here? Connected to the Brothers?

Guillaume Gourdon Comines. Merchant. Card player. Wealthy.

Clavis Dusmenil. Gente. Last of a big family. Running out of money—watch for activity. Good card player.

Jacquemin Erdannes. Former sailor, possible pirate. Messy in appearance. Seen with the Mistigri (Cassell).

Sæmunder Magnús Handar. Principe (Leader) of the Séminaire. Lives in the Tower. *Avoid*.

Nathan Laciaume. Séminaire Brother.

Munnrais. First name unknown. Likely leader of Les Royaux gang.

Honoré de Niver. Baron. Gente. Owns lands outside of town. Has a rogue for a son.

Marguerite Quinol. Of the Dockside Hoque family of ivory traders. Married to Valen.

Valen Quinol. Financial clark. Low-level gambler. Name has come up a few times—anything doing? Married to Marguerite, née Hoque.

Stéphane Trouluc. The "Secret Broker". Values the secrets at the Forbearance Game. Would know a lot of it weren't for that crown.

Mme. Vabanque. Owner of the Syncretic Club. The place gets loud, but it's clean.

APPENDIX II
CATALOGUE OF GAMES

Excerpted from Salen's *Index of Diversions:*
Name, Type – Play Type, Deck used (if cards). Note.

Atouts, Card – Patience, Satique. Cross formation.
Beaufils, Card – Trick-taking, Satique (abbreviated).
　　Traditional to Cadogna. Traditionally four-handed, but a
　　two-handed variant knows some popularity.
Blots, Dice – Race.
Burny, Card – Patience, Satique. Nine piles.
Carambol, Skill. Involves running balls through hoops and
　　around obstacles on a table-top playing surface.
Carré, Card – Matching, Fanzago. Extensively popular in
　　L'Ombre.
Clips, Card – Comparison/Matching, Satique. Bluffing variant
　　of littre. Valtivan. Called 'Fool's Littre.'
Crow's Cross, Skill – involves throwing small chips in
　　patterns. Accompanied by a child's rhyme.

Dieuroi, Card – Prediction, Satique (3 decks). In essence a controlled lottery, with players betting on what card will come next.

Flinks, Skill – involves throwing small chips in patterns. (cf. **Crow's Cross**).

Fornal, Card – Trick-taking, Satique. Six-handed.

Hagens, Strategy – Elimination. Uses a custom board with multiple pieces which move and capture in different ways.

Henpenny, Card – Fishing, Fanzago. Simple and fast. Named after the quick movement of the hand required to grab coins when matches are made, reminiscent of a hen pecking at grain.

Joccas, Dice – matching, four four-sided. Traditionally played with 'knucklebones,' from the ankles of hooved animals.

Littre, Card – Matching, Satique. Traditional to Cadogna, rarely played past childhood.

Oakey, Card – Matching, Satique or Fanzago. Traditionally uses a board and pegs to keep count of points, a practice which is widely presumed to be the result of the popularity of this game among sailors; pegs in holes are less likely to roll around in rougher seas.

Pass-The-Word – Social. A child's party game in which a phrase is whispered in secret and repeated. Non-competitive.

Signaux, Card – Trick-taking, Satique. An oddity in the type, having no partners. Popular mainly in Valtiffe.

Six-Man Sessin, Strategy – line-forming. Widely thought to be one of the oldest games in existence.

Skiptop, Skill. A child's street game played with 'knucklebones' (See **Joccas**).

Stomach, Card – Comparison, Satique. Fast-paced clips variant with a single card drawn by each player.

APPENDIX III
EXCERPT FROM
THE FANZAGO DECK: A BRIEF HISTORY

THE FANZAGO DECK has been the standard for playing cards in casinos, taverns, and clubs throughout the Ombrian coastlands and the adjacent countries for over two centuries. Originally manufactured in the port city of Anillar and sold to sailors for petty coins, the Fanzago worked its way from the crumbling docks of Mola to the noise and color of sunny Torreçon as naval trade grew in the relative security of the post-war decades (circa 1010-1030), and has made an indelible mark on our cultural history.

Each card in the Fanzago deck bears an illustration of a pastoral scene, all cleverly drawn so that the images on the cards align perfectly when placed next to each other. Distant mountains form an uninterrupted horizon behind foreground depictions of farms and castles, beasts, and streams. Rearranging them to form pretty landscapes and little stories is a common diversion in both nurseries and salons, but their main use is, and has always been, in gameplay.

Prior to the Fanzago, one could not enter into a friendly round of carré without first inquiring as to the nature of the deck being used. The suits, the values, even the number of cards in the deck would vary from town to town, and in the cities even from borough to borough. We are all familiar with numerous variants of a game as simple as, say, henpenny; it seems every family has their own odd rules, mainly perpetuated—and in some cases outright invented—by the elder members of the clan. Imagine having to review not only the house rules before play, but the contents of the deck itself!

Out of this chaos arose the discrete packet of wonderful design and ease of use that is the Fanzago deck. Determining the precise timing of the very first Fanzago's creation with any certainty has gained the status of a folkloric quest among historians, but we can say without any doubt that the first professionally-printed run was in the year 1013 by a small company known at that time as Anedas Printing and Engraving. Sorya Anedas y Lida, the proprietor, had no interest whatsoever in cardplay or gambling, and saw the project as all but a waste of resources. Her wife, Benigna Anedas, was something between a socialite and a rake, and had developed the deck's original design with her struggling artist friend Orland Fanzago. Sorya agreed to a small run to help Fanzago earn a little cash from his drawings and perhaps settle some small part of his debts, most of which were owed to the Anedases.

Orland Fanzago had attempted to make a name for himself as a landscape artist, but found himself on the tail end of that sort of art's popularity. By all contemporary accounts, Benigna Anedas was a masterful card player, dealing through dozens of games most nights of the week. Local legend has it that the two struck up a conversation about the poor design of most cards when Anedas lost a sizable sum in one hand because she was under the impression that the three of stones was the five. If you find yourself in Anillar, you can treat yourself to dozens of retellings of this snippet of legend by asking any of the residents. The exact table at which the fateful hand was played is claimed by at least six different taverns within the town's borders.

When Benigna Anedas brought the idea to her wife, Sorya accepted on one condition: an enchantment. An apprentice from the Séminaire had come to Sorya with a concept for his Master's Spell: he had developed a way to keep water from damaging paper, and wanted to combine this with the printing process to make weatherproof nautical maps in volume.

Knowing that sailors, and especially navigators, are hesitant to accept any sort of change to their time-honored and superstition-laden processes, Sorya had tried to turn him away. The young man was insistent, though. The Anedas shop's maps were well-respected for their fine lines and clear inking. He didn't want his talent wasted on a lesser product.

Sorya knew less about life at sea than she did about cards, but she knew the unfaltering truth that sailors like to gamble. Under her supervision, the first run bore a light enchantment to stay dry. It quickly became the favorite of every sailor in the region. The delicate scrollwork of the Fanzago cardback became synonymous with dependability, a reputation which it enjoyed even as later runs were printed without the enchantment upon which its original popularity was based. Within a decade, no decent club in any city for hundreds of miles would use anything but a Fanzago.

The fact that the name of the original artist has now become the name of the standard style itself is surely something which descendants of the Anedas family find frustrating. Sorya was so sure these cards would never make it past their first run that she refused to have the printer's mark pressed on to the boxes, choosing instead to put her wife's foolish friend's name on them.

While the original Anedas cards were simple two-color woodcuts, printers everywhere did their best to improve upon the imagery of the original while being sure to keep true to the general shape of the figures. Even today, if you were to stop by your corner shop and pick up any deck, you would find the laborers on the two of stones in the same pose they were placed in by Orland Fanzago himself.

The use of the cards for the telling of fortunes, while widely practiced today with varying levels of seriousness, did not come about until the beginning of the last century. Dilettante oracles could be found in many cities, often doing their works in public despite the objections of the Brothers. The assignment of mystical values to each of the cards is attributed to Belmiro Sansa, the noted soothsayer and performer.

Sansa distributed a pamphlet of the designations which he wrote under the assumed name of 'Daniel Derrinda.' The pamphlet begins with a roughly written first-person account of the hapless Derrinda stealing a book from the great magician Belmiro Sansa, but not understanding its contents and offering them to the public to interpret. This marketing coup fed the puzzle-solving egos of Sansa's patrons, who paid handsomely for thousands of copies.

Small improvements in the clarity of the suits and values have been made over the decades, but the basic design of the deck is mainly unchanged from that first labor of love. Individual cards from the original run of the Anedas Fanzago, the veracity of which can often be determined simply by pouring water over them, can be found on occasion in the finest antique shops, but full decks are practically unheard of in this day and age.

APPENDIX IV

REFERENCE TEXTS

A Gamester Abroad, de Tabanne, Jerôme
Leather-bound and cloth-bound editions (Very common)

One of the most famous pieces of literature in the Cadois language. Having becoming a household name thanks to his popular newspaper column and the success of *The Gente's Manual,* de Tabanne sent regular letters to the *Charger* as he travelled the world over the course of five years. Upon his return, the letters were collected into a single volume and published with a new introduction by the author and detailed maps of the locations he visited. 'Gamester tours' can be hired in every major city, retracing his steps.

Beaufils Wisdom, Llewell, Jacob
Cloth-bound (Rare)

An attempt to bring Salen's approach to game writing found in *Signaux Argot* to the game of beaufils. Llewell's work did not find as much of an audience. The book offers some entertaining views of club life in Soucisse, but little in the way of memorable information on the game.

Dishonest Play and Players, de Tabanne, Jerôme
Paper pamphlet (Uncommon)

Nearly long enough to be a book in its own right due to de Tabanne's customary verbosity, this pamphlet had a decent run in Voet but never found success in other cities. Sections from this work have been included in later editions of *The Gente's Manual*.

The Fanzago Deck: A Brief History, de Alodesal y Juegon, Ariadna. Trans. de Tabanne
Leather-bound (Uncommon)

De Alodesal y Juegon proves herself to be a capable scholar in this short work which details the development of the Fanzago deck of playing cards used most commonly in L'Ombre. Illustrations of the cards and their versions through the years are to be found in both the L'Ombrais and Cadois versions. The book represents the only time de Tabanne translated a foreign work for publication. His reasons for doing so are unknown, but his extensive annotations have led many to believe he wanted to ensure the work did not help carré take off in Cadogna.

The Faithful Scholars, Barberaque, Emile
Originally on broadsheet, later bound (Very common)

A later Barberaque play, and representative of the shifts in comedic style taking place in the coastal cities at the time of its first production. Most satire before *Faithful* targeted the foibles of the gentry in an inoffensive and gently teasing manner, but later Cadois plays took their characters from the merchant class more often than not. Whether or not *Faithful* prompted this change or was simply indicative of its times is a subject of scholarly debate.

The Gente's Manual of Card and Dice Entertainments, de Tabanne, Jerôme
Cloth-bound (Common)

The work which made de Tabanne famous. This extensive catalog is considered the standard reference for the rules of all manner of parlor games, though many serious gamesters criticize the work for being heavy on etiquette and light on the more complex or arcane situations one might find in play. Additions are made every decade or so in an attempt to keep up with the latest variations, but the author's original text remains untouched. It is a common gift upon reaching one's majority, often given with the enjoinder to read the book with an eye towards how to behave in polite society.

The History of Blots, Salen, Guillaume.
Cloth-bound (Uncommon)

Salen's scientific mind makes this wide-ranging history of the ancient game of blots a rather dry read in parts, but many of the anecdotes and tangents shine with the author's charming voice. De Tabanne providing the introduction ensured the popularity of the book among gaming aficionados.

Lives of Gamesters, de Tabanne, Jerôme
Cloth-bound (Common)

A collection of sketches on many of the most famous game-players in history. While many of the figures presented are known for other accomplishments (e.g. General Rousselot, whose passion for blots famously delayed his invasion of Cadaval), most are people who either made their living at the tables or were gentes who contributed to the history of gamesmanship in a notable way.

Notes on the Disease of Sharp Play, de Alodesal y Juegon,
Ariadna. Trans. Salen.
Paper pamphlet (Rare)

An influential series of essays on cheating of all levels, from simple childhood misbehavior to complicated cons. Alodesal ties any type of dishonest play to the gravest of sins and errors, and provides extensive historical context to support her claims. The pamphlet had little success in Cadogna.

Of Corte and Courtship, Salen, Guillaume
Leather-bound (Common)

This memoir provides a gente's view of the elegant world of casino gambling in the world's most famous destination for gamesters. Salen spent several seasons in Torreçon competing in that city's card tournaments, and returned with the material for this lovely book on L'Ombrais high society.

The Rake's Price, Barberaque, Emile
Originally on broadsheet, later bound (Very common)

A galloping farce, unique in its use of audience participation. Several bit parts are played by volunteers from the night's crowd in traditional productions. Many of these short lines have become common phrases in the Cadois language, though the source of them is often forgotten.

The Rolls of Blots on the Juegon Board, de Villa y Lonza, Serca.
Trans. Salen.
Leather-bound (Rare)

The full list of every game played on the storied Juegon blots board. Each new champion of blots in L'Ombre takes on the role of editor of this tome. The original starts with several sheets of scrap paper on which the very first games were documented by hand. Salen's translation is a true oddity, of interest only to the most passionate fans of the game or to historians, whose ravenous desire for names, dates, and locations is well known.

Sharping Easy, Unknown
Paper (Scarce)

A rough topic and rougher language made this pamphlet a hot commodity when it was first run in Voet by a printer who did not leave his mark. It details the methods by which cheating at cards, dice, and common parlor games can be effected. While the descriptions are crudely written and often opaque, this pamphlet set the standard vocabulary for sharps everywhere. Reprints can be found, but not often.

Signaux Argot, Salen, Guillaume
Cloth-bound (Uncommon)

A slim volume which includes the full rules of the game and its variants, an introduction to the basics of strategy, and several pages of aphorisms and adages on the finer points of play. More popularly known for his translations, Salen was one of the great proponents of bringing the Valtivan game of signaux to Cadogna.

The Soucisse Courant, n/a
Paper broadsheets (Extremely common)

The oldest running newspaper in Soucisse. Distributed widely.

The Voet Charger, n/a
Paper broadsheets (Extremely common)

The self-described 'Gente's Paper' of the city of Voet. Reprinted daily in major cities. De Tabannes' column *Table Talk* was featured for years.

FIND US ONLINE!

www.rebellionpublishing.com

/rebellionpub   /rebellionpublishing   /rebellionpublishing

SIGN UP TO OUR NEWSLETTER!

rebellionpublishing.com/newsletter

YOUR REVIEWS MATTER!

Enjoy this book? Got something to say?

Leave a review on Amazon, GoodReads or with your
favourite bookseller and let the world know!

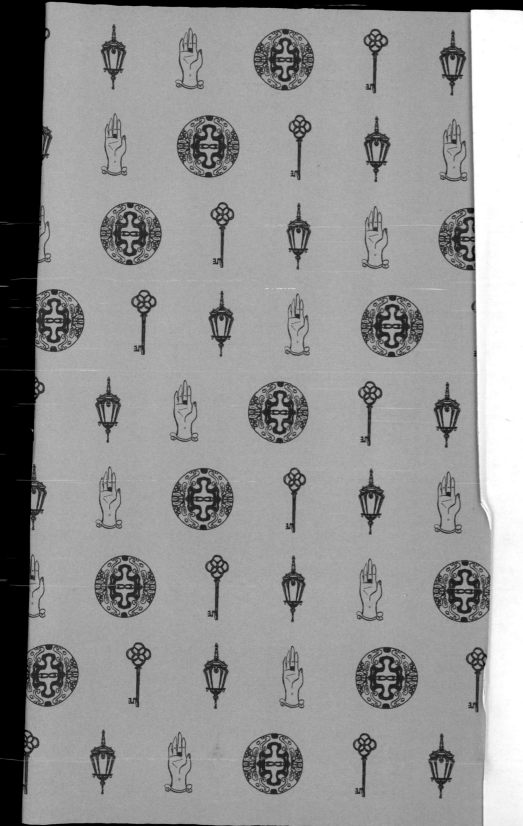